The Memory Stones

CAROLINE BROTHERS

BLOOMSBURY
LONDON · OXFORD · NEW YORK · NEW DELHI · SYDNEY

Bloomsbury Paperbacks
An imprint of Bloomsbury Publishing Plc

50 Bedford Square   1385 Broadway
London   New York
WC1B 3DP   NY 10018
UK   USA

www.bloomsbury.com

BLOOMSBURY and the Diana logo are trademarks of Bloomsbury Publishing Plc

First published in Great Britain 2016
This paperback edition first published in 2017

British Library Cataloguing-in-Publication Data
A catalogue record for this book is available from the British Library.

ISBN: HB: 978-1-4088-4449-6
TPB: 978-1-4088-7282-6
PB: 978-1-4088-4451-9
ePub: 978-1-4088-4450-2

2 4 6 8 10 9 7 5 3 1

Typeset by Integra Software Services Pvt. Ltd.
Printed and bound in Great Britain by CPI Group (UK) Ltd, Croydon CR0 4YY

MIX
Paper from
responsible sources
FSC® C020471

To find out more about our authors and books visit www.bloomsbury.com.
Here you will find extracts, author interviews, details of forthcoming
events and the option to sign up for our newsletters.

For Lorna

La muerte me enseñó que no se muere de amor. Se vive de amor.

Death has taught me that you do not die of love. Love keeps you alive.

> Juan Gelman, *En el hoy y mañana y ayer*
> (In today and tomorrow and yesterday)

There is a land of the living and a land of the dead, and the bridge is love, the only survival, the only meaning.

> Thornton Wilder, *The Bridge of San Luis Rey*

*And Demeter, goddess of the harvest, furious that
none of the gods would help her, descended from Mount
Olympus to scour the earth for her daughter. Crops withered.
The fields lay barren as Demeter searched and grieved for the loss of
Persephone, abducted by Hades and imprisoned in the Underworld.
Finally Zeus, alarmed at the desolation befalling the earth, sent his
messenger Hermes to bring Persephone back. But the woman who
returned was not the same maiden who had vanished. For those
who sup with the Dead must remain forever with them,
and she had done so; though restored to the Living,
she was obliged to return to Hades' realm for
long dark months each year.*

CONTENTS

PROLOGUE

ENDINGS AND BEGINNINGS

Buenos Aires
Late June 1999

A young woman running through an airport, heels clattering like marbles dropped on a floor. Around her, flight numbers and desk numbers and gate numbers juddering on screens.

Crowds surge towards her and she strives against them; they part then close behind her like a stream. Harried, she's searching for something, some window, some counter, a place to buy a ticket; then shouldering herself – *Permiso! Permiso!* – to the front of a check-in line.

Overhead, words flare and blink in manic unison: NOW BOARDING. No, she has no luggage. No cigarette lighters. No knives. NOW BOARDING. ALL PASSENGERS. LAST CALL.

A thud, and an emblem flowers in her passport like a bruise. Turning, there is one last stretch and she hurtles into it, crimson raincoat flapping at her sides. Signs bleed like they're underwater, for duty-free things, for Argentine leather, perfumes. The departure lounge is empty; the staff are switching off their terminals; a suspended screen is flashing in alarm or consternation: GATE CLOSING. GATE CLOSING. She hurls herself through. GATE CLOSED.

The entrance to the plane is a fish-mouth and she tumbles into it, staggers down the ribs of seats. Her door-keys drag like ballast from the life that she is fleeing, a deadweight in the pocket of her coat.

She is in shock; the tangible world is real and at once unreal to her; her swollen mind is numb and she cannot think. She is running to escape the falling, and flying to escape the running; amid the splintering that's both inside her and outside her all that matters is the lift-off into flight.

Mexico City
July 1999

Sunlight is filtering through the leaves of the jacaranda, between the slats of the wooden blinds. The sounds of a Mexican morning – the thwack of the doorman's broom inside the stairwell, the hawkers' calls as their barrows rattle over the cobbles – have at last receded, leaving me alone with my thoughts.

I am trying to prepare a class while the apartment is empty, but find I cannot settle to the task. My mind has been numb for days after all that has happened, the surge of possibility and then the silence, the hope that I'd held for so many years unravelling in so few hours.

Perhaps it is the way the light falls that triggers it, an impression of other trees and other sunlight, that this morning carries me back. My thoughts become untethered, vaulting over the years that have intervened till they alight on this one thing. A memory, just one memory. A season, which at the time we didn't know would be memorable at all.

It was 1976 and the summer, which that year had been so reticent, descended as if by ambush, trapping us in a prism of heat and light. Outside Buenos Aires, the dusty roads that vanished into the pampas now dazzled with mirages; on the eastern side of the city we were hemmed in by the river that stretched to the horizon, blinding under a merciless southern sun.

We'd lived through heatwaves before, but this was different. There was something fierce in the relentless rise of the mercury, something sullen in the humidity's leaden drag. Traffic lights begrudged their slow permissions. Ambulances veered down the weary streets with wails that stretched then sagged like old elastic.

In the airless night we silently cursed our wakefulness, and searched for a strip of mattress not afire with our own body heat. By dawn, defeated, Yolanda would rise to prepare the coffee; I'd follow her into the kitchen, hollow-eyed. But Graciela, oblivious to everything – the sun, the assault of jack-hammers on the footpath, the radio we had on low for the weather forecast – slept on through the morning, undisturbed.

That summer, our youngest daughter was transformed. The exams were over and she was home for the weekend, back in her childhood room. She padded around the house in her nightdress, forgetting where she'd been going before she got there: the end of the song she'd been humming; an anecdote she'd started to recount. She strummed her guitar, or lay on the grass staring up at the trees, dreaming. She was nineteen, and radiant, and in love.

Everyone who could get away had gone to the coast, to Mar del Plata, to Punta del Este, to villas or apartments or beach shacks down by the sea. That year, for a change of light and scenery, we'd rented a house in the delta and were going to Tigre.

Julieta, our eldest, had flown down from Miami and gone on ahead of us, staying with a friend in San Isidro on the way.

The rest of us, abandoning the car, took the train from Retiro station, rattling past the shantytowns and along the marsky coastline to the port. The boat from the fruit dock wound through the reedy waterways, past stilt-houses tottering between the pine trees, past private jetties with doll's-house roofs at the ends of them where the speedboats and the water-taxis moored.

'This is Venice before anyone thought about building Venice,' Graciela had said as we'd glided through the silty water, past men hunched over fishing rods and women cocooned in hammocks on the ends of the piers. 'This is Venice before they buried it under stone.'

They weren't the last words she spoke to me, but they might have been. Amid the chatter of everyday existence, they are the last that I remember, these words from another epoch, an echo from another life.

More than two decades have passed since that last summer – the last I was ever to spend in a country that had always been home. For years now I've been living in Mexico City, thousands of kilometres to the north. But if ever I find myself pulled onto a boat in Xochimilco, and we're drifting among the reeds and islands that once were the Aztecs' gardens, I remember her, I remember Tigre, I remember those days before the world lurched sideways, the last days before everything went dark.

In Tigre, in the lushness of the delta, there was a breeze, and if the breeze faltered there was the emanation of coolness that the river carried with it on its long journey south towards the sea. It had come to us from the rainforests of Brazil, through the gorge at Salto del Guairá in the years before its eighteen mighty waterfalls were dynamited and dammed. It had plunged through the arena of Iguazú, its cascades gleaming white-lipped through the jungle, the air alive with butterflies and the crash and roar of the falls. Then south again, Paraguay in one arm, Argentina in the other, until, reddened with silt, it meandered into the delta and lolled into the Rio de la Plata that was not really a river at all, but rather an estuary that spilled into the Atlantic's inky shoals.

Ours was a holiday house on the eastern side of the Abra Vieja, a narrow finger of the delta, lent to us by a colleague at the clinic. It had pointed eaves half hidden by the pine trees, and stilts concealed by hydrangea shrubs with blooms like babies' heads.

Even before we docked there, I knew which room she would choose. From the water you could see straight into it, to the iron bedstead and wooden dresser tucked under the isosceles roof. Sunshine was pooling on the bedclothes; flung there by the river, diamonds of light scattered across the wardrobe's mirrored door.

The sealed-up rooms when we'd entered them were hoary with desiccated moths. We threw open the windows and shutters; we swept the dustsheets off the furniture in wide flamenco swirls.

Outside, lilies clustered like bridesmaids, and irises shimmered in profusion in the garden of the house next door. The neighbour's house was locked up for the summer, but Graciela was already advancing with a kitchen knife, and soon returned in triumph with her quiver of pilfered spears.

Easter lilies, then, and irises that fanned like paintbrushes over the belly of the milk jug, stolen flowers with purple petals that dripped onto the tablecloth like tears.

Afterwards, all through siesta, Graciela waited for the water-taxi's thrum. Too distracted to read, she was deaf to the din of cicadas, to the squeals of children leaping into the swimming hole, sending clouds of insects spiralling into the air.

When finally José arrived, her lassitude evaporated. We heard her laughing as she showed him around the stilt-house, as they photographed each other under the droopiest willow tree. Later we heard her protests as, hand after hand and just as her sister used to, he called her bluff with the *truco* cards.

Julieta joined us early in the evening. We ate at a table in the garden, leaf debris helicoptering onto the tablecloth, and afterwards we lingered, sleepy with wine and the exhaustion we'd been carrying with us for days. Yolanda told old stories of the delta, of its pirating past and the fugitives who'd hidden there, of the jaguar hunters who'd given Tigre its name. And when the stories ran out we stayed on listening to the stillness, to the calls of the owls and the lapping water, while the fireflies burnt their time-lapse trails in the air.

She'd been so full of plans. Not just for the weekend. Not just for what to buy when the fruit launches docked or where to swim in the late afternoon. Graciela already knew, with a conviction that sobered me in someone so young, that this man José whom she'd known for a year was the one that she wanted for life.

In the early hours of the morning, long after we'd gone to bed, the stars went out. Magnesium flashes of lightning turned the trees to skeletons and, far away, thunder rolled over the rooftops of Buenos Aires. I rose to fasten a rattling window. All around the islands, the water was electric with rain.

The delta was a drug; it helped us forget. It was an oasis after the tensions of the city. We could see it gleaming in the distance if we turned into one of the waterways that threw open the horizon, but in Tigre it had still been possible to believe we were a world away. All over Argentina people were braced for another coup; in the darkness of the churches people prayed for it; nobody believed that Isabel could last another week.

I remove my glasses and, setting them down on my notes for next week's lecture, press my fingers into the corner of my eyes.

Outside the study window, the breeze disturbs the leaf-shadows that fall like feathers onto the rug on the floor.

There was too much we couldn't know, too much that was inexplicable yet to come. But at least we had this: this place, this moment in our lives. At least we were granted Tigre.

I fold it away with care, a small envelope of time to which I entrust this one last salvageable thing. For this is how I remember her, how I choose to remember, how it soothes me to remember her. Blurred, diaphanous, memory leads us astray, it orphans us in the past, but this I keep always close to me, hard against my heart, its silver surface smoky as a daguerreotype and lustrous, even as it fades.

PART I

THE NIGHT OF THE DOGS

1976–1978

I

Buenos Aires
March 1976

Out of the darkness, two sounds: the scrape of metal on concrete, and a low, lupine kind of snarl.

I watch through the bathroom window. After the first night I have started to wait up for them: for the flick of a tail, the flitter of shadow across stone. I observe them from above with the lights turned off as they slink through the deserted streets. Under the curfew the quietness is eerie; against the silence, their noise sets my nerves on edge.

No one knows where they come from, whether they are feral dogs that have infiltrated the city, or city dogs that hunger has turned wild. They invade the night-time suburbs like scavengers in the wreck trail of disaster. From the window I see them streak across the playground, heads down, tails low, in furtive silhouette. Lured by opportunity, they salivate at weakness, aroused by the possibility of spoils.

Since the day of the coup there has been no garbage collection, and the rubbish cans now totter under their burden of sacks. Each day more accumulate, so that the cans swell into hillocks and then small islands, the bloated bags on top of them as taut and obese as seals.

And nightfall is when they come to feed. One moment quietness, then suddenly that metal sound, and shadow creatures are tearing at the carcasses, eyes a-glitter, breath steaming through ivory jaws. They trapeze on bony haunches, seeking the moist organs inside. The air trembles. The membranes spill their warm intestines; the gutted plastic releases its stench of rot. Drooling, the hangers-on emerge from hiding and trot towards the action; others lurk in the shrubberies to pace, to watch and wait.

Some nights the excitement boils over; some nights feast degenerates into fight. I've seen it: the flash of fang as hunter rounds on plunderer, as young blood turns against the old. Beneath the branches, in the stippled streetlight, they converge in a seething mass. Then the mass shifts shape and staggers sideways, and suddenly something snaps. Growling, yelping, some cur breaks free in triumph; the vanquished skitter and skulk away. They limp into the bushes with limbs slickly gleaming in the lamplight; when morning comes, the footpaths are smeared with detritus, and dotted with scarlet trails.

'Come to bed, Osvaldo,' Yolanda says.

I turn, and see her standing in her nightdress by the doorway, watching me watching by the window, as if vigilance alone could protect.

'I'm coming now, *amore*,' I say, and go to follow her.

But then another shadow passes by the window, between the patterns the *ceiba* trees are casting on the footpath, and I cannot pull myself away.

It is the dogs above all that fascinate me, even more than the army tanks. It doesn't occur to me that there might be some connection, that the feral and the disciplined might not be opposites after all, but merely different facets of the same thing.

The tanks we felt before we saw them, a low vibration that made the leaves of the pot palms shiver and the lids on the saucepans jiggle as if over steam. At first I thought it was an earthquake: things were tilting; things were coming unhinged. But the sounds grew louder, and new ones followed: the scrape of steel as the behemoths ground around the corner, gouging out the cobblestones like teeth. Then, at the intersection where the cobbles gave way to asphalt, the grinding turned to a rumble that grew louder as the column drew nearer; behind it, personnel carriers purred. Conscripts crouched in the back of them with anxious eyes and guns that spiked the air like accusations. There they are, I thought, our soldiers, bodyguards of the nation, summoned to subdue the unquiet land.

And subdue it they have, quarter by quarter, street by street locking us down. On television we saw the tanks encircling the Casa Rosada; overnight, Isabel had been hustled away. Even now, in daylight raids, people are being wrenched from suburban houses, helicopters throbbing overhead.

Across the city, army trucks are stationed on every corner. Machine-guns peer like telescopes down the wide, deserted streets.

All this, yet it's the dogs that haunt me, the way they appear at night where by day the soldiers have been. The mangy gang-land dogs, the watchdogs and the runaways and the lap dogs, the shantytown dogs with washboard ribs out running with the greyhounds and the mongrels, agile beasts and cunning ones that are reckless now with instinct and eager to do better than just survive. They hunt in packs, these mastiffs and these slack-papped bitches, they remember their old proclivities and unleash them. They pick over the reeking garbage like hyenas, all of them, the household pets and the abandoned ones that are everyone's last priority now that the coup that has long been expected, that many have secretly yearned for, now that the coup itself has finally arrived.

2

Buenos Aires
May 1976

'Osvaldo!'

Half the bar swings towards me as Hugo bellows my name.

I move towards the corner they've taken over, smiling at the cluster of empty glasses, at the upturned faces of friends. Hugo, slightly drunk, embraces me, and I work my way around the table greeting each of them in turn.

It's a Friday night and a group of us have gathered at the Paradiso, the bar that Hugo gets us all to patronise chiefly because it's three doors down from where he works. Gleaming with brass fittings, it has the old-world aura of a ship's saloon, while the haze of smoke inside it makes the outside world more opaque than it already is. The beers, however, are passable, and the wine is sometimes excellent, and the bar's number is taped to a newsroom pillar so that Hugo can be phoned there from the desk.

And if ever a call should come in, Gustavo gesticulates as if he's guiding in an aircraft till Hugo dashes to the receiver; he can sprint to the office and be back again before his beer goes flat.

'What'll it be, Osvaldo?' Hugo is saying. 'The next round's on Heriberto, I believe.'

It's a running joke with all of us that Heriberto, a movie critic with vitriol for everything but 1940s Hollywood, finds endless ways to wriggle out of his turn.

'After the pittance you pay for my pieces – when you happen to remember?' says Heriberto. 'You publishers are all the same, exploiting the bohemian poor.'

Hugo guffaws. 'Exploiting!' he says. 'Who's doing the exploiting when a writer engaged on an exclusive contract recycles his opinions up the road?'

'Slander!' cries Heriberto. 'You have no . . .'

But Hugo waves his protests aside. 'Actually, we've discussed it with accounting. Payroll has no objections to paying you in kind. And Gustavo here is more than happy to set you up a tab behind the bar.'

Heriberto nearly chokes on his beer. 'What, and have you lot guzzle away my meagre earnings? When what you pay me for the wisdom of years would barely cover what you feed those goldfish of yours?'

Heriberto is short and portly and myopic, which letters-to-the-editor have unkindly suggested might explain his views on cinema; he wears a Borsalino battered beyond pretentiousness to cover his vanishing hair. He looks older than his ID says he is – an image he has cultivated since his twenties; now he is well past forty he has started to grow into the part.

'Why not? Two birds with one shot,' says Hugo, glasses flashing. 'We wouldn't have to bother about sending you a cheque and you wouldn't have to worry about buying us rounds.'

'I wouldn't say "worry" was quite the right word,' says Diego, chipping in.

Heriberto, suddenly uncertain whether Hugo is joking, rummages in at least five pockets for his lighter, then holds it to his girlfriend's cigarette.

Sofia – or is it Sonia? From Heriberto's glare when I greet her, I realise I've got it wrong again – is half his age and seemingly devoted to him, though I have trouble taking them seriously as a pair. A freelance writer with ambitions, she is a good head taller than Heriberto and buxom in her figure-hugging blouses; shamelessly, he strings her along by name-dropping about his connections on the national press.

'Still, it's a great idea, trading goods for services,' Diego continues through the paisley whorls of smoke. 'Though governments tend to hate it. You can't tax a barter economy, after all.'

Diego, whom Hugo and I have known since we were all at high school, we once teased for his stocky legs and his fashion-free taste in clothes. Now we rib him for being a dour economist, though in reality he holds unorthodox views that he defends like a conspiracy theorist; he still goes about in an orange pullover that no one can persuade him to discard.

Gustavo is working around the table, empty glasses clinking as he two-by-twos them onto his tray.

'Just a Quilmes, Gustavo,' I say, in response to the eyebrow he's raised.

'Sure it's a nice idea, this cash-free system,' says Marguerita, with whom Diego has been in love since he reversed into her car at university, though he still hasn't mustered the courage to propose. 'But it can only work at a micro level – you know, for crates of tomatoes, film reviews and the like . . .'

Heriberto, put out at hearing his profession placed on a par with market gardening, scowls as he returns the lighter to his jacket on the back of his chair.

Marguerita, these days an established actress, has a husky voice to go with her Spanish features, and a weakness for French silk scarves that some dealer in San Telmo ferrets out. Jet-eyed under the sweep of her black eyebrows, she has the quickest mind of all of us, and dissects our arguments with the kind of intensity that Heriberto reserves for the Hipódromo racing guide.

Hugo likes to hear her take on things, which he adds to all the other opinions he accumulates so that you never quite know which are his.

Diego, however, disagrees with her about the limits of the cashless economy, and swiftly their dispute escalates. The rest of us scramble to keep pace.

I'm sorry Yolanda hasn't accompanied me this evening – she intervenes only judiciously, but appreciates the sparring like a high-speed spectator sport. And she likes the Paradiso, with its chandelier dangling bell-shaped from the ceiling; it reminds her, she says, of the *salóns* where, years ago, we used to go to dance.

Tonight, however, she is buried under a backlog of marking, so she has sent her love to the rest of us and dispatched me here on my own.

Hugo was my best man when Yolanda and I got married, though he insists he has never been tempted to indulge in such folly himself.

'One malfunctioning relationship is enough,' he says, whenever we quiz him about the girlfriends he has presented to us over the years. 'You know I'm wedded to my job.'

We form a band, of sorts, Yolanda and me with Diego and Marguerita, Hugo and Heriberto. Others have come and gone, moving in and out of our loose circle, but our best discussions and our most boisterous evenings take place when all of us are there.

I have my back to the bar, but in the mirror I can see Gustavo, our shipboard master of ceremonies, sliding a cassette out of the tape deck and slotting another one in. We try to curb his penchant for some of the more maudlin tangos; Hugo is convinced he puts them on on purpose when our arguments start to heat up.

Since the coup, however, the atmosphere at the Paradiso has changed. It is the first time I have been here since the generals announced they were taking over, and the difference is perceptible even to me. It is not just the ban on certain pieces of music, forcing Gustavo to weed out Discépolo and Pugliese, even some of Gardel's tangos, from his collection. It's as if something has interfered with the barometer, pressure added to the air we breathe.

'This curfew's bad for business,' Gustavo mutters darkly, bottles of Quilmes weeping as he sets them down. He curses the fact that the buses now stop before midnight; he predicts the demise of the Paradiso, of café life itself.

The bar, it is true, is almost empty – unusual for a Friday, particularly in so busy a part of town. Idle behind the counter in his jacket and starched white apron, Gustavo complains that even his regulars are dwindling; if they show up at all it is singly, or at most in pairs.

'Nothing but espressos, that's all they want,' he says, eyebrows lowered in one of his heavier scowls. 'I haven't served a bottle of Malbec in days.'

I don't know whether it's the same all over the country, but here at least, no one seems to vent about the news unless it's football, or launch into a debate about politics with a stranger at the table next door. At lunchtime these days the outdoor cafés are deserted; with the ban on assembly, even the students are staying away.

Weeks have passed since the generals seized power and I've scarcely spoken to Hugo since they did. '¡CAYÓ ISABEL!' the headlines screamed, and nobody seemed to be sorry she was gone. Yet strangely, the relief we'd all been expecting hasn't come.

We've had coups before, of course, but I'm unsure what to make of this one: the endless parades of jeeps down Corrientes, the edicts descending so fast we can barely keep up. Communiqués interrupt the television broadcasts, and repeat till our minds turn numb on the radio waves. I sense it's not what's said so much as what they stand for, but I have no gift for unscrambling the military's codes.

I do know that 'subversion' is the word they use for terrorism, but there hasn't been a bomb in ages now, and since the army has taken over, it's hard to believe that the terrorists haven't all been caught.

In practical terms, what bothers me most are the random roadblocks, which three times now have made me late at the hospital; the police are either arrogant or jittery, and you'd better watch your movements when you reach for your ID.

'They've removed Isabel, they've taken power,' I say to anyone at the table who's listening. 'Surely now they can lift this state of siege?'

'Lift it? Why would they?' says Heriberto, glad of the change of subject, Borsalino nodding as he speaks. 'It suits them better to keep us battened down.'

'I think he's right,' says Marguerita. 'Have you noticed how no one is saying anything about elections? This is it. It's how they plan to rule.'

Though politics is Argentina's greatest obsession after football, I have no natural feel for it, like being born tone deaf or colour blind. Beyond my family, what matters to me most is my profession: the treatment of my patients, changes at the hospital. Politics in the wider sense has always seemed abstract.

Now, as I sit with my friends at the Paradiso, ears half-tuned to the lilt of conversation, I feel a sense of unreality at this new chapter in our country's life.

'What makes you think this lot will be any different?' someone is saying. 'Generals are always rescuing us from ourselves.'

'Not from ourselves, for themselves,' somebody quips, and everyone at the table laughs.

As they talk, I find a pen in my pocket and start doodling on the back of an envelope, as I sometimes do to relax or to while away time. As a child, I filled sheets of butcher's paper with drawings of made-up creatures, and progressed to pictures of classmates when I got to school. To impress Yolanda, in the first months of our romance I did sketches of our fellow students, and caricatures of the anatomy professor we all lived half in fear of; later, I teased our girls with cartoons of them as kids. Once in a while, for want of a better subject, I'd turn my hand to a politician: Onganía, say, or Evita or Perón. But it was never anything more than an idle pastime, and never something I considered in a professional light.

But now, as I drift in and out of the conversation, some-thing surfaces through the diktats and the menace, through the Junta's tone and the barking voices that track us along the radio dial. Suddenly I am remembering my schooldays, how the master treated the slow kids in the classroom: the humili-ation, the patronising tone of voice. Perhaps it is that, some residual anger, that drives the strokes of my pen.

Three blind mice.

On my hospital envelope I scribble away at the Junta's three top generals. While the others pursue their arguments, I depict our leaders in a series of ridiculous poses, with and without their hats and medals and uniforms, testing how far my metaphor holds up.

With his beady eyes and pointed chin, the Army general looks more like a rodent the longer I stare at his photo in Hugo's *Clarín*. I give him a stripy T-shirt, a generous sprinkling of stubble, and a giant sack that he's hoisted over his shoulder, 'A-R-G-E-N-T-I-N-A' stencilled down the side. Suddenly the *ratón* has become a *ratero*; the mouse, a thief – but a blind one, blundering around with his bag of loot since I've blacked out his burglar's mask.

Around me the discussion grows more animated; words like 'capital' and 'import substitution' wash over me, then something about some bulldozers in the shantytowns. I barely notice when Gustavo selects a slow Di Sarli tango to calm us down.

I am absorbed now by the nose of the Navy general – its bulbousness surely a cartoonist's gift. I curl his bushy eyebrows over the rims of his blind-man's glasses; I garnish him with cauliflower ears. I place him on the quarterdeck of a frigate, his tail a-droop in the ocean air. White cane aloft, he's issuing orders to fire the frigate's cannons, while from the stern, sailor rats are rushing to abandon ship.

The music swells and the voices drop. I drift in and out of an incident Marguerita is recounting: something about a police raid on the *Fac* she lives next door to, something about some students taken away in vans.

The third blind mouse has radar ears and is blindfolded with the Argentine flag. Since he's the Air Force General, I draw him playing Blind Man's Bluff with his pilots, who buzz him in their aircraft before bailing out in parachute descents.

'Phenomenal!' cries Heriberto, surprising me with his approval, cantankerous old critic that he is. Swaying slightly, he slaps me on the back and calls me '*Amigo!*' and whisks my scribblings out from under my hands.

Sonia and Marguerita lean forward to admire my artistry; Marguerita adds some shantytown dogs of her own. Diego, cheeks aflame in the radiance of his sweater, says he likes the first one, even if I've left the economy out.

Hugo loves them.

'Osvaldo,' he says, 'we have got to publish. Do them up in ink for me, in black and white; get them to me by Monday if you can.'

The next two issues have already been planned but he wants them for the first one after that.

'Come on, Hugo,' I say, embarrassed. 'I'm not a proper cartoonist; this isn't a professional's work.' The pictures are not even sketches; they are more like the sort of jottings I'd do on the back of a telephone pad.

'All the better, Osvaldo. It's precisely because you're not a professional. You're a doctor, and people trust their doctors. They know you're not political. They know you're on their side.'

'That's rubbish, Hugo, as well you know,' I tell him, laughing. 'Doctors have opinions, just like anyone. Doctors vote.'

'Not under dictatorships they don't,' says Marguerita.

'My point exactly,' says Hugo. 'In any case, you know what I mean, Osvaldo. As a profession you *médicos* are seen as neutral. No axes to grind. Unaligned.'

In their wire rims, Hugo's circular glasses throw up triangles of chandelier light. Give him an idea and he'll run with it on pure adrenaline; he is beaming now as if we were still eleven-year-olds playing nick-knock on the neighbours' front doors.

There is vanity at work, I admit it; I'm not insensitive to the praise of my friends. I think of that afternoon's patients: a case of severe glaucoma; a boy who'd collected a black eye in the playground – I've had a spate of them at the clinic since the coup. There are different rewards for the work of a cartoonist, I can see that – a satisfaction that's more immediate than the process of healing and care.

'They don't look too childish?' I ask Hugo. I think of my colleagues at the hospital, and wonder how they might react.

'Of course not – but what would it matter if they did? If they puncture the pomposity . . . Come on, Osvaldo! It's only a bit of fun.'

Hugo flatters me with his excitement and wears me down with his arguments, and in the end I concede. In any case, it's not as if that many people will see them; *Focus* is an entertainment weekly with a modest circulation, even if its listings are the most reliable ones in town.

'Whatever you do, make sure he coughs up,' says Heriberto, wagging a finger. 'Never let it be said I didn't warn you . . .'

'Of course we'll pay – ignore him,' says Hugo. 'Just don't go flogging your work off to the competition.'

Hugo promises to write an editorial to accompany my drawings. Diego, making amorous eyes at Marguerita over the glow of his tangerine jumper, describes a mid-air circle with his finger, and Gustavo brings us another round so we can toast the edition's success.

━━

Around us, things are evolving fast.

Without our noticing when it happened, fear has insinuated itself into our lives. Suddenly our restless nights are punctuated by the pop-pop of gunshots, curious-sounding at first, then unmistakable, sometimes just a block or two away. Yolanda, ever a light sleeper, clings to me when they wake her and I hold her, and can't be sure if it's her heart that is racing or it's mine. In the thin hours of dawn we rise red-eyed with sleeplessness and drink black coffee at the kitchen table. Yolanda makes anxious phone calls to Graciela, and reassuring ones to Julieta in Miami, where she's been living with her husband for the past year.

The security guards who appeared in our street some time ago still patrol the houses of our neighbours, acquaintances with corporate jobs and kidnapping fears. Driving home after dark, we are stopped by police with searchlights, and once, a twilight shoot-out makes us reverse all the way up our road. At school Yolanda hears whisperings; at the hospital there is talk about 'hunting accidents'; there are the colleagues of friends who, from one day to the next, fail to turn up at work.

But no one ever talks about what is happening. Life goes on in the city as if we alone have heard the gunshots, and if others ever witness anything it is not discussed.

My sketches start to worry me. I call Hugo from the clinic; he tells me we have two more days till they go to press. Since I am in the neighbourhood, he drops out of a planning meeting and we duck in for a sandwich at the Paradiso.

Gustavo is looking more cheerful; he has just clocked on and welcomes us, making a show of pouring our beers.

Hugo listens to my concerns and takes them seriously. At the weekly meeting, he says, they talked about changing the headline, about softening the editorial thrust. They went back and forth over whether to pull the text and simply use the pictures, or whether to ditch the entire spread. It's a listings magazine, someone insisted, not Timerman's *Opinión*; others were better placed to analyse the regime. But in the end, they decided that self-censorship wasn't their remit; that if press freedom were ever in need of champions, it was then and not when times were easy; that exercising excessive caution would be doing the Junta's work.

I do not feel particularly reassured.

'I'm out of my depth here, Hugo,' I confess to him. 'I'm not sure I have your stomach for things like this.'

'These bands of steel, you mean?' he says with a laugh, and pats the belly that has started to gain some prominence in recent years.

But he understands what is making me nervous. My days are spent at the clinic, examining haematomas in the eyes of footballers and brawlers; it's a world apart from lampooning a regime.

'Do you want to withdraw them?' he says.

I hesitate. He is offering me an exit, but I don't take it. Perhaps I am over-reacting. I don't want to be seen as cowardly in the eyes of my oldest friend.

'If I do, will you still publish your editorial?'

'Publish and be damned, as they say.'

I waver. I profess to share his values. It feels like a kind of test.

'They are only cartoons, Osvaldo,' says Hugo, trying his hand at doctorly reassurance. 'If anything is problematic it'll be my words and not your pictures. Your drawings are innocuous. If these generals want a shot at governing, they're going to have to learn to take a joke.'

In any case, he says, they have raised the matter with the publisher, who took a few minutes between meetings at *Gazeta Hípica* and *Autos Hoy* to consider it. They have calculated the cost.

'The cost?' I say.

'Look, we're an entertainment weekly – we print theatre reviews and list what's on at the movies. It's not as if we're

Clarín or *La Nación*. But I suppose if the generals aren't happy they could seize a few copies if they feel like it. Close us down for a week or two. At worst, stop publication for a month.'

I feel relieved. They have examined it and weighed the consequences. If they are going ahead, if Hugo's publisher is standing behind him, I don't feel quite so exposed.

'Okay, Hugo. You can have them,' I say.

'Good man,' he responds, and pats me on the back. 'You should see the mock-ups. They're going to look tremendous in print.'

'I haven't told Yolanda yet,' I tell him. 'I want it to be a surprise.'

He smiles. 'Perhaps you should fill her in beforehand,' he says. 'You know. Just in case.'

He pays the bill, pocketing the receipt, and we embrace and go our separate ways.

I am waiting at an intersection, negotiating the lunchtime traffic back to the clinic, when his last words come drifting back. *Just in case*, I think, and wonder: in case of what?

~~~

Yolanda looks at me, when I tell her that night, with disbelief and anxiety meshing in the tiredness of her face.

'They probably won't even notice,' I say, trying to sound more confident than I feel.

'Osvaldo,' she says. Her eyes are round with foreboding. 'I'm sure Hugo knows what he is doing, but for pity's sake be careful. Everything is different this time.'

'Different how?' I say.

'I don't know. It's just a feeling. Their methods. Their brazenness. That man they pulled out of the restaurant the other day . . .' She is struggling to put her finger on it. 'They want to make sure we know we are vulnerable. They want to give us reason to be afraid.'

—

Retribution in the event comes swiftly, and is not delivered in words.

Hugo cannot ring me from the magazine the morning after publication, and I am not at the clinic; from the bar of the Paradiso he tries me at the hospital, and the switchboard pages me there.

'I can't talk for long, Osvaldo,' he says, when finally we connect. Fresh from theatre, I am standing in the doorway of the nurses' station at Recovery, which is where I've intercepted his call.

From Gustavo's phone he describes the ransacked scene. Phone lines yanked like ivy through the plasterboard. Typewriters smashed, their keys wrenched out like so many disarticulated words. Downstairs in the print room, where other magazines besides *Focus* use the presses, loading belts dangling in the void.

'My God, Hugo,' I say, as his words sink in.

And in his office, in a puddle of water among the shards of glass on the floor tiles, the bodies of his goldfish, glistening like orange pulp.

'I suppose you could say they've expressed their appreciation,' he says.

I look around at the walls of the nurses' station, at the noticeboard with its rosters scattershot with coloured pins.

'I see what you mean about their sense of humour,' I say. 'I guess it'll be a collector's item now.'

Her back to me, a senior nurse is sifting through the admissions files, pretending not to overhear.

'I doubt it, *amigo*. Too dangerous. In any case, they've pulled the entire print-run. From here to Ushuaia you're not going to find a single copy on sale.'

A shiver passes through me: awareness of what we have done, the huge mistake.

'Will you be okay?' I say.

The nurse's back straightens almost imperceptibly.

'It's a warning, and we're paying attention,' he says. 'That should go for you too.'

Before I can reply, his voice changes swiftly, becomes brusque. 'I have to go, Osvaldo. Listen to me: take care.'

This sharpness isn't like him. I wonder if suddenly he has company at the bar.

'You too, Hugo,' I say. But my words are lost under the sound of the hung-up phone.

That morning, running late, I took the Subte to the hospital, preferring the crush in the underground to the peak-hour traffic on the road. Late in the day there are complications, then an emergency operation; I am unable to leave the hospital before dark.

Ford Falcons are all over the roads in Buenos Aires; the *patotas*, however, have a particular affinity for those in khaki green. Yolanda and I see the hit squads all the time, we all do; sinister as reptiles, they patrol the streets with gun barrels jutting from their windows and wires where their number plates once were.

That evening, when I emerge from the underground station, one of the *patotas* turns its attention to me.

With its windows down, the car crawls a few paces behind me, block after block, all the way up Scalabrini Ortiz. I tell myself not to look, to walk calmly, not to engage. But from the corner of my eye I glimpse their guns and my heartbeat accelerates. When I turn into a one-way street I lose them; it takes me all my willpower not to run. They may not know who you are, I tell myself; don't give them any reason to find out. Then, before I've realised, they are back. It is winter; night has fallen and the streetlights flicker on, casting their jaundiced glow upon the world. I pass a laundrette window and see the car's reflection: elbows, sunglasses smeared with lamplight, the dull black metal of their guns.

I reach the ironwork gate outside our house and the Falcon stops. The engine hums. Thick-fingered, I fumble with the key. In it slides at last, and I sense their expectation. They are waiting for me to look at them – as they know I will, they are sure of it – when I go to close the door. I move slowly, an actor playing myself as the man I was before my cartoons had ever been thought of, but the urge is stronger than I am, and after all an innocent man would turn.

Casually, I lift my eyes. I let my glance slide their way.

The man at the kerbside window is ready for me. I've seen his weapon but he doesn't use it. Instead, he raises his hand through the open window and points at me, grinning behind his sunglasses, curling his fingers into the shape of a gun.

I am still shaking when I find Yolanda in the kitchen. She hugs me for a long time, stilling me as I lean into the warmth of her, the scent of jasmine fading under the dust of class-room chalk.

'They followed me,' I whisper.

I feel her shoulders tense.

I tell her what Hugo told me about his offices. She saw the cartoons yesterday on her way to school, before the magazine vanished from the stands. She understands how we might have thought them humorous; she understands how the generals did not.

'What was he thinking? What were either of you thinking?' she says, and I know she is as angry with Hugo as she is with me.

'He gave me the chance to retract,' I tell her. I feel foolish now; how stupid I was not to see. 'He's probably in more trouble than me.'

'You're both in trouble, Osvaldo. You'd better have no doubt on that score.'

I feel a wave of coldness coalescing, as it did when I spoke to Hugo, the implications surfacing on my skin.

'It might have been a coincidence,' Yolanda says. She is talking about the Falcon, the men who trailed me along the kerb. 'But if they weren't sure before, they will be now. They'll have put it together. Now that they know your face.'

She breathes deeply and sets me away from her, cupping my elbows the way she does when she has something important to say. Under the kitchen light, her eyes are flecked with brilliance, gold and red flashes on green.

'Osvaldo,' she says. 'Listen to me now. They may have made a mistake tonight, but they are not going to make another. We both know they are not playing games.'

I cut her off, seeking to reassure. 'I'm not important enough, Yolanda. I'm not political. I'm just a doctor.' It is only when I say it aloud that I realise how feeble it sounds.

'They came for a teacher at school today, for something much less than this.'

I look at her, and know what she is about to say. Already I feel the things I love slipping from my fingers like leaves.

'Tonight. Right now. Before the curfew.' Her words are an urgent whisper. 'Take your passport. Go to the Aeroparque.'

'Yolanda,' I start to say, but she silences me with a look.

'If they find you, they won't forgive you, Osvaldo. There isn't going to be a second chance.'

3

Buenos Aires

July 1976

Yolanda receives a letter.

It is brought to her on a Wednesday afternoon, after the final bell, while she is sitting in the stillness of a classroom pungent with orange peel and adolescent sweat. Chalky light hopscotches through the windows; her head is bent over the hieroglyphics of a fifth-year biology test.

At the back of her mind she is worrying about certain changes being announced to the curriculum. *The Little Prince* has already been removed from the library, and now she's been told that creationism is about to be introduced. She hasn't dared ask about her units on reproduction and evolution, but if they have to change she would rather not teach them at all.

She looks up at the sound of footsteps scuffing the quiet corridor. She sees a dome of bouffant hair bobbing along the inside windows where the second years have put up their projects on plants.

A gangly teenager taps twice on the door's glass pane then lopes towards her, a pale pink envelope in his hand. Gabriel has always been one of her better students; lately, though, his concentration has deteriorated. The paper he has submitted, somewhere in the pile she is correcting, will determine whether or not they'll have to have a talk.

'Some man at the side gate handed me this,' he says.

She raises an eyebrow.

'He asked who studied biology, and when I stepped forward he told me to give it to you.'

Away from the jostle of his peers, she notices for the first time how quickly he has grown: a beanpole adolescent with angry skin, tripping over his feet into manhood. He stands before her in his *guardapolvo* that is suddenly too small for him, his too-long arms dangling from its too-short sleeves.

She smiles and takes the envelope he holds out to her, as if she has been expecting its arrival all along. In a script she doesn't recognise, she sees her name, Sñra Yolanda Ferrero, spelled out in slanted capitals. As she turns it over, some half-heard talk floats back to her from yesterday in the common room, something that had happened to a pupil's father, a union man, and it occurs to her that perhaps that father was Gabriel's. She will have to ask the physics teacher discreetly: an endless font of gossip, Borovich seems always to have the gravity and relativity of what's going on mapped into a theory, like astrophysics.

She turns the envelope back again, puzzling at the lettering, at the strange pink stationery, when suddenly it occurs to her that Graciela might be involved. In a rush, the outside world, kept at bay beyond the sanctuary of the classroom, returns like an incoming tide. Graciela has been distraught since Monday, when José failed to come home to her; last night she wasn't even answering the phone.

Osvaldo, thinks Yolanda. Not for the first time she turns to him before remembering he is nowhere within reach.

'Thank you, Gabriel,' she says in her schoolteacher's voice, grateful that the role still steadies her when all else seems awry.

Gabriel is already retreating towards the door. She waits for him to tread, as she knows he will, on the squeaky floorboard, watches him step backwards to open the door.

'Gabriel, before you go . . .' she says.

He pivots towards her with surprising grace.

'Did the man say anything else?' she says, her mind suddenly focused. 'Did he say who he was?'

'Nope. Just some guy. He took off on his motorbike right away.'

Was that all? She was always hammering at her students to be observant, to be precise in their descriptions. Although they were making progress in the classroom, she could see it was going to take longer for them to apply the lesson to life.

'Okay, Gabriel. Thank you,' she says, dismissing him with a nod.

She holds the envelope up to the light and shakes it, as if foreknowledge might be the harbinger of luck. Then, blunt-fingered, she saws it open in a jagged frill.

Mamá, I am fine. Don't worry about me. I am with friends. I can't say any more, except that I'm praying for J. and thinking of you and Papá and Julieta. All will be well. Love you. Graciela.

Yolanda reads the note over and over. She exhales audibly, doesn't realise she has been holding her breath.

Graciela is in hiding: she understands it right away. Someone must have persuaded her it wasn't safe to stay. She had insisted, when Yolanda had implored her to come home to her, that she couldn't leave their apartment, that José might try to telephone, that she needed to remain where she was.

The letter, thank heavens, is in her daughter's handwriting. She must have asked someone to find an envelope and deliver it, someone who had also written the address. Yet the colour of the envelope is so girly – was that somehow significant? The same pink as the geraniums in the garden . . . Could she be somewhere with a floral name? Flores, Florida, Floresta, suburbs all . . . Yolanda shakes herself, stilling her overwrought mind.

Her daughter is probably holed up on the coast somewhere. Or in some small town inland.

Relief floods her bloodstream, it flushes her face. Graciela is all right, thank God she's all right; she is safe.

Yolanda's spine stiffens.

She is not all right. Why else would she send word like this? Why else would she have to flee?

For the third time in a week Yolanda goes to see José's parents. Some years older than she is, they've been lurching between panic and paralysis since the day of his disappearance. They can't understand why no one is able to help.

'Arrested! Cheché hasn't been arrested!' Maria is saying, emotion mounting in her voice. 'If he had been arrested, then someone would know where he was!'

Rain has been hammering the city since morning. Maria's hair is windblown and she has forgotten to remove her raincoat, which is dripping onto the floor. She is still holding the bag of food and clothing she had packed for José and taken to the police station, and has had to bring home again.

Neighbours who used to chat to them now cross the street when they hear what has happened to their son.

On the table, unwatered, miniature rosebuds are dying in a pot of soil. Unopened mail is piling up in the kitchen. A yellow-eyed tabby ropes itself around their ankles in the hope of being fed.

'He's been abducted, not arrested, Yolanda,' Maria says in a kind of sob. 'That student we talked to said they were plain-clothes men who took them. No uniforms. No number plates. No names.'

Yolanda gets home exhausted by these visits on top of her day at school. Their helplessness unnerves her. And as for Graciela . . . She is too frightened to think.

Eduardo, José's father, sits in ashen silence, waiting for Maria's shuddering to stop. He is undone by her hysteria, Yolanda sees that, is barely able to cope with his own fears.

Was José on someone's list? she wonders. Or was he swept up by mistake?

It is delicate; she doesn't know how to ask them; she doesn't want them to think she's been showing up only for her daughter's sake. But she needs to know if José has been involved in anything, if only to assess what danger Graciela might be in.

On the doorstep, at last, she finds a way.

'Have you spoken to any of his friends?' she asks Eduardo. He is a tall man, and was probably a striking one in his youth. He's like an ancient lion, she thinks, heavy-faced and digni-fied despite his dulling hide. 'Are they involved in any kind of group?'

Eduardo knows what she is asking and her heart constricts when she sees the pain in his eyes.

'José is a good son,' he says. The lines in his cheeks look like crevices scoured into rock. 'Extremist politics has never been Cheché's thing.'

Yolanda flushes. She hadn't meant to imply that he'd embraced violence – only that certain affiliations, anything with even the vaguest link to *peronismo*, might prove a dangerous thing.

Grave-faced, Eduardo clears his throat. 'They have been going to the *villas miserias*, however,' he tells her after a moment. 'It's the only thing I can think of. They've been teaching literacy in the slums.'

They? Does he mean José's university friends? Does he mean Graciela went too?

He anticipates her question before she voices it.

'A few of them have been going along together, and I understand that Graciela recently joined in. I spoke to Francisco – he's a friend of José's – who said that she was planning to start her own class, although for some reason she didn't accompany them last time.'

Yolanda takes in this news. Graciela had been unwell at the weekend, she remembers now, and had cancelled lunch on the Sunday; it makes sense that on that Monday, she might have decided to stay home.

'It can hardly be that though, can it?' she says. 'Teaching the alphabet can hardly be considered a crime.'

Or could it? She turns it around in her mind. How would the regime see it? Surely not as organising, or radicalising the poor . . .

'This literacy programme – is it run by the student union or by some group at the *Fac*?' Suddenly she is worried. She wonders whether political tracts were distributed with the books they took to the poorest *barrios*; whether some party provided the funds.

'José hardly ever talks about his volunteering,' Eduardo says, 'so honestly I don't know how it works. But he would be in it for the teaching, not for the student politics; he wouldn't care whose backing it had.' His German accent thickens with emotion. 'He's never been one for joining things, Yolanda. But he does have his convictions. "How can anyone improve their life if they can't even read?" – he said that to me once. And also that this teaching was the best thing he'd ever done.'

Yolanda smiles to hide her own anxiety and puts her hand on his sleeve.

'We will find him,' she says after a moment, waiting till she can trust her voice. She has promised to help them draft some letters, and go with them to the Interior Ministry next week. 'We just have to be methodical. Someone will know where he is.'

Eduardo nods, and they stand in silence a moment, looking out at the rain in the trees.

'Have you heard from Graciela?' he says to her, just as she moves to go.

She looks at him, at the paw-like hands protruding from his woollen jacket, the one she guesses he keeps for special occasions, and has worn today for visiting the police.

Yolanda lowers her voice. 'Not since the note. But that was more than a week ago.' She says it like a confession, confiding in him because she needs to talk to somebody and cannot keep it any longer to herself. 'I am sick with worry, Eduardo,' she tells him. 'I have no idea if she's safe.'

⁓

They stand together in lines outside government ministries. They go to army barracks and police stations and jails. They speak to parish priests and to any church official who will receive them; to newspapers, thinking the editors might know something, or write something, that they might be keeping a tally of names.

Weeks go by. Nobody has any information. Nobody has any news.

They would file a petition for *habeas corpus*, if they could find a single lawyer who wasn't afraid.

A mistake has been made, Yolanda thinks. The spelling of José's surname. A page from a list of prisoners that has somehow been misplaced.

She hadn't imagined, none of them had, a silence this profound. It's as if he had plunged into a well so deep that it had swallowed even the echo of his fall.

—

If Yolanda's outside world has widened, at home her world has shrunk.

All week she has been irritable at school. When the sixth-years complain that she hasn't returned their assignments, she snaps at them and doubles their homework load. It's unlike her, she knows it. She sees them exchanging glances from under the springy canopies of their hair.

She has to remind herself how much she loves being a teacher, that her exhaustion is not their fault. But sometimes, when she has spent her entire morning queuing, or being shunted between the offices of bureaucrats, she has no patience for their adolescent games.

She makes an effort for a single pupil. She has learned what happened from Borovich, who takes Gabriel for physics; it was indeed Gabriel's father who was marched off the factory floor. She is harder on Gabriel than all the others because he's the brightest and she will not let him squander it; what has happened to his family has destabilised him, but she refuses to let him slide.

Though Julieta phones her weekly from Miami, Yolanda is still not used to this: to Graciela being God knows where, to the hollow feeling Osvaldo has left at home.

The night he left Yolanda paced the rooms of the life they had built together, knowing that without his weight beside her, she would find it impossible to sleep.

His washing was still entwined with hers in the laundry; his elbows still creased the jacket where it hung on the back of his chair.

She put his things away. She dried the cup he'd had his coffee in that morning. She folded his underwear and paired his socks and placed them in their corners of the drawer. She bookmarked the page and closed the book that he had left facedown on the floor.

She was putting his things in order and it comforted her. There would be no footprints in the bathroom in the morning, no warmth on his side of the bed. Yet performing these tasks in some way brought him closer, as if she could still speak to him through the myriad private gestures out of which they had woven a life.

Downstairs, his papers still lay on the desk where he did their accounting, on the desk where he must have worked on his cartoons.

The records he'd last played for them were scattered across the sideboard, and one by one she fitted them into their sleeves. A seventy-eight sat mutely on the turntable, its butterfly label pinned under the Perspex lid. A triangle of light came on as she lowered the needle onto the record, waiting for the song he loved to start.

'Toda mi Vida' – a tango by Aníbal Troilo. They'd danced to it before they got married, and now she listened closely, to the heartfelt words of loss and longing and love. When it came to an end she picked up the needle and played it again, trying to hold the essence of him, conjuring him back through this sound.

And as she listened she looked at the drawings they'd hung above the sideboard, cartoons that he'd done years ago of the girls. She'd smiled at his depiction of Graciela, all giddy on the swing that she had wound up in the playground, of Julieta stuck on a pony that refused to budge.

She turned the volume up so she could hear it when she went into the laundry, allowing the melody to accompany her through the house. She passed the dining room and the room that the girls had grown up in, the shelves with their child-hood things. She wanted the music to fill her, to fill all the spaces they had occupied, the intimate geography of their lives.

She stood before the washing basket, enveloped in the song as she unwound the arms of his shirts from around her cloth-ing, releasing the slow tangle of his embrace.

She laid out his undershirts on the bench top and folded them and unfolded them and folded them again, and when she was done she closed her eyes and smoothed the soft ma-terial, remembering the contours his body made, his warmth against the skin of her palm.

Osvaldo.

Crying would not help things, she knew that.

She wanted him far away in safety. She needed him there by her side.

4

Paris

October 1976

There is a surreal quality to my life in Paris. On Saturdays the markets jostle with shoppers selecting from infinite varieties of apples, buying butter in slabs from the cheesemongers, sizing up the quality of the shellfish heaped upon pillows of ice. The *pâtisserie* windows glister with constructions that emerge in polyhedrons dangling from golden strings.

I move through it but on the outside of a city intent upon pleasure, present though my thoughts are elsewhere. I see but do not hear the buskers on their accordions; I see the cheeses displayed like pieces on a chessboard, but am not curious how they taste.

My alibi is a shopping list that Carla drew up this morning: artichokes and pumpkin, mushrooms and asparagus, and strict instructions for only the red Anjou pears. Baguettes I can pick up later, on condition that I get them from the baker she knows. The fruit stalls are indecent with colour as I join the line in front of them, out of place in this rainbow-hued world.

I've been in France for five months now, cobbling together an existence that still feels tentative because I cannot tell how long I am going to stay. My horizon stretches only to Yolanda's phone calls, and my thoughts turn constantly to home.

Yet not even this tenuous foothold could have been achieved without François' help. We met a decade ago in Rome, when Yolanda and I attended the congress of the medical association that François and I belong to, and which is held in a different city every year.

The last one we went to was in Nice, in February just before the coup. That congress proved a lifeline in ways I could never have imagined, since the visa I'd had to obtain for it was still valid when I'd had to escape.

'Three kilos . . . three,' I tell the Tunisian who serves me, as he leans onto his pumpkin-slicing knife. When he weighs the enormous wedge that he has cut for me, his estimate proves exactly right.

An eye surgeon with a passion for Piazzolla, François came to collect me when I phoned from Orly airport, and he and Hélène introduced me to their friends. François had met Arturo years ago in Paris, in a line for Piazzolla tickets when Arturo was here researching, and the two had stayed in contact ever since.

Exiled like me from Argentina, Arturo lectures part-time at one of the history institutes; Carla works as a translator for a publisher in Spain. In their first-floor, inner-courtyard apartment, they'd needed a tenant to make ends meet.

And it was François, again, who'd helped me find a job. My qualifications are not recognised in France so I am barred from medical practice; I was cleaning cinemas in the Latin Quarter when François arranged an interview at a friend's pharmaceutical firm. I have no vocation as a salesman, but I also know how lucky I am that they decided to give me a chance.

Now I keep my one suit pressed by hanging it over a chair in the living room, and knock at the doors of doctors who were once my peers. Medipharm sees marketing value in my experience as a practitioner; I spend my days convincing the profession of the superiority of Medipharm drugs.

They only have white asparagus, and Carla didn't specify, so I add a bunch to my hillock of brown paper bags.

'Anjou pears – the red ones,' I say, holding up six fingers when the Tunisian asks.

It's only temporary, I tell myself; the job means I can pay the rent and still send money home. And in any case, with any luck, I'll be back in Argentina within a year.

The visa I obtained for the congress expired months ago. Though my grandmother was French and French is my second language, France owes me no assistance, and I appeal to the Italians instead. My grandfather, who'd had a choice between New York and Buenos Aires, emigrated to Argentina in the 1900s, and because of him I qualify for an Italian passport; thanks to Italy, I am able to extend my stay. Every few months I cross the border to renew my interim visa until my Italian papers are ready; Medipharm schedules me visits to clients en route.

I pay the Tunisian and arrange the bags of vegetables in my basket, pumpkin on the bottom, mushrooms as Carla instructed on the top.

In this place of safety I am trying to put some order in my life, yet still I find I cannot be at peace. My eldest daughter's anger keeps pursuing me – perhaps because it echoes what I already feel.

'How could you abandon Mamá and Graciela?' Julieta had said, when I'd called to tell her I was now in Paris. And when I told her the reasons: 'How could you have been such a fool?'

I could picture the colour rising on her cheekbones, the cleft in her otherwise strong chin. She couldn't know how little I needed her admonitions, how bitterly I already reproached myself.

I reach the front door and buzz myself into the building, vowing to leave my unhappiness outside.

It is only when I have carried the basket upstairs to the apartment, and Carla has come to the door and thanked me and taken the basket from me, that I realise I have forgotten the bread.

—

I sit up in the darkness on my borrowed folding bed. The bookshelves lean over me in the dimness; I see the sofa looming like a hunchback, the unsteady standing lamp.

I have dreamed again of Yolanda. I slept in happiness and woke again to the loss of her. She is not here; we did not properly say goodbye.

Closing my eyes, I try to re-enter the dream. Shreds of it trail around the corner, recede like lamplight under a door.

It is no good – I cannot go back into it, so I try instead to remember it. I still my mind and concentrate, willing myself back into its warmth.

I've known her half my life, and in my dream I'm aware this is a leave-taking, so that the dream unfolds like a slow farewell to all the women I remember her to have been.

I take the hand of the shy young student I met at university, who'd hesitated beside my row of seats as she left the lecture hall. She turns, and there she is, in her emerald dress all loveliness, the Yolanda I took out dancing on Saturday nights. She steps away from me, then moves towards me with the rhythm of the music, and becomes the blushing Yolanda who married me with tiny yellow roses in her hair. This time I turn, and when I look back she has become the Yolanda who bore our daughters, the woman I feared I'd lost but who came back to me after Julieta's complicated birth. I see her in the hospital, with Graciela the miracle baby when no more babies were possible, or so we'd been led to believe. As I pull her towards me she becomes the forthright one, the Yolanda who makes me laugh with simply a look, who can convince a classroom of teenaged boys that they can all be better than they are. And coexisting with that woman is another Yolanda, the pragmatic one, the intuitive one, the Yolanda who sent me away.

Yolanda. I'd awoken with her scent on my skin, the curve of her spine under my hands. She was so vivid I ached for her; she was so present I'd reached for her in my sleep. She had changed all the time and I hadn't seen it happening; she'd kept growing beside me and I hadn't known. Gathered from all these women who were still alive within her, her wisdom had outpaced mine and grown deeper, until it had become the anchor to my life.

The reality is that the night I left, there had been no time for farewells. Pressured by the curfew, we'd thought only of the moment. I'd hugged her and held her close, but hadn't imagined a separation that was anything other than short-lived.

Yet it is lasting; soon it will be half a year. In her absence the dream had brought her closer, but then it let her go.

And as it recedes, a wave of coldness rushes over me that has nothing to do with the draught blowing down through the chimney, nothing to do with the chill of the room. I didn't say goodbye. Not to Yolanda, not to Graciela. Julieta was living in North America, but Graciela – she was just a few *barrios* away. I could have made the detour. I could have just stopped by.

It was a calculation. It might have been too dangerous for both of us. I had to get to the airport. It would have used up precious time.

It was, it might have been, it would have. Yet the fact remains: I didn't even try.

~~~

5

Buenos Aires
October 1976

A face that Yolanda doesn't recognise peers between the wrought-iron curlicues, through the frosted glass of the door. A young woman, a stranger to her, is hovering on the front steps.

'I am Silvia, the girlfriend of José's friend Tomaso. May I come in?'

Yolanda swallows. She studies the girl and scans the street as she closes the door behind her.

It has been three months. Three months since José was abducted. Three months since Graciela went into hiding. Three months without word of where she is.

There is something disturbing about this girl, Yolanda thinks, fighting a sudden reluctance to let her inside.

Insect-thin, the girl has shadows under her eyes and clothing that seems to unravel the more she speaks. A twisted scarf slides backwards off the blue-black hair it is meant to hold in place. It, the cobwebbed cardigan, the skirt over laddered stockings: all are black, or an historical black, faded to a washing-machine grey. Among the silver rings that click as she moves her fingers is a gothic cross that catches on her sweater so that the front of it is ragged with pulled threads. Behind clotted mascara her pupils are wide and her skin has the greyish tinge to it of a smoker on minimal sleep.

A night-flier, Yolanda says to herself, unable to dispel the image; a clawed creature with membranes for wings.

'I'm sorry to show up like this,' says Silvia. A row of silver bangles, oxidising black, jingle tinnily on her arm. 'I got your address from José's parents. I wanted to come in person.' She pauses. 'It's about Graciela,' she says.

Yolanda freezes where she is standing in the hallway, her welcome dying before she can shape it into words. Graciela – what about Graciela? Something is wrong; with immediate conviction she knows. And in the same flash, she realises she doesn't want to know. As long as she can stop this girl from speaking she can inhabit the 'Before' when nothing has yet happened, like holding back the turning of the tide.

She moves mechanically through the gestures of hospitality as she shows the girl into the sitting room. She forces her feet to carry her to the kitchen, gropes for water jugs and glasses, for coffee cups and the *mate* tin and those small hard almond biscuits. She opens cupboards and closes them again, opens drawers and shuts them again, delaying things by looking for things, anything to postpone listening to what this torn-winged messenger in her living room has travelled here to say.

Nothing, the girl doesn't want anything besides water; she wants, she needs, to talk. Yolanda needs not to hear. She stands in the kitchen with her forehead against the door of the refrigerator, its hum matching the thrumming some-where inside her, readying herself for what cannot be readied for.

'I need to tell you what happened,' the girl says.

She will not be delayed, Yolanda thinks. Whatever it is, she is going to wade right in.

Yolanda hesitates between the kitchen and the living room, holding a glass of water, forgetting what she is doing mid-step. She can hear a distant tinkling, like a bell in some mountain temple: the sound of ice trembling against the side of the glass.

Graciela Graciela Graciela, she thinks. Let her be safe, let her come to no harm. Let her remain how Yolanda remembers her, the whimsical second daughter who came to them when she thought there'd be no more children, Graciela the graceful, the one she'd always wanted to protect.

The girl begins. There is no stopping her now.

She was bringing them provisions; she had missed the train. She arrived on the very last one, the late one that came from the city terminus, and took the side entrance to the building because it was quicker when you were coming that way. Unusually, the elevator was out of order, so she had had to take the stairs.

Yolanda forces herself to concentrate over the roaring in her ears.

Silvia could hear voices, then shouting as she climbed the steps and found the lift jammed open – it was whining in high-pitched protest on an upper floor. The apartment door was ajar, she could see into it from the stairwell; all the other doors remained shut. Then a wave of sound reached her with a time lag, like an explosion on a far horizon: there came a thudding and a screaming and a cascade of smashing that hit her like the crunch of her own bones.

Through gritted teeth Yolanda can imagine it: the shattering of glass under metal; a boot grinding the carpals of a hand.

Then, through the sliver of doorway, Silvia glimpsed what she didn't want to see: a knee in Tomaso's back; Tomaso's arms being trussed with electrical cable; Tomaso's head wrenched backwards by the hair.

And in the seconds that passed in a kind of paralysis, she noticed another thing: that the men who were inside the apartment, driving another boy's head into the carpet, had dressed as if for a party, disguised in platinum-blond wigs and jokers' masks.

Silvia is twisting her fingers as she relates this, compressing them till the rings indent the phalanges and the metalwork cuts off the flow of blood.

Yolanda cannot bear to watch. She cannot bear to hear.

The girl couldn't think what to do so she continued up the staircase as if she had been headed all along to a higher floor. She went up and up till there were no stairs left and no higher floors to reach. Every step felt like a betrayal, but some other instinct was driving her; she could think only of getting away.

At the top of the stairwell she found a door and opened it, and went out on to the building's roof. There, behind a ventilation duct, she crouched under the rolling black clouds.

Shaking, she prayed they hadn't seen and wouldn't follow her. She was trembling so violently she was sure the building was rocking; surely all of Flores knew she was there.

So it happened in Flores, Yolanda thinks. She remembers the pink envelope. Here in Buenos Aires. Only a few *barrios* away.

There was someone called Tomaso; there was another student; but where was Graciela? Yolanda hardly dares breathe.

'Suddenly there were noises down in the street – a sound like the howling of dogs, and shouts and car doors opening – so I peered out over the parapet, and that's when I saw them come out.'

Silvia releases a sound that is almost a sob.

'There were eight of them, those men,' she says, 'they had Graciela and Tomaso, and Tomaso's friend Guillermo, and another girl whose name was Susana, I believe. They got everyone. They marched them out with their hands bound behind them and blankets thrown over their heads, and straight away they shoved them into those cars.'

'And they made them wait while four of the men went back and stripped the apartment. They took the television and the stereo. They took the crates of records. They carted out the barbecue set and a bike.'

And from above, she said, she could see the masks – a laughing clown, a Miss Piggy snout, a Planet of the Apes gorilla – where they'd pushed them up off their faces.

Silvia swallows hard when she has finished. The skin of her fingers is yellow where she has squeezed them against her rings.

Yolanda is staring at her. Graciela was there. Her mind cannot move beyond it, beyond this simple fact.

Slowly, she drags her thoughts back to Silvia. Who is this girl? she wonders. A friend of her daughter's? An acquaintance? The traitor who gave them away?

'I'm sorry,' Silvia says, unable to read the expression on Yolanda's face. 'I only knew Graciela a little – we met at the *Fac* last year. I don't know who those men are, or where they've taken everyone. I just thought you would want to know.'

Yolanda sits with her head in her hands for a long time after she has seen the girl to the door. The ice melts into a ring under the glass on the polished tabletop and turns dark in the layering dusk.

She had feared it but she has not prepared for it. She is incapacitated by what the girl has said.

She feels the earth turn and the night fall and somewhere a tide receding as she sits on into the darkness, trying to think what to do.

———

6

Paris
October 1976

'I'll come back, Yolanda. I mean it. There's no question of your doing this alone.'

I am sitting on Arturo's lumpy sofa in Paris, winding the spiral phone cord around my finger, pressing the black receiver against my ear.

Far away, at the end of the line in Argentina, other voices are chattering over our call.

It's five days since I picked up the phone and heard her utter them: four words like nails hammered into my chest.

They have taken her.

Knowing immediately who she meant. Shock, and then denial. Around me, a world in collapse.

Yolanda has rung from yet another *locutorio*. She picks telephone offices at random for the sake of anonymity, and because it's far too risky to call from home. But today the glass between the cubicles provides no insulation, and our conversation breaks into non-sequiturs that snag on other lives.

I have thought it out. I am insisting, though she forbade it from the first call.

'I can do it clandestinely, Yolanda. I should have done it the minute you called.'

'Are you out of your mind, Osvaldo?' Her voice is ragged with fatigue. 'I forbid you to take such a risk.'

I have no strategy, no plan. I know only that I am wasting time, that I should already have gone.

'For pity's sake, Osvaldo,' she says when I can hear her again over the babble of interference. 'You're on their list yourself.'

And if the literacy project had nothing to do with it? What if they took Graciela only because they couldn't find me?

But Yolanda has no time for my sense of guilt. She is not interested in how responsible I feel.

'What did you have in mind – a prisoner swap?' She lowers her voice. 'You don't see it, do you? What's going on is not lawful, Osvaldo. They're not playing by those rules.'

People are being snatched from buses and wedding receptions, she tells me, from football stadiums and in pre-dawn raids at their homes. If I come back, and she is adamant about this, then I will be joining their ranks.

'Yolanda, you have to see it from my point of view . . .'

She cuts me off. 'And you from mine,' she says.

'How can I live with myself if I don't look for her?'

'How can I live with myself if you do?'

I don't ask how she is coping with the searching. I don't ask how she manages it on top of school. I don't ask what it's like to try again at doors she has already knocked on, to wait in line for officials who never receive her, to clutch in her hand a number that never gets called.

All I hear is rejection. Her prohibition against my coming home.

In the gulf that yawns between us, we cut our dialogue short. The receiver clatters as she hangs up the phone.

I hug myself in the cold of the night-time apartment. Graciela Graciela Graciela. Her name reverberates down all the years I have known her. How can Yolanda expect me merely to stand by?

I miss my wife but I am angry with her, and hate this rift, and hate the way our conversations these days seem to end.

I stand in the bleakness of the living room, the light bulb sending its pale illumination across the courtyard, my daughter's absence stabbing at my heart.

We will get through this, I tell myself. We will find her. We have made it through so many things.

We got through the two miscarriages.

We got through Julieta's accidents: the time she crashed her bicycle, the time she broke her arm in a fall from a horse.

We got through Graciela's illness when she was a five-year-old, when her scarlet fever was diagnosed only just in time.

We got through our financial troubles. We got through the first years of my practice; through Yolanda's changes of school.

The next time we speak, I tell her I won't come home. I tell her I still miss her, that I'm sorry we keep arguing, that I will do what I can from here.

She says nothing for a moment, and when she speaks again, her voice is full of sadness.

'I love you so much, Osvaldo. Not a single moment of a single day goes by without my wanting you back.' She pauses, then goes on. 'I can't tell you how hard it is for me to say this, but if you love me at all, if you love Graciela, I need you to make me a promise: that until this situation is over, you will not try to return.'

7

Buenos Aires
November 1976

Shuffling feet. Women in low-heeled shoes and raincoats. Men in office lace-ups, briefcases planted like milestones on the ground.

The line spills down the steps of the government building, hugs the wall under its balconies, and disappears around its eastern flank. She thinks of it as a breadline for information, all of them queuing for a small ration of hope.

Yolanda, who has been here since six, is among the first twenty people in the line-up, which means she has a chance of being seen. Turning, she recognises a face or two behind her and nods at them: all of them like earthquake survivors searching for a name.

'Who are you looking for?' they ask each other, for there is plenty of time to fill. The refrain ripples up and down the queue that leaps from the Interior Ministry to the police commissariats, from the Defence Ministry to the law courts, from the prisons to the offices of the church.

My daughter. My son. My brother. My sister. My husband. My father. My wife.

They inch forward in pairs or singly, feet aching, backs hurting, rehearsing the words they will use. Like Yolanda they've risen early, taken buses in the dark or the first metros, arriving hours before any of the staff.

When finally it is Yolanda's turn, the dough-faced bureaucrat thrusts a clipboard list at her and tells her to run through the names. She can tell, even before he passes her the register, that he is ranked too low to help them, and high enough to keep them at bay.

Neither José nor Graciela is recorded there, even when she checks a third time, even making allowances for misspelling.

'Why aren't they included?' she asks him. What does he advise her to do?

'If they are not on the list, then they have not been arrested, Señora. Perhaps they have taken a vacation.'

Yolanda stares at him in stupefaction, until she realises she hasn't misheard.

'They have not gone on vacation,' she says slowly. 'They were taken away, separately, by plain-clothes police.'

'Señora,' he says, 'if they were arrested by the police then they would be in prison and their names would be on the register. Since their names do not figure on the register, then we have to conclude that they cannot be under arrest.'

'Then where are they?' she says.

Other family members are pressing forward in the line-up, impatient for their turn.

The man sighs and rubs his brow as if dealing with a particularly obtuse child.

'Señora, this is not a bureau of missing persons. Your daughter and her fiancé are grown-ups; they are responsible for themselves. If you really think they have vanished, if you're sure they won't show up next week with a Florida suntan, then I suggest you report them as missing to the police.'

At the diocese, where she is received – after days of petitioning – by a bishop who is a cousin of the wife of Yolanda's brother, the discourse is more or less the same.

'What were they up to, Señora?' the churchman says. 'No one is arrested without good reason. Perhaps they have involvements of which you are unaware.'

His fingernails are yellow and longer than a guitarist's; he bends each one and flicks it back while he pretends to listen, sunk in his purple chair.

'Graciela has not "been up to" anything, Your Excellency,' Yolanda is saying. 'She has been swept up in some crackdown by mistake.'

The bishop continues as if she hasn't spoken. 'Pernicious influences are afoot, Señora. We must be vigilant, and keep watch over our children at all times.'

Yolanda, who has hardly eaten for days and scarcely slept, wonders if he's heard anything she has said.

'Your Excellency, my daughter and her fiancé are not children. Graciela will be twenty in a month.'

'We are all children in the eyes of God,' the bishop says. A yellow fingernail bends so far back she winces, and waits for it to snap. 'It behoves all parents to inform themselves of their children's whereabouts, and of those with whom they associate. A moment's inadvertence, they mingle with the wrong people' – his hand circles in the air – 'then suddenly they have strayed from the righteous path.'

Yolanda feels her anger mounting. She has seen the Junta's warnings, like some twisted joke, on television: *Do you know what your child is doing right now?* She swallows hard to keep her emotion in check.

'Of course, if your daughter is innocent,' he continues, 'if nothing is weighing on her conscience, she'll have nothing to fear and no reason to have run away.'

'With the greatest respect, Your Excellency,' Yolanda says, 'Graciela has not run away. She was abducted. You are a man of conscience, a man of influence. I am begging you to intercede on my behalf, to find out where my daughter is being held.'

'If your daughter was engaged in subversive activities, then I will intercede for you in prayer.'

Subversive activities? Yolanda flushes. Anger roars inside her, and the desperation that has been building in her for days. But she holds it, she manages to hold it. Instead, she shapes it into a retort that she delivers with an equanimity long-honed before classrooms of recalcitrant boys.

'My daughter is not a terrorist, if that is what you mean to suggest,' she says. 'She is no guerrilla and she is not a subversive. She is a student at the University of Buenos Aires. She is studying psychology; her fiancé is majoring in modern languages. I had hoped you might have found, by virtue of the privileges conferred upon you by office, something more to offer us than your prayers.'

He responds without missing a beat, without lifting his eyes from his fingernails, without raising the tenor of his voice.

'God's hand moves in mysterious ways, Señora.' A fingernail the colour of nicotine clicks against the cushion of his thumb. 'If God wants your daughter to be found, He will ensure it. Be humble and have faith. Go in peace. Do not question His will.'

He rises from his velvet armchair to signal the meeting is over. As he does so, it comes to her in a flash of intuition: he knows. If not where Graciela is, he knows what's going on. He knows exactly how to find out.

In his imperious robes he means to usher her through the doorway but Yolanda holds her ground, resisting the extreme awkwardness of the moment, facing him over the carpet that creeps in florid opulence across the floor.

'I will not take one step from this room without your solemn oath, as a man of God, that you will find out where my daughter is, as well as the man she intends to marry.'

'Are you threatening me, Señora?' His expression has lost its bland impassiveness; she sees a mix of mockery and displeasure in his face.

'Your Excellency, I am imploring you.'

He sighs, as if with tedium. To placate her, she thinks later, or merely to get her out of his office, he tells her to return in a month. He will enquire, he assures her. He will be sure to inform her if there is any information to convey.

At home, she marks the day a month hence on the kitchen calendar. Mid-December, she thinks. For the church, a charitable time.

Four weeks later she returns to the diocese offices. The secretary to the secretary to the bishop regrets to advise her that, the affairs of the church being at once so manifold and so pressing, the bishop will be prevented from receiving her that day.

Nor can he do so the next day, or the next, nor on any of the days that follow, nor during any of the subsequent weeks.

The secretary to the secretary to the bishop advises that he has added her name to his list. The bishop will see her most certainly, the moment he has anything to report.

It is nearly Christmas when she learns of it, more than two months since Silvia's visit to her home.

'All I want is something to help me drop off at night,' she tells the doctor. 'Osvaldo's away and I need something to steady my nerves.'

It's a Saturday morning and Yolanda is in the consulting room, observing the Japanese prints on the doctor's wall. There is a famous one, of a wave that is breaking over some boats in front of Mount Fuji, the sky alive with water and flying foam. She has seen it a hundred times, but now she properly looks at it, and is surprised to see that the boats contain tiny people, men in pigtails clinging to the deck as if all they could do was pray for the storm to pass.

The doctor, who has treated them all since the girls were children, won't know about Graciela's disappearance. Circumspect, Yolanda has resolved to keep it to herself.

Fat as a cigar, his fountain pen seems to scribble the Valium prescription on its own. 'You must be thrilled at the prospect of becoming a grandparent,' the doctor says, inking his signature with an expansive swirl that travels across the bottom of the page.

Yolanda stares at him.

'Julieta isn't expecting,' she says. 'We've just spoken on the phone.'

The doctor looks up from his prescription pad, pen poised as if it's about to drop ash where he is meant to add the date.

'I'm not talking about Julieta,' he says. There is a puzzled expression on his face.

Yolanda's mind is whirring like a machine.

'Graciela was at the end of the first trimester the last time she came to see me,' he says. 'I gave her some advice for the morning sickness and a referral to the best gynaecologist I know.'

Yolanda is reeling. Graciela pregnant? She is not quite twenty. Yolanda can scarcely make sense of his words.

'She was ecstatic, I must say,' the doctor continues. Under bristly eyebrows, his glasses flash opaquely in the sunlight; Yolanda adjusts her position to see his eyes.

'She couldn't wait to tell her fiancé,' he says. 'She wanted him to be the first to know.'

Concentrate, Yolanda tells herself. Stay calm. Collect the facts.

'Can you tell me the date of that appointment?' She tries to say it lightly, then holds her breath, centring by force of will the pieces of her that feel like they are flying apart.

The family cards lie between them on the desk, four interlocked narratives of sickness and health nestling in a worn manila sleeve.

She sees his perplexity shade into reluctance. He has said too much, he must be thinking; now he will be worrying where it will lead.

She watches him twist a cufflink, a tiny red and gold chessboard, between his fingers.

'Please,' she says, praying that this family doctor is also a family friend.

He looks at her with an expression she cannot decipher. She feels suddenly self-conscious in last year's teaching dress, her untrimmed hair grown frizzy for lack of care.

'As her mother,' she adds, and fears the moment already lost.

He hesitates. All she has asked for is the date. Is it patient confidentiality that's worrying him? she wonders. Yet surely, in the case of pregnancy, for the patient's mother an exception might be made.

'Since you are next of kin . . .' he says, twisting the harlequin cufflink the other way.

Next of kin? she thinks. That's what you say about the dead.

He picks up the filing cards, salmon-pink and stapled together where new ones have been added over the years. Taking a moment to examine it, he slides out one that has 'Graciela' inscribed in blue letters across the top.

'It was July the twenty-sixth,' he says.

She leans forward and he shows her where it is written, this last trace of Graciela, her beautiful second daughter who is missing, and who it seems is now expecting a child.

Speedily Yolanda makes the calculation. 'So she's due in January,' she says.

He nods. 'About January the twenty-second. In roughly one month's time.'

One month. So, she thinks, right now her daughter is eight months pregnant, and the doctor confirmed the pregnancy in July. On July the twenty-sixth, he'd said – and Yolanda knows that date. That's the day when José disappeared.

Had they spoken? Had Graciela told him he was going to be a father – or had she been waiting for him to get home? With Yolanda there'd been no time for talk of babies when the night was embroiled in panic, when the phone was engaged with Graciela's frantic calling, when midnight passed and still he hadn't come back.

A day or two later Graciela had gone into hiding, and no one that Yolanda knew but Silvia, diaphanous Silvia in her gothic garb, had seen her for the next three months.

Yolanda tries to remember. It was still too early, the last time she'd seen her daughter, drinking tea at the kitchen table in mid-July. The pregnancy wasn't yet showing, and Graciela hadn't yet mentioned it to anyone; after Yolanda's own miscarriages, she would have been waiting until she was sure.

How in God's name was she coping? Was she ill? Had she been suffering from constant nausea, as Yolanda had done herself? With mounting panic she wonders in what conditions her daughter is living, if she is getting the care she is needing: fresh food, vitamins, light.

Yolanda looks up. Over his glasses the doctor has been scrutinising her, and she looks him straight in the eye.

He knows, she thinks. He has guessed.

Can she trust him? She longs to, but isn't sure of him; she has no knowledge of where he stands. Here in the doctor's office, where she has sat so often with that pain in her chest or a feverish child on her knee, she decides to take the risk.

'I don't know where they are holding her.'

In desperation she has blurted it out, and blindly she ploughs ahead. A door is ajar and she keeps her foot inside it because no one else has helped her, because everyone else has patronised or humiliated her, and every path has ended in a wall.

'Since she is pregnant,' says Yolanda, the precariousness of Graciela's situation dawning, 'is there some place she might have been sent?'

His mind is clicking over, she can see it: he has made a mistake; he shouldn't have mentioned the pregnancy; he doesn't want to get involved. He has his connections – that much she assumes – but like everyone else, he's afraid.

'I'm sure the authorities will be able to help you,' he says. The door to his concern slams shut as if yanked by a draught.

The appointment is suddenly over because he is standing, he is handing her the prescription, he is smiling his urbane smile. A moment later he is ushering her past the defeated pot-palms, out towards his secretary, out into the remnants of the day.

That night, in the slow moments before the Valium lifts and rocks her, a new thought enters Yolanda's mind.

Could he have known about Graciela's disappearance before she made the appointment? Had he let slip about the pregnancy on purpose? Had he wanted her to know?

⸻

She calls from a phone box on Avenida Callao. Over the roar of the traffic, Osvaldo reels from the news.

'Graciela's expecting a *child*?'

Yolanda begins enquiring at the maternity hospitals. Sometimes she can manage three of them if she starts out early on a day she isn't teaching, but there are scores of smaller clinics on her list. She makes her way to the public wards and tries to catch the midwives, who generally prove more helpful than the obstetricians. Have they examined any women in jail?

They look at her as if she were out of her mind.

She persists; this is her one best hope and she will not be deterred. Do you recognise this woman – she is now in her third trimester? She is eight months pregnant. Look at her, surely you'd remember her face? She thrusts the picture on top of clipboards, into reluctant hands. They barely glance at the photograph. It is one that José took of Graciela last summer, the most recent one Yolanda has of her, Graciela framed by a willow tree at Tigre. Please, she begs, do you recognise her, is there nothing you recall? The doctors are uncomfortable; caught off guard, they can't dislodge this woman who won't withdraw without an answer. They avoid her, they try to evade her questions. Do you have an appointment, Señora? Have you registered at Reception? We don't discuss our patients. Can't you see these people are waiting? I will have to call security. Please step aside. Señora, we are trying to work.

She weeps into the telephone. It is hopeless. There are too many clinics, too many doctors, too much suspicion and fear.

They keep track of the weeks. They count down the January days.

The baby, Yolanda thinks, must be somewhere with its mother, once they guess that the time has come. Its birth must be recorded somewhere, and with it, Graciela's name.

At the start of February, with the summer sun beating down on the tiled footpaths, Yolanda begins checking the hospital lists. She tries register offices for lists of new-borns, and paediatric wards in case of complications. After a while, she turns to the orphanages. She turns to the adoption courts.

There is one place they've both thought of but cannot bring themselves to mention. Then one day Yolanda tells Osvaldo she has taken a map and circled all the cemeteries. She tells him it is just to make sure.

8

Paris
January 1977

My first winter in Paris. I cross the grimy courtyard, past the garbage bins huddled in their derelict shelter. Under a ferrous sky, pigeons shiver on the window ledges. The cobblestones are oily as dead birds.

Darkness departs reluctantly in these low January days. Dawn doesn't break; the mornings creep up stealthily, a pale extension of night.

A switch on the wall sheds its mandarin glow and I lean on it and count a beat, waiting for the click that releases the lock on the door. I swing my body behind the handle and hang there a moment, counterpoised to the great weight of it, before stepping out into a corridor of sound.

I am still unused to the assault of it: the wail of sirens, the churn of buses, the motorists' hair-trigger horns.

A flotilla of headlights navigates the dimness. My eyes stream from the cold, and the cough I've acquired – in this foreign land I am prey to every illness – feels like it could shake my ribcage loose. I hunch my shoulders against the breeze that fingers my collar, that wheedles through button-holes and seams.

New Year has come and gone; the forecast has turned Siberian and the *mairies* have strewn the thoroughfares with grit. Discarded after Christmas, moulting fir trees slouch against the limestone. The footpaths crunch with pine needles and salt crystals as I set off for my first appointment as if walking through a forest by the sea.

Right now in Argentina it is summertime. People will be on holiday at the beach.

I picture Yolanda waiting beside hospital elevators, inter-cepting the orderlies for word of Graciela. Ever since her abduction we've been turning in frantic circles, our nights disturbed by terrors we dare not name.

Along the boulevard I glance at the still-closed doors of travel agents and hairdressers and search for her reflection, the shining eyes and the freckles that vanish in the winter months. I search for her at the bakery and in the line at the dry cleaner's; once I think I see her strap-hanging at the back of a bus. Reflexively, in this city where I recognise no one, where nobody shares my memories, I look for her in every stranger's face.

And now – I cannot fathom it. *The possibility of a child.*

Did she go full-term? I wonder. Hands swollen with cold, a gang of Moroccan fruit sellers is unloading crates of arti-chokes from a truck. Did it all go well? I ask myself, and shudder as I remember her sister's complicated birth.

I am haunted by my worst imaginings. They are with me before I wake, before a lighter shade of darkness prises through the living-room shutters and hauls me into another recalcitrant day. They are with me as I stand in the icy bathroom, speckling the sink with hyphens as I shave. They are with me as I spoon coffee into Carla's battered percolator, as I spill its talcum softness onto the worktop, as I map mental routes between the meetings that punctuate my ineffectual hours.

I am tormented by my inability to help her, by the fear that I might be to blame.

Black ice: they've been predicting it on the radio. They discuss it like an omen from the underworld: an occult force that could snatch the living away. This morning, however, the roads are dry; sediment streaks the gutters like an afterwash of aspirin. Underfoot, puddles shatter like quartz and the TV antennae rasp the lowering sky.

Beyond the intersection I approach the metro entrance, its twin lamps peering bloodshot into the feeble light of dawn. Tempted by the underground warmth, I vacillate, then decide to continue on foot. The salt is going to leave tidemarks on the shoes I polished this morning, but if I walk fast I can be on time and save on the metro fare.

Arturo and Carla have lent me a pair of driving gloves, and a knitted scarf that seems to grow longer with every wearing. I have a woollen hat that Carla gave me, and a cashmere coat that we picked out at a charity shop in Passy. Thanks to them I am kitted out for winter; I move about this hard-edged city enveloped in other people's lives.

I have been camping in their two-roomed apartment for half a year and never once have they suggested it's been too long. I fold away my makeshift bed in the mornings, and although it's harder in the winter months, I make sure I am always the first one up and try not to be home too much.

Hungry for news, they are always inviting new arrivals back for dinner, if we're not visiting the Argentines who form the nucleus of our social life. Carla, dressed in the poncho that Arturo gave her for Christmas, passes around the *mate* or her *dulce de leche* creations, while Arturo puts Piazzolla on the turntable, or a tango if he's in the right mood. Deracinated, homesick, and worried about our families, we gravitate towards each other in search of reassurance, or just to hear our language spoken in our sibilant accent, while we learn to match our heartbeats to the rhythm of those who are safe.

And the conversation almost always turns to politics: what's happening in Argentina; what, over here, we can do. I find myself paying attention to their discussions, listening for any development that might bring Graciela home.

There is little enough reporting of Argentina in the newspapers we get in Paris, but every mention I do my best to absorb. I scour the Spanish papers that Arturo retrieves from the institute as we try to pierce the censorship, and analyse the rumours that pass for facts among the exiles here.

The problem, according to Arturo, is that here in Europe, the coup in Argentina is not understood the way Chile's was, where the death of Allende, and the killings in the stadium, made everything so clear. Because Isabel had been so incompetent a president, because Argentina before the coup had been swept by waves of violence, the perception here is that the Junta's arrival was welcome and long overdue.

'That's only because our generals learned their lesson from Pinochet,' Carla is saying. 'Our lot are keeping their abuses hidden from view.'

'Except for the occasional glimpse behind the curtain,' says Arturo. 'Nothing controls better than fear.'

'Well, it's a brilliant strategy, really. Disappearance allows them to wash their hands. No body, no crime, after all.'

And it's working, I think to myself. The stories that are seeping out of my homeland fill me with terror. As the north wind howls down the chimney flues at midnight, I tremble for Graciela, and pray for her, and cling to the hope that motherhood will win her release if innocence isn't enough.

'We've got to find a way to get this talked about,' says one of the exiles, blowing his nose as he battles another French cold. 'Writing letters is all very well, but we've got to get more coverage in the press.'

Over *mate*, someone suggests enlisting help from showbiz – Montand and Signoret have shown they're sympathetic. Then somebody mentions athletes, and suddenly we're discussing the World Cup.

'A boycott? Of next year's Cup in Argentina?'

'Are you crazy? They'll try to stop us. Overwhelm us with propaganda.'

'We'd need slogans. Something powerful . . .'

'And posters. Something visual . . .'

'A logo to counter theirs.'

'And FIFA?'

'What *about* FIFA? We can't expect anything from FIFA.'

'No – I mean what leverage would we have?'

'We'd have to go straight to the players. The captains, the strikers . . .'

'And make a start with Sweden. Some place that still has principles.'

'The Dutch too. And West Germany, since they are the reigning champions.'

'I don't know about Germany. After what happened at the Games in Munich . . .'

'You mean what happened at the Games in *Berlin*, if you want to bring in the Olympics.'

'That's brilliant, we should use that: the 'thirty-six Games and the Junta's Cup.'

I replay the conversation as I approach the overpass, the Paris ring road roaring underneath.

It occurs to me, for a second before I dismiss it, that I could pitch in with a few cartoons. But I have vowed never to draw again – at least not until Graciela comes back.

The day has lightened; the cars are switching off their headlights; the street lamps flicker in unison and die. A northerly wind is wheeling off the plain beyond the airport; I wind my excessive scarf in an extra loop.

In fact I'm already involved, informally at least, with another kind of boycott: of the international cancer congress that Videla, the Junta's leader, has just announced. They plan to hold it in Buenos Aires shortly after the World Cup as proof of the Junta's concern for human life.

A couple of French oncologists have approached the association of Argentine doctors and proposed a 'counter congress' on the same dates. They want to hold it in Paris as a protest, and as a show of solidarity with their colleagues in Argentina, since a number of them have vanished since the coup.

Ahead of me, the hospital's ad hoc ugliness rears above the underpass. My fingers are ice inside my gloves and the footpath's cold is seeping into my feet.

My instinct is to discuss these matters with Yolanda, and reassure her that I'll do nothing to put her at risk. But another part of me understands that the less she knows the better, and that anything I do must be discreet.

An ambulance yodels past me, complaining through the traffic as it carves a path over the intersection and in through the emergency gate.

Inside, the bustle of a hospital morning: orderlies wheeling patients towards the elevators, drip bags wobbling like jellyfish as they bump over the linoleum floor.

Iodine and detergent. My heart clenches for a moment. I am back in my old hospital in Buenos Aires, inhaling the same aroma of neglect and care.

I follow the hand-drawn signs to Pharmacology, and wait for an eternity by the lift.

Will they do any good, these boycotts? I ask myself. Is there any way they could tip some balance that might bring Graciela back?

Upstairs, I stop off at the washroom. I remove my second-hand coat and loop my too-long scarf through one of its sleeves. In the sepia light I straighten my tie, and with my handkerchief do my best to erase the chalky tidemarks from my shoes.

The telephone shatters the silence like a cascade of breaking glass. Wrenched from sleep I fling myself towards it, since from my camp bed in the living room I'm the nearest, and get there after only two rings. It must be well past midnight; behind the unpleated shutters, the slumbering rooms are dark.

'*Allô?*' I try to say it the way that Carla does, though I can never get the inflection quite right. Groggily, I pat the book-shelf for the pen that's always rolling off it. The notepad seems to have vanished again; I tug a newspaper off the seat of a chair.

'Osvaldo?'

The voice is so faint I can barely hear it.

'Yolanda?' I say. My mind heaves awake. Today is not the day we'd agreed to talk. She never calls me this late.

I look up to see Arturo's nose and his stripy knee in the gap of the bedroom door.

'Is everything all right, *amore?*'

Softly, he closes the door.

There is a pause before her answer reaches me. Barely perceptible, it travels through the hissing and echoing while a dozen scenarios flash across my brain.

'Yes. No. I don't know,' she says. 'I've woken you all, haven't I? I'm sorry to call so late.'

Where are you? What time is it there? Can you talk? We speak over each other and through each other, unable to find a rhythm in the phone line's trip and lag.

'It's early evening here,' she says. I grind my ear against the receiver. 'It's still light. I'm not far from home.'

'Has something happened?' I say. I'm whispering now, worried I'll keep the household awake.

'No, nothing's happened,' she says. 'Nothing's wrong – at least nothing new.'

I'm fully awake and my heart is thudding, not sure whether or not to feel relief.

'You sound different,' I say. But the line is poor; I cannot identify what's changed.

'I just wanted to hear your voice.'

Our words skid and slide towards each other in irregular formations, a necklace being strung from both ends.

Something *has* happened, I think. Or she's seen something. Something's made her distressed.

She pauses, then speaks so softly I scarcely catch it. 'I just feel so afraid.'

'Afraid?' I say. 'What's made you afraid?'

'Nothing. Everything. It's all the time,' she says. Her voice is trembling and she takes a breath as she tries to order her thoughts. 'It's not one thing. It's what's happened and hasn't happened. You know, with Graciela. Not knowing anything. Not hearing anything . . . I get these feelings of foreboding, Osvaldo. I can't see how this is going to end.'

I can hear in her words the strain of it, day after day confronting what's there and isn't there to confront.

'Yolanda,' I say. I wish I could be there beside her, that she'd allow it, that she weren't so alone.

'I was downtown today, in Florida,' she is saying. 'They were dressing the Pacífico windows . . . the place was heaving with shoppers. Suddenly I found myself in front of that photo studio – you know, the one with the old cameras in the window . . . The street was sparkling in the sunshine, people were spending money and drinking coffee and buying their boxes of *alfajores*, and all I could do was stare at the photographs of the brides, and those cherub babies . . . And there was one photograph, a mother and child . . . Osvaldo, it looked so much like her . . . And when I looked up again I'd lost all sense of time. I couldn't remember where I was or which way I'd been going, whether I'd been there a only few minutes or a couple of hours.'

'Oh, Yolanda,' I say. 'I'm so sorry, *querida*.'

She doesn't say it, but she thought we'd know by now – we both did. It is the middle of February and January the twenty-second, which we'd believed was Graciela's due date, had been a sort of deadline; I think we'd both convinced ourselves that by the end of the month we would have heard something, that surely they'd have ordered her release.

In the darkness I survey the shapes around me: the sofa sagging like an ancient warhorse, the cone I have made of my bed cover, the glint of the breakfast bowls. I don't know what to say to make things easier. I don't know how to make us feel less far apart.

'You know what's hard?' she says. 'It's that for everyone else, life goes on as normal: the buses run and the shops are open and people go out to restaurants. They laugh, they watch the football, they're out buying their flashy cars and designer clothes. I feel like I exist in some parallel universe. I can't sleep at night without my tablets, and when I get to sleep I dream that we have found her, and every morning I have to relive her loss.'

'*Amore*,' I say, not knowing how to comfort or help.

I dream about Graciela also – a recurrent dream where she is a little girl running fast and giggling over her shoulder, running without looking towards the edge of a road where she cannot hear my shouting, where she misreads my panic for encouragement as I hurl myself towards her, where it's all a game, until she runs across.

Sometimes it's my own cries that wake me, that must also bother Carla and Arturo; other times I jolt awake and find myself bathed in sweat.

There is no answer so I just listen to Yolanda speaking. The two of us are imprisoned in our separate circles, unable to go backwards or advance.

'Are you looking after yourself?' I ask her after a while. I think about the things I want to tell her – about the boycott, the rival cancer congress – but know I cannot raise them without multiplying her fears.

More than anything I want to tell her that I'll come back: a word from her and I'll be on the next flight home. But she has made me promise not to raise the subject; she has made it clear that it's not something she is willing to discuss.

Instead she tells me about school: how the old fifteen-minute flag ceremony in the morning now takes the best part of an hour; how rote-learning is to be favoured over reasoning; about her request to work part-time. She thinks she can get by on half her salary as long as I can continue to send money home.

'You know I will,' I say.

I am shivering now in the stillness. I stretch the cord as far as it will go and burrow back down in my bed.

'And what about you?' she says. 'Is work all right? Are you doing okay over there?'

'As well as I can without you.'

I picture her as she's speaking, the formal way she has of sitting, the angle of her chin as she holds the receiver to the soft incline of her head.

'It's not that easy, for either of us,' she says.

And she wants to ask, I can tell because they are my questions too, but she stops herself because she knows there are no answers, that I have no answers to give.

How long till we find Graciela?

What has happened to our grandchild?

How long will this separation last?

'Yolanda,' I say. And it comes out now in a way there is no stopping, all the things I have been wanting to express.

I tell her how much I love her, how without her I feel lost to myself. I tell her how stricken I feel about our family, and about these endless months apart. I tell her how ashamed I feel when I remember my pledges when we got married: how I'd vowed never to leave her, how her happiness would always come first.

'None of it's your fault, Osvaldo,' she says. 'The world has been upended and none of us saw it coming. What could any of us have done?'

At that instant I want so much to take her in my arms. But we have only our words, and when the words run out we drift on through the silence, listening to the sound our breathing makes, and to the hollow sounds the cable makes that might be in the air or underwater, and to the quietness of the earth revolving, which is all the intimacy we have.

I have to sleep, she has to go home from wherever she is ringing. I worry about her, alone in the darkening streets.

'Will you be all right, *amore*?' I say.

I can hear her smile and the way it's laced with sadness when she answers.

'Sleep well, *mi amor*,' she says.

72

9

Buenos Aires
November 1977

From a distance they look like doves in their white head-scarves.

Every Thursday they have started turning up there, circling the square opposite the Casa Rosada, because as long as martial law is in force it is forbidden to assemble and stand. In their sandals, in their sturdy shoes and compression stockings, they walk in silence holding their big photographs, and those who don't have photographs hold up hand-drawn signs instead.

'Where is my daughter?' the placards say. 'Where is my son?'

This is the end of the road. This is where the mothers come when there are no more avenues to try.

A hundred pigeons take flight. They billow over the monument like a mainsail, then circle it before vanishing into the sky.

Should she join these women? Yolanda asks herself. Would it do any good?

She wonders what Osvaldo would think, what sharp-tongued Julieta would say. Though she'd had misgivings when her eldest daughter told her they were moving to Miami, again and again she gives silent thanks that Julieta and her husband are half a continent away.

Julieta had wanted to come home as soon as she'd heard about her sister, but Yolanda would not countenance it. She couldn't bear the strain of it, a second daughter unsafe.

Then she thinks about Graciela, her precious second-born, whom she loves as much as but differently from her first. More like her father than Julieta ever was, Graciela will now have been a mother for the best part of a year, experiencing these transformative months of her life with no one from her family by her side.

That is what Yolanda tells herself, what she needs, what she has to believe. In the depths of her heart she knows there are other alternatives, but none that do not end in a chasm of pain.

Yolanda scans the faces in the square. There are mothers, housewives and grandmothers, ordinary women and professional women, mothers of teenagers and mothers of retirement age.

Demure in their white headscarves, they could be the Junta's ideal of womanhood if it weren't for their lack of passivity. Yolanda knows, because she shares their fury, that they will march until their children are returned.

Rain begins to fall, fine as a summer mist. The women walk in silence, forming a circle around the pyramid in the square.

Surely it is safe, Yolanda thinks, watching them pace like schoolgirls in their knee-length skirts and sensible, buttoned-up coats. Surely there would be an outcry, she tells herself from her vantage point in the portico of the cathedral. Surely it would be a step too far if they started arresting mothers before the Casa Rosada.

Yolanda was in her early twenties and not yet married but clearly she remembers it, the last time Evita addressed the crowd from the balcony overlooking the square.

'Osvaldo,' she says. She is in another *locutorio*, her exasperation evident despite the faintness of her voice. 'I've been to all the ministries. I've been to army barracks and police stations, court houses and orphanages. I've been out to El Devoto and the other jails.'

He knows her list is long because he, too, has made suggestions. He has racked his brains for the names of former patients, for colleagues at other hospitals, for anyone they could call upon to help. Together they identified lawyers and churchmen, journalists and bureaucrats, even friends with some distant relative in the army.

'You have to believe me,' she is telling him. 'There *is* no other place to turn.'

He has no idea who these women are, why she thinks they could help, how she imagines this could possibly be risk-free. Yet far away in France, with only a telephone line between them, he cannot dissuade her from going to the Plaza de Mayo – even if, as she insists at first, it is only to stand and watch.

The next Thursday she goes again. This time, everything is different; the air is crackling with tension; Yolanda can see but can't get a sense of what's going on. The women are marching again in silence but this time their banners are screaming: '*Que Aparezcan Con Vida Nuestros Hijos*' – 'We Want our Children Back Alive'. She turns, and suddenly horses are bearing down on them; the mothers trip and scramble but refuse to disperse. They are insisting: they want a meeting with the Junta, and will not leave until their demands have been met.

On the third Thursday she watches from closer by. The women are walking in their circle around the pyramid; Yolanda peers at them over a copy of *La Nación*. The 'Mother, Home, Child' section is full of *Futura Mamá* ads; her heart constricts at the displays of maternity clothes.

She is awash with conflicting feelings. Instinct urges discretion but discretion has yielded nothing. By marching, the mothers are insisting on visibility – that she understands immediately, having been dismissed so many times herself. Yet to her mind, they look terribly exposed.

She is afraid of visibility, afraid of the horses, and especially she is afraid of the police.

It takes her one more Thursday to find the courage. Pedestrians are hurrying past the cathedral, commuters are rushing to the Subte, the police are taking positions for a show of force. This time the mothers are holding life-size paper cut-outs of the missing. And at their front, a new banner catches her eye.

'*Dónde Están Los Centenares de Bebés Nacidos en Cautiverio?*' it says. Ice slithers down Yolanda's spine as she re-reads it. 'Where are the Hundreds of Babies Born in Captivity?'

Hundreds? Can that be right?

Awareness strikes her like a cascade of freezing water. Whatever this is, whatever they're caught up in, she knows she cannot do this on her own.

There is a signature beneath the banner, and she takes note of it: the Grandmothers, the *Abuelas*, of the Plaza de Mayo.

Grandmothers? Well, she is a grandmother now, she must be, and she is one of these women, whether she marches with them or not. She grasps it now in the most visceral way, the knowledge hard inside her like a stone. She is mother and probably grandmother to people who have disappeared.

As soon as the march is over Yolanda moves against the stream of pedestrians, keeping her eye on the sign being rolled away. The women are embracing each other and parting; they are pairing up and peeling off towards the Subte; she has to reach them before they disperse.

She catches them up at the zebra crossing. Among them is a woman a little older and a good head shorter than Yolanda is, round-faced behind glasses that are perched on a small, blunt nose. Yolanda sees, when the woman removes her headscarf, that her hair is silver where the gold is growing out.

Suddenly she remembers the rosebuds she saw at Maria's house, their colour fading because, in the panic after José's abduction, no one had thought it important to water the plants.

The woman has cheeks like winter apples and, around her wrist, a green elastic band.

In the way she stands – short-legged and sure-footed in her brown no-nonsense footwear – Yolanda is suddenly reminded of her own mother, and feels drawn to her because of a welling need for mothering herself.

The woman looks up at her approach. Yolanda is startled by her eyes; against the grey of the city, they blink from behind her glasses in a flash of cornflower blue.

'Who have you lost, *querida*?' the woman says, before Yolanda can introduce herself with the words that she's been practising for days.

Yolanda is taken aback. Was worry etched so deeply into her face?

'My daughter,' she says. The words come out hoarsely, and the rest in a kind of whisper. 'Her fiancé. And maybe their child.'

The blue eyes scrutinise her, and make their lightning assessment. 'Meet me at the Santa Cruz church on Saturday, any time in the afternoon.'

Yolanda nods with gratitude; she is swaying with relief. Perhaps these women can help her. Perhaps she need not feel so completely alone.

'Thank you,' she says, steadying herself on the woman's extended arm.

'When you get there, just mention my name: Constanza.'

She flashes Yolanda a smile as the lights change, then hurries off across the intersection, a diminutive figure with a rolled-up banner, dwarfed by the passing cars.

In the end it had happened so quickly: a single question, the instant trust.

Yolanda is awash with gratitude.

After all these months, somebody, finally, has said yes.

'*Dios mio*,' Constanza says. She clicks her tongue. 'It just won't do. Haven't you got a bigger one than that?'

Yolanda shivers into her jacket. Inside the church the air is chilly. They are standing among the rows of pews and the woman she met at the Plaza de Mayo is studying her handbag with a frown.

Yolanda gives her a puzzled look. She never carries her shoulder-bag downtown; though petty crime has all but ceased since the coup, she isn't one for taking chances; anything larger than the one she is carrying would only be inviting trouble.

Constanza disagrees. 'That one's no use at all,' she says. 'You need something you can leave open at the top.'

'I could pin a sign on it too, saying "Pickpockets Here"!'

Constanza chuckles, forgetting that they're in a church. Yolanda notices how much she likes the sound of it, thinks how little laughter there's been over this past year.

'It's just the opposite,' Constanza says. 'It's so people can put things in.'

'You've lost me now, Constanza,' Yolanda says. She bites her lip the way she does in the classroom, when a pupil comes up with an answer they both know doesn't make any sense.

'It makes it easier for the *denuncias*,' Constanza says.

Yolanda shakes her head. Denunciations? Who would be reporting anything to them?

'People will come up to you, Yolanda,' she says. 'On the Thursday marches. "Are you the Mothers?" they say. Or "Are you the Grandmothers?" And they'll press a piece of paper into your palm, or slip a message into the top of your bag.'

Yolanda's eyes widen. 'People are smuggling you information?'

'Not all the time. But often enough. It makes sense when you think about it though, doesn't it? Who else is there left to tell?'

Yolanda takes this in. It sounds far-fetched, but maybe this way she will hear something. Maybe one day, someone will bring a tip-off for her.

'Believe me, you don't always want to receive them,' Constanza continues. 'Sometimes you unfold a scrap of paper and it's a death threat. Don't look at me like that. Of course we get them. At other times it's misinformation, or outright lies. Sometimes they say things that are deeply hurtful. But we read them all and then look into them. And sometimes we get valuable information. Usually it's anonymous, and it might just be a detail, but for one of us, it could be a life-changing clue.'

Yolanda's head is swimming. 'What sort of things do they say?'

'It could be anything. They might report on someone they believe is involved in these abductions. Or it might be something quite specific, a record of something they've witnessed, or just something that struck them as strange. Last week, for instance, someone told us they'd seen a toddler abandoned on the steps of the Casa Cuna, at the orphanage in Córdoba.'

Yolanda takes a step backwards. 'Are babies showing up like this?'

'Not often, I don't think, not that we really know. In this case we got in touch with the orphanage. It turned out that the *denuncia* was right – a two-year-old had been left there on the steps. But it's delicate. If the child is old enough, it can sometimes remember its name, perhaps that of a sibling. But we can't always be sure a particular child is one of those we're looking for. We're still working out how to proceed.'

Yolanda reflects. 'I don't even know if Graciela had her baby,' she says. 'She was three months pregnant when she went into hiding; six months when the abduction took place. If they kept her in some kind of jail,' and she shudders at the thought, 'it's quite possible she lost the child.'

She doesn't say it but she is remembering her own history: the miscarriages before Graciela. She swallows, and pushes her past grief from her mind.

Taking her by the shoulders, Constanza fixes her with her cornflower gaze.

'Yolanda,' she says, 'you can stop that right now. You don't know it, and you cannot assume it. If she was pregnant when they took her, you have to start from the premise that she had her baby. Until someone informs you otherwise, you have to assume they are both alive.'

Yolanda absorbs Constanza's words. Still, she thinks, if they've been separated, if Graciela's child has been dumped somewhere like the one they found in Córdoba, how could she hope to identify it? She knows nothing at all about it: not its gender, not its date of birth. She doesn't even know its name.

'You know, Constanza, no matter how I look at it, I still don't understand. What use to them is someone like Graciela? What do they want with pregnant women, with nursing mothers? None of it makes any sense.'

Yolanda's eyes run across the sparkling altar; they travel over the candelabra, over the marble chapel of the Virgin, over the pillars and the ceiling vaults. She is not fooled by the pretty, stained-glass windows. They form a barrier like all the others that have walled her off from her daughter and her grandchild, an obstacle she would tear apart with her naked hands if only she knew where to start.

Constanza hugs her because she has no answers and no other way to reply. And the gesture releases something that Yolanda has for long months been withholding, because the next moment she is weeping on Constanza's shoulder, for the first time giving into it, letting herself weep.

Her tears leave indigo patches on Constanza's second-best dress, turning part of the scalloped neckline a darker shade of blue.

'When they abducted my son and daughter-in-law,' Constanza tells her after a moment, 'the men, whoever they were, thrust the baby into the arms of a neighbour and took his parents away. But the next day the *patota* returned. They knocked on the neighbour's door and demanded the baby too. What did they want with a baby, Yolanda? He was seven months old but they came back for him – and nobody, it seems, saw anything, nobody knows a thing. The neighbour who kept my grandson overnight – she couldn't even describe the men. And of course no one has any clue where his parents are, or where my grandson was taken. Well, frankly, Yolanda, I don't believe it. I don't believe nobody knows.'

The two of them sit side by side on the hard wooden planks of the pew.

'People don't just vanish into thin air, you know. The Junta aren't magicians. We will find them, Yolanda. God knows, we will shame them into giving our children back.'

Yolanda squeezes Constanza's hand. She knows this woman is right. But she can't help feeling as if she's lost in a blizzard in some Antarctic wasteland, and that all her senses have been confounded by a world of depthless white.

'Well, there is something about a snowstorm,' Constanza says, when Yolanda tries to describe her disorientation. 'I should know, I was caught in one once when I was a girl, up there where I come from in Bariloche.' Constanza toys with the elastic band around her wrist. 'If there are two of you, you have one thing that you don't have on your own, and that's perspective. It changes everything. You can see where you are in relation to the other person, and you can see the lie of the land. That's your starting point. It's the beginning of finding your way out.'

Yolanda smiles through her tears, and nods. They sit on in the vaulted silence, breathing the aroma of wax and incense, reflecting on the rage and sorrow that have delivered them to this place.

After a while Constanza gets to her feet.

'One important thing I forgot to tell you,' she says. 'These accessible handbags I was telling you about – they have another use.'

She opens hers and tilts it so that Yolanda can peer inside. There is the sound of clinking and rolling, and something glints in its depths.

It is Yolanda's turn to stare.

'Marbles?' she says.

'I borrowed them,' says Constanza, her blue eyes twinkling in the stained-glass light that is splashing onto the flagstones at their feet. 'From my other grandson. We all carry them now – they're for under the hooves. In case the police try anything with those horses again.'

Buenos Aires
December 1977

It's a Sunday morning and Yolanda is sitting on the end of the bed. She has the door open onto the garden, letting in the tentative sunshine, though the ground outside is soggy from the overnight rain.

In their pots outside her window, the geraniums have exploded into flower. She tries not to look beyond them to the flower-beds that reproach her with their exuberant crop of weeds.

The house is quiet, as it's always quiet these days. This morning she isn't going to do the weeding. She isn't going to file her correspondence, or climb the ladder to clear the guttering, or attend to the faulty faucet above the sink. She is tired. She is worried about what distance is doing to her marriage. She is anxious about her daughter. She wants her family near.

She has brought out all the photo albums, the fat white ones of their wedding, the family ones with their layers

of filmy paper, and the tall thin ones that the girls themselves arranged.

She has spread the books out in rough chronological order
across the bedspread and is going through them page by page.

Here is the wedding photograph of her parents. It was
retouched by the studio artist, which is how she knows
that the roses her mother carried that day were yellow, matching the bud in her father's lapel. Here is Yolanda as a
five-year-old in her favourite frock – she recalls how the fabric
thickened where those daisies were embroidered onto it –
sitting on the steps of her childhood home. Ricardo, her
brother, who is standing beside her, must have blinked at the
wrong moment. She smiles now at those maroon-coloured
knitted shorts.

From its corner holders she slips out a photo of herself
beside Osvaldo, taken when they had first started stepping
out. There are flowers on the table, and cards to mark their
places, though she can't for the life of her remember where
it was. Osvaldo has his arm across the back of her chair
and the shutter has gone just as he is about to speak. She
sees how round her face was, how smooth her skin, how
very young she looked. She frowns a little at the hairdo.
Ah, but she still remembers how glorious she felt in that
dress.

And Osvaldo, slender, with darker hair, and lots of it. She
traces the side of his face with her fingertip. When he looked
at her, how her heart caught. How it spun.

And there they are, outside the church on their wedding
day. Hugo, as best man, is standing beside Osvaldo, and there
is Franca, her dear old friend from schooldays, and Yolanda
herself with roses in her hair. Later, at the reception, Osvaldo
had leaned across to her and whispered that he'd just got
married to the most beautiful woman in the world.

She leaps ahead, and comes to pictures of the girls. Julieta the adventurer, always first on a jungle gym or a horse. And there was Graciela – forever trotting after her – suddenly a teenager on the beach. And Julieta again, so grown-up already – Yolanda's heart ached that night, she remembers – her eldest daughter going out on her first date.

She folds back the rice-paper pages, each photo opening a tunnel into the past. Graciela again, dancing on her fifteenth birthday. Julieta's wedding – there's Hugo chatting to Osvaldo. She loses herself in reverie, remembering, loving her life.

She pulls the last album towards her, and an envelope slides out of the back. The paper is old and fragile, and tears as she pries it open; inside she finds a collection of Osvaldo's cartoons. She must have slipped them in there for protection, then forgotten where she'd put them; from time to time she had wondered when they'd turn up.

Then suddenly she is laughing aloud. She remembers these drawings now she sees them: Graciela doing a headstand in the garden, legs wobbling, eyes popping, blood rushing to her head. And Julieta – who didn't like this one, Yolanda remembers – doing a cartwheel, straight into a pile of dog turds on the beach. There are more, some scribbled in biro on the backs of envelopes, others done on holiday when he'd had more time.

He will be pleased to know she's found them; she must remember to tell him next time she calls.

As she slides them back in she notices a second envelope wedged inside the first one, and works it free, the paper soft as cotton in her hand.

She opens it, and there it is. After all these years, when she had searched in drawers and in the backs of books and believed it lost, she has found it. The first drawing Osvaldo had done of her, a sketch and not a caricature. The one he'd done in secret, and had worked and reworked to present to her on her birthday. The one that made her realise she'd fallen in love.

'*Amore*,' he'd said, and she remembers the first time ever he'd used it, the Italian endearment he reserved for no one but her.

So long ago it was. Yet seeing it now, she is suddenly that girl again. She remembers her, she remembers her ardent heart.

She looks out at the dripping garden, at the sun filtering down through the trees.

Somehow she will find a way, she tells herself. She will stitch this family back together. Surely soon it will be safe for Osvaldo to come home.

Paris
March 1978

Three brown eggs are bouncing in a saucepan on the stove.

Carla is in our tiny kitchen, her chestnut hair tied back amid the billowing steam. She is cramming brie into a baguette with her right hand and lowering the gas with the left. Both she and Arturo are apprehensive about my journey and I am touched by their concern.

It's only as I prepare to leave it that I realise how much of a family we've become. There's been no milestone to indicate it; it's happened without our noticing how or when. Thrown together by circumstance and held there by necessity, we've been rubbing along in this too-small space as if we'd never lived any other way.

I will be away for only a couple of days but Arturo is full of warnings. The night train to Rome, he insists, is notorious for thefts.

'It's endemic in the *couchette* cars,' he tells me, eyes streaming from the hay fever he is so susceptible to in France. 'Even the cops are in on it. Everyone's taking their cut.'

It sounds far-fetched to me, but Arturo, who now breaks out into a riff of sneezes, is adamant about this point.

I'm travelling light, I reassure him. I don't even own a suitcase and I don't have money to spend on a sleeping berth.

Arturo's caution, I know, is his way of reminding me to be vigilant in other ways. Still shaken by the disappearance of two close friends in Argentina, he takes these matters seriously, but over the past few weeks he has been more than ever on edge.

A wave of paranoia swept the Argentines here a month ago after Cecilia, an ex-detainee only recently arrived in Paris, recognised one of her torturers at a meeting to which Arturo had also gone. The man had passed himself off as an exile, had spoken with one or two people, then vanished as soon as he realised his cover was blown.

Cecilia could only be calmed with sedatives. The rest of us were shocked to learn how easily we'd been infiltrated, how relative our safety; how each of us was potentially being watched.

Perhaps that's when Arturo's attitude to the World Cup boycott changed.

'The more noise we make,' he'd said when we were discussing it a few days ago, 'the less they are going to tolerate it, and the more dangerous it is going to get.'

His new-found reticence startled me. This wasn't the Arturo I knew.

'But, Arturo,' I said. 'Don't you think it's the least we can do?'

I was thinking about Graciela and her baby, I was thinking about the disappearances, what we'd heard about the secret jails.

'What matters are results,' he'd said. 'Take that slogan, "Football between the Concentration Camps". All that does is wave a big red flag that is going to invite retaliation.'

'And over here, what are they going to do?'

'They've sent their hitmen out, Osvaldo. You saw what happened to Firmenich in Mexico.'

'Firmenich's a guerrilla leader. And that raid was a debacle – the Junta got caught red-handed, sending their goons into a foreign country. They're not going to try that again.'

'They're capable of anything, we both know that. Just ask Cecilia what she thinks.'

I could see how tired his eyes were; his hay fever was debilitating, and he had developed a twitch that kept making him blink in an effort to cover it up.

'We have to face facts,' Arturo continued. 'The generals are incredibly sensitive about their image at the moment. With the French worked up about those two nuns who got abducted, and that Swedish guy making all that noise about his disappeared daughter, they desperately need this Cup. They'll do anything to ensure it's not derailed.'

'Look, the boycott might not come off – we know that, Arturo. But the campaign will at least get people talking. Even if the matches do go ahead, Argentina will be packed with foreign journalists. And after the games, they'll be looking for stories to write.'

'So get to them privately, before they go,' Arturo said, before dissolving into another bout of sneezing. 'I just think we need to keep our heads below the parapet. There are other ways to fight.'

I didn't agree, but I didn't want to argue with him either. I didn't understand why suddenly he'd become so obdurate when I knew where his sympathies lay.

Perhaps it is the European winter, dragging on interminably when by rights it should be spring. The three of us seem attenuated somehow, our faces pale, our nerves all the time on edge. Our conversations dart like dragonflies, unable to settle anywhere for long.

Proximity has made us intimate in myriad private ways. We know each other's preferences for breakfast; we know the colour of each other's underclothes as they dry on the bathroom rails. Perhaps, I think, my absence will be good for us. It will give them both some privacy. It will give us all some space.

'Here, take this,' Carla says with a smile. She places the baguette she has wrapped in foil on top of my borrowed travel bag, along with an apple, an *empanada* and the eggs.

'By the way,' Arturo says, 'if they do steal your bag on the train, apparently you can reclaim it from the police in Ventimiglia the next morning – minus any valuables of course.'

'I'll remember that, *amigo*,' I say, as we fold each other in a hug. He has lost weight since the day that François introduced us; the thatch on his head is thinner now and his shoulderblades saw through my embrace.

Carla, whose birthday we'd celebrated the month before with thirty-four candles on an orange cake, slips something into my pocket as we stand for a moment by the door.

'It's a secret weapon, Mr Bond,' she says in response to my puzzled look.

I pat my hip and discover an origami envelope about the size of a postage stamp. There is something in it when I shake it: it makes a scratchy sound, like sand.

'It's for the railway Mafia,' she tells me. 'If you catch them fishing around for your passport you can fling a pinch of pepper in their eyes.'

'So it's not for their hard-boiled eggs?'

'Well, it was meant to be for yours. Though I suppose you could use it for ransom if they won't give you your passport back.'

'Ah-ha,' I say. 'So really it's travel insurance.'

She smiles and shakes her head. 'Off you go now. Have a safe journey. Don't talk to strangers,' she says.

'And I thought we were the strangers around here.'

She laughs. 'Then don't let anyone talk to you.'

As I hug her goodbye, I realise suddenly how I love her for her lightness, as I love Arturo for his friendship despite our differences, despite the strains in the way we live.

'*Suerte, amigo,*' Arturo says, blinking in the doorway. 'Good luck with it. I hope you find your man.'

———

A tangerine dawn is breaking over the railway yards when the night train from Paris pulls in at Termini station. The early swallows are already lassoing the sky.

I've only been once to Rome and that was a decade ago, for the congress where I first met François. Because Yolanda was with me, the city now flashing past the taxi windows is familiar not just in its own right, but for the way I saw it with her.

I remember it framed by the lens of my camera: Yolanda wearing the cashmere scarf she'd bought in the via Condotti; Yolanda doing a movie-star pose on the rim of the Trevi fountain.

I didn't get robbed on the train. I did get cheated by the taxi driver, who tripled my fare with a scenic tour that skirted the Spanish Steps and the Coliseum.

I am too tired to dispute it. We who visit from elsewhere excuse Rome everything because of her grandeur, I tell myself as he deposits me in a gloomy street at the back of St Peter's Square.

From Paris I'd booked a room in a *pensione* that a dour woman with a cross on her bosom mercifully lets me occupy right away. Doilies froth over glossy surfaces in a building with a cage for a lift. Room number eight, scorning the baroque promise of reception, overlooks a lightwell colonised by pigeons; a row of loggias glowers down at them over the top of the Vatican wall.

I take a shower and sleep for the next three hours. When I awake I am ravenous, and go outside to find coffee and something to eat.

This afternoon I have an appointment with a bishop. I am not a religious man but Bishop Traversini has connections in Argentina, and I hope he might have word for me, some sign at least, some news about Graciela.

A fleet of Vespas takes off with a roar at the traffic lights. I stand for a moment in their slipstream, taking in the sharpness of the Roman air and the fumes and the southern light.

That I have this appointment at all is serendipitous. Though the French won't let me practise as a doctor, the Latin Americans in Paris occasionally ask me for consultations, and since few can afford a specialist, I try to help them out. A friend of Carla's called one Saturday night in a state of panic, and as soon as I examined her twelve-year-old – he'd hurt his eye while messing around with a power drill – I realised he needed surgery right away. With François' help, we got him to Emergency at a hospital where a colleague of his could operate, and undoubtedly saved his sight in that eye.

The boy's mother had wanted to repay me but I refused to hear of it; it was the surgeon who deserved her thanks. But after she spoke to Carla and learned my story, she realised how she might be able to help.

She had, it turned out, a relative who was close to a bishop in Rome. A few days later, through Carla, she sent me an Italian phone number with instructions to dial it in a month.

'We would expect to see you at the Vatican in person, Señor Ferrero,' the secretary had said when four weeks later I'd called. 'If it's convenient for you, Bishop Traversini' – he spells out the name to ensure I've noted it correctly – 'will receive you this coming Thursday, at three in the afternoon.'

There are still a couple of hours before my meeting. A queue of sightseers is shuffling towards the Vatican Museums and I fall in with them, and soon find myself inside. Moments later I am gazing upwards at the ceiling of the Sistine Chapel, tumbling upwards into its infinite skies.

I stand there for a long time looking up at it, looking up at the hand of God. Fingers entwined, Yolanda and I once stood on these floors and marvelled until our necks were aching, at the magnificence of the sight.

Then, it was all discovery, and we were awed by the artist's work. This time, it's as if some other painter had taken over, or I myself were looking through different eyes.

Now, I can scarcely see the beauty. Instead, what swims before me are endless cycles of creation and destruction, of death and disaster and expulsion, like the one that has my country in its grasp.

Alone among the chattering tourists, I am shaken when I get to the end. I am a humanist more than a believer, yet even I can hear the drumroll that descends from those lofty ceilings, pounding out its message: There is no escape.

Suddenly I need to get out. I plunge from the chapel into the soaring vaults of St Peter's, and seek a pillar to lean against among the tour groups and the pilgrims and the guides. In the whispering basilica I close my eyes and stand for an age with the cold stone knuckling my backbone, listening to the scrape of chairs and the click of cameras in front of the *Pietà*.

With clarity it comes to me: I don't want Michelangelo's magisterial vision. I don't want this eternal struggle between good and evil that not even his God can contain. I want ordinary life in all its insignificance. Pleasures so small they scarcely register. Banality. The minutiae of routine.

Like the tiny figures in the background of a Flemish painting. Anonymous ice-skaters. Swimming children. Farming people dancing or ploughing the land.

Like Yolanda recounting her day to me on her side of the bed in the evenings.

Like Graciela and Julieta teasing me and passing the *mate* across the garden table.

Like stopping at the baker's at closing time to pick up the loaf they have kept for me, the aroma of yeast accompanying me as I walk home to my daughters and my wife.

Theatrical in their blue and gold stripes, the Swiss Guards allow me into a courtyard where a young priest comes to meet me and guide me through the Vatican maze. His robes sway like backstage curtains as we navigate staircases and cloisters with hidden gardens. Citrus trees strung with lemons glow like fairy lights.

We stop before double doors of oak. The priest knocks twice, then opens them in unison without waiting for an answer; they give onto an enormous chamber with a view over the rooftops of Rome. The priest nods once before retreating, closing the doors while stepping backwards like an usher at an opera-house box.

Before me, the bishop dressed in a long black cassock and a purple sash stands with his face to the window. When he turns I see he is quite a bit older than I am, a clean-shaven man with cropped white hair that clings to his head like lichen.

His hands, thick-fingered, are as broad as a farmer's. I wonder how he manages the small black buttons that cascade from his larynx to his shoes.

He grips my hand in his peasant's paw and greets me with warmth in his eyes. 'Osvaldo Ferrero?' he says.

'Eminence,' I say, and instinctively bow my head. I sense the generosity in him despite the austerity implied in the jet-black sweep of his robes.

We make small talk about my trip from Paris, about the brisk spring weather in Rome. He asks where I am from in Argentina, and in his rumbling voice informs me that he spent many years there as a missionary, and feels a great affection for my land.

'Will you walk with me?' he says after a moment. It's more of a command than a question, but he says it gently; it's understood that I'm to follow his lead.

We descend another flight of stairs and emerge inside a courtyard with a fountain. He takes a diagonal path towards it and I accompany him to a low stone bench among rose bushes that have been mercilessly pruned.

My mind has been on a rollercoaster for days now, dreaming about Graciela's homecoming, wondering what the bishop might say. Yolanda, who's been through countless versions of this meeting in Argentina, cautioned me repeatedly against hope.

'For them, this is just another appointment,' she'd insisted, even as I made her promise to ring me immediately after my return. 'If he's seeing you at all, he's only doing it as a courtesy to Carla's friend.'

Still, now that I'm in Italy, inside the Vatican, inside this courtyard, I can't help thinking: could they have made me travel so far in vain?

I sit beside him in the lemony sunshine and wait for him to speak. The fountain textures the quiet with its pattering; the water arches back on itself, forming a shape like a glass hibiscus as it falls.

He must know something, I think to myself. My heart is thudding. There must be something he has managed to find out.

From somewhere inside his cassock he produces a pair of mittens the size of bed-socks, and wriggles his great paws inside.

'Circulation,' he says, almost in apology. 'At my age, one tends to feel the cold.'

I nod. The air is clear as crystal. Far above us, with its angel's-eye view of life on earth, an aeroplane traverses the sky.

'I have been informed of your situation, of your great suffering,' the bishop begins, and suddenly every fibre in my body is alert. 'I know you are in need of information about your daughter. Unfortunately the circumstances in Argentina are very complicated. I'm afraid we have not been able to ascertain very much.'

My heart falls so heavily it must be audible. He is preparing me for the disappointment Yolanda intuited even before I caught the train. He knows nothing. He has found out nothing. He has nothing, after all, to share.

I breathe in, and breathe in again, trying to steady my mind. But my thoughts are already racing backwards, back towards Roma Termini, back up the spine of Italy, back across the south of France and north to the station in Paris. Already I am back in our poky apartment, back where Carla and Arturo will have finished lunch and be laying out their books to start their afternoon's work.

I will thank the bishop for his trouble. I will take my leave. Politely, I will walk away.

'This is what I can tell you,' he continues. 'There was a child that lived.'

I freeze. The planet halts its slow rotation.

'*A child that lived?*'

'That is what I am able to tell you.'

'A child? Is it a girl? Is it a boy?'

He looks at me with eyes that return only the reflection of my own.

'This is all I have learned; it is all I have been told. Had it been possible to find out more, I would have informed you of any further facts.'

My mind is spinning. Though he is speaking carefully, I cannot absorb his words.

'*A child that lived* – does that mean the child is living still?'

'I understand your anguish, Señor Ferrero . . .'

'Your Eminence, I implore you. The child's mother, my daughter, Graciela?'

Preserve this, I say to myself. Hold tight this slender thread.

'Señor Ferrero, I am sorry. This is all the information I have for you. I hope it brings you some peace.'

I am desperate now; he will walk back to his office, the double doors will close and it will be as if this dialogue never took place.

'Could you go back to them?' This is my one last chance and I am pleading. 'I beg of you, Monsignore. Would you ask them again?'

He has a line of communication. He has only to keep it open to find out more.

But he is standing and he is waiting for me to stand. When I do, he places his hand upon my forearm and stills me with the anchor of its weight.

'Your family is in my prayers,' he says. There is empathy in his eyes. 'I do not underestimate your pain.'

He will not do it. Or cannot.

I watch his figure recede across the courtyard, slender in his long black robe with its shock of purple, a good man who perhaps discovered long ago that goodness, too, has its limits. Nevertheless, he has tried, and he has managed to prise open a door. Yet it isn't enough – how could it be? Peace? He must have known I'd find scarce solace in his words. I am furious with him, and grateful to him, and shaken by the violence of what I feel.

Graciela! I want to shout her name from the bell towers, from the obelisk and the great dome of St Peter's, from the cupolas and the bridges and the ruined monuments of a city unashamed of its scars.

I look up in search of the horizon, but it is obscured by the high stone walls. Beyond the fountain beyond the courtyard beyond the parapets and defences, swallows swoop in vertiginous orbits, painting a Sistine chapel in the sky.

The bishop leaves me a few moments of solitude before sending the priest back down.

We walk in silence, our footsteps echoing through the endless passageways, the hem of his cassock darting again at his heels. And as we walk, the words of the bishop return to me like a flame in the depths of the labyrinth:

There was a child that lived.

⁓

THUD! The cork rockets skywards and plants a round grey kiss-mark on the ceiling. It remains overhead like a full stop between one life and another one, a turning point we have sealed with an explosion of joy.

It is the night of my return from Rome. Arturo, dumb with happiness, is standing beside the table, champagne cascading over his fist.

Carla had declared at dinner that she had important news. Bolognese spirals decorated our mismatched plates, nubs of bread lay strewn among the dishes, and dregs of Bordeaux lingered in the glasses that were recycled mustard jars.

Carla hadn't touched her wine; she was beaming and clasping Arturo's hand.

'We're expecting a baby,' she'd said.

They had wanted to tell me on the eve of my trip to Italy, but because I was preoccupied had decided to await my return. Now I was back they couldn't contain it a moment longer; they wanted to tell me before anyone else.

I am stunned for a moment, then thrilled for them; they are shy, nervous and excited as they accept my congratulations; then we are embracing and uncorking the champagne.

We rinse our glasses and toast the age-old marvel of it, the fact of it, like a flag in the earth, where everything had felt so tentative before.

'God, amid this uncertainty,' says Arturo, blanching a little and grinning like a kid. 'We must be crazy. Are we crazy, Carla? Osvaldo, tell us we aren't completely insane.'

'Ladies and gentlemen, I raise my glass in honour of the fact that you are both totally out of your minds.'

'You hear that in there?' Arturo says, his ear on Carla's belly. 'You'd better prepare for the worst.'

'He's told her to tap twice for "yes",' Carla explains. 'But I didn't hear anything, did you?'

'It could be a he,' Arturo says. 'Anyway, he's probably asleep.'

'With this racket? Not likely,' I say.

'My God, Osvaldo, I'm going to be a father!' Arturo shoots me a panicky look, as if the act of telling has brought the reality home. 'I don't have a clue what to do.'

'What about me?' says Carla, laughing. 'At least you don't have to give birth.'

We drink to the delight of it, to optimism, to happiness that seems so elusive these days. I throw my arms around the three of them and enfold them in another embrace.

Carla only sips at her glass but Arturo and I are a little drunk, and we laugh a bit and cry a bit together. It is the release of something we've shared without ever discussing it: the constraints of our patchwork existence, the struggle for a foothold in Europe, the anguish of too much loss.

'We want you to be the godfather, Osvaldo,' Arturo says after a moment.

'Would you do it?' says Carla. She says it solemnly, both of them staring at me with round eyes.

I realise that their elation is mingled with trepidation: about being parents, about embarking on this adventure with nobody present from home. And I am touched that, perhaps because of what has happened in my family, they want to include me in theirs.

'I would be honoured,' I say with a bow.

'Of course there will be a lot of responsibilities,' says Arturo.

'Don't listen to him,' says Carla, cutting him off with a dig in the ribs. 'No matter what he likes to imagine, he won't be palming off his parental duties onto anyone else.'

Perhaps, I think later, staring at the shadow-play on the ceiling as I stretch out on my camp bed by the bookshelves, perhaps this explains why Arturo has been so wary lately of standing up for what he believes. We live on tenterhooks about what's going on in Argentina; we all live with our residual fears. But Arturo is going to be a father. He has a new life to protect.

For me, at just over fifty, the joy I feel for them is genuine, but I realise as I try to untangle it that it's not a pure thing. It is shadowed by what I wake to every morning: the worry about my own family, the missing that has become a constant ache.

So Graciela has had her baby, even if the bishop could tell me nothing more. Perhaps this annunciation in Paris is a kind of affirmation: a promise that things will someday return to normal; that it isn't foolish, after all, to hope.

They haven't dared ask what I learned in Rome; tomorrow there'll be time enough to talk. Yet it seems to me that tonight in celebrating the promise of Carla and Arturo's baby, I was also welcoming my grandchild into the world.

One other thing I realise is that the arrival of Carla's baby will have practical implications for me. It will bring to an end the household we've created, despite our occasional chafing, despite the strange dynamics of being three. It feels like a coda to this phase of my exile. I will have to find another place to live.

PART II

THE GARDEN AND THE WILDERNESS

1979–1984

I

Buenos Aires
August 1979

There are roses, hydrangeas, a *mate* bush that could be used for making tea if you felt industrious, and a pomegranate tree – she is proud of this – that last year bore its first fruit. But the best thing about Constanza's garden is that it isn't overlooked.

It is her idea. More and more mothers have been joining the Thursday marches, some cautiously like Yolanda, others in distress and disarray. Some, like Yolanda and Constanza, are searching for grandchildren as well as children and have joined the group of Grandmothers; tip-offs that concern young children are usually channelled to them.

Constanza pats the pile on the table. Five or six items, on lined paper and notepaper, and one scribbled in the margin of a newspaper, are waiting to be filed away. *Denuncias* the Grandmothers have looked into and that seem genuine, they are at once dangerous because their allegations are so sensitive, and useless because they are meaningless on their own. For the women who are searching for missing grandchildren, it's like trying to solve a jigsaw puzzle starting only with a middle piece of sky.

Nevertheless, they are precious. The Grandmothers know, or pray, or believe that someday they will come across corroborating evidence. Something that will allow them to make a connection. They will cross-reference this information against a name, a date, a signature on a document, someone registered at a particular address. A memory alone might do it, if it confirms another memory. A hunch. Some other *denuncia*. A guess.

Yolanda picks up one of the items. A single typewritten paragraph floats in the middle of the page.

> *In my neighbourhood, in Bella Vista, at Garibaldi 941, a woman in her late 40s, the wife of a navy officer, claims God has heard her prayers. She says someone abandoned a baby in a cardboard box in a park on Easter Sunday, and that God has entrusted the infant boy to her care.*

And in blue biro on squared paper yanked from a notebook:

> *I work at the public hospital in Quilmes. On 12 June I saw a woman in an advanced stage of labour being brought in by the police. She was some kind of special prisoner and we were forbidden to communicate with her. She was blindfolded throughout the delivery and gave birth with her hands in shackles. Immediately after delivery, the infant girl was listed as NN – no name – in the hospital register and deposited in the nursery. The woman was removed, and a few days later the newborn was taken away.*

Swallowing, Yolanda puts the paper down.

'How many of these have you received?' she says.

'So far, since we started? Ones like those two?' Constanza considers. 'About eleven.'

Eleven. Yolanda holds the paper missives in her palm. The weight of a child's life, she thinks. As light as a butterfly's wing.

'Women are giving birth in handcuffs, and their infants are being taken away?' Yolanda says. She cannot believe where her mind is leading her.

Constanza stops what she is doing and peers over the top of her glasses.

'We don't know, Yolanda,' she says. 'Maybe these are exceptions. Take that hospital one. If it were common you'd think we'd have heard about it by now. But people are scared. Or they pretend they haven't seen what they have seen. It's hard to tell how widespread any of this is.'

'Do you think the babies are being adopted?'

'Perhaps we should call them appropriations,' says Constanza.

'Do you think that that's what's happening? Appropriations?'

Constanza looks at her. 'Would it surprise you?'

Yolanda's mind, already staggering from one possibility to the next, reels as she absorbs this one too.

Constanza slides a box of plastic bags across the table and puts her hand on Yolanda's arm.

'You are the only person who knows about this,' she says. 'No one, not even the other Grandmothers, must know.'

'Know what?' Yolanda says. They are whispering, though neither has suggested that they should.

'Where I put them,' says Constanza.

The Grandmothers' greatest fear is that they will be raided. It is something they treat with the utmost gravity, terrified as they were two years ago by the abductions from the Santa Cruz church. Thirteen people disappeared at that time, including three of the founding Mothers and two French nuns who were close to them, betrayed by a military spy. There is danger for those who bring them information, they know that. There is danger for those who receive it. And there is the danger of failing to recover a child if any of these fragments are lost.

No one, however, could think where to hide the clues. Filing cabinets and desk drawers were too obvious. Bank vaults were immediately ruled out. They'd thought of floorboards and skirting boards and even ironing boards at their last meeting, held as it happened at Constanza's house with the radio and the vacuum cleaner on. Which was when she'd looked up from her kitchen table and contemplated her own back lawn.

The other Grandmothers are not here today, so Yolanda and Constanza get to work. They roll the messages in separate sheets of baking paper and slip each one inside a double set of plastic bags. The bags they seal with the elastic bands that Constanza has been collecting for the purpose. Then, from where it is drying in the dish rack, they take a re-sealable jar, now empty of cherries, and finish it off with the hair dryer. Finally, they place the scrolls inside it and screw on the water-tight lid.

Then, with a trowel she wields as deftly as a cake-knife, Constanza carves a jar-size circle in the grass. They take it in turns to saw through the roots and dig out the dirt, then press the jar down into the topsoil, burying it there like a tulip bulb that they hope will bloom in the spring.

Constanza sits back on her heels and catches her breath.

'How many of these have you done?' says Yolanda softly, casting an eye over the lawn.

'Oh,' says Constanza, winking. 'It depends on the weather. The amount of rainfall. There may be one or two others planted round about.'

Afterwards, they press the grass back like a pastry lid, patting it down with the toes of their shoes. The excess soil they sprinkle on the flower-beds under the pomegranate tree. Then they count their steps to the back door, and count their steps to the fence. Double-checking the distances with a tape measure that Constanza retrieves from her sewing basket, they stash the coordinates in the back of an atlas, to be guarded like a treasure map of hope.

2

Buenos Aires
September 1979

Nothing could be more important than this rock.

'Ana darling . . . Don't make Mamá late, *corazón* . . .' Then some longer words that don't have any meaning, just notes and colours and whooshing sounds that make Ana think of the wind.

Her hands on the stone, she is squatting beside the flower-bed, the hem of her skirt getting damp in the pointy grass.

This one is a little bit heavy, and at first she thought it wouldn't move at all. But now she has found an edge, and she has all of her fingers under it and is pulling, and just when it seems impossible, it gives and rolls onto the lawn.

Wriggle wriggle wriggle!

Ana's eyes dart everywhere, looking at everything that scurries and slithers and crawls. Exposed to the light, earthworms twist like acrobats. Ants stream in all directions rescuing ant-sized grains of rice.

She giggles, she claps her hands. It is so funny how they go.

A centipede – 'Mamá, come and look!' – curled in a tight black coil. A fat white slug that simply sits there, not knowing what to do.

Filaments lie tangled up with other ones, all flat in the space that is smooth as a bowl and the opposite shape to the rock. Inside it there are patches like cotton-wool, and cobwebs the same colour as the dirt.

'Ana sweetheart. I've popped Liliana in the car. Do you want us to leave you behind?'

She pretends that her ears are full so that there isn't any room for hearing, like going underwater in the bath.

Earwigs! They thought they could hide by sitting still but now they are in a frenzy. They have snippy pincers for cutting things though she's never seen how they work. She tries to catch one to pick it up but it's too fast for her fingers to grip.

There are some baby snails that don't go anywhere. They think that no one can see them if they stick to the bottom of the rock.

'Ana Lucia – for the last time! Come and get in the car!'

Sometimes, when she pretends she doesn't hear things, she has noticed that they end up going away.

Oh! She nearly missed the beetle with horns on its head and a shell that's good for hiding in the mushroomy dark.

But the funniest of all are the woodlice. They scuttle in all directions until you touch them, when they roll up into little grey peas.

Suddenly from nowhere, from somewhere high above her, something clamps her under the armpits and she is flying up through the air. She doesn't want to look at the trees or see the streaky colours; she doesn't want to go anywhere in the back of the car. She kicks her legs like a beetle when it's been flipped over onto its back. She fills up her lungs and releases a yowl and shuts out the stripy world.

When she lets the light come in again, it has gone all blurry. But she can see the sparkle of an earring, the whorls in her mamá's ear.

She knows her mamá is cross from the way they're walking. The ground is juddering up and down and the wail that Ana is making keeps jumping about.

'Ana, what did you promise me this morning?' Her mamá's voice has that funny spiky sound. 'What did you promise you would do when your mamá called?'

But Ana isn't listening. She is thinking about the rock lying upturned where she left it, and all the creatures scurrying away through the grass.

—

112

3

Buenos Aires
September 1979

Yolanda's ears are buzzing, her heart is racing, she has been unable to concentrate all day. She is desperate to call but has to wait until she can get to a public telephone; it is evening in Paris when she manages to rush out during a break between classes at school.

'She's safe, Osvaldo!' she cries. 'She's safe! She's safe! She's all right!'

'Yolanda?' Osvaldo says. 'What are you saying? Slow down!'

In the middle of the night Yolanda received a phone call. The man wouldn't leave any number; she has no way to telephone him back.

'He wouldn't even leave his name,' she says. 'For security reasons he said he couldn't. It doesn't matter, Osvaldo. He knows her. He's seen her. She is all right. After all our worrying! He says Graciela is fine.'

Osvaldo's voice is cautious, but it might simply be the distance. He wants to know exactly what the man has said.

'That he was a friend of Graciela's. That she had asked him to call on her behalf. That she can't ring herself but she is safe and is being well looked after. That she sends her love and asks us not to worry.'

'Not to worry? Yolanda, it's been over two years.'

But Yolanda isn't listening. 'He even called her "Ela" – he knows her childhood nickname! And he said that she needs our help.'

'What kind of help?'

'He said she has run up a debt.'

'A debt? What sort of debt?'

'He didn't go into the details. Maybe he doesn't know. We didn't talk for long. He just said that she had asked if we could give her some financial support.'

'It's odd though, don't you think? You know how she is with money. It's not like her to borrow . . .'

'It's not like her to vanish, either. It's not surprising she's had to ask for help.'

'How much does she need?'

'He said she needed two thousand dollars.'

'Two thousand dollars?'

'That's what he said. He said "Two thousand dollars should tide her through."'

'What did he say about the baby? When can we see them? Where did he say that they were?'

'I don't think it's like that, Osvaldo. I don't have the impression she's somewhere we can visit. Otherwise I'm sure he would have said.'

'But did you ask him?'

'I asked about the baby. But as soon as I did, he said he had to go. "I'll ring you back," he said, and then he hung up.'

'Jesus, Yolanda.'

'Maybe it's dangerous for him to ring us. Perhaps he can only phone at certain times.'

'Perhaps. But it makes no sense to me. We hear nothing for two years, she has a baby somewhere, and the next thing we know she gets some friend to call you to ask for money? Why wouldn't she call us herself?'

'Maybe she can't, Osvaldo. What do we know? Nothing is normal any more.'

'Yes, but borrowing two thousand dollars? It's not the sort of thing she'd do.'

'Well, she will have had expenses for the baby. What if the child's been ill? Or she has? She'll have had to buy medicines, clothes, things like bottles and nappies . . .'

'So you are going to send it?'

'How can we refuse? God knows what state she's in. She's probably in one of those re-education facilities down in the south, where they won't have any supplies.'

'What re-education facilities?'

'Down in Chubut, or Santa Cruz. Somewhere in Patagonia. Some of the Mothers talk about them. Not that anyone seems to know very much about them, but that's where some of them reckon their kids have been sent.'

'You think she's in Patagonia?'

'I don't know, Osvaldo. She could be. She could be anywhere. I'll ask this man when he calls.'

'And in the meantime, where are we going to find a spare two thousand dollars?'

'I'll sell something. I have my mother's wedding ring. The engagement ring you gave me. There's that necklace of my mother's, the gold one . . .'

'I could ask for an advance at Medipharm.'

'And by the time you've paid the transfer fees and the exchange commissions it'll be half gone. It's probably better if I handle it here.'

'But your mother's jewellery? They're the only things of hers you have.'

'She would have wanted me to use them like this, Osvaldo: for our family, for Graciela. It's why she left them to me.'

'Be careful, Yolanda.'

'Be careful of what?'

'I don't know, exactly. It doesn't feel right to me.'

'Don't worry, he's a friend of Graciela's; he wants to help . . . My God, Osvaldo – after all this time! I always knew she'd find a way to get in touch.'

A few months later, at half-past eleven, the same voice comes rasping down the line.

'Hello, Yolanda,' he says.

'Where's my daughter?' Yolanda says. 'I want to know where she is.'

He hangs up.

She trembles afterwards at her boldness. She paid the two thousand dollars. She took out a loan and made the other payments he also asked for. Now she is tired of this game.

The calls continue, irregularly, as the late summer turns to autumn and then to winter. Sometimes he doesn't telephone for weeks. She never knows when the calls will come, or how much he will ask her to provide.

She has long since sold her pieces of jewellery. She has sold the television and her sewing machine and the other house-hold appliances. One day, she sold the car.

He tells her Graciela is sick. The next time he tells her she is improving but her health is still precarious. One day, just making conversation, he asks what the house is worth.

Yolanda is ill with worry. She fears Graciela has been separated from her baby – why else would the man not have mentioned it, or asked for money for the things it requires?

Even so, and after everything, his next request still takes her by surprise.

The phone rings just after midnight, on a wind-lashed winter's night. She's been tracking the forecast for places like Trelew and Ushuaia, watching the temperatures in Patagonia plunge. Each time, she cannot help it, she hopes the caller will be Graciela herself.

She recognises his smoker's voice. Though she's drowsy with sleep, the *porteño* accent is familiar now, even if she still cannot estimate his age.

'She wants you to knit her a pullover,' he tells her.

She isn't sure she has heard correctly.

'She says she is feeling the cold.'

And so Yolanda, who hasn't knitted since the girls were children, rummages in the upstairs trunk she has long been meaning to empty, and fishes her needles out.

'You're not going out in this?' Borovich says, seeing her pulling on her raincoat in the common room as the trees whip around in the wind.

With rain-soaked shoes she dashes through the downpour to the knitting shop and selects the finest wool – fibres that are not itchy, because Graciela always did have sensitive skin. She decides on green to match her eyes, and a roll-neck pattern because it's warmest, and asks for advice on keeping the tension loose.

For three nights and four days she works at it, purl and plain, purl and plain, as she twists the strands together, straining her eyes in the lamplight over the cable stitch of her love.

When he doesn't call back she decides to continue. She knits a scarf, and a hat, then wonders if she could manage a pair of mittens. She wonders if there is time for a second pull-over, and starts it, since one might not be enough. When she is done, she wraps the items in tissue paper, and ties them with purple ribbon, and puts them in a basket beside the front door.

When finally he calls back, the man says he will be in Buenos Aires on Wednesday and promises to deliver the parcel if Yolanda can bring it to him by noon. He tells her to meet him in the Botanical Gardens, just beyond the green-house, beside the statue of the Roman wolf.

Two days later she goes to her assignation. The park is nearly deserted late on a weekday morning, the red gravel paths turned soft by the overnight rain.

Fattened by neighbourhood widows, runaway cats glare at her from the roots of the *tipu* trees. In frozen vigil, an eagle waits in the spokes of a monkey-puzzle tree; she notices it high above her only after feeling its stare on her back.

Yolanda shivers into the sleeves of her coat as she stands before the statue, observing the expression on the she-wolf's face as it suckles the orphaned twins. She has sold the watch her father gave her for graduation, but the plastic one she's wearing tells her there are still ten minutes to go.

She is impatient for the man's arrival; she has so much she wants to ask him; heaven knows, he might even bring a message from Graciela herself.

It's an overcast day made darker by the density of the foli-age and the ivy that has spilled out of the rockeries and is inching like a tide across the lawn. Yolanda finds herself turning to check it hasn't crept up on her, then laughs at herself for imagining herself brought down by the tendrils' snare.

Her hips start to ache and her legs grow heavy as she adjusts and readjusts her weight. Her heart seems to have resumed its odd tripping rhythm, but she puts that down to her nerves. There are no benches in this corner of the gardens; she's been standing for fifty minutes and the basket handles are cutting into her hands.

Romulus and Remus crouch beneath the she-wolf as Yolanda wonders what is holding the man up. She is grateful the rain hasn't started again, though her shoes are damp from walking. Drops of water blown from the leaves keep finding the back of her neck.

In the glaucous light there are no shadows by which to measure the passing of time.

Suddenly she sees a figure, a dog that's part Alsatian, gliding through the gloomy trees. Collarless, ownerless, it moves through the ivy towards her as if on a mission to find her, baring its teeth in a growl. Nervous since a child around big dogs, Yolanda retreats as it keeps advancing; she can see the hard white of its canines, the mottled pink flesh of its gums. Its angry eyes lock on her and she stares back at them, clutching her basket to her like a shield. The animal snarls; her throat constricts; it could fell her with a single leap.

Then, from across the gardens, a fusillade of barking, and the dog's flattened ears shoot up. It snarls again, then abandons her and races towards the sound.

Shaken, Yolanda paces briskly up and down the pathway. She spots a distant bench where she can rest and still keep an eye on the statue, but she retraces her steps when she finds it is wet from the rain.

Her legs and feet are numb when, four hours after she got there, she understands that the man isn't going to show up. Something has gone wrong, she thinks, some accident or obstacle, some insurmountable delay. Hungry, deflated, she limps towards the gate that leads to the Plaza de Italia, watched by the eagle and the half-wild cats.

She waits a long time at the bus stop. When the *collectivo* finally gets there the seats are already taken, and no one seems inclined to relinquish theirs.

As they lumber across the intersections Yolanda sees herself in the window. A middle-aged woman stares back at her, hair frizzed by the damp and the winter, raincoat tugged about her like a sack. Tied with its purple ribbon, the parcel sits unopened in her basket, the tissue paper pockmarked by the rain.

But the basket itself is lighter now because the other things it's been carrying, hope and longing accumulated over these long months of absence, and the promise this man held out to her, are trickling away through its weave.

At 2 a.m. the phone rings, tearing Yolanda from her Valium sleep.

Is it Graciela? Is it Osvaldo is it her brother? Is it Eduardo is it Constanza is it Julieta in Miami is anything wrong?

She is flushed with panic and disoriented when she picks up the receiver in the hall.

The silence she hears sounds hollow. She can tell there is somebody there.

'Graciela?' she says.

She holds on, scarcely daring to breathe. She waits. She waits.

And then it erupts. No words, nothing but a voice. A man's voice. And the voice is laughing. Great guffaws of laughter that have an edge to them, and more than that, a sneer in them; that echo down the line and ring in her ears as she shivers in her nightdress in the hallway, as the malice seeks its target and bores into it, searing her heart like a brand.

4

Buenos Aires
May 1980

All night rain rinses the pollution from the streets, and the sunrise wrings out mornings of luminous blue. Buildings sway like paper cut-outs against the azure skies and the evening sunshine sets the trees aflame. Men go to work in shirt-sleeves; in the citrus light of evening women linger in thin cotton frocks.

By rights it should be autumn. Plane trees fill the gutters with leaves that curl like wood-shavings; behind the stadium in La Boca, ash trees sprinkle the footpaths with golden stars. But the temperature in Buenos Aires has climbed back into the twenties, and people's spirits have lifted with it – a windfall second summer on borrowed time.

Banked up for blocks behind the level crossing, the traffic is immobile, and Yolanda is impatient to be on the move. Halfway down the bus, she is nursing a shopping basket by the window and examining an address she has circled on the map in the *Guía 'T'*. She hadn't trusted the forecast, and as the sun beats down on the grimy glass she regrets having worn her raincoat over the top of her too-heavy dress.

Behind her are two other Grandmothers who will alight at the same time she does, if the train ever lets the traffic through.

The *denuncia* came handwritten on heavy, plain white notepaper. Yolanda hasn't asked how it reached the Grandmothers; she knows only that it was sent a month ago by the director of a kindergarten, and that it is genuine because the Grandmothers have followed it up.

'*There is a confidential matter I wish to discuss with you,*' the letter had said. '*Please send someone I can trust.*'

The Grandmothers at first were wary, uncertain whether this might be some kind of trap. But they investigated, and took precautions, and two of them volunteered.

They agreed on a neutral place, and Patricia and Marta were waiting when the director arrived. Immediately she expressed concern about a child enrolled at her kindergarten. She was worried about a discrepancy between her date of birth and the results of her medical exam.

Though apparently not quite three, the girl – whose name was Ana – seemed older than her birth certificate would have it, so the doctor requested a copy of her medical records at birth. The documents, duly provided, did nothing to diminish his perplexity. Either the entries had been confused with those of some other child, or the documents' dates were erroneous, because his own observations did not correlate with a child of that age.

Since the girl was a late enrolment, the director knew little about her, only that she came from an irreproachable home. She'd met the parents in person, Señora Bielka sitting straight-backed in her office in a slim-line sleeveless dress, a chiffon scarf knotted at her throat. A little older than the other mothers, she was also twice as elegant, and carried herself with poise. Still, the director thought, there was something about her, perhaps some strain or brittleness, behind the layers of mascara and kohl.

The father, in full uniform, was overdressed for a kindergarten meeting; she appraised him against the hundreds of other parents she'd invited into her office over the years. His unctuousness oppressed her and bordered on condescension; his self-assurance was a little too loud. He had neatly combed hair, and a narrow face, and a look in his eyes of a man used to getting his way. The couple didn't hold hands like other first-time parents, and it occurred to the director, just fleetingly, that he might have been seeking to deflect her attention from his wife.

These, the director stressed to the Grandmothers, were purely subjective impressions. She filed them at the back of her mind for refining or correcting over time.

A fastidious woman, however, it was the paperwork that left her uneasy. She'd seen birth certificates before that had been signed by military doctors; numerous military families had enrolled their children with her over the years. What bothered her in this case was that the documentation failed to match up.

The discrepancy niggled, but she kept her concerns to herself. She had no explanation, no appetite for conflict, and no desire, should it come to that, for entanglement with the board. Still, it troubled her when facts were not in order. She sensed there might be a matter of some delicacy to confront.

On the other hand, she knew about the Grandmothers – she herself was of their generation. When her doubts refused to dissipate, she resolved to take the unusual step of raising the issue with them.

Two of the Grandmothers were searching for children whose age might correspond to that of the little girl concerned. One didn't know the sex of the child she was looking for. The other, as it happened, was searching for a little boy.

So it is that Yolanda comes to be getting off a bus and walking towards a kindergarten one unseasonably warm May lunchtime, Constanza and Patricia at her side. They stop at a bench to rest their legs just as the children pour into the yard.

Of all the shouting-tripping-giggling three- and four-year-olds, Yolanda knows immediately which child the director meant.

A little girl hangs back inside the doorway instead of scrambling into the courtyard; she stands with one foot on top of the other one as if hesitant about going outside.

But before Yolanda can indicate anything to Constanza, a woman in a pink sheath dress and stylish heels swoops across and scoops the child onto her hip. She kisses her and smoothes her hair and talks to her, then sets her back down on the stoop. They descend the steps together, the little girl taking them from side to side, her mother holding her firmly by the hand. Then the woman straps her into the back of an American sedan that is double-parked opposite the gates.

Yolanda's heart is thudding. She presses her hand against it but she can't tear her gaze from the girl. Isn't that Osvaldo's forehead? Aren't those Graciela's eyes? And isn't that how Graciela used to stand when she was little, one foot on top of the other in her red leather shoes with the buckles, getting dust on the bridge of her socks?

Yolanda thinks she is right but she can't be certain. A child's stance in a doorway is proof of nothing, she knows that; she needs evidence that would stand up in a court of law.

And yet, and yet. The possibility beats insistently at her chest. Surely this is her grandchild, surely this is she.

And then it becomes unbearable to her to imagine her grandchild's life: being kissed by strangers' lips, her naked body bathed by strangers' hands. She has to get nearer . . . The traffic up ahead is slowing; when the cars come to a halt there will be a brief second to act. The sedan is nearly in front of them; Yolanda is measuring the distance between herself and the vehicle's windows, with no plan other than slamming the roof and pounding till they open the door.

All she needs is to embrace her, to bury her nose in the nape of the little girl's neck. She knows she will know from the scent of her, from the texture of her skin, whether this child is blood of her blood, flesh of her daughter's flesh.

Suddenly a hand is gripping her by each elbow. Patricia is on one side, Constanza on the other; as the car slides towards them they see the expression on Yolanda's face. The hands stay on her arms as the car moves level with them and then continues, as she stands there in an agony of confusion, letting the moment pass.

She watches the trees bend and the buildings arch and the falling leaves eddy in the reflection of the windows as the vehicle accelerates through the sunshine, whisking the little girl away.

They discuss it in a café on the other side of town, out of earshot of any eavesdroppers who might be lurking near the school.

For now, they will keep watch over the girl, it is decided. They will take photographs of her, discreetly, from between the cars and the trees. They will learn her routines and follow them and keep note if anything should change.

Yolanda will be the one to take the photos since, rummaging for some papers in the back of Osvaldo's desk, she came across his camera the other day. Either Constanza or Patricia will accompany her, keeping watch at her side.

But first, Yolanda must establish herself in the neighbourhood. She has to shop at the greengrocer's and the bakery, have coffee at the corner café. She should blend in with the residents, passing the kindergarten so often she becomes invisible, so that anyone who notices her will think that she lives nearby.

'She needs a dog,' Constanza says with a laugh. 'Who's got a dog they can lend?'

'A dog!' Yolanda says. 'I don't think my knees would hold out.'

'I'm serious,' Constanza says. 'People see the pet and not the person – it'd be the perfect disguise.'

'Not in that *barrio*,' Patricia says. 'Didn't you see those dog-walkers – eight animals at a time? That's the way they do it over there.'

'Even better,' Constanza says. 'We can get Yolanda a job.'

'Hold it right there,' she says. 'I already have a job, if you remember. It might be part-time at the moment, but I still have to show up at school.'

But Constanza isn't listening. 'Oh, God,' she says, blue eyes lighting up. 'I've just had an idea.'

'Don't even think about it,' says Yolanda. She cuts her off because the same thought has also occurred to her: how to learn more about the family; how to get close to the child. 'Not a dog-walker, not a nanny, not a maid,' Yolanda says. 'They'd see through me the second I walked through the door.'

'What about an Avon lady? A demonstrator of Tupperware wonders? A holder of private showings of baby clothes?'

Yolanda laughs, then turns sober when she sees Constanza's face.

'He's a military man, Constanza. To go into their home . . .' She imagines it for a second, and then dismisses it.

'Let's start with the photos,' she says.

A week later, when Yolanda and Constanza arrive outside the kindergarten, the grounds are different. Child-sized chairs and trestle tables stand in a horseshoe beneath the jacaranda. Woodchips clinging to their clothing, two fair-haired boys hang like fruit bats from the jungle gym; most of the other children have gone indoors. But, deep in concentration, the little girl is out there, sitting at one of the tables. Smock rolled up to her elbows, she is immersed in finger-paint.

Yolanda's finger is on the shutter. She has found a way to work the camera without her glasses, and has framed the child between the tree and the kindergarten fence. The two of them are locked in concentration, Yolanda focused on the little girl who is focused on the peacock brilliance under her hands.

In the soundlessness of that moment, the world seems to hold its breath. A single leaf-curl flutters free and lands on the child's hair.

Aware perhaps of the stillness, the girl glances towards Yolanda the moment the shutter clicks. To Yolanda, it sounds as though the jacaranda has been struck by lightning; she braces herself for it to come crashing to the ground. But the girl goes back to her painting and Yolanda, mesmerised, hides inside the tiny square and hurriedly winds on the film. She is about to press the button again when the girl looks up and smiles directly at her, and holds her two palms up to her, like orange and lilac butterflies hovering behind a wire fence.

Yolanda squeezes, winds on again. A third time she releases the shutter before the girl plunges back into her artwork, seascapes of green and purple escaping from the colour blue.

Yolanda is taken aback, she turns hot and cold with the shock of it; she had thought herself concealed by the cars. Could this be her grandchild? She is almost certain, she wants it to be, she can't be completely sure. But the child's gaze went right through her, and her heart is still rebounding from being seen.

Constanza leans towards her, shifting a bag of groceries from arm to arm. 'Did you get her?' she says softly, as if the trees themselves could hear.

'I got two or three shots,' Yolanda says. 'But I think she noticed me.'

'She saw you?' Constanza looks stricken. 'Come on,' she says. 'Let's go.'

Yolanda slips the camera down beside the celery and fights an overwhelming urge to turn and wave. She needs the girl to forget her; she needs her not to talk about what took place.

They leave it a week before they return. They watch till all the parents have come to claim their charges, but the little girl is nowhere to be seen.

'Perhaps she stayed home today,' Constanza says. 'Children are always giving each other their germs.'

But Yolanda is worried. For days now she has had an uneasy feeling, after what took place last time.

'They've gone,' the director says, when finally, discreetly, Patricia reaches her by phone. 'They said they were moving away.'

Yolanda, standing beside her friend as she dials the number, feels faint when she overhears the words.

Away? Where away? Across town? Another city? Abroad?

'They took her out of kindergarten last Friday,' Patricia says as she replaces the receiver. 'The director understands the father has been transferred to his next assignment; she presumes he wasn't allowed to say where.'

Yolanda's knees give way. She subsides into the nearest chair.

Patricia comes and sits beside her.

'I'm sorry, Yolanda,' she says, taking Yolanda's hand in her own. Then, after a moment, 'If it's any comfort, we have copies of the documents, the birth certificate and so on. I've given them to Constanza to keep safe.' She stops talking for a moment, and clears her throat. 'There is one thing we are going to have to bear in mind, however: this family is going to be difficult to trace. We tried looking up the Bielkas when they first came to our attention. There isn't even an entry in the telephone book.'

Yolanda looks at her, unable to speak.

'We'll keep looking, of course we will. But it's not going to be easy. Even if we could be certain about the little girl. Even if the father were not a military man.' She pauses. 'And we have to keep an open mind, Yolanda. The little girl might not be the Bielkas', but she might not be yours either. It might even turn out you are looking for a little boy.'

Head swimming, Yolanda delves into her handbag for an aspirin, or for something to take in order to steady her heart beat, and finds Osvaldo's camera there instead. She curls her fingers around it and holds on to it, firm in its soft leather case.

The film is still inside, waiting for her to finish it, the negatives scrolled up tightly within their shell.

⁓

In a long thin park that runs beside a railway line, Yolanda sits on a bench overlooking a lawn that's reserved for children and a sandpit that's reserved for dogs.

Slouching towards adulthood, a huddle of teenagers are perfecting smoke-rings in a gap between the trees alongside the line. A couple of girls with beads in their hair twirl and untwirl on the swings. In the distance, smaller kids argue about the positioning of a goal.

The tomato-coloured envelope rests fatly on her knees. She is readying herself for disappointment, yet hoping her hand was steadier than her heart as the shutter worked and the girl stood up and waved at her with her bird-of-paradise hands.

At the store where she had gone to collect the photographs, they'd told her that her set of prints was lost.

When she'd pressed the assistant to check again, he'd produced a basket overflowing with envelopes and lifted it onto the counter. A layer of them sheared off onto the floor.

It took her a moment to understand what she was seeing. She'd thrown the assistant a questioning look but he'd shrugged and avoided her eyes.

So many of them: Could that be right? So many unclaimed lives?

With shaking hands she'd helped him sort through the hillocks that quickly mounted on the counter. None of them bore the number on her receipt.

Had they been destroyed or confiscated? Was someone in the photolab a spy?

She'd kept her nerve and insisted he check once more among the weekly dividers. And suddenly he'd discovered it, lodged under the wrong day of the week.

Behind her, a string of railway carriages rattles into the suburbs. A red and yellow ball lies abandoned in a puddle like a beach-toy at a miniature dolphin park.

She puts on her reading glasses and peels the envelope open. The black-and-white squares slither onto her lap like fish.

With them is a small paper pouch that she opens first to check that the negatives are inside. Holding them by their perforated edges she counts them: four-and-a-half strips of celluloid, the reverse imprint of ghosts.

The most recent pictures are sitting on top of the pile. And there she is, this child who has lived in Yolanda's mind so vividly for the past few weeks, confronting her with proof that she is real.

There are three photographs of the girl. One is blurred but in the next she is sharply in focus. Yolanda shivers; the child has seen her, she is looking directly at her and smiling and raising her arms.

And there she is again. In the third photograph she has her hands aloft, smiling still, though the smile is beginning to fade.

'Here I am,' the girl seems to be saying. 'Look at all the colours I've become.'

Yolanda drinks in every detail: her height, the shape of her face, the curve of her three-year-old's arms.

That is all. Two decent pictures, snatched from the reel of her life.

But Yolanda pores over them. They are proof, but proof of what, exactly? That light glanced off her limbs, that light illuminated a forehead that might have been Osvaldo's, that light reacted with chemicals to affirm that this child exists.

Proof of everything, then. But proof of nothing, too.

Yolanda's throat constricts and there's a rat-a-tat rhythm in her chest. She feels close to certain about this girl. She cannot bear to think that they had lost her almost as soon as she had been found.

Blindly she shuffles through the rest of the pictures, scarcely seeing them, scarcely caring what's there. Since Osvaldo left and Graciela disappeared she's had no need for photographs; she's had nothing she has wanted to celebrate, nothing she has wanted to record.

Then, with something like wonder, she starts to look more closely at the other prints. There are photos of Julieta with her husband Felipe that Osvaldo must have taken the last time they were home in Argentina. There are a couple of shots from Easter in La Plata, her brother's grandchildren on plastic tractors doing damage to the garden shrubs.

She slows right down, preparing herself for what surely is yet to come. And suddenly there she is: Graciela in an old wicker chair on the veranda; Graciela in a sundress in the garden; Graciela in the background while a gaggle of children grapple with ice-cream cones.

The sight of her daughter jolts her. She is beyond tears now but not beyond the shock of it, not beyond the ache. For a moment she is euphoric at the sight of her, and then what's happened rushes back.

She scrutinises the photographs for signs of it: signs of the coming turbulence, signs of the stalking night. It isn't there between the trees or in a corner of the garden; no fleeting figure hovers at the edge of the frame. Yet it was present, she has no doubt; the spores of catastrophe were all around them, hidden in the fullest light of day.

Across the park, the kids are shouting again as the football flies through the air. The smoking teenagers are scuffing the dust and eyeing the girls on the swings. To all of them she is invisible, a nondescript woman alone on a bench against a background of railway trees.

None of them sees her stand. None of them sees her thrust an envelope into her handbag and hurry along the footpath towards the overpass, towards the homebound train.

Dusk falls. The puddle on the edge of the playground, deserted now, lies too low to be stirred by the wind. But the tiny beachball shifts, and shivers, and rolls a little distance through the water, describing a slow revolution in the breeze.

5

Buenos Aires
October 1981

The house is squeaky with balloons. They have been bouncing around the den and in the dining room; they have come to rest on the soft chairs in the living room; there is one behind the door in the toilet, and five on the stairs, and a blue one and a yellow one that escaped and burst on a tree.

There have been fizzy drinks and *empanadas* and cupcakes, and a game of pass-the-parcel; and now a dozen seven-year-olds are tearing around on the grass.

Intimidated by the bigger children, Ana lingers in the kitchen with the housemaid, who is tossing half-gnawed pizzas into the bin. Her papá and Sancho's papá have gone out to get more lemonade, leaving the women to fuss over the goodbye gifts and Ramón in charge of the party-goers outside.

Today is Ana's cousin's birthday and Ana is the smallest guest. Sancho's friends are two years older than she is, and stronger and quite a bit rougher, making her reluctant to join in their games. Instead she hides out in the kitchen, and busies herself with an army of jellies that jiggle as she wobbles them on the tray.

This is the moment she has been dreading since the morning, when she woke up and remembered, when her tummy first started to hurt. It didn't go away when she helped wrap Sancho's present. It didn't go away even after all the pink meringues.

Ramón, who is her papa's best friend and Ana's godfather, always makes them play it – even when it is somebody else's birthday – and he always makes Ana go first.

'There you are!' he calls to her, spotting her behind the jelly tray, blindfold dangling from his hand. 'Get over here, Ana – hurry up! We're waiting for you to start!'

Ana thinks he looks even fatter without his uniform and the police hat with the shiny badge that he leaves in the front of his car. She doesn't like calling him uncle because he isn't one, though it's what everyone makes her say.

The next thing she knows he has yanked the blindfold so tight that it hurts her eyes. The red and purple lozenges that smear the inside of her eyelids make her queasy; she feels panicky when she cannot see the light.

Then Ramón's big hands are patting her chest and shoulders, turning her around and around. The pain in her tummy turns into a kind of stabbing; she feels dizzy behind the blindfold and her scalp feels like it's burning where her hair has been caught in the knot.

Ramón for some reason finds the way she reacts amusing; she can hear him making his sideways sort of laugh. Then the world is pressing in on her and she starts breathing very quickly; agitated, she stumbles on the lawn.

Now it's the children's turn. With sticky hands they pick her up and spin her, chanting the rhyme about hens and thimbles and haystacks, before scattering all over the yard.

'Stop!' she calls a moment later, knowing that the only way out is forwards, that she has to go through with the game.

Giddy, Ana fights a wave of nausea, listens hard over the thudding in her ears. Something's rustling to the left of her, quite close to the hydrangeas; then someone suppresses a giggle to her right. She lunges, arms flapping at emptiness; the garden sinks and rises like a boat.

Then somebody sneezes and abruptly she changes direction, following her outstretched arms. She trips, to gales of laughter, but then discovers that the obstacle is attached to a leg. Patting the arm and shoulders, she comes to the wingnut ears.

'César!' she cries and her guess is correct, because someone is yanking her blindfold off and now it is César's turn.

The other kids tie the blindfold over his eyes as Ana – freed, breathing fast, and surprised to find she is nowhere near the hydrangeas – rubs her own eyes in the too-bright sun, looks up at the cauliflower clouds.

She turns, and as she does, she sees Ramón is watching. He grins his strange grin down at her from the step by the kitchen door.

6

Amsterdam
November 1981

Delayed after a stop in Iceland, the flight from the USA is late and it takes them an age to clear immigration and recover their bags. I've had meetings all day and my back is aching as I lean against a pillar, watching for them to emerge through the Arrivals door.

Medipharm moved me to Amsterdam five months ago, asking me to supervise their junior reps and manage a few of accounts of my own. This evening, on their first visit since I moved to Europe, Julieta and my grandson will arrive.

It will be the first time I meet Mateo, a pint-sized bundle of energy hurtling headlong into life. I am thrilled at the thought of seeing him, and impatient to see Julieta. But my anticipation is mingled with apprehension: Julieta has been angry with me for some time.

Finally the doors slide open and there she is, the boy on her hip, a gigantic suitcase dwarfing them on a trolley she is struggling to turn. She stops for a moment, looking for me among the handsome, blond-haired families and the chauffeurs with their cardboard signs. Then, when she sees me hurrying towards her, her face breaks open in a smile.

I feel a surge of love for her that overshadows our partial estrangement; I blink back tears and hug them both for a very long time before I can trust my voice.

'Meet your *abuelo*, Mateo,' she tells the boy, proffering his head for me to kiss.

'Hello, young man,' I say to him, taking his curled-up hand.

He opens eyes that could swallow the universe and fixes me a moment, then closes them, exhausted by being awake.

Julieta lifts him to my chest and I hold him to me, the way I first learned to hold her. My grandson, I think. Around us the airport blurs as I marvel at the tiny fingernails, the curve of his lengthy eyelashes, the whorls of his seashell ears.

After the excitement of flying – 'We are next to the clouds, Mamá!' – jetlag has felled him. His head slumps onto his mother's neck as I pass him back into her arms.

'He didn't sleep much on the plane,' she says by way of apology. 'It's good we've arrived at this hour though – with any luck he'll sleep right through the night.'

'Julieta,' I say, and start over because my voice is catching. 'Let me look at you.' I hadn't realised how much I've missed her, how overwhelmed I would feel just seeing her face.

Her light brown hair is shorter now and darker, and she has dressed smartly despite the length of the flight. And suddenly a memory comes back to me, as random as it is luminous: Julieta at Mateo's age, running towards me in her new white shoes, leaving skating tracks across the dewy grass.

'How are you, Papá?' she says. She is standing back, scrutinising me in turn. 'It's wonderful to see you at last.'

We tread carefully so as not to spoil this moment, both of us anxious for it to be smooth. The 'at last' rankles but I let it pass. She is here – the two of them are – that is all that matters; at least we have made a start.

I have a two-roomed apartment up three flights of stairs that rise abruptly as if inside a ship. From the rafter above the bed I have made up for him, I have strung my summer mosquito net so Mateo can dream he is sleeping under the rigging.

We take a bottle of wine into the living room, leaving Mateo's door ajar. Later I will bunk down here on the sofa, with the flicker of the canal's reflections playing along the top of the wall.

I pull the two spare blankets out of the cupboard and hand one to Julieta; we drink to our reunion enfolded in tartan squares.

We step around the subjects we know are delicate. Julieta asks me about life in Holland; I ask her about her plans to return to work. She tells me about Felipe, how the record company has put him in charge of all of Latin America, how these days he spends half his life on planes.

I'd have liked to have seen him again, and to have heard his views on developments in Argentina. In another way, however, I am glad that she and Mateo have come alone. It's been far too long since my daughter and I have had a chance to talk.

And now that it can, the conversation turns towards more difficult things.

Never shy about stating an opinion, Julieta believes Graciela was abducted because whoever did so failed to get their hands on me. She says the cartoons I drew were reckless; my giving them to Hugo, culpable. And she holds me responsible for everything that's happened since.

She blames me for her sister's disappearance. She blames me for breaking up the family. She blames me for leaving Yolanda to cope on her own.

I listen in silence until she is done. I do not try to defend myself, but I try at least to explain: how the board of *Focus* had weighed things up and decided to publish anyway; how fleeing had been an attempt to protect her mother and Graciela, as much as to save myself.

But she cannot hear or isn't finished. 'What could you possibly have thought you were achieving?' she says. 'It was a military Junta, for God's sake. Did you think you could save the world with your stupid cartoons?'

Julieta is used to speaking freely. She can't imagine what it's like when that freedom disappears.

'At the time we didn't know,' I tell her; 'we couldn't have known; we believed it was important to speak out.' It was still too soon; we couldn't have foreseen the consequences of our actions. 'Do you think I could have imagined for one second that Graciela could get swept up in it? That we'd have gone ahead had any of us known?'

'Well, you should have guessed: you, Hugo . . . those friends of yours who were so obsessed with politics.' Emotion flares in patches on her cheeks. 'You should have seen where it was heading. I can't believe how naïve the lot of you were.'

Hugo, Diego, Marguerita . . . Yolanda has heard nothing of any of them since I left.

'That's easy to say now, Julieta. But we lacked the benefit of hindsight at the time.'

'Hindsight? How about foresight? How about insight?'

'I don't think anyone could have had that sort of insight, not at that moment,' I say slowly. 'As it is, I have to live with my guilt.'

And yet, I think, there are things Julieta doesn't know about her sister. I am not trying to excuse myself, but there were other factors that might also have imperilled her, even without my cartoons.

Julieta hasn't known, so I tell her now, about José's teaching in the slums. She has heard stories from Felipe, after his business trips to Argentina, about unionists being arrested in their place of work. But she isn't aware that teaching literacy in the *villas* is also considered subversion. She doesn't know that Graciela went there with José regularly, that she had plans to start a class of her own.

'It might mean nothing or it might mean everything,' I tell her. 'I'm not trying to shift the blame.'

There are other things, too. Psychologists, I'm beginning to realise, like journalists, like lawyers, were being targeted as a profession. Though she was only a student, psychology was Graciela's field.

Julieta is quiet as she thinks through the implications. 'We might never know,' she says, 'since there seems to be no record of her being arrested, let alone of any charges being brought.'

For the millionth time I ask myself whether there could be some door we haven't tried.

Julieta shivers, and pulls the blanket around her. 'It was always so hard having her as my little sister,' she says.

I look up, startled by her words.

'She was everyone's favourite, wasn't she? The baby everyone adored.'

'Julieta,' I say. 'Do you really believe that?'

'It's true, Papá. You and Mamá both know it. I know it probably better than anyone, having shared a room with her for all of those years.'

'We've never loved one of you more than the other, Julieta — you must know that. You are very different people, that's been obvious since you were tiny. But you cannot think that because of it, we loved either of you any the less . . .'

'You say that, Papá, but that's not how it felt. You gave her so much attention. You were both so protective of her. I don't know, perhaps she really was more fragile after that scarlet fever episode. Or maybe it's because she came along after Mamá was told she'd never have another child.'

'Oh, Julieta,' I say. 'You were our first-born, and I can't tell you what we both felt – how extraordinary it was, how you transformed us the day you arrived.'

'It's not that, Papá. It's everything that came later. Though I was older, it was as if I were constantly overshadowed in your affections. I always had to earn the things that came to Graciela as a gift. It didn't make things easy between us . . . Then, when we were growing up, my boyfriends started getting crushes on her. Do you remember Alejandro? Do you remember Marcelo, who I'd been so in love with – the one she went out with before José? Do you know how she met him – do you? She couldn't help it, Papá. Graciela was like a kitten – she needed attention. Why do you think I pushed Felipe to take this job in Miami? When she started to look at him like that, I couldn't bear it. We left before anything could happen.'

'Julieta, surely you're imagining it . . .'

'See, Papá, even now you refuse to face it. It's even worse now that she has vanished, and you and Mamá have transformed her into some sort of saint.'

I try to respond but she prevents me.

'Don't say anything, Papá. Just hear me out. I know you haven't had an easy time, I understand, I really do. But never once have you come to visit us in Miami. Mateo's two and a half now, and never once have you bothered to come. I know you're sending money home but we'd have paid your flight

– we said so several times. As it is, I've had to bring Mateo halfway round the world so that he can meet his only grandfather. Anyone would think you care more about this child of Graciela's than you do about my son, about the grandchild you actually have.'

I hadn't realised. I hadn't realised any of it. That it wasn't enough to love her so much and simply assume that she knew.

'Julieta, I'm so sorry,' I say.

'It's okay, Papá. It's not like anything's changed. But it breaks my heart, that's all. And do you want to know the worst of it? It's not like I don't care . . . about Graciela, I mean. She's my little sister. God knows I love her too, despite everything, in spite of what I've had to forgive her. And the idea of there being a missing child . . .'

She stops for breath. I can tell all this has been weighing on her, that it has cost her, too, these past years.

'I'm just saying, Papá: don't forget you have another daughter. Don't forget you have a grandson, too.'

On the second evening we're in the kitchen preparing dinner when Felipe calls from Miami. I pass the phone through and close the door to give Julieta some privacy, and construct a fortress around Mateo with the piled-up sofa cushions.

After a while, she nudges the door open with her toe.

'Mateo,' she says. 'Come and say hello to Papá.'

'Hello, Papá,' he says as Julieta holds the receiver to his ear. Silence for a moment. 'Yes . . . Yes . . . We nearly got run over by a bicycle. Then we went on a boat.'

Julieta laughs and takes back the phone and explains about our tour of the canals.

She mimes a question while she's listening, asking if I want to say hello.

'Felipe!' I say. The receiver is warm from the ears that have been pressing against it. 'How are you? I hear they've locked you up in your corner office.'

He groans. 'And swallowed the key. I wish it *were* a corner office – at least I'd have a bit of a view. How are things in Amsterdam?'

'We're all good. The rain's held off. I don't suppose there is any chance you can get away?'

'I'm still trying, Osvaldo, but I'm not too hopeful. The new director's just started' – he drops his voice because he's calling from work – 'you know what they're like.'

'Well, we're missing you here. But your wife and son are doing fine, if it's any consolation. Mateo says the canals are like moats. He's on the lookout for crocodiles.'

After the call I go back to chopping vegetables. Julieta has already fed Mateo and is about to put him to bed.

'I want *Abuelo* to tell me a story,' Mateo says. He is standing in his fortress in his sheriff's pyjamas, four books sliding down his belly.

'Have you brushed your teeth?' Julieta says.

He gives her his Cheshire Cat grin.

'Did you do *pipí*?'

He nods.

'You sure?'

'Yes, Mamá.'

'Okay, then hop into bed and wait for *Abuelo* to tuck you in.'

'Sounds like Felipe is pretty tied up,' I say, as Mateo gallops off to his room.

'Yes, I know,' she says. 'In one way I am proud of him, but that company is turning me into a corporate widow.'

She makes light of it, but I know how disappointed she is that he hasn't come.

'We'll still have a good time, just the three of us,' I say.

I hug her briefly and dry my hands, and follow Mateo through the bedroom door.

After five stories – the first one twice – my grandson finally agrees it's time to sleep.

'Will you make me some cartoons, *Abuelo*?' he says before closing his eyes.

My back stiffens. Has he overheard some conversation of Julieta's? I haven't touched a sketchbook since Hugo published my drawings, and do not intend to as long as Graciela remains missing.

'We'll see, Mateo,' I tell him, smoothing his hair. 'Now, how about you pretend you're a sleepy stowaway, just like the boy in the book?'

Ginger and garlic fill my small Dutch kitchen with aromas of the tropics. Julieta smiles as I join her over the stove.

Our talk the night before has affected us, but it may also have done us some good. Julieta seems less edgy with me, though our relationship will still take time to repair.

At dinner our conversation drifts back, as perhaps it must, to the absence at the centre of our lives. All day we've been stepping around it as if around a chasm in the fog.

'You know, I see her sometimes,' I tell Julieta.

She is sharing out the last of the prawns she has grilled for us and stops, spoon poised in mid-air.

'What do you mean?' she says.

'I see Graciela. In the street. Once, in the Paris metro. I know it sounds improbable. I doubt it myself sometimes.'

'It must have been someone who looked like her, Papá. It happens to me too.'

'It felt like more than that, though, this time. It was the day before you arrived. I only saw her from the side but I felt so certain. She was with somebody, some man. I followed them until they went into a building on the Herengracht. I even wrote down the address.'

'Oh, Papá,' Julieta says gently. 'It makes no sense.'

So I tell her the little I know – what I've learned from anecdotes passed on by other exiles. That occasionally they liberate a detainee, one they consider 'ideologically recuperated'. That they make them check in regularly with their minders, like an offender on parole.

'Maybe Graciela is among them,' I say. 'Maybe she's one of the ones they've released.'

Julieta puts her hand on my forearm. 'What would she be doing in Amsterdam, Papá? Why wouldn't she have got in touch?'

'Maybe they've imposed some deal on her – you know, that she can go abroad on condition that she severs all ties.'

'What, like some sort of witness protection programme?' She bites her lip. 'I don't think it's possible, Papá. I don't think they do that sort of thing.'

'I tell you, Julieta. It had to be her.'

I don't tell her how it affected me, the likeness in every detail, from her gait to the colour of her hair. How I raced along the Herengracht trying to catch her, out of breath, a cramp in the soft place under my ribs. How long I stood waiting opposite the building, among the passers-by and the cyclists and the end-of-workday traffic, before I realised she wasn't coming back out.

'And she just happens to be here in Amsterdam? Where you're living?' Julieta shakes her head, then speaks slowly. 'Papá, don't do this to yourself – you'll go crazy. You know, I hate to say this, but it's been so long and we've had no word . . .'

I anticipate what she's about to say and halt her before she says more.

'You know, don't you, that for ages your mother was getting phone calls?'

Julieta looks up sharply. 'What are you talking about? What calls?'

'From some man, some friend of Graciela's apparently, asking us to send money on her behalf. First it was to settle some debt she'd run up. Then it was for other things. You know she sold your grandmother's jewellery. She sold things from the house. She sold the car.'

'Oh, God,' Julieta says. 'Why did she never tell me?'

'What would you have said? To stop doing it? As long as there was any possibility Graciela needed us, she would give them whatever they asked. That's why she has stayed on in the house, though I've urged her to join me here. And though she hates those calls, she doesn't want to miss one – in case Graciela really does need our help. And if one day Graciela herself should ring . . . Your mother can't bear to think of her trying to call and there being nobody to pick up the phone.'

'But she never has, has she?'

'No. Not as far as we know. And in March, whoever the man was stopped ringing. Though I suppose it could resume at any time.'

'It's been five years, Papá,' Julieta says. Then, quietly: 'You know what I've been thinking? That if there really is a child, as the bishop said, then maybe that's what we should concentrate on. I know Mamá's looked for birth records, for any kind of document. There was that dead end at the kindergarten . . . But now that the child is older, there must be other things: health cards, vaccination cards, school records . . . There must be something that will lead us back to Graciela.'

What she is saying makes sense, I think: somehow to follow the child. Yet still, what we lack is a lead.

We have finished dinner, and the emergency candles Julieta found in a cupboard have almost burned down to their stubs.

'We should turn in,' I say, glancing at my watch. 'It's after midnight. We can do the dishes in the morning. Do you think you'll be able to sleep?'

'I'll take something if I can't,' she says, and gives me a jetlagged smile.

I hear her brushing her teeth in the bathroom, and recognise the same *andante* rhythm she used as a child. When she kisses me goodnight I smell the mint of her toothpaste, the faint apple-scent of her hair.

'I'm glad you've come, Julieta,' I say.

'Me too,' she says, and squeezes my hand. 'Goodnight, Papá. Remember to get some sleep.'

She closes the door and I go over to the window, and gaze down at the silent world. A white mist is rising from the water, turning the street lamps into silkworm cocoons.

Below me, the water is blacker than the sky. Its surface reflects the fairy lights and the gingerbread houses opposite, transforming the half-moon bridges into perfect Os.

All across the sleeping city, across the spider's-web map of its waterways, bridges stand like this one, spanning the canals with arches that transform themselves into circles only on nights as still as this.

They look like tunnels, I think. Like secret passageways. Gates to a parallel world.

~

The sky is a fat grey hammock slung low to the horizon and the hump-backed bridges rise to meet it halfway. Pedestrians cross like tightrope walkers balanced between two parabolas, their reflections shimmering below in the brackish glass.

On one of the canals a dredger is working, hauling abandoned bicycles out of the murk. It swings its neck out over the water, pincers loose as a dislocated jaw. Toxic iridescence fans outwards like paisley plumage, smearing the surface with its sheen.

The dredger pivots swiftly, then plunges its Jurassic neck into the silt. Nuzzling the floor a moment, it strikes some submerged obstacle, locks on to it, and pulls.

Bent frames and twisted handlebars cling to the sludge beneath the water, reluctant to relinquish their hold on the velvety filth. But the dredger insists, pulls harder, and noxious bubbles escape its sulphurous kiss. Bilge water streams as the dredger lifts and rotates slowly, then releases its haul of debris onto a barge. Rotting metal clatters down the pile like broken femurs; tibias and scapulas catch in the spokes and chains.

Osvaldo quickens his pace and hurries past it, averting his gaze. It spooks him in ways he can't enunciate, the naked ribs, the stench of fetid water, this vision of the macabre.

7

Amsterdam
April 1982

Disoriented with sleep, I fumble for the telephone. Its shrill-
ness disassembles the dark.

At first I can't identify who is speaking; it takes me a
moment to register it is Julieta, back in America these past
five months, dragging me from the warmth of my bed. But
Julieta never rings this late; like Yolanda, she is careful about
gauging the time.

Since her visit here with Mateo we have called each other
more often – we try to do so every couple of weeks. I am grateful for this new closeness, despite the fact we live so far apart.

But her voice this time is strange and I have to force myself
to concentrate. She is flying to Buenos Aires at midday;
Yolanda's brother telephoned her from La Plata; it was Ricardo
who asked her to call.

Have I understood correctly? Could I have heard?

She says it again but I don't believe her.

'It was her heart, Papá . . .' Sentences reach me down the line in pieces; I try hard to catch them and pin them down. '. . . Ricardo thinks the lift must have been out of order . . .' What lift? I think. Where was she? '. . . They found her in the stairwell, on the sixth floor of a building in Belgrano . . .' I can't think of anyone we know in Belgrano, a single reason that would take Yolanda there. '. . . She was on her way to Patricia's . . .'

Patricia, I think. A Grandmother. One of her friends.

What Julieta says next is distorted by her weeping. 'They called an ambulance and took her to the hospital, but when they got there . . .' She halts; she is struggling for breath. 'She didn't make it, Papá. They tried to revive her. But she was gone by the time they arrived.'

I sit on the arm of the sofa in the moonlight. The trees whisper, the water mirrors the night outside my window, here on the dark side of the world.

'This can't be true, Julieta,' I say when I can find my voice. 'Ricardo is mistaken. They have confused Yolanda with somebody else.'

At the end of the line Julieta is fighting her tears. 'Papá, listen to me,' she says. 'Ricardo had to go to the hospital. They asked him to identify her.'

There is a noise like buzzing in my ears. I find my fingers wrapped around the telephone cord, its spirals like a tourniquet around my hand.

When she speaks again, I feel as if I'm returning from some great distance. My mind spins and gains no traction. I cannot grasp this aberration in the order of things.

'I'm catching the first flight down there – Felipe is taking care of Mateo,' she is telling me. 'What will you do, Papá? Is it too dangerous for you to go back?'

Woodenly, I tell her I will find a way.

I hang up the phone. My mind reels through states of numbness, then roars refusal. Yolanda was fifty-two last birthday. We spoke only two days ago.

Let night resume its circumnavigation of the planet; when dawn breaks, let her live, let her still be alive.

But Julieta's words swoop down at me from the rafters. Fragments of her sentences bounce back at me from the walls.

In the stairwell.

Didn't make it.

It was her heart.

———

I arrive to a paroxysm of patriotism in a city that has been transformed.

Flags flutter from the tops of skyscrapers and from people's balconies; they fly like capes from the statues in the parks. They decorate schools and traffic islands; they sprout from aerials and the mirrors of trucks. Blue and white stripes hang everywhere like a veil over the ravaged economy, like a veil over the ranks of the missing, like a veil over the well of my loss.

Amid the fervour, I forget to be afraid. I didn't expect the sort of euphoria that I remember from four years earlier, after the boycott failed and the World Cup matches went ahead and were broadcast on French TV. This time, the banners are about the Malvinas, those islands pinned like butterfly wings to the blue of the South Atlantic. Slogans like '*Abajo el colonialismo!*' and '*Las Malvinas son Argentinas!*' hang from apartment windows; they decorate the trunks of the trees. '*Down with colonialism!*' I read as we crawl through the traffic. '*The Malvinas are Argentine!*' leaps in giant capitals across a wall.

The British are nothing if not tenacious, I think to myself; what makes the generals so confident they'll let the Falklands go?

Nothing, anymore, seems real. Beyond the taxi window the world unfolds apart from me, like the film of some stranger's life. I am inside myself but also outside it, functioning automatically, but disintegrating inside.

I've flown from Amsterdam to Montevideo and crossed the river by ferry to Buenos Aires, not daring to risk a direct arrival by plane. I am still in shock. But it was not shock that protected me when I disembarked with my false identity. Instead, it was the recklessness of grief.

As we roll through the febrile capital, familiarity and alienation sweep over me in waves. I am home, I can scarcely believe it, yet never have I felt so estranged. I am not Osvaldo Ferrero, the man who escaped six years ago, creeping home in secrecy to bury his wife. No, I am this other man, the one in my false passport, and I am grateful for this alibi that proved easier to obtain than I'd ever surmised. I lean on him, this Vicente Carlucci, I will myself to be him as we pass the sports fields and the Aeroparque, the cafés and the mansions on the tree-lined *avenidas*; I inhabit his life as we travel these bitter streets.

Six years. And to come back for this . . . I should never have listened to Yolanda's warnings. I should have taken the risk.

We pull up beside a police car at the traffic lights. I stare ahead as the occupants observe me through the window, and breathe again when finally they pull away.

Soon we reach my *barrio*. The newspaper kiosk has disappeared from the corner where it huddled between the footpath and the traffic lights, blocking the view of the street from the Colibri. Behind its window I see the ancient waiter shuffling as he always shuffled between the tables, then claiming his old observation post at the bar. But the footpath florist, her buckets bright with gerberas, has vanished; her slow-burning plumes of incense no longer linger on the polluted air.

My mind moves like a concertina, in and out of reality, observing everything, forgetting everything, then remembering why I have come.

I move as if underwater, slow motion in a time before sound. I climb the steps and turn the key that left Argentina with me, and pause on the threshold of the past.

Then I shut the door behind me and stand in the afternoon stillness, letting the tide break over me in this homecoming that is really a farewell. The autumn sunlight filters through the windows, a world revolving in the motes of dust.

She is still here.

She is all around me in the silent house that no one has entered since she locked the door four days ago and left it, not knowing she was never to return.

I walk towards the kitchen, passing the girls' old room. Graciela's guitar still leans against the bedstead. Julieta's bear still slumps on the windowsill. The line is still faintly visible across on the floorboards where Julieta, in territorial assertion at the age of twelve, divided the room in two.

'Yolanda,' I say quietly, wanting her to know I've come home.

Her breakfast plate is leaning in the dish-rack. Her coffee cup is sitting where she left it, her one last kiss upon its rim. I pick it up, and close my eyes, and press the cold hard china to my lips.

I move through the silent house, a ghost of myself in search of another ghost.

She is still here; I can feel her presence everywhere. She is in the wrinkles in the tablecloth, the folded-back pages of the newspaper, the leaf litter that has blown in through the garden door.

'Yolanda,' I say, more loudly now, calling to her, wanting her near.

From the cupboard where it belongs in the kitchen, I remove the glass jug and fill it, and water the plants in the living room, mindlessly, pointlessly, just wanting them to live.

I lift a jar from the bathroom shelf and open it, and suddenly jasmine blossoms in the air. This is the night-blooming scent of her, when I closed my eyes and waited for her, as she talked the school day out. The container is cold and heavy, an egg of cobalt glass. I trace the groove she has traced along the inside, my finger where her fingertips once were.

'Yolanda,' I say, and call her name to the emptiness, refusing this new intimacy of loss.

I sit on the bed that was once our bed and stare through the sliding glass door. Weeds have invaded the flower-beds; the garden is looking forlorn. By her bedside I open the book she was halfway through and close it again, the page she was reading still marked.

She was here, she is here, she has gone out just for a moment, any minute now she will be back.

There are photos of the girls on the dressing table: one I've never seen, of Graciela under a willow tree in Tigre, and a wedding photo of Julieta and Felipe. In the bedside drawer I find her reading glasses, and the tablets the doctor gave her to help her to sleep. And beneath them lies an envelope, a brown one that is velvety with age. I take it out and open it, careful that the edges don't tear.

What's inside I haven't seen for thirty years. I don't recognise it, then recognise it with a rush.

It is the drawing I did when I first met her, the first sketch of her I ever made. I hold it now, amazed that she still has it, remembering as I turn it towards the light. I see where the tentative lines grow confident, the hatching lightest in the shadow beside her face. I was trying to capture something so elusive. I was trying to draw the way she lifted my heart.

She'd kept it. She'd held on to it all these years.

'Yolanda,' I whisper. 'Stay awhile, *amore*. There is no hurry. Stay with me, now I've finally come home.'

The wardrobe door is ajar and her clothes are lined up neatly: the things she wore on school days, the things she wore to go out. And in the drawer where she'd always kept it, I find the cashmere scarf that she'd bought when we went to Italy, that she'd worn at the Trevi fountain, that she'd worn to remember Rome.

I take this thing she loved and fold it inside my shirt inside my jacket, its softness and her perfume close to my skin.

Then I pull her pillow from its place beside mine and hold it. I inhale her scent and hold it to my chest and breathe it in again, breathing in all that was good in her, the weight of her when I held her, the weight of her life on my life.

And in the moving air of this silent room she comes and sits beside me, and enfolds me in her arms. And together we wait in silence until the knowledge comes, till the weeping comes in shudders, till the raw, animal hurt of it comes.

———

I wander like a phantom through the protocol of funerals, embracing strangers, sharing words of comfort I do not feel. Julieta is there, red-eyed and trying to be strong. Ricardo is there, bewildered by the shock of it, stumbling through his loss. Elisa, his wife and Yolanda's sister-in-law, holds on to him; acquaintances bring condolences and support.

We bury her at the cemetery in La Plata, not far from the house where she grew up. There are Grandmothers standing with us beside the rose bushes; for the first time I meet Patricia and Constanza, eyes of startling blue in an ashen face. Eduardo and Maria – José's parents – come to the ceremony but not to the graveside; for Maria it has proved too much. There are school teachers, a physics teacher called Bukovich or Borovich, and one of her former pupils who said he was studying medicine, whose name, I think he said, was Gabriel.

There are smiles amid the mourning. People see me, and greet me, and then they touch me: they squeeze my arm or embrace me in disbelief that I am here and still alive, that Yolanda is the one who is gone.

I have too little time with Julieta. I hug her tightly, wordlessly, both of us needing comfort, neither of us with anything to give.

I leave Argentina shortly afterwards, clinging to my alibi like a friend. Ricardo and the Grandmothers urge me to hurry; they insist it is still unsafe, that I must not stay to sort out Yolanda's affairs.

Somewhere, on the other side of the world, a British fleet is sailing towards the South Atlantic. As my plane takes off from Montevideo, I stare out of the aircraft window, down at the upholstery of clouds. Beneath them, the world keeps turning. I feel estranged from it. Bereft.

~~~~~

Julieta stays in Buenos Aires ten days longer, and calls once she has returned to the United States.

'I found out what happened, Papá,' she tells me.

Both of us had been disturbed by it: why Yolanda was found lying on a staircase when the lift hadn't been out of order at all.

'She took the stairs because the Grandmothers always take the stairs,' says Julieta. 'They do it for security reasons. So the doorman can't tell where they're meeting from the number above the elevator door.'

A little at a time, like a patient testing a limb after an operation, I allow myself to think about my wife. I let glimpses of her slip between my fingers like a child with its hands to the light.

I think about the heart that let her down. I think about the way she would never give up. I think about her dying alone in the stairwell, the Grandmothers waiting one floor above and wondering. I think about Constanza arriving after her, and finding her there where she lay.

'Julieta,' I say, and want to continue, and find I cannot speak after all.

'You know, Papá,' she says after a moment. She is learning to do this now, to rescue me at times when the words won't come. 'There is one thing I discovered when I was going through the house.'

She tells me about a box she found in the bottom of the linen cupboard, how it was tied with purple ribbon, how there were layers of clothing folded in tissue paper inside.

'I didn't know she'd taken up knitting again,' she says.

The box was full of children's clothing, all of it made by hand. There were tiny sweaters and woollen hats and scarves with stripes or fringes, a double set of everything, in colours for a boy and a girl. Yolanda had made each a little larger than the previous one, working her way through the sizes, with the smallest at the bottom of the box.

Yolanda had told me about the things she had knitted for Graciela; about the day she had waited for hours in the gardens for a man who had never shown up. But she never told me that afterwards she had continued; that year after year she had knitted things for her grandchild without knowing if it was male or female, preparing for the day it was found.

It takes Julieta a moment to find the words. 'I was going to give them away,' she says, 'unless a sweater or two fitted Mateo. But maybe we should keep them . . .'

'Let's hold on to them, Julieta,' I say.

8

Buenos Aires
June 1983

'Mamá, look!' she says. 'It's wobbly!'

Ana tests it again with her tongue. It gave her a shock the first time she found it could swing like a hinge, its sharp edge jutting over her gum. She can feel the fibres stretching when she pushes it, and for a second panics that it might not spring back into place.

'Mmmmm,' her mother says, then looks up from her gardening magazine. She makes big eyes at the fang-face Ana is pulling. 'Don't play with it, sweetheart. It will come out when it's ready all on its own.'

'Do I look like a savage tiger in the jungle?'

'You look like a very scary tiger indeed.'

'What'll happen if I swallow it by accident?'

'Oh, darling. It will just go through you like a birdseed and there'll be a great big gap when you smile.'

'But how will the Tooth Mouse find it?'

'If that happens, we'll still leave him a glass of water. He knows when little girls have lost a tooth.'

Ana can't stop exploring it – it's as if her tongue has a mind of its own. The tooth is much bigger than a birdseed, she tells herself; if she swallowed it she would feel it travel all the way down. She imagines it looping through her insides like the pipe-slide at the swimming pool; she imagines it sticking in her belly and taking root. If she died and they had to cut her open, they'd find a tooth-tree growing inside.

At lunchtime, she has to chew sideways so that her loose tooth doesn't go down with a pasta shell. Her mamá cuts her apple into bite-sized shapes and *caramelos* are Strictly Not Allowed.

But at school on their purple cushions she can't help it: while their teacher is reading aloud to them, Ana's tongue keeps worming to the spot. She turns to María Magdalena who is sitting beside her and makes her giggle when she gets the tooth to move.

The sing-song voice continues but Ana, absorbed by the mechanics inside her mouth, has missed a bit of the story and now she has lost the thread. The tooth is bending further; she pushes some more to see how flat it can go. Suddenly she feels a snap, and something enormous lodges on the cushion of her tongue. She spits into her palm and is surprised at the diminutive trophy, hardly even the size of a bead. Its underside is hollow and slightly pinkish, and there is a flavour in her mouth like salt or something metal; she hadn't realised that teeth could taste of the sea.

María Magdalena makes her open her hand to show her, and soon the rest of the children are crowding around.

The teacher stops her reading and peers over. She wraps the tooth in a handkerchief and puts it in a pencil case so Ana can carry it home.

Now her tongue keeps travelling to the empty spot. Her mamá said a new tooth would grow in place of the missing one, but so far nothing has happened; the space still feels smooth and soft. When her papá comes in to kiss her goodnight she bares her teeth like a deep-sea shark and pokes her tongue through the gap.

At night, in her elephant pyjamas, Ana switches on the bedside lamp. The tooth has grown bigger in the glass of water it's sitting in so that the Tooth Mouse can find it in the dark. Carefully, she picks up the glass and carries it, using both her hands, to the end of her bed where Liliana, whose eyes blink shut when she lays her down, is sleeping among the other dolls in her pram. Ana apologises for forgetting to show her earlier, but luckily it's not too late.

In the morning the tooth has vanished. Sitting in the water at the bottom of the glass is a coin that seems to ogle like her Polish grandmother does when her reading glasses are on.

'What can I buy with this, Papá?' Ana says.

'Not a lot,' he tells her, because a Bad Thing called Inflation is eating it up. But he promises to convert it into something nice if she tells him what she would like.

She has her answer ready; she has had it in mind for weeks.

'I want a baby sister,' she says.

He stiffens, and looks at her with an expression she cannot decipher.

'That's not how babies get here,' he says.

9

Paris

October 1984

'Osvaldo,' he says. 'Can you come back to Paris? There is someone here I think you need to meet.'

I am thrilled to hear Arturo's voice. Though we spoke a lot after Yolanda died, our conversations have grown sporadic, so I am all the more delighted to find his message, in the secretary's neat handwriting, on a square of office notepaper on my desk.

I didn't realise how much I had been missing them until I rang him back and Santiago picked up the phone.

'I'll get him,' my godson says in his six-year-old's voice, the receiver clattering in my ear. 'Pa-a-a-a-pá-á-á-á!' I hear him shout, the receding syllables hiccuping as he runs.

'*Amigo!*' Arturo says. In my office cubicle I am ambushed by emotion. I am glad he cannot see my eyes.

We chat for half an hour. The circle of exiles we used to know in Paris is diminishing. He mentions various names, how the homesick ones went back soon after the election, buoyed by newfound hope of rebuilding their lives. For others, though the Junta has gone, the feelings are still too complicated, the losses and betrayals too raw.

Arturo and Carla are among those who are planning to stay in France. Arturo has a chance at tenure and Santiago has just started school. Once he has settled in to it, Carla will work full-time for the Spanish publisher she's been translating for as a freelancer since she arrived.

Santiago at school already! Arturo says they are still living in the same first-floor apartment but they are looking for a bigger place. That, he confides, is partly for another reason: they are trying for a second child.

Hearing him reminds me that I too have decisions to make. I am fifty-seven now and cannot imagine ever again living in Argentina. Yet here in Europe I feel rootless, and increasingly adrift.

Julieta continues to phone me every few weeks, as she has since she and Mateo came to stay. She and Felipe keep inviting me to visit them in Miami, and I did go once, but no matter how much I love seeing them, I've never made it a regular thing.

Julieta I know is worried; she thinks that I have buried myself in the past. She says I should socialise more, even think about remarrying. She doesn't understand I have no interest in what she calls moving on.

I feel bullied by her insistence and dig in my heels in silence; our differences risk resurfacing between the seams of our patchwork entente.

I don't know whether Arturo senses any of this: my stagnation, my rudderless years. What neither of us could have foreseen is how this phone call would become a watershed in my life.

'Come to Paris,' he says again. 'Stay with us. There is someone here I believe you need to see.'

~~~

It is strange being back in the old apartment. The cork mark is still up there on the ceiling; the old sofa still subsides towards the living-room floor. Carla has had her hair cut short while Arturo is properly balding; Santiago, in Luke Skywalker pyjamas, is constructing Lego-block towers on the stretch of floor where once I'd had my bed.

We embrace; we smile and blink at each other, observing the small ways we have changed. Santiago gives me a distracted hug before the Leaning Tower of Pisa collapses into a mountain of rubble.

'We've missed you, Osvaldo,' Carla says, as Arturo uncorks a bottle of Bordeaux.

'We have *mate* if you prefer,' he says, remembering.

I shake my head. 'Wine would be perfect,' I say. I don't add it, but I need something to steady my nerves.

A sort of museum now ornaments the bookshelf. With a stab of nostalgia I take in the tango figurines, the silver *bombilla* in its handmade *mate* gourd, the pair of salt-carved llamas from Jujuy.

'Welcome back to Paris,' says Arturo, raising a proper wine glass in place of a mustard jar.

'And to your home away from home away from home,' Carla adds.

'To you both, and to my godson,' I say.

Carla is cooking something to do with aubergines and vanishes into the kitchen with her glass. Then she pops her head back out through the door.

'I'm afraid I haven't acquired too many Michelin stars since last time,' she says with a wry expression on her face.

'Well, as long as they haven't taken any away . . .'

She smiles and her head disappears.

'We had an *asado* on the balcony of a friend's place out in the suburbs last weekend,' Arturo tells me, 'until the neighbours got upset about the smoke and complained to the fire brigade.'

'They let you keep your steaks at least, I hope?'

'Fortunately, though they could have done with another five minutes. Santiago was the only one who didn't mind – he got a tour around the block in the cabin of the firemen's truck.'

'They showed me how to turn the siren on and make the ladder go up and down,' Santiago says, looking up from his building site.

'And did you get to fight any fires?' I ask.

'Not this time. They said I have to wait till I am big.'

Arturo smiles. 'Inés will be here in a moment,' he tells Santiago. 'Now go off and brush your teeth.'

'I already did that, Papá,' he says, adding the final cross-beam to a helicopter landing pad.

'Good boy. When she gets here you can say hello but then I want you to skedaddle off to bed.'

Earlier, Arturo had come to meet my train. We'd hugged and then stopped for a beer at one of the brasseries opposite the Gare du Nord.

'So who is this Inés you are so certain I have to meet?' I asked him after a moment, as the waiter set our glasses down on their matching cardboard mats.

Arturo waited for him to leave us, then moved closer and lowered his voice.

'She's an *ex-desaparecida*, actually,' he said. 'I only learned she was coming ten days ago – she's seeing that UN committee on disappearances, the one in Geneva I'm trying to help.'

I nodded, slowly taking this in.

'They held her clandestinely in Pozo de Quilmes and Banfield. And she was in ESMA for a very long time.'

I stared at him. The Escuela Superior de Mecánica de la Armada. The biggest torture centre the regime had devised.

'There's more, Osvaldo,' he said, and hesitated before continuing. 'They made her work as a kind of midwife when she was inside.'

'Jesus Christ, Arturo,' I said softly.

'I know, I know. I would have told you before you got here but I didn't want to discuss it over the phone. I met her on Monday. She says she is here to see Danielle Mitterrand, then she is going to London and on to Geneva. I thought you might want to speak to her yourself.'

My mind spun. Had Arturo told her anything about me? Did she know why he had invited her to his home?

'Even if she does have any information, do you honestly think she'll want to chat about her experiences over dinner?' I said, protesting.

'We can go gently, and maybe later on she will feel up to discussing things. You're a doctor, Osvaldo, you know how to talk to people. I think it's worth asking. There might be something she can recall.'

I appreciated the good intentions, but how could he contemplate such a thing?

'Osvaldo,' he said, as if reading my thoughts. 'She's here because she wants to help.'

Now, with Inés's arrival imminent, I feel anxious. If she knows anything, if she can tell me any detail . . .

Carla pops her head around the kitchen door again, her hair turned curly by the steam.

'I've met her too, Osvaldo,' she interjects, after I ask Arturo how easy he found Inés to talk to. Carla sends me a reassuring glance. 'Don't worry,' she says. 'It's going to be all right.'

⸺

Inés Moncavillo is late for dinner because she has walked. She walks everywhere now, no matter where she happens to be or what country she happens to be in. In Paris a week, she has walked all over the city, and out of the city on a radius that spikes into the suburbs, along railway tracks and bleak arterial roads. Wherever she has to go, at whatever time it is, in whatever weather, she walks. And if she has nowhere to go she sets out anyway, walking till some ring road stops her, or she is turned back by the start of a motor-way or by roads that end in cul-de-sacs in deserted loading yards.

A petite woman with hardness in her eyes, she looks a decade older than her thirty-nine years.

Arturo buzzes her into the building and finds her standing stiffly under the light bulb on the landing after she's rapped at the apartment door. Outside it has been raining, and water sparkles like broken glass in the weave of her too-heavy coat. She wears it belted tightly around her abdomen like a carapace, wrists poking out of the ends of her sleeves like forks.

There is an edge to her, some mistrust or impatience that borders on intolerance. She tenses as we greet her in the entrance; even before we are introduced I feel discouraged about the prospect of her help.

At dinner we talk about life in Europe, about university politics and office politics and Argentine politics, about acquaintances who are and who are not going home. Inés sips her wine but barely touches the food that Carla sets before her, as if eating were a pleasure she denies herself, or the part of herself that has not yet been freed.

Carla goes to check on Santiago. I stack the dishes and ferry them into the kitchen where I build my own Tower of Pisa, on top of the salad bowl on top of the saucepan on top of the stove.

Arturo produces a bottle of whisky and we sit amid the debris at the table, amid the rinds of cheese and the mandarin peel and the woody husks of walnuts, talking until long into the night. The candles sink to the rims of the wine bottles, then plunge into the darkness beneath. Their extinction forms a hiatus that might have ended the evening, had Carla not found replacements in a drawer.

And now, at last, Inés begins to open up.

There are certain things she wishes to make public, she tells us; others she'll share only with the families of those who didn't make it, partly to alleviate what she feels is the burden of having survived. She has notebooks in which she writes down details that come back to her, even after having given testimony, since her memories often surface unbidden.

Reaching for her handbag, she pulls out a school exercise book that seems incongruous for what it must contain. It is crammed with minute handwriting, as if the words themselves were cowering on the page. Inside she jots down names as they return to her; lists dates when she can remember, crosscheck or deduce them; describes the voices of torturers whose faces she couldn't see.

She wants to purge her mind of them, so that her sweating, dread-filled nightmares might give way to ordinary dreams. Externalising them onto clean white sheets of paper she hopes will bring her a measure of peace.

Then, in the flickering darkness, she tells of unspeakable things. She has passed through the gates of hell and learned that everything that lies beyond them was created by the hand of man.

Dying holds no terror for her now, nor sickness, nor physical pain. She has been to the frontier of endurance and passed over it. The cruelty was in the hauling back.

What she fears are not electric volts in the tenderest parts of her body, nor rape, nor bilge-water drowning, nor being slammed against cold metal doors. She fears none of their other methods with their playground appellations for searing the body with pain. Like some secular Inquisition, it was not even about obtaining information. Instead, it was a perversion that ravaged bodies in order to break what lay inside them: the kernel that made them human. Then it eliminated the bodies, too.

No, it is not dying, nor anything physical she fears. It's the return to the tribe of the living, now that she knows what it's capable of.

'We are God,' they'd told her. 'No one remembers you.'

And from inside, from beyond the gates of the underworld, she and the other prisoners could hear the world they had left. Chained in their attic kennels, high above the officers' mess and the basement torture rooms, the shouts of school kids drifted up to them, the cheers of fans at their football games.

With a fingernail, with the sharp edge of their shackles, through the blackness behind hoods and blindfolds, they had scratched the names of their loved ones into the walls. Intimate as Braille, the letters had turned out crippled, lopsided, yet the deformed calligraphy of yearning had kept alive the memory of who they once had been.

Carla blinks back tears in the candlelight. Arturo squeezes her hand.

Inés tells us she is one of the few to have survived the torture centres, and attributes that to her usefulness in the birthing room at ESMA, the naval academy that doubled as one of the

Junta's most iniquitous dungeons, when those who ran that particular realm of darkness discovered she'd had training as a nurse.

Once liberated – perhaps because they considered her implicated, or ideologically 'recuperated', or simply because they were convinced of their own impunity – she stayed in Argentina just long enough to testify before the National Commission on Disappeared Persons before departing. She has no intention ever to return.

She tells us the things she told the people from the commission, the things that would not fit into their final report. She wants there to be no secret about what happened. She wants it to be known where the disappeared went.

Then she speaks of the women she helped in childbirth, of the women she says saved her life. But it was not the existence of the birthing room that protected her. Rather, amid the savagery that surrounded them, it was the shreds of her own humanity that those women allowed her to cling to – by giving her the chance to assist another living being.

Sometimes delivery happened in a corridor; more often, on a table in what must once have been a sort of kitchen, the mothers sometimes in blindfolds, sometimes in chains.

Prurient as pubescents, the guards muscled in to leer. Once, when a birth was breech and she'd called for a doctor, they tossed her a plastic cup. Often, after a child was delivered, they'd force the exhausted mother to clean the afterbirth off the floor.

I can't bring myself to ask her, but finally I must. And somehow, even before she answers, I've guessed.

Yes, among the women she'd helped in labour, there had been a green-eyed one with chestnut hair and freckles slowly fading for lack of sunlight, a woman whose name she recalls as Graciela.

Graciela Ferrero – she remembers because of how young she was, and because all of them made it their business to memorise names and surnames, to know who else was there.

She'd arrived when she was six months pregnant and given birth at the end of January – to a baby girl with eyes she must have inherited from her mother.

So it was true. The words that have held so much hope come back to me, tracing the ellipses the swallows made as they swooped over the vaults of St Peter's, over the cloisters and the Vatican gardens. *There was a child that lived.*

I am flooded with emotion, but dare not interrupt.

Inés consults her notebook, the cramped columns of dates. 'It's here,' she says. 'I've listed it. It would have been January the twenty-sixth.'

And then something comes back to her that she had forgotten until this instant: Graciela had taken the suture needle, the only instrument they were allowed by the military doctor, and marked the new-born infant behind the ear.

Inés thinks for a moment, folds her arms into a cradle. Yes, it was the right ear, she is sure.

'It was almost beyond her,' Inés says, 'it was almost beyond the two of us to scar that perfect child. But I held her as tight as possible while her mother made the incisions, cutting three small crosses into her skin.

'"Somebody will remember her," Graciela said when at last we'd stopped the bleeding. It was the sort of thing you'd notice, she said, at a clinic, or perhaps an orphanage, if for any reason her daughter should go astray.'

So she'd foreseen the possibility, I think. She had guessed. And blindly, maybe desperately, she'd sought a way that her child could be identified.

'Then,' Inés says, 'she sang. She sang to the child and whispered to her, four syllables of a single word. Over the following days she must have said it a thousand times, over and over like an incantation, singing it to her like a lullaby, burning it into her memory, singing to her her name.'

And then she sings, as Graciela had sung, but in a voice so ravaged it could barely carry the notes:

Liliana Liliana Liliana,
Liliana my love, luz de mi vida,
Light of my life, Liliana.

The building is in darkness except for our window. The lacerated melody lingers in the stillness, a promise unpinned by any hope.

So, I think, it was a girl. She has a name. She has a place and a date of birth. She has her mother's love inscribed upon her skin.

After more than seven years of knowing nothing, this suddenly seems so much.

'They were together for about ten days,' Inés continues. 'Despite being so thin, Graciela managed to breastfeed her, but the infant was so hungry that they had to get bottles delivered from outside.

'When they took the baby away they told Graciela, as they told the other mothers, that they would take it to her family. They told her to write her parents a letter that they would deliver along with the chid.

'The day after that was a Wednesday, and that was the night she was transferred.'

Transferred?

Transferred where? To some other secret dungeon? One of those re-education facilities Yolanda used to talk about? I cling to the ambiguity, knowing but refusing to countenance what else this word could mean.

Graciela, I think. My brave, beautiful daughter.

I weep for a while; I think we all do. It is some time before I am able to speak.

'Is there more?' I manage to ask. I look at Inés, and know immediately that there is. There are things that will have happened to Graciela that, because I am her father, she will try never to tell me, that she will try to protect me from.

We sit for a long time in the semi-darkness. Carla hugs Inés, but Inés cannot bend into her arms.

When I can, I thank her: for telling me the things she has remembered, for reliving things that otherwise would have been lost.

She nods and sits another moment in silence, a waif-like figure reflected between the glasses and the candles in the window, a survivor, still struggling to return.

There is something else I need to know from her, though I am almost too frightened to ask.

'Did you ever hear what happened to the baby, to Liliana?' I manage to say. As I say it I wonder if I am the first person, apart from her mother, apart from Inés, ever to have used her name.

But no, she never heard where the child went.

'There was a rumour,' she says, 'about a list being managed by the obstetrician at the naval academy – I once overheard a conversation between two of the guards. The impression I got was that it was all top secret, something reserved for police and military couples, and perhaps for others who were friends of the regime.'

A list? I think. Of course: a waiting list. My mind revolves. Did money change hands? Did the wives come up to the academy to select an infant? Or were their husbands simply allocated a child when their turn came around?

My stomach churns. I cannot still my thoughts.

Arturo goes to pour another round of whisky, but Inés slides her hand across her glass.

'It's getting late,' she says. 'I should probably be going soon.'

She rebuffs Arturo's offer to call a taxi, though he presses her to take one to be safe.

'I will walk, I need to walk,' she says. Then, aware she has spoken sharply, she makes an effort to soften her tone. 'It's all right, Arturo. I know it's late, but I prefer to go on my own.'

My legs give out when I go to stand. Graciela has gone but I cannot mourn her; Liliana lived but vanished within the first few days of her life.

Inés turns back before leaving and gives me her hand. It is bony and cold in my own.

'I know these things are not easy to listen to, Osvaldo,' she says. 'All the same, I hope they have been some use.'

And suddenly I understand what she is struggling with, and how badly I misjudged her at the start. What I took for antipathy is the thing that has come undone in her. Out of what she has left of faith in human nature, she has travelled back into the darkness in order to give me her help. But she is also trying to fix the broken circuits, to relearn the patterns of empathy. She is trying to relearn how to feel.

I look her directly in the eyes. 'Thank you for what you did for Graciela,' I say.

She smiles her first smile of the evening, and slightly bows her head.

'You would have been proud of her,' she says.

And then she is gone, a solitary figure lost among the great boulevards of Europe, walking, because at last she is free to do so, endlessly into the night.

I stand for a moment in the darkness of the landing, wanting a few minutes alone before returning inside.

I need to talk to Yolanda. She will want to know every detail. We will comfort each other and bolster each other and resume the search together. Then, with a jolt, it returns.

This is how it happens, how it always happens: I reach for her before remembering she is gone.

All the same, when the lights are out and I'm back in my old camp bed between the Lego watchtowers, I try out the syllables in the silence, sounding out the rhythm in them, feeling their shape on my tongue.

'Li-li-an-a, Lili-Ana, Liliana.'

Four lilting syllables that make me think of lilies, of the flowers her mother so loved.

And suddenly I am back in the delta, back in that long-ago summer with the heat and the fireflies in the lushness, with the lapping of the water from the passing boats and the shouts of the swimming children. There is the reflection of the river in the windows, and the smell of silt, and strains of music drifting across the islands. And I am back with the lilies and irises she collected for the house on the water, back with the flowers she stole from the garden in Tigre.

⁓

'I want to mark her, Inés,' she whispers. 'As a sign, so somebody sees.'

Inés is remembering. She is walking through the streets of Paris long after midnight, and as she walks she replays the scene she had forgotten but tonight has remembered, and now cannot help remembering. She walks and walks, heading south along wet avenues with the traffic lights reflected on the footpaths, till she arrives at the edge of the river and it is dawn.

The longboats are still sleeping. The obelisk that came all the way from Egypt rises behind her; further along the river-bank, the lime trees in the Tuileries stand in their tall straight rows.

She had forgotten that incident with the needle, and wonders how that could be. She remembers the ferocity of Graciela's love, and the despair in it, because in some part of her – of this Inés is certain – Graciela knew.

Inés had clasped the baby to her. She remembers the wet mouth at her neck; she remembers the small heart hammering against her own. As Graciela broke the skin and cut her, deep enough to make her bleed, broad enough to scar her, Inés gripped the writhing infant and talked to her, trying to still the bellowing grief that seemed to express their own immense distress.

It was done.

Ten days later, Graciela picked up the pencil and wrote. Though she must have known, she would have clung to the smallest hope. She'd shown the letter to Inés when she had finished it – then taken the paper back.

Not under her name but down the margin she drew crosses like three small kisses, the middle one misaligned the way the marks were misaligned at the back of her daughter's ear.

What was she thinking? Inés had asked herself. That her daughter might one day wonder about those crosses? That in case of separation, someone might match the letter to the child?

Inés had had her doubts. She didn't believe such letters were delivered, even before she'd heard mention of a list. She'd had no proof of anything. But she didn't believe they took the babies home.

Buenos Aires
February 1977

A piece of paper, a scrap really, lies where it has fallen beside the rubbish cans, slipping from the top of an open sack when it was tossed into the garbage men's truck. A blast of exhaust sends it cartwheeling across the car park like somebody's runaway shopping list escaped from a pocket or a bag.

It snags on the crenellated trunk of a cedar tree and is pinioned there, quivering, torn a little along one fold. The breeze is loath to release it, but once it does it slides down the trunk and lodges amongst the leaf litter, in the woody crook of a root.

> *Dear Mamá, Papá . . .*

There it loiters, waiting for the wind to change. The breeze doesn't shift, but its conviction fades, and in one freak gust it lifts the paper and propels it over the car park's edge. Aloft, it gathers momentum and spirals higher on a counter-current all to itself. It sails over the outsized links of the anchor chain cranked taut to halt arrivals, but lowered for vehicles to roll across with a head-banging double thud. It toys with the branches of a *ceiba* tree before a downdraught pulls it lower, and it skims the last metres to the boundary fence over stripes of freshly mown grass.

I can't tell you of my joy at feeling close to you, thinking of you reading these brief lines.

The barrier is a net of diamond wire and the paper is pegged against it by the wind. Thrumming like a moth it hangs there, while the words inscribed on its underside slowly dissolve. Js become Is, Ms become Ns, and even the Xs in the margin become the shadow of themselves as minute quantities of graphite dust rub off in the afternoon breeze.

I want you to know that I am all right, as I hope you and Julieta are too – that is the most important thing.

The paper struggles against the mesh for several moments, but the wind is boring into it, insisting until something gives and the flimsy scrap slips sideways and is suddenly through.

Mamá, Papá, I need to ask your help.

School is not yet out. The ice-cream van is edging through the traffic. Ants are carving supply channels through the grass beside the pathway while a flock of parrots chatter their green parrot chatter at the top of the trees.

I need you to look after my daughter, your beautiful granddaughter
Liliana, till I can return and care for her myself.

Windborne! The letter soars and dives and tumbles along the serpentine footpath; it clings to the shin of the first passer-by. It's a woman who is strapping a toddler into a pushchair, but to her the paper is refuse that she shakes off with an irritated kick.

The thought of being separated from her is more than I can bear.

She doesn't notice the mineral words dissolving; she doesn't notice the address where it could still be sent. She doesn't notice that the longer words, like *granddaughter* and *separated* and *important*, are vanishing from the page.

Will you tell her every day how much I love her? That she is the centre of my universe, the reason for my life?

Lighter now, since its ballast of verbiage is shrinking, it floats in dreamy circles towards the trees. It catches the eye of the toddler, who stretches his arm towards it and giggles at the way it spirals against the afternoon sky. The woman, who has found a bench and is sitting there, thinks he is gurgling at the parrot flock and returns to her movie-star news.

José will be so proud of her. Tell him that I love him with all my heart, that not a day goes by without him in my thoughts.

Somewhere along an avenue the letter flutters earthwards, relinquished by the inconstant breeze. A second later it is sucked into the slipstream of a speeding vehicle, then is pulled under a semi-trailer's wheels. Torn, dirtied, embossed with grit, its words are barely legible under the herringbone print of tyres.

I miss you all and love you always,
Graciela

The letter rips in half. One piece tumbles towards a storm-water drain where it washes over the edge and disappears.

The other, stuck beneath the shoe of a passing pedestrian, resurfaces on the floor of the twenty-nine bus. It travels behind the ticket punch, is crushed under sneakers and boots and shopping bags, until the vehicle rolls at last into the terminus sheds. There, a cousin of the driver who has lost his job at a factory slops out the bus with a mop and soapy water, and the pulpy tatters disintegrate when he washes them down the steps.

eart
alw
ciela

11

Buenos Aires
October 1976

A double thud as we pass into the shadow world.
Suffocating under blankets, under boots on the floor of a vehicle,
Separately we all feel it, all those who enter here.

Chained for hours in the corridor, my body cries, then numbs.
When they come for me, I have lost the ability to stand.

I don't –
Sliding, when I hit the wall.
Room for two in there? Laughter.
A blow, and the howling is mine. I am inside this animal sound.
The room falls silent, deferential. Then it resumes.
Sing for me, sweetheart. Come on, a nice little tune.
Singeing. The stench of urine. Beyond, some strange perfume.

We are not human.
Swollen-bellied, I squat naked on a paint-tin in my blindfold before an audience of guards.

The metal bedframe cuts.
Face down this time, beneath my blindfold, I glimpse the splashes on his shoes.
My ears tear with someone else's pleading, with weeping.
Again, that bestial howling.
Suddenly the world turns to wire every nerve in me is burning.
I think: my unborn child.

Hijo de puta, *she loves it. The little whore, she's begging us for more.*
Time bends out of all proportion. I am molten metal. A laboratory of pain.
When they bring me to: sniggering.
Purple saucers! Check out what happens to their tits.
Again it starts. The screeching air convulses.
Then darkness, such soft darkness. I am floating floating floating
Then they haul me back to the light.

The Wolf, that's what they call him. The one they all defer to.
That perfume. Does he pomade himself in the bathroom, then kiss his wife goodbye?

Somewhere, outside these walls, the ice-cream vendor passes.
When the morning sessions are over, I hear his tinkling tune.

José, are you here? Are you somewhere inside?
I scratch your name into the floorboards.
Caress the broken splinters with my lips.

I lose count of the times.

It's not facts any more, or names. It's some other thing they want.

The *parilla*, they call it. The barbecue. Its neat crosshatching of burns.

I am thirsty, so so thirsty. The others here all warn me not to drink.

Musk, is that what it is?

Cloying, when he works himself up.

Dance for me, honey. I'm saving the last tango for you.

I'm here, José, don't go –

At 200 volts the cattle prod makes the television go static.

When the football's on, the guards upstairs complain.

Words peel apart from meanings: the Operating Theatre. The Clinic.

Oh yes, the Maternity Ward.

Peel till there are no words left.

Just different registers of screaming that echo down the Avenue of Joy.

And in this special hospital, a doctor's standing by.

I recognise his hands, the stethoscope's cold lick.

He has changed his beard again. The thin disguise of his hair.

The Wolf is back. I know him by his smell.

All night long the dogs bark. Their jaws rip holes in the dark.

Confess, my child, the priest says.

Car horns sound. Far away, a wedding, or a victory.

Then, from some bright stadium, a paroxysm of cheers.

Confess, when I have forgotten my own name?

What priest is this, who inhabits the Underworld?

Through the corner of my blindfold I see where the shackles weep.
Bruising. The sweet puckering of burns.
God's busy, they tell us. *We are The Almighty.*
You are this vermin. This filth.
My hair is ash. I panic as it disintegrates in my hand.

Hooded, I know it's night from the sound of moaning, sometimes the sound of sobs.
José, *mi amor*. Come closer –
There is nowhere it doesn't hurt to lie.

A clanking sound as someone struggles with their chains.
Medieval, the new guard said, stumbling in on us by accident today.

The baby, they decide, requires vitamins. They deliver me a salad and a steak.
This is power: these arbitrary acts.
To give. To take away. To choose.

Someone called Roberto died this morning.
They brought his body up to us to give him the kiss of life.
Downstairs in the Operating Theatre, they couldn't tell if he still had a pulse.

The night guard gives me a *caramelo*.
Pregnancy excites him. He wants me for himself.
When he is done, he wipes himself and talks about his wife.

We are beyond purgatory now. This is the inferno.
A child is hope, which makes it worse.
In this darkness, close to mine, I cradle its beating heart.

You cannot escape if you are already dead.
Inés, what will happen to my baby? But Inés shakes her head.

Dear God, please spare this infant. Please let this baby live.

The iceman cometh, again I hear his tinkling.
The iceman taketh away.

PART III

THE DOUBLE HELIX

1985–1992

I

Amsterdam
March 1985

Far away in Vatican City, the telephone rings many times. I'm about to hang up after the fifteenth ring when somebody picks up at the other end.

I ask to speak to Monsignor Traversini. After the conversation with Inés there is more I want to ask him. Perhaps he can help us again.

'*Mi dispiace, signore.*' A man's voice, cultivated, urbane. 'We have nobody here of that name.'

I try the Vatican switchboard, spelling out Traversini three separate times. I try the Vatican press office. He appears on nobody's list.

'He's a bishop,' I tell them. 'Surely he figures somewhere in your files.'

'Perhaps he has retired by now.' The voice I've reached this time is trying to be helpful. 'Or perhaps he was just a temporary visitor to Rome.' The bishop, he suggests, might have returned to pastoral work; the Vatican, after all, is such a crossroads; there are always so many people passing through.

Julieta, on reflection, thinks it may be just as well I cannot reach him. My questions might alert someone to our search.

The long darkness is dissipating in Argentina. The Malvinas are lost, the economy is still in tatters, but the Junta has been gone for more than a year. The commission of inquiry that Inés spoke to delivered its findings six months ago, and now it has published its report into the disappeared.

I have a copy of it here on my table in Amsterdam. *Nunca Más*, it's titled, 'Never Again', and most of it I cannot bring myself to read. In the privacy of my canal-house rooms I open it, examine a few pages, and close it again. Sometimes I have to go for a walk outside.

They have identified more than 300 secret prisons. They have interviewed the few survivors, who have spoken of unutterable things. They have documented 9,000 disappeared and are still counting. And among the 50,000 pages of depositions that fed the report's 500 pages, there are accounts of babies born to captive mothers, just as Inés described.

I cannot read it, yet force myself to look. On every page I search for Graciela, by name or implication. And because I cannot find her, I imagine her in every account of horror; I see her face in every unbearable line.

And what I read, and what Inés has told me, becomes something I cannot shut away. I dream of botched Caesarean sections, of basement torture chambers, of instruments devised for obscene permutations of pain.

I see lilies floating down a river, and Graciela, my sweet daughter, floating with them, clasping her child as they drown.

It is fury I feel, and then revulsion, and after that an immense, bone-marrow kind of sorrow, that human beings should be capable of this.

And then the anger returns. I cannot believe, I refuse to, that silence should be the end of it. That nothingness is all there shall be.

The opposite of life is not death, I realise; it is disappearance. It scorns us with its impunity. It incarcerates us in its no-man's-land of silence. It denies us the ability to act.

Well, for Graciela, for Liliana, I reject it. There must be answers, even if they've been hidden somewhere, even if buried under layers of stone. There must be a crack where a blade of grass might push towards the sunlight . . . And that is when I decide to make a stand.

First I discuss it with Julieta, now pregnant with her second child. I raise it with my brother-in-law Ricardo, and with José's father Eduardo, though he is struggling with Maria's ill health. I tell Constanza and Teodoro, my lawyer in Buenos Aires. I explain what I intend to do.

I draft it one Saturday morning at my window, a dredger clawing its way down the canal outside. Here, among the peaceable Dutch, I take a step, a small one that's all but certain to be ineffectual. But it's the only way I can think of to fight back.

Teodoro sends the notice to all the national newspapers in Argentina, and all the local papers in Buenos Aires, including those devoted purely to sports. It appears in their Saturday editions.

Constanza collects them all and mails them in one fat bundle; I pick them up in Amsterdam where she sends them care of *poste restante*.

I spread them out on my desk and shuffle through them, scanning the flimsy pages of print. MISSING MISSING MISSING, they cry as I arrange and rearrange them, as if reordering them might make sense of the inexplicable, or bring an answer to what is really a double plea.

Liliana: may you, or someone who cares about you, see this message.

May it bring you and your mother safely home.

London
March 1986

The laboratory I work for is expanding, and is setting up an office in London; before the winter is over the company proposes to transfer me there.

I've grown attached to Amsterdam, to the plain-speaking Dutch and my attic rooms overlooking the ziggurat skyline, and now I feel reluctant to leave. Yet my manager is persuasive; they are offering me a promotion; and part of me feels ready for a change.

My schoolboy English is rusty, the city's range of accents is overwhelming, and Londoners seem to be permanently on the run. But Medipharm signs me up for a month of language classes, and the job is mainly administrative, liaising between London and Paris from an office in the centre of town.

Our building, a recent renovation, is white and light and open, branding us with clinical flair. Yet it is an anomaly in this part of the city, tucked away in a courtyard in a maze I keep getting lost in, in the streets behind New Fetter Lane.

The revolving door ejects us into a lane that burrows into Fleet Street's fume-laden fug. Double-deckers churn like paddle steamers past the newspaper buildings. Upholstered like old hookers in tat and ash-pocked velvet, pubs sway on their timber haunches, their rooms giving onto other rooms that worm into the city's heart.

The sales reps are young and eager, and we have to get started somewhere, so we divide up London's hospitals using a map and a list of the saints. Once Mark, Mary, Thomas, George and Bart are allocated, we move on to the Royals, and include with them the Princesses, Kings and Queens. The rest are named after universities, boroughs or body parts: Hearts and Eyes go quickly, and we share out those that remain.

There is some trading according to drug type and geography, then the teams submit their lists to me, and I coordinate strategy with marketing, finance and sales.

Every so often I stare out of my window at the transparent English rain. And I wonder sometimes how I got here, when it was that the temporary became so permanent, and how it happened that, in my life as in my profession, I feel as if I've lost my way.

To lift myself out of my brooding I go walking. At lunch-time I cover the length of Fleet Street, passing the obsidian façade of the *Daily Express* building and the unicorn spire of St Bride's. Then invariably I head south, across Blackfriars Bridge as far as the griffon statue, even when St Paul's is shrouded in cloud. It does me good to watch the play of light or rain on water, the way the tidal flow of the river connects with something larger than itself.

And as I walk, I think about the abandoned bridge that runs beside the one I'm crossing, the solid Victorian pilings so resistant to the current's pull. There is something reassuring in the way the phantom bridge accompanies the existing one, its pylons sunk in the ancient silt under the imaginary reach of its spans.

Yet living in London takes more adjusting than I'd expected; London strikes me as a city for the brave. Not for the faint of heart are its broken footpaths and heaving underground carriages, its rain-lashed railway platforms exposed to the wind. Here, resilience is not a quality. It's a requirement to survive.

'You have to be patient,' says Daniela, a Chilean exile I have met through Carla, shouting over the Friday-night roar of a pub near Charing Cross. 'Once you make friends here, everything changes. But you have to accept it takes time.'

'How much time?' I shout back at her over the smoke and the din and the jostling, lip-reading more than I can hear.

She has very dark eyes, and silver rings on all her fingers that clink on the glass she hands me from the bar.

She laughs and yells an answer into my ear. 'What's that expression the English use? How long is a piece of string?'

I've rented a basement flat in the west of London, and have a bit part in the great commuter struggle up and down the Central Line. I've seen the people at Amnesty about my family, and told them that there is also a missing child. They have my case on file; they are pressing it along with others in Geneva; but so far they have little to offer beyond sympathy and the shaking of heads.

Daniela, who works in radio, introduces me to one of her contacts, a trades union man whom I visit up near Tottenham Court Road. He has some good connections in Latin America, though they are limited; those who survived are still in exile, but he promises to consult his counterparts in Spain.

These fruitless meetings discourage me and compound my frustration; Daniela is the only person I know who understands.

Even so, it surprises me when one day she takes me by the hand.

The simple gesture marks a turning point, though it is difficult to say when it was that our relationship changed.

She is twelve years my junior and lost her husband, Sergio, when Chile lost Allende. Her father was born in England, so when she fled, she went first to stay with relatives outside London, and supports herself now doing shifts at the BBC.

Her eyes have laughter in them despite her sadness, and we have our foreignness in common; we step carefully around each other, aware that getting closer might also hurt.

What we most need is friendship, and in London we find ways to do the things we might have done back home. We go to Spanish-language movies; we listen to Latino music in the booths at Tower Records; we discover new jazz collections and tangos I've never heard. We frequent an Italian bistro I've found near Cambridge Circus that is just about as generous as the ones in Buenos Aires. She finds me a *mate* seller in Camden market, and we pass the hot tea back and forth in the gourd he also sold us, and laugh at the mistakes I make in English, and sleep together in my basement bed for solace, and then for joy.

I don't tell Julieta about her, at least not right away. My relationship with Daniela still feels tentative; I don't want my daughter advising me, or bossing, or making plans.

But I do tell Daniela about Julieta, how her family has just grown bigger with the arrival of Paulina, how I flew to Miami just days after the baby was born.

'You're proud of Julieta, aren't you?' Daniela says; and I realise, despite our difficulties, how much I am.

She tells me in turn about a schoolfriend who has just turned up in Toronto, someone she feared had been killed in Chile, and who has now shown up, alive.

And that reminds me of Hugo, and Diego and Marguerita and Heriberto, and the boisterous nights we spent at the Paradiso.

'I've lost sight of all of them,' I tell her. 'I have no idea where any of them might be.'

'Maybe you should go back and look for them.'

'Perhaps,' I say, and consider it properly for a moment. 'Though I'd hardly know where to begin.'

'It's not just that though, is it?' she says, and I know she understands what I cannot bear to articulate: that losing my wife and daughter and grandchild has been sorrow enough, without adding a roll call of friends.

I shake my head, grateful for her intuition.

'I'm not that brave, Daniela,' I say. 'It was hard enough going back that once. I don't imagine I will ever return.'

How little we know, how little we can foresee, I understand only later, after the phone rings late in the evening and I've answered, and spoken for a few moments, and hung up.

'Is everything all right?' It's Daniela, calling from the bedroom.

My mind is racing. I have to go back to Argentina right away.

I go in to her and sit beside her, by her pillow at the top of the bed.

Daniela sits up. 'What's happened?' she says, anxiety suddenly shadowing her face.

'That was Eduardo. José's father.'

I take her hand, see the soft silver glint of her rings.

'He says they have found José.'

3

It is dark inside the wardrobe when she climbs into it, so she holds the doors together with her fingers, allowing in a narrow spit of light. Inside there is the musty smell of wood and fusty clothing, and an old paper sticker glued to a panel that she carefully peels off with her nails.

There are all kinds of furniture and household objects in the warehouse. While her father attends to the inventory or is busy taking deliveries, she plays among the dining sets and the dressers as if she were in some Alice-in-Wonderland dolls' house where everything was made life-size.

The building must have once been a kind of factory, because the space consists of a concrete floor with grease marks in some places, and high brick walls without any windows apart from a row just under the roof.

She accumulates a nest of discoveries. There's a green enamel button and some *peso* coins she dived for under the armrests of sofas, and a silver star from a necklace, and a screw-on coral earring she retrieved from the back of a drawer. She has made a chain from paperclips and dislodged a photo from where she found it, stuck down the inside of a desk.

Risking splinters and the sharp ends of nails, she explores for secret compartments in the backs of drawers, in the panels of the writing desks.

After hunting for things, what Ana likes best is hiding in the wardrobes. Some have keys in their curlicue locks but others have to be tied shut with string. From the inside, all of them smell different; Ana decides it's because of differences in the dust. Some have sawdust dust, others have old-clothes dust, or resiny dust, or dust that's more like grit from the bottom of shoes.

Now that the client who was browsing among the dressing tables has left, the coast is clear for Ana to pull out her secret objects; she holds the photograph up to the strip of light. A young man with heavy brows and curly hair stares back at her, a blurry puppy wriggling out of his arms. He wears a skinny shirt tucked into his flares and his name, Ana knows, is 'Leo' because it is written in blue biro on the back.

She imagines all sorts of things: that Leo is her special friend, or perhaps an older brother with whom she embarks on adventures. Today she pretends that the two of them have stowed away on a galleon after finding a stash of treasure made up of coins and silver stars. Pirates, however, are also after the bounty and believe Ana and Leo have stolen it, so they've commandeered the ship and locked all the crew in the hold. Ana hears a bell and the sound of footsteps – the pirates must be scouring the deck in search of them. She is vaguely aware of talking; of somebody giving orders; there are rising voices and suddenly a woman's screech.

Ana freezes where she is hiding, presses her eye to the crack in the door. A woman in a purple scarf is shifting in and out of the light. She sees a man put his hand on her sleeve, but the woman only shrugs it off. The woman's shrieks grow louder; she is hurling insults at Ana's father; she has to concentrate to hear what is being said.

'I remember you!' – that much Ana picks up through the wooden panelling – 'You were the one in charge.' Then there are some swear words, and others Ana doesn't recognise. 'And you remember me,' the woman says next. 'By God, you sadist, you do.'

Words are flying like bullets and Ana is paralysed. Should she run to defend her father, or stay hidden inside the wardrobe, or rush outside for help?

When she looks again, the man is tugging at the woman's elbow but this time she wrenches her arm free. Then she leans across the counter, her purple scarf all twisted, and spits in Ana's father's face.

'Get out of here!' he roars at her. 'Get off my premises right now.'

'Or what?' she says. 'Come on then. What do you think you might do?'

The world falls silent for a moment, then Ana hears more footsteps, the tinny sound of the bell.

Ana stays where she is, head between her knees, tension still crackling in the air. But her legs are starting to get cramps in them and she needs to stand and stretch.

She clambers out of the wardrobe, stashes the pirate treasure in its hiding place and goes in search of her father at the front of the store. She finds him combing his hair before an antique mirror, a wet patch like a medallion on his shirt.

'Why was that lady screaming, Papá?' she says.

His reflected eyes, so brown they are almost black, look back a little wildly through the glass.

'Oh, she's just another nutter, Ana. One of those crazies. There are plenty of them around these days, now that Democracy's flushing them out onto the streets.'

She wants to ask what it was that the lady called him. It was a new word, an adult word, and Ana suspects a bad one, but she knows he doesn't like her learning words like that.

He drags the black-toothed comb across his skull, but the lines come out all crooked, like her homework when she does it on the bus.

He sees, and he sees Ana see. Then he smiles.

The comb scrapes across his head again, over the pink canopy of scalp. But the furrows this time are perfect, the narrow ridges properly aligned.

Ana is awash with relief. There is nothing he is afraid of, not even lunatics on the attack. She feels proud of him, and safe with him. There is nothing he cannot master, she thinks to herself, no circumstances he cannot control.

4

Colonia del Sacramento, Uruguay
October 1976

A couple of stories appear in the Uruguayan newspapers. Tiny pieces, really, just a few lines at first in the human interest columns of the Montevideo dailies that keep an eye on the provinces, towns like Rosario and Colonia del Sacramento, which lies opposite Buenos Aires on the Río de la Plata shore.

The local papers, of course, make quite a fuss about it; the bodies, after all, are washing up on their doorstep, and it's only human to be shocked by the macabre, or when events occur that disrupt the natural order of things. And when male and female cadavers start lodging in the reeds along the river, naked, bloated, and with quite a bit of damage . . . that, to the coastal residents, is an aberration in the order of things.

The first one bobs ashore just below the Santa Rita ramparts at Colonia. It is found on a Saturday morning by a couple of kids who have cycled there with fishing rods strapped to their bikes. Having had no luck with the spinners they've been casting from the breakwater, one of them decides to try his hand upstream.

The cry he releases into the morning soon brings his schoolmate running. When he gets there, he finds his friend is throwing up into the grass.

Their fathers are alerted; the police and an ambulance are summoned; the body is wrapped in heavy-duty plastic and carted off to the morgue. The hospital pathologist examining the corpse looks grave in the photographs printed in Sunday's paper, and troubled behind his solemnity when interviewed on local TV.

Glasses glinting above his sideburns, he speaks into a fuzzy microphone. He says that the body he's examining, of a young man in his twenties, is in poor condition after spending several days afloat.

'But what I find most disturbing,' he adds, 'are all the broken bones.'

There is speculation about a car crash, or a savage murder by hammer blow before the body was tossed to the waves. Barstool pundits extemporise about new forms of thuggery, and ghoulish jokes start surfacing about the diet of the river fish.

There are changes to restaurant menus to account for the withdrawal of the local bream.

But there is nothing to identify the body, no rings or tattoos or any items of clothing, no evidence beyond what might be derived from examining the victim's teeth.

Even in a quiet place like Colonia, the talk might eventually have faded away had no more bodies turned up. But two days after the first discovery, a woman wheeling her pram on the south side of town faints when she sees that a second cadaver has floated in to shore. This time the body is a woman's, naked too, and dragging in the reeds. From the way her head is lying, her neck appears to be broken, and one of her arms seems to be bent the wrong way.

Over the coming days, another seven corpses nudge in to land, four of them close to Colonia and the other three further down the coast.

All joking dies away; a serial killer must surely be on the prowl. Parents triple-check the locks on doors and windows, and accompany their children to and home from school. The mayor imposes a draconian curfew. Teenagers invent a game of dare that involves nocturnal walks with flashlights, but most of them are too skittish to venture far. The hard-pressed hospital pathologist takes photographs and copious notes to assist with his post-mortems, but his descriptions correspond to no one reported missing to the police.

Then, early one morning, a contingent from the Uruguayan army arrives. The pathologist is told to halt his examinations and to cease updating the press. Reporters from the national papers, and even from the international news agencies, are repelled at the doors of the hospital, and camera crews who insist on gaining entry get roughed up by paramilitary thugs.

Meanwhile, residents start to complain that their phone calls are being cut off.

The army captain orders the bodies removed from the morgue at the hospital, though the post-mortems are not yet complete. Simultaneously, the sextons at the cemetery out-side Colonia and at another downstream from Montevideo are each told to prepare a pit. When the bodies are delivered to their graveyards, they are entered as 'NN' in the register – the initials that are applied to indigents, and to those of no known name.

There they are interred while the police conduct an investigation, but it is closed in a matter of days.

Very occasionally, another body shows up to disturb the peace. The local authorities, however, have learned their lesson and keep the matter quiet, and the corpse is discreetly added to the cemetery's common grave.

The rest is down to the sextons who, having looked death so often in the face, have a sense of something larger, and a feeling of responsibility towards those entrusted to their keep. And the sextons are offended. It insults their professional pride and their sense of civic duty that so little effort has been expended on identifying the newcomers in their care.

They make sure that what details they have are entered into the registers correctly. And when the five-year tenure expires, and the NN graves are meant to be turned over for use by newer claimants, they make alternative arrangements because they take a long-term view of things, and know that someone some day will come looking for the missing, especially when those missing are individuals as young as these.

Occasionally a rumour reaches them: that the currents have brought a body or two ashore on the opposite coast. But fifty kilometres lie between them, and they are too wise to go about making enquiries across the river, and the rumour is never confirmed.

What none of them, not those who had curtailed the examinations, nor those who had silenced the reporters, nor those who had imposed a swift solution to conceal the disturbing evidence, what none of them had known was that the sextons, in fact, were not mistaken: that people would indeed turn up at the cemetery gates and ask them to reopen the collective graves.

Nor could any of them have guessed at the advances that would be made one day in the field of genetics, in anthropology and in archaeological forensics; or that DNA could be made to speak with such precision, even in the face of missing generations; that samples would be collected and answers sought.

So it was that the Uruguayans had found José years before a team of Argentine forensic anthropologists turned up to enquire about the NN graves. At the time, nobody in the town on that side of the river had had any way of identifying who he was.

He isn't the first to have shown up dead in a country he never visited in life. But when the hospital pathologist examined him, and found every bone in his body broken – the multiple fractures to the ribs, the pelvis fissured, the ulna shattered and even the femur broken – he could only fill in the dental templates as best he could in the diminished time available, with no time to investigate the savage perforations on his skin.

Instead, he entrusted the body to the sexton at the cemetery near Colonia, along with the others they had fished from the reeds and the rocks.

5

Colonia del Sacramento
March 1986

Because there are so few members of José's family, I fly from London to Montevideo to be with his father, and arrange to meet him directly in Colonia. Maria, too unwell to travel, has stayed behind in Buenos Aires. Her mind is slowly clouding and Eduardo, with health worries of his own, isn't completely sure she has understood.

I make copies of the documents Eduardo has collected: the results of the DNA tests, the old and new dental records, what notes the forensic investigators have made. At the cemetery they copy the relevant pages of the register, and let us photograph his burial place. Eduardo and I do not discuss why we are doing this; it is not something it occurs to us to discuss. Gathering these last traces of José's existence seems to help us believe that what has happened has happened; for Eduardo, these are the last things he can do for his son.

We stand under the pine trees in the graveyard, staring at the garden of crosses, the white tops of the graves. The breeze comes in off the water and strokes the feathery branches, carrying the sounds of life from beyond the walls.

She is not here, I know that. The investigators have been thorough in their analyses. Graciela was not with him in this place.

But José's bones have lain in the loamy soil, anonymous, unknown to us, even while some part of us had hoped that he might have survived. For ten years his parents have longed for him and been unable to grieve for him, existing in the half-light of his absence, as do all of us who yearn for the disappeared.

'The ache of it,' Eduardo once said, 'is how I know my heart is still alive.'

We go to the waterside at Colonia together, knowing now the extent of it, knowing at least the end. The waves tangle and untangle the reeds; they slap and fall against the rocks.

I've seen those pages in the official inquiry, felt the shudder in the investigators' words: the stupefying Pentothal injections; the night flights over the river that runs to the sea.

I'm a medical man, these days a drug-selling man; I know what Pentothal does. Did they blink awake in the shock of cold air, falling? Did their nerves shoot pain at the crack of bone on water, fracturing on waves like cement?

'Let's take him home,' Eduardo says, his crevassed face more worn than the cemetery stone.

They give us the splintered bones of his son in a box, to bury or burn.

On the Argentine shore we stand on the grassy embankment and cast rose petals by the handful into the river that's as wide as a sea. Despite his coughing, Eduardo says a blessing as the dots of red recede like so many footprints, dancing their invisible dance on the silty tide.

We watch them bob and toss as the current tugs them into a trail that recedes towards the horizon. We watch until the light fails and our eyesight falters, till the ribbon of brightness drifts towards the vanishing point where the sky lifts off from the sea.

Attended by the young woman they increasingly rely on, Maria is with us in her wheelchair, disoriented, a blanket over her knees.

Eduardo goes over to her and bends his giant frame down to her and takes her in his arms.

'It's all right, *mi amore*,' he says to her, not sure if she knows why they've come. 'He's going on his journey, sweetheart. It's time to let him go.'

And from the depths of the things she's losing, memory, vocabulary, through his own grief and heartbreak, she astounds him by finding the words.

'Adieu, Cheché,' she says.

6

Buenos Aires

March 1986

Before I return to London I have one last thing to do.

Eduardo, since he's been there before, comes with me in the taxi. The hospital's rust-red towers soar above the glass-and-concrete entrance where the nurses loiter smoking; the smell of disinfectant greets us as we walk through the door.

In the entrance Eduardo hesitates before recollecting the way. I take in the head-down march of the junior doctors, the orderlies' rubber-soled squeak on the polished floors. A trolley rattles past us, and the sound of it catches me in an updraught of nostalgia at being back in an Argentine hospital, back where I once felt at home.

We negotiate endless corridors. An old woman and a child kneel in the hospital chapel, draughts tugging at the candle flames. At the billing offices, the accountants' windows are lined with streaks of Sellotape, as if marking the height of floodwaters, where notices have been taped up and then removed.

At last we find ourselves in Immunology – a passageway with seven doors and a fire hydrant glowing at one end. On the wall, a cartoon mosquito warns of dengue fever. Children slither over the backs of the seats while a cleaner in blue overalls skims a mop over the floor.

We sit in silence amid the hubbub, waiting for my name to be called.

After a while Eduardo clears his throat.

'He was a good person, Osvaldo,' Eduardo says.

I look at him, at his big bear's head, the great span of his workman's hands.

'I know, Eduardo,' I say.

The past few weeks have exhausted him, the repeated explanations about José since Maria cannot remember what he has said. He looks taller now than I remember him, and I realise he must have lost weight.

'He loved your daughter very much.'

'I know he did,' I say, and then fall silent. A taciturn man, he has things on his mind I sense he is wanting to say.

'I think it was because of that, because of his kindness, that he died,' Eduardo says after a moment. 'You know. The teaching. Those places they went.'

He stops, trying to bind the facts he knows into something that might help them make sense.

Then he shakes his head. 'I can't stop thinking there must have been something we failed to teach him, something that might have saved him, or at least have preserved him from harm.'

'What could you have taught him, Eduardo?'

'I don't know. Some quality that might have armoured him. Scepticism. Less idealism, perhaps.'

'And made him into someone other than he was?'

He looks at me with pain in his tired eyes. 'Yet maybe he would still be alive.'

Though José had been missing for a decade, for Eduardo, for his family, it is as if he has only just died.

'José was twenty-two, Osvaldo,' he continues. 'When I think about his childhood . . . It went by like that, in the blink of an eye. It was all we had. He was with us for such a short time.'

I think about the years of silence, how the long unknowing has been neither help nor preparation. I think how language fails us. How there is no word like 'widow' or 'orphan' for the parent who loses a child.

I put my hand on his arm.

Then suddenly the nurse is calling my name. We rise in unison and traipse down the line of doors.

I tell her I am there for the database; that I want to give a genetic sample; that I – that the two of us – are looking for people who have disappeared.

'That's why we're here, Dr Ferrero,' she tells me. Her voice is clinical but not uncaring. 'That's why they set us up last year.'

Peering over her green-framed glasses she explains to me the procedures, how the genetic maps they are building require as many relatives as possible to take part.

I tell her about Yolanda's brother, and about Julieta who is living in Florida. If Julieta cannot come to Buenos Aires, the nurse informs us, there is a partner hospital she can use in the United States.

I fill in the forms while the nurse examines my documents. I transcribe names and numbers, provide addresses and secondary contacts, put my signature to the necessary permissions.

The tourniquet pinches for a moment; I ball my fist as she swabs my arm and inserts the needle into my vein.

And suddenly, watching the thread climb blackly up the needle, I am gripped by the absolute conviction that Liliana exists. She lives not just in my imagination, not just in Inés's memory of her birth. She is alive, with my genes and Yolanda's, with Eduardo's and Maria's, in her body; our missing children are living on in her.

The nurse extracts the needle and makes me sit a moment longer – in case of dizziness, she says. Eduardo is standing by the window, staring out towards the Parque Centenario that is half hidden by the monkey-puzzle trees.

It's like starlight, this database, I want to tell them. It's like shining a lamplight down the generations that follow on from us and believing that whatever we want to call it, this leap of faith, this feat of genetic biology, might re-establish origins and set things right.

Then, the immensity of this endeavour overwhelms me. Liliana is just one child in the universe. Finding her will defy every law of probability, and all this database can do is confirm or deny.

Eduardo has his back to me, immersed in the world outside. When I glance up at him, I see his shoulders shake. Just for a moment, just a tremor, imperceptible to anyone who wasn't already watching, to anyone who didn't already know.

Then I remember the other reason for these samples, how they have already proved their worth.

And their worth may extend to Graciela. I dread the thought of receiving the call that Eduardo must have answered, that this vial of blood might be needed for an out-come that would extinguish any last hope of her being alive.

The nurse who left us for a moment returns with water in two paper cups. As she passes me one, I realise that dizziness was not what worried her. In the privacy of this small office, she has witnessed these emotions before.

Eduardo turns back from the window and thanks the nurse and places his cup on the table. He has composed himself; it's as if nothing had taken place.

'Don't lose heart,' the nurse says to us. She gives a slight bow of her head, then looks at us over the green frames of her glasses as she steps back to open the door.

My flat is chilly and smells of the damp when I get home from the airport; London is only grumblingly awake. It's too early to call Daniela so I boil the water for *mate* and wait by the basement window. The shins of the early commuters flicker past the railings as they hurry along the footpath above.

The letter I wrote on the plane is still in my pocket. I flatten it out and examine it, the nudges and bumps of turbulence apparent in its uneven lines. Almost without thinking, I reach for a sheet of paper and begin to transcribe.

I stop, pen poised mid-sentence. I can almost see her; she is standing in my blind spot, only just out of sight. I can hear the swish of her clothing; I can see her shadow shifting on the wall. I don't dare turn but go on writing, each loop and stroke a kind of summoning, conjuring my grandchild into being.

What is it going to take, I wonder, to find the bridge that spans our separate worlds?

The envelope sits there, propped against the windowsill, for weeks. I stare at the blue letters of her name, Liliana

Thurmann Ferrero, that has José's name and Graciela's name, which is also my name, within it. I stare at the wide white space below it filled with everything I don't know about her: a name without a person, a letter in want of an address.

———

7

Buenos Aires
September 1987

Her mother has returned from the nursery with a new type of rose. She unwraps it from the newspaper, hacks through its plastic pot with the secateurs, then sets it aside while she works at deepening the hole.

Ana glances at the angry leaves, at the anorexic branches malevolent with thorns. She is mystified by what her mother sees in roses, even the ones she's taken such care over grafting; the stems themselves are treacherous, the plants as ugly as skeletons for most of the year.

Her mamá catches the look in Ana's eye and laughs. Those small brown nobbles will soon start sprouting leaves, she tells her, and the blooms will be exquisite, their scent more lovely than any perfume.

Then she hides the tag with a picture of the rose bush blossoming – she wants to keep the colour a surprise.

Ana can't remember the last time she had an hour alone with her mother; sometimes it feels as if her mamá doesn't live with them at all. She doesn't help Ana get ready for school in the mornings; it's her papá who sets out the *tostadas* and the breakfast jam. After school, and though the nuns insist she has to practise, Ana can't sit at the piano because her mamá is having a sleep or is fighting a headache – it's the first thing that Luisa, hurrying from the laundry in her pale blue apron, tells her when she opens the door.

This morning, her father went out early to see his accountant; her mother ventured downstairs soon after he left. It's the first time Ana has seen her out in the garden in ages, despite the fact that roses are her favourite thing.

Ana has missed her. When was the last time they varnished their toenails China Town red, she wonders, or flipped through the pages of magazines to size up the fashions abroad?

A gust of wind snatches the sheet of newspaper the shrub came wrapped in and flings it across the lawn. Ana chases after it and stomps on it with her sneaker. Then she bunches it into a cabbage and goes to kick it between the fence posts when her mother intervenes.

'It's dirty, darling,' she says to her. 'Be a good girl and drop it in the bin.'

The gardening bin sits around the side of the house on the way to the passion-fruit vine. It is already full of rose cuttings and dead branches that are no use on the compost heap.

Ana tosses the newspaper ball on top of it, and just before the lid crashes down she glimpses an intriguing word. 'MISSING', it says, and after it, 'CAN YOU HELP?'. She is just about to retrieve it to see if a reward is offered when she hears her mother call.

'Anita!' she says. 'Can you come and give me a hand?'

Ana releases the handle and the lid falls shut with a thud. She bounds over the grass and skids to a stop an inch from the Autumn Damask, earning her a momentary frown.

Her mother is holding the new shrub by the base where the thorns are scarce.

'Will you take it for me? Carefully now. I can't do it with just one hand.'

Ana pulls on her gloves – with a frisson of fear that a spider might be lurking in the fingers – and replaces her mother's grip. She is surprised to find how heavy the plant is for what is mostly a collection of sticks.

Grit and soil rain onto the grass as her mother fans out the roots. Then she takes the shrub back and lowers it into the hole.

'There,' she says, rubbing an itch on her nose with the back of her wrist. Ana, who has already yanked her gloves off, leans over to help her scratch.

'Thank you, *corazón*,' her mamá says with a smile.

Ana, who can hear Adriana shouting at Paco to stay away from the pool while the pump is working, basks for a moment in her smile. Ana is not allowed next door any more, not since the accident she had in the swimming pool, but she still likes their neighbours and sometimes drops by quietly to say hello.

The watering can sounds like the arpeggio she hasn't practised when Ana goes to fill it at the tap. Her elbows lock under the weight of it as she wobbles across the garden, trying not to water her feet.

After the watering comes a layer of straw to ensure that the roots stay warm.

'It's like putting a baby to bed,' says Ana, watching her mother pat everything down.

'It *is* a bit like that,' her mamá says, with a laugh. 'When you arrived it was a toss-up, you know, but you were lucky – we decided to give you a cot.'

Ana pictures her infant self in a pile of hay, and giggles; it's been ages since her mother has made her laugh. Her mamá smiles and kisses her on the forehead, and that is when she tells her about the baby.

How, a few years after she married Ana's father, she got pregnant. How the baby arrived too early. How it died soon after it was born.

Ana is stunned. She is ten years old and has always believed herself an only child, the pivot of her parents' world. She can't imagine sharing them with anyone with a prior claim.

'Would I have had a brother or a sister?' she asks after a moment, her ears still buzzing with the shock.

'You'd have had an elder brother, my darling,' her mamá says. She gives Ana a squeeze with the crook of her arm because her gloves are all covered in dirt.

Suddenly, Ana thinks about Leo, the secret boy whose photo she keeps hidden in the back of a warehouse drawer.

'What was his name?' she says.

'We didn't get around to naming him, sweetheart. He died too soon. We couldn't even get him baptised.'

Ana ponders her words.

'And where is he buried?' she says.

'We couldn't bury him either, *querida*. I don't think your papá wanted to. The hospital just took him away.'

Ana's head is awhirl. It gives her a funny feeling to think about having a brother; she wonders in which room he would have slept. It makes the balance of their family life feel different, their rapport somehow unsettled, as if a shadow family were hovering behind the family they were.

8

Isle of Skye, Scotland
September 1988

'Scotland.'
  'Sussex.'
  'The Hebrides.'
  'Brighton.'
  'Skye.'
We've known each other for two years now, but never have we managed to go away. When Daniela tells me she has a weeklong break in her schedule, I tally up the days I'm owed by the company and suggest that we travel somewhere.

'The Isle of Skye?' Daniela cocks her head over the map of Britain we've unfolded on the kitchen table. 'Brighton's so much closer, you know . . .'

'The further the better,' I tell her, tracing the craggy relief of an island that is shaped like a half-submerged hand. 'Since we have this opportunity . . . let's go and see what's there.'

After so much time in cities, I am drawn to how I imagine it: all mountains and wind-rush and sea.

'You *do* realise,' she says, with the one-dimple smile that appears when she has yet to be persuaded, 'that it's one of those places they mention on the Shipping News.'

Daniela once met the person who presents it, while standing in line at the BBC canteen. Later, we'd tuned in to the midnight broadcast to hear its incantation, like eavesdroppers on some ancient Saxon rite.

'So we won't be short of weather,' I say.

'That's one thing you can count on,' she says.

We catch an overnight train from London, shooting past cities with famous names and streets I cannot picture, ascending the spine of a country I barely know. Sometime around dawn we cross an invisible border and are stunned by views of the sea. Then we're stumbling into Edinburgh, disoriented by the earliness of the light.

We order eggs and bacon in a café near the station, filling in time before we go to pick up the car. Under her mug of tea, Daniela unfolds the map of Scotland, which suddenly looks more daunting now we're actually there.

'Three hundred and eighty kilometres to go,' she says. 'Ready for a little drive?'

The journey is a blur of forests and russet hillsides, of castles returning to the stone they once were hewn from, of mercury rivulets rushing to valley floors.

Rain curtains us in, then lifts to dazzling sunlight, to rainbows presaging other rainbows, and lochs that are linked to other lochs by rivers that that are shallow and fast. Cloud erases Ben Nevis from the landscape. We stop for coffee anyway and the publican, in a dialect Daniela later translates for me, tells the story of last year's hikers who vanished off the mountain in the snow.

Fog envelops us as Daniela takes over at the wheel. Hail batters the roof like golf balls, then sunshine bleeds through the clouds. We pass ruins and restorations, and bridges to prickly islands, and sites of long-ago massacres that soaked the glens in blood.

Suddenly the road flies over a saddle of rock, and the earth plunges like it's the Rift Valley floor. We pull over, stilled by the sight of it. The landscape, like a silver-nitrate photograph, is refracted through a thousand raindrops that the sun has tinted golden on the windshield – the world afire through a globe of ice.

'You never told me it'd be like this,' I say.

She smiles back at me, black eyes aglow in the orange light. 'You never asked,' she says.

It's still daylight when we catch the ferry at Lochalsh and arrive at last on Skye. In Kyleakin we pick up the key and a few provisions, then follow the coastal road. We travel inland before the sea comes into sight again; the road gets narrower and narrower until it runs out altogether, ending in a jetty and a tumble of lobster pots.

There is a shingle beach and the house is set just back from it, a whitewashed fisherman's cottage sheltered by a low stone wall and a tree. The mountains glare at us like intruders from across the water; behind the house, the top of the cliff is rusty with reddish grass.

We are too tired to cook so we unpack the car and drive back to the pub we noticed on the way. We toast our arrival with whisky from a local distillery that the barman through his whiskers recommends.

Over the next few days we explore. We puzzle over ancient standing stones whose existence seems to have outlasted what they mean. Rugged up in all our clothing, we scramble along the trails of mountain chains whose summits we never see.

We hike to the Pinnacles on a coastal path that cuts through grass so green it looks electric.

Daniela clambers up to a cluster of rocks while I wait for her at the bottom of the path. I see her bobbing and disappearing between the outcrops before she emerges at the summit and waves. She sits there awhile staring out at the sea while, high above, an eagle slips and regains its hold on the wind.

From below, I watch her descend. Buffeted by a breeze that is full of the ocean, she inches along the path. Hunched into her anorak, she is alone against a backdrop of sea.

There is such solitude about her, I think, as she gets closer. Behind her vivacity there is a quietness as unknowable as the standing stones.

When she reaches me I take her in my arms. She stands there, hair in her eyes, hands thrust deep into her pockets, leaning her weight against me as I shelter her from the wind.

We stop at a pub beside a bridge medallioned with lichen, over a stream racing with runoff from the hills. Salmon is on the menu so we eat there, and sink into the warmth of an alcove, our faces still tingling from the cold. By the time we leave it is after nightfall; we carve tunnels with our headlights through the dark.

We turn onto the road that is meant to lead to our cottage, but familiar forms shift shape and make us doubt. Was this the farm? Was that the stand of trees? The road pushes back when I press on the accelerator so I ease off again, slowing into the undulations of the land. We round a curve, pass the bulk of a barn that is protected by trees meshed into a wind break, and come face to face with a stag.

I stop the car and dim the lights so as not to blind him. Antlers aloft, he towers over us like some mythical beast. He stands for a long time watching us as we watch him, none of us daring to move.

Then, as suddenly as we've come upon him, he tosses his head and bolts. He rears out of the earth in a single movement, bucking as if in response to a secret summoning, and swerves through a gap in the trees. The smell of peat and sea-borne cold streams through the open windows; we roll forward to see if we still can see.

But he has vanished; the starless night has swallowed him. The only proof that we encountered him lies in the syncopated thudding of our hearts.

'Did I dream that?' Daniela says as we wind down out of the valley, the two of us still in awe.

'I think we both did,' I say.

For people who live here, such creatures must be as familiar as the landscape. For us exiled South Americans he is a thing of wonder, an enigma that stepped out of the wild.

Inside the cottage the air is freezing and the bed sheets have stiffened with the cold. Daniela's rings clink like ice-cubes against the glass-topped table; she slithers under the blankets bringing a draught of icy air.

'I have one word for you, if you'll allow me,' she says, slipping an arm across my ribcage, fitting her knees into the backs of mine.

'Tell me then,' I say, ready for any of a hundred things.

'Shipping-news.'

'Shipping News? That's two words!'

'Not if you use a hyphen – as in shipping-news report.'

'Okay,' I say, picking my battles, 'so you were right about the weather – although to be fair, today it didn't rain.'

'You forget the wind-chill factor,' she says, feet icy on the backs of my calves.

'Okay, so it's been a little chilly.'

'Chilly!' she says. 'You're talking to a Latina, remember!'

'Come here,' I say, turning to face her, and hugging her to warm her, hoping that that might also thaw the sheets. 'Apart from the cold, do you think it's been worth coming all this way?'

'That's a big "apart from",' she says, but then concedes: 'I did like seeing the stag.'

'The stag!' I say. 'Is that all?'

'Is that all? That stag was amazing!' she says.

'I know,' I say. 'But has that been the only good thing?'

'Well,' she says. 'Not only that.'

'So – what else then?'

'Well, the salmon was good.'

'The salmon!'

'Yes,' she says. 'Very fresh. Very good.'

'And the walk on the cliffs?'

'Oh, yes, that too, that was quite good,' she says. 'A little windy, maybe . . .'

She lifts her head and smiles at me in the darkness.

'Quite good?'

'Okay, yes, it was very good.'

'And the standing stones?'

'Oh, yes, I forgot them. So earnest, yet so forgotten. Yes, I liked those stones very much.'

'And the pub with the bridge? And the whisky?'

'Oh, yes, I liked them too. And the whiskery barman selling the whisky.'

'So you like everything!' I say. 'You are having a good time!'

She laughs out loud. 'Did you doubt it?'

'I don't know. I was worried. You were right – it is quite a long way. And there is a bit of a breeze . . .'

I have been teasing her but behind the teasing is another question that's been hovering for a while between us, and she picks it up right away. She knows that I mean Sergio, her husband who was killed in Chile, how she feels about coming away with me.

'Out there on the path today, when I was climbing those rocks and the cloud lifted for a moment and you could see right over the sea to those other islands, and there was that eagle . . .' Her voice becomes suddenly serious. 'I couldn't help thinking about him, you know.'

She has released me and is lying back on her pillow, staring up into the dark.

'It's like that sometimes. He comes back to me at certain moments. Sometimes he seems so present I can almost feel it. And then the sense of him recedes. And the strange thing is that it feels okay. Honestly. Here, and in London too, I am fine with it. It feels – I don't know how to say it exactly – peaceful somehow. That he would be all right with it, with my being with you, with my going on living, that is.'

I rest my forehead against her shoulder and let her speak.

'You must have moments like that too, sometimes,' she says. 'It must be strange for you to be here with me, as if I'm taking Yolanda's place.'

I leave my head where it is and try to think how to respond. It's been six years, but it is so rare, and therefore still so hard to hear her name. I will never forget; it is not possible . . . But Daniela leaves me that private space that I leave her, and just as I accept Sergio, she seems to accept Yolanda as part of who I am.

'Strange – I don't know. A bit, sometimes. But it doesn't feel contradictory . . . Perhaps these things are just different,' I say.

I don't know how to express what I feel without it sounding like a demand for reciprocity, so I think a moment more.

'I've wanted so much to go away with you,' I say finally. 'And if it weren't for you, I wouldn't be here on this weathery island, travelling so far north it'll soon be south, subjecting you to freezing winds and a bed of frosty sheets.'

'You're not subjecting me to anything, Osvaldo,' she says, taking my hand and bringing it to her face. 'Everything that's happened, I've wanted to happen.' She pauses a moment. 'I'm happy we're together,' she says.

~

9

London
January 1990

The rain has stopped and the streets, rinsed clean, are gleaming; tyres suck at the tarmac, and exhaust fumes from the buses and taxis billow on the clarified air.

Night has already fallen when I go to meet Daniela and find her waiting at the entrance to Bush House. I kiss her and ask her about her day as we set off through the city; the rings I expect to feel cold on my skin are warm from the heat of her hand.

We cut through Covent Garden and head towards Cambridge Circus. The West End's neon turns the puddles to cathedral glass that is shattered by the passing cars. We are heading to the Italian bistro that, even on a Friday evening, always finds a way to fit us in.

Beads of moisture race down the steamed-up windows; inside, the tables are crammed with students going on to the movies or the Comedy Store.

We tear open the packets of grissini, and suddenly, fleetingly, I am reminded of the girls as children: of the breadstick duels they engaged in, the orchestras they pretended to conduct.

We start on the wine before the cannelloni arrives in dishes that sear the tablecloth as if marked by a burning tyre. Pepper is added from a grinder the length of an axle and the Parmesan comes in a bowl with a hubcap lid.

The warmth inside the restaurant is soporific. When the cinema rush thins out we order espressos, and Daniela fights and then succumbs to the temptation to smoke.

The food and wine make me feel expansive, and though I hadn't intended to revive the issue this evening, the subject seems to arise of its own accord.

'Daniela,' I say, my hand on hers. 'You know, I've been thinking about Mexico again.'

She looks up at me, curls of smoke tangling with the rain-damped twists of her hair.

'Thinking what about Mexico again?'

Too late, I realise I should have waited. But now that I've started, I have to plough on.

'About going,' I say.

She throws me a guarded look, trying not to anticipate my words.

'Going – what – for a visit? For a holiday? Forever?'

I take a breath, and tell her. 'I want to go back to Latin America.'

Suddenly the things that have been building come pouring out, unstoppable as the morning's rain. That I'm getting older. That I want to move to some Spanish-speaking place that isn't Argentina. That I'm tired of living this rootless, provisional life.

I can see her face adjusting. Her dancing eyes are wary, trying to gauge how set upon this I am.

'We all miss home, Osvaldo, and moving to Mexico won't change it. It will only give you another place to miss.'

Her rings catch in the skeins of her hair as she runs her fingers through it, then she folds her hands on the table in the form of an X.

'I know, Daniela. But I can't keep doing what I'm doing. This job, this whole commercial thing . . . It was only meant to be for a little while.'

'Perhaps principles are a luxury for an exile,' she says, surprising me with the bitterness of her tone.

I know how hard she works to make ends meet in London, how in Chile she'd once had a career that she believed in, how her shifts at the BBC are never enough. I know how long it has taken to have her own programme, and now that she has one, what a difference it has made. I feel a rush of shame at what I'm asking, knowing what she would have to give up.

'I don't suppose any of us asked to be an exile,' I say. 'I just didn't expect to lose so much of myself.'

'And Mexico is going to fix that?' she says. Her cigarette is turning to ash between her fingers. 'You'd go back to surgery over there?'

I shake my head. 'It's not very likely now. But I might be able to teach at one of the medical schools. As far as I know' – I try feebly to joke – 'anatomy hasn't much changed.'

'Have you thought about Spain?' she says after a moment. 'You could go to Madrid, or Barcelona. It's less expensive than London, and it would feel more Latin. At least we wouldn't be so far apart.'

Something slips inside me. She is not coming. She will not leave with me.

'I can't see any point in moving to Spain,' I tell her. 'I might as well be in France or Holland or England. It's just as far from home.'

'Home,' she says. 'For me that's England now.'

She doesn't want to go back to Chile, she has always said so, even now that Pinochet has gone.

'Daniela,' I say. I reach for both her hands across the table. 'I want you to come to Mexico with me.'

Her gaze goes deep inside me, touching all the histories of my heart.

'And start all over again in a whole new country, with neither home nor income, where the currency collapses every six years?'

'It's Latin America,' I say. 'We both know it's full of problems. But so is the United States. So is Europe . . . I don't fit in here, Daniela, not really. The language, the humour – God, I even miss the weather. I know you miss them all too.'

'Don't start, Osvaldo. You know it's not fair.' She withdraws her hands, sits back.

But I want this, and I don't want to go without her, so I continue.

'Why shouldn't we have these things, Daniela? In Mexico we'd both be closer to where we come from. I'd be closer to Julieta and her children. You'd find work in Mexico City. And it's full of other exiles, people like us.'

She doesn't interrupt so I keep going.

'At work, the company has expanded and now they want to restructure; they've been talking about it for a while. Soon they'll want to retire me in any case. If I talk to them, I'm sure we could sort out something. Maybe we could even buy a place in Mexico City, some place big enough to give you an office at home.'

'I don't know a soul in Mexico City,' she says. Her voice is flat. She is leaning way back in her chair.

'We'll find people. Arturo, Carla, they'll have friends there. Maybe people at the radio . . .' I take a deep breath. 'It's not only for emotional reasons, Daniela. I don't know if it's self-ish, but it would be easier for me, you know, with regard to Liliana, to Graciela. It would help to be in the right hemi-sphere, in the right time zone, in case there are things I need to do . . .'

I pause to let my thoughts catch up.

'But it's not only that,' I say. 'I'm tired of drifting. I want to shape the next part of my life. *Te quiero*, Daniela. I love you, and I want you to be part of it. That's why I want you to come.'

She remains silent, then notices the ash that's inching towards her fingers. She stubs the cigarette out like a full stop.

'Have you decided when you're going?' she says.

I flinch at the 'you'. Her voice is soft but I know that she is upset.

'Nothing's decided, Daniela, nothing. This is the first time I've formulated it properly. I wanted to see what you thought, if you could contemplate it.' I take another breath. 'I don't want to choose between Mexico and you.'

'Don't do this, Osvaldo. This is your decision. You can't make it all hinge on me.'

'But that's how I feel,' I say, helpless, not knowing what else to say.

She is toying with her espresso cup, trying to thread the handle with the spoon.

'I can't decide just like that, Osvaldo,' she says. 'I have a life here. I need to think.'

'Will you do that?' I say, heart lifting because she hasn't said no, hoping. I take her hand and hold it across the scars on the tablecloth. 'Will you do that?' I say. 'Will you at least give it some thought?'

Province of Santa Fe, Argentina
April 1990

'What's "Due Obedience", Papá?' Ana says.

They are in the car, just Ana and her father, driving to her uncle's *quinta* in Santa Fe. They've had the radio on but her papá, who gets annoyed by all the lies the journalists broadcast, switches it off a few moments into the news.

Ana has never heard of this obedience thing and wonders how it will affect them at school.

But her father explains that it is a very good law that the president brought in a few years back to protect soldiers who followed their orders.

'So why are they talking about it now?' she says.

'Oh, some crackpots are agitating to get rid of it.'

Still, Ana is puzzled. Aren't soldiers meant to follow orders? She doesn't understand why they need a special law about it. Nor, now that they have one, why anyone would want to take it away.

It's in response to all her questions that her father decides to tell her about the war.

He explains how the armed forces were heroes who saved the country from terrorism and the communist peril. He says there are people who fail to understand what the police and military have done for them, and who think that those who defended the nation ought to be punished instead.

Ana is struggling to keep up. She's heard about the war in the Malvinas; she was only small at the time but she can remember the streets full of flags.

'So these people think those islands ought to be British?'

'Not that war, Ana. I'm not talking about the Malvinas. I'm talking about the one that went on before.'

Ana is surprised. She had no idea there'd been another war.

'It began before you were born, and was over by about the time you were starting school.'

'Where did they have it?' she says, scanning the farmland stretching flatly to the horizon. She imagines barbed-wire fences and trenches, and tanks rocking over the top of them the way she'd seen in films.

'It was everywhere,' her father says. 'All of Argentina was under threat.'

Everywhere? She hasn't seen any ruined buildings, or army tanks rusting in the streets.

'But where did they have the actual fighting?'

'It wasn't like that,' he tells her. 'The whole country was crawling with subversives – they were hidden among the general population. They were murdering people and kidnapping people, they were stirring up trouble in the factories . . . We had to be smart and fight by different methods – by gathering information. By using intelligence.'

'Intelligence?'

'We brought them in for questioning. Cross-referenced what they told us. Built up a picture of who they knew and what they did.'

'And did it work?' She turns to look at him but his eyes stay focused on the road.

'We got a lot of them, but that sort of battle – to purify the country – it's never-ending, you know.'

'So why do people want to punish the soldiers?'

'There are people who don't understand things properly, Anita. Human rights people. Lawyers. Those Grandmothers they sometimes talk to on TV.'

'Like that lady who came to the warehouse?'

Her father stiffens. 'What lady?' he says.

'You know, the one who screamed at you that time.'

'Who?' he says, and then remembers. 'Oh, that woman? That was years ago! No, she was harmless. A loony.' He taps the side of his head. 'You know. Psychologically deranged.' He clears his throat as he changes gear. 'What I mean is, there are people out there who have never accepted what the country was up against, or even what their own children did. And now they are looking for revenge – for instance, by getting rid of laws like Due Obedience, and sometimes, by breaking up people's families. Especially ones in the military and the police.'

Ana looks up. 'Are we in danger, Papá?' she says, suddenly afraid.

'Of course not, Anita,' he says, smiling at her sideways. 'I'm just telling you so you know what's going on.'

'Then why doesn't someone explain it to those people? They probably don't know all the facts.'

'They don't want to listen, Ana. There are people like that. Brainwashed people. Fanatics. People you cannot reason with.'

Her uncle's *quinta* lies just beyond Rosario and they pull in at the top of the drive. Apart from the stables, there is a big house with a swimming pool, and hammocks on the veranda, and a giant barbecue they use for the Saturday *asado*. Her aunt and uncle go there nearly every weekend.

Often Ana finds it tedious, being roped into rounds of table tennis with César, or going kayaking with him and Sancho on the river, while her father and uncle go indoors for their military chats. She's not keen on the watchdogs either, German shepherds that growl at her, and force her to take the long way round to the stables to keep out of their path.

That's because, more than anything, it's with the horses that she wants to spend her time.

She grows to love the smell of straw and sawdust, and the astringent reek of ammonia, as she walks Jacinta in circles around the yard. Soon she has made such progress that she is allowed to go further afield.

She glows with pride when her father, who sometimes comes to watch her, praises her riding posture or her skill at keeping the horses under control. This time, watching her set off through the tall grass by the creek-bed, he cheers when she and Jacinta clear the fence.

Always, driving home on Sundays, the two of them stop for hamburgers, always at the same hamburger place. She barters her fluorescent tubes of mustard for his portions of tomato ketchup; they drink Coca-Cola through double straws and pull faces when the bubbles make them burp.

At an outside table on the homebound road on Sunday, they're finishing their fries and are about to go back to the car.

'How'd you like to have your own riding gear?' her father says all of a sudden. 'If you think you'd get good use out of them, you're probably big enough now to have your own helmet and boots.'

Ana stares at him, for a moment unable to speak. She cannot think of any greater happiness. She leaps up from her side of the table and flings her arms around her father's neck.

'Thank you, Papá,' she says.

When they get home, she goes to see her mother and finds her where she'd left her, still in bed. Her father says he is tired from all the driving and pours himself a whisky, then switches on the TV in the den.

Ana sits on the edge of her mother's eiderdown. A feeling a little like guilt, a little like disloyalty, prickles at the back of her neck. She has much more fun with her father than she has ever had with her mother. She decides she will not mention the helmet and boots.

'How was it, *corazón*?' Her mamá turns towards her in her lilac nightdress, the same one she was wearing when they'd said goodbye.

'Good, Mamá,' she says. Ana sees the broken veins on her mother's cheekbone, and wonders when the last time might have been that she'd brushed her hair.

'Did you have a nice time with your cousins?'

'It was okay. I played ping-pong with César again.'

'Oh, dear – well I'm sure he appreciated it. How are your aunt and uncle?'

'They're good, Mamá; they send their love. Pascual's knee is getting better. Lorena had to go into Rosario so I didn't get to see her all that much.'

'And did you ride Jacinta?'

'Yes, Mamá,' she says. 'We went a long way up the creek. I saw a dead fox.'

'I hope you were wearing a helmet, Anita. I don't like your going off on long rides on your own.'

'It's fine with Jacinta, Mamá. She's very gentle. She's not a nervous horse.'

'Well, you mustn't do any jumping. I don't want you carted home with a broken leg.'

Ana thinks about the fence, but doesn't mention it. Her mamá hasn't directly asked her . . . She wonders whether it's dishonest not to say.

'Mamá,' she says instead, and pauses. 'You should come with us next time.'

If her mother would only come to the *quinta* with them, she could see Ana ride for herself.

Her mother looks at her and smiles. 'Next time I will, my darling,' she says, patting Ana on the back of her hand.

Mexico City
January 1992

'Why don't you write to her?' Daniela says. 'Why don't you write her a letter and publish it in the Argentine press?'

The morning sun is filtering through the windows, through the branches of the jacaranda that has already lost most of its leaves. The shouts of a hawker selling day-of-the-dead effigies well after the *Día de Muertos*, and Judas puppets well ahead of Easter, reach us above the clatter of his wheels. Daniela leans over the window-ledge, over the branch pecked bald below us where the neighbour's parrot perches, to see what the noise is about.

More than I'd ever dared hope, Daniela has taken to Mexico City and loves living in this old neighbourhood, where the cobbled streets and glimpses of mountains remind her of the place she grew up. On top of that, she has managed to pick up freelance work for Mexican and US radio, as well as for the BBC.

'I should have known they'd burn the Judas dolls here, too' she says. 'I'd love to do a piece on that.'

She looks beautiful this morning, I think. She has cut her hair so it is just above her shoulders, and both of us are more relaxed than we ever were in London, despite this city's panoply of stress.

'What do you mean, publish a letter?' I say.

Since learning what I learned from Inés, for me the end of January has never been an easy time. It's the anniversary of Liliana's birthday, and it reminds me how fast the years are passing without any breakthrough in my search. The 'Missing' notice I update each year for the newspapers raises my hopes for days beforehand, only to have them dissipate in the silence that ensues.

'In Toluca I hear they blow them up with fireworks,' Daniela is saying. Mexico's enthusiasm for the Judas figures fascinates her; the ones the hawker is trundling past our apartment, papier-mâché devils with horns and sombreros, are roughly as big as an infant and painted a fire-engine red.

'Daniela?'

She turns back to me from the window.

'I'm sorry,' she says. 'A letter, yes, why not? You could write to her "on the occasion of her fifteenth birthday" and publish it in the papers. It occurred to me on Sunday when all those *quinceañera* girls were gathering outside the church. Don't they make a big deal of it in Argentina when you turn fifteen?'

She's right about the fifteenth birthday parties, though they're nowhere near as elaborate as the fiestas here. Still, the idea of a published letter makes me nervous. I feel reticent about making public the details of what until now has been a family affair.

'I don't know, Daniela. Don't you think we ought to be careful who we alert?'

'Your Missing notice may have already alerted them, Osvaldo. And, anyway, isn't exposure the whole point?'

'And if it's seen by whoever she's living with?'

'Well, isn't that what you want? If they're good people they might respond to you. And if they've appropriated her – well, what are they going to do? And who knows? Maybe someone who recognises her will tell her about it. Maybe she will see it herself.'

I stand beside Daniela at the open window. Wood pigeons are brooding in the jacaranda's upper branches; soon the parrot will notice and scare them away. I put my arm about her waist and lean my forehead against her head.

'And if it has the opposite effect? Frightening her. Pushing her into hiding, as it were . . .'

'Then you won't have lost anything, will you?' she says. 'And at least she'd have something to think about while she hides.'

In the back of my mind I'm nervous on other grounds. A public appeal might entail unspecified dangers, after all the amnesties and the pardons they've been handing out.

'Not if you go through Teodoro,' Daniela says, when I finally give voice to those fears. 'You don't have to publish your name.'

Our conversation is punctuated by the whistle of a passing knife-sharpener, then by the racket of the gas deliveryman, whose passage is signalled by the chain of metal rings he drags along the cobbles behind his truck.

'We could record some good sound if we went to Toluca.' Daniela is thinking aloud. 'We could use the Judas dolls to explore Mexican ideas about betrayal, which would lead us to La Malinche, and maybe La Llorona, the mythical woman who weeps for her missing children, and how the two of them sometimes get confused.'

I'm listening with only half an ear to this talk of weeping women and Judas dolls. Daniela's idea of a letter is starting to make sense.

I show what I have written to Daniela, since she is better than I am at expressing her thoughts in words. Both she and Julieta suggest a couple of improvements before I fax the page to Teodoro. He promises to show it to Constanza and José's parents, and get a copy to Yolanda's brother Ricardo in La Plata.

There is a bit of a commotion in the media when the letter appears. Though Teodoro sent it in as an advertisement rather than a news item, it gets picked up by national radio, and a couple of papers write stories about it of their own.

Extracts from my 'Birthday Letter to my Unknown Granddaughter' – Daniela suggested the title – appear under headlines like 'Where is Liliana?' and 'Girl with the Wrong Name'.

Again, Constanza bundles up the copies and posts them to Mexico City; the letter, she says, even got a mention on the television news.

Over the following days I jump at every phone call, and invent excuses to visit the post office, though Teodoro, I know, would have called if there'd been any word. To get out of the house I make trips to the local bakery, returning with pastries we have no need for, and make detours that go past Sanborns to pick up newspapers that have no news.

But after the initial excitement, nothing transpires. No fifteen-year-old gets in touch with Teodoro, nobody writes to say they know who she is. The letter floats away unanswered, like a feather on the surface of the sea.

What does arrive is an envelope sent by courier, postmarked the United States. It is large and yellow and contains a note from Julieta, as well as two hand-drawn cards.

'*It was the kids' idea,*' she tells me in her spiky handwriting. '*When I told Felipe you were writing a birthday letter for Liliana, the kids piped up saying they wanted to send one too.*'

The cards have been folded into separate envelopes, and both have Liliana's name across the front. Paulina has plotted the letters in pea-green marker pen, with circles above the 'i's and hearts in a crayon procession around the edge. Mateo, who is left-handed, has written the 'L's in Liliana sloping backwards, like a skater slipping backwards over ice.

Julieta has left the envelopes unsealed, guessing I would want to have a look inside.

Paulina, at six and a half, has drawn a giant rainbow with flowers and hearts floating in an open sky. Julieta must have given her some help with the spelling.

> *Happy Birthday Liliana,*
> *I am sad that you are lost but when you are found I will show you*
> *my tadpoles.*
> *Love from Paulina*
> *xxxxxxxxxxxxxxxxx*

Mateo's is decorated with hand-drawn animals, alligators and jaguars and *guanacos* – which he loves all the more since hardly anyone knows what they are.

> *Dear Liliana,*
> *Happy Birthday to you.*
> *We are looking everywhere for you. I hope you read the*
> *newspapers in Argentina, because* Abuelo *put an ad in there.*

You may not have noticed because you might not have recognised your name.

When we find you, if you want you can come and live at our house. We live in Miami USA. If you don't speak English we will teach you. It's good here, except for my sister.

I hope to see you soon,
Lots of love from

Mateo xoxoxoxoxoxox

I stare at the cards and smile at the way they imagine her, at how naturally they accept she exists. For them, I suppose, the age of storybooks is not so distant: Hansel and Gretel escape, after all; Red Riding Hood finds her way home. Perhaps it is less of a leap of faith than I'd imagined, for them to assume she'll be found.

And as I read their words and look at the drawings they have done on shirt-box cardboard, something shifts in me too. They have dislodged Liliana from abstraction; she is a person they draw cards for and make plans for; they fill me again with hope.

There is a P.S. at the bottom of Mateo's card. 'Put yours here,' he has written, with an arrow to the cardboard's edge.

I turn it over. On the back, in orange crayon, he has traced the outline of his hand.

PART IV

THE CAVE OF THE HANDS

1994–1998

I

Mexico City
December 1994

It is our third winter in Mexico City and our jacaranda is shedding its leaves early this year. Last year's seedpods hang like pilfered purses from its branches, while its roots dislodge the footpath tiles as if the tree itself were straining to get away.

Tethered to his perch, the parrot perfects his rumba moves behind camouflage getting thinner by the day.

More and more I love these Mexican winters. It is chilly in the mornings but by noon the temperature has climbed back up to the twenties; the sun still has some warmth in it and there are months to go before the seasonal rains.

Julieta has brought Mateo and Paulina to stay with us for Christmas, and Felipe has managed to accompany them this time, too.

Daniela, who has been working down in Chiapas, has just at this moment returned. Watching from the window, Mateo sees her alight from her Beetle taxi; then I'm embracing her in the doorway, smelling the wood-smoke in her clothing, my face in her jungle-combed hair.

As I relieve her of her recording equipment, I sense how tired she is, how difficult the week has been. But she is thrilled to see the children, who have adopted her as their *abuela*. Mateo, fifteen now, is closest to her and she spoils him like a grandson, but talks to him like a man.

'Daniela, can we get a *piñata*, a real one?' says Paulina, jumping up to hug her as soon as I step away.

Mateo is hard on his sister's heels. 'What was it like in the jungle?' he says, his excitement spiking in a high-pitched note that sends Paulina into a fit of giggles.

'Kids, let Daniela at least get through the doorway!' says Felipe.

'And,' says Julieta, 'whatever happened to saying hello?'

'Hello, Daniela!' they chime.

I catch Julieta's eye with a glance that transforms her frown into a complicit smile. She's been a mother for ages but somehow it still astonishes me: the little girl I used to have to admonish for her exuberance, admonishing these children of her own.

Daniela kisses everyone and flops into the nearest chair. She unlaces the boots she says she has practically slept in; she has brought back a spare set of footprints in the mud in the tread underneath.

'It was fascinating, Mateo, in answer to your question,' she says. 'Though it was freezing cold and the roads down there would shake your fillings loose.'

'I don't have any fillings,' says Paulina.

'And no brains either,' says Mateo, dodging his sister's swipe.

Daniela tells them about the villages they slept in: the frost on their blankets in the mornings; entire communities completely cut off by the rains.

'Did the wild animals keep you awake?' says Mateo.

'Want to know what kept me awake? Roosters! They started crowing at four a.m.'

'Four a.m.! That's the middle of the night,' says Paulina, who hates getting up in the mornings. Julieta has endless battles waking her in time for school.

'Weren't there any real animals?' says Mateo. 'Jaguars and pythons and things?'

Daniela laughs. 'One snake, but it was already dead and it wasn't a python. And no jaguars – not any more – they've all gone,' she says. 'These days the most dangerous animals all live in the towns.'

'Do jaguars live in the towns?' Paulina says, eyes wide.

'Dummy, she means people,' Mateo says.

Felipe fetches us beers from the kitchen. Paulina has climbed onto my lap, though by now she is too big for it; Mateo sprawls on the cushions at Daniela's feet.

'What a welcome!' Daniela says, taking a beer and relaxing into her chair. 'I can't believe we've got you all here at once!'

'Can I feed the parrot?' says Mateo, leaping up to the window and leaning towards the tree. Having cocked its head, the bird is peering up at him, unused to entertainment from above.

'You'll have to ask the downstairs neighbours,' Daniela says. 'Actually, speaking of food, shall we stay in tonight or do you want to go out to eat?'

'Out! Out!' the kids say. They are crazy about Mexican food: they want *quesadillas* they want *enchiladas* they want *chiles rellenos* they want *nopales*.

'Calm down, you kids – Pauli, you too,' Felipe says. 'Daniela's just got back from travelling. She might like a night at home.'

'No, let's go out and celebrate,' Daniela says. 'There's even an Argentine steak house round the corner if you feel like it. We can stay in and cook any time.'

I smile helplessly at Julieta.

'I think it's been decided,' I say.

The apartment we have here is larger than the ones I had in Amsterdam or London; there is a sofa-bed in the living room and another room with bunk-beds for the kids. They have climbed into their pyjamas and wriggled under the blankets, and the chattering has finally quietened down.

Felipe is already snoring in the living room. Julieta has at last stopped rummaging; she has found the earplugs she'd been looking for in her bag.

I pull Daniela against me under the bedclothes. It feels good to have her back again in my arms.

'Did you miss me?' she says.

'All the time,' I say. And it's true.

She asks how my week has been. I fill her in on the sights we've seen in her absence: the pyramids, the Zócalo, the Opera Bar with Pancho Villa's bullet hole in the ceiling. I tell her about my lecture, and how the Medical School has invited me to teach an additional class. Then she tells me about her reporting, how the material was so much better than they'd expected, how they might have to do a follow-up programme next year.

We discuss our plans for Christmas, what we'll need to buy from the market, the presents we still have to find. In the distance I hear the whining of a siren, then one of those five-tune car alarms repeating its full repertoire, then some shouting that soon fades away.

We find that we are both whispering; then I follow her into sleep.

'When are we going to meet Liliana, *Abuelo*?'

Paulina is sitting under my desk as I organise my papers, catching the ones that slide off onto the floor. Felipe and Julieta have gone souvenir-hunting with Mateo in San Angel; Paulina, still adjusting, she says, to the altitude, slept in this morning and missed them. Daniela is going through her interviews while the house is still.

I stop what I am doing and look at my granddaughter, a curious, fuzzy-haired nine-year-old in pyjamas sprinkled with stars.

'I guess that's something fate will decide.'

'That's not a very good answer,' she says. She is her mother's daughter, I note, unafraid to say what she thinks.

I smile and explain that finding her isn't something predictable, that we are doing whatever we can to put luck on our side.

'When we find her,' she says, 'will she stay with you in Mexico or will she come and live with us?'

'You can invite her,' I say. 'But she's nearly a grown-up now. She is about to turn eighteen.'

For Paulina, that presents no obstacle. 'I can't wait till we find her,' she says, crawling out and sitting cross-legged on the rug. 'It will be like having a big sister. I get sick of having a brother all the time.'

I ask her to pass me a birthday card that has slipped out of the folder onto the floor. I'm filing the 'MISSING' notices in with the cards that she and Mateo have sent for Liliana over the years.

'What do you think she'll be like?' I ask.

Paulina's answer is immediate, as if it's a question she has already considered and resolved.

'She'll be very tall, with jet-black hair that she can sit on because she has decided not to cut it until she is found.'

'The problem, though, is that she may not know she is lost.'

'Sooner or later she'll guess. She'll notice she doesn't look like anyone in her family, that no one has the same nose as her and no one has the same-colour hair. Then, she'll start looking for clues.'

I nod as she hands me a drawing Mateo did two years ago, when Liliana turned sixteen. 'I hope you are right, Pauli.'

I'm sorting through all the papers I've collected about Graciela and José and Liliana, placing them in the filing cabinet that we lugged home from *Tepito* one weekend. I need to find things easily; I need to order my correspondence with Teodoro, with Amnesty and the OAS and the UN committees in New York and Geneva, and the documents I gathered with Yolanda over the years.

But there is another reason for this sorting. I want it all to be accessible. Before they leave I want Julieta to be able to locate these papers, if ever she has to take over where I've left off.

'*Abuelo?*'

'Yes, Paulina.'

'How will we know she's Liliana when we find her, if nobody has seen her before?'

The way she asks the question, the way she tilts her chin towards me in the sunlight: for a second it could have been Julieta when she was a child. I set aside the papers I am holding and pull her onto my knee.

'We might be able to tell. There might be a feeling, something about her that we'll recognise. She might look a bit like her mamá did when she was about the same age. But nowadays there are ways to check scientifically; with a drop of her blood she can do a test to make sure.'

'Like the princess who pricked her finger on the spinning wheel?'

I smile. 'A bit like that,' I say.

'So is her blood the same as our blood?'

'It will have elements she got from our family and others from the family of her papá. That's what the scientists look for. To see if the elements match up.'

'What if they make a mistake?'

I put my arms around her and hug her. 'They do it very carefully and they check it lots of times. And they ask another laboratory to test it too, to make sure the results are the same. The chances are so small that if you do get a match, then you can rely on it ninety-nine point nine nine nine per cent.'

I'm relieved she doesn't ask how Liliana went missing. Julieta must have found a way to explain it to the children, because Paulina doesn't ask what happened to Liliana's parents, or about the circumstances in which she disappeared.

'Now, Miss Bedbug,' I say, setting her back on her feet, 'some of us have work to do. Are you planning to get dressed before the others get back, or do we get to admire you in your star-spangled pyjamas all day?'

My desk is piled high with folders. Apart from the reams of correspondence, there are articles about laws laid down and then rescinded, about sentences pronounced and then revoked. I shift aside the papers that have yet to be put in order to give myself room to think.

Liliana is turning eighteen. When she does she will no longer be a minor. If there were some way I could reach her, if I could write to her and this time if she saw it, legally she would be entitled to act.

I decide to write her another birthday letter. It has to be for the twenty-sixth of January, though I know she may not know the true date of her birth.

In longhand, I try to formulate my thoughts.

My dearest Liliana, I begin, then hesitate. Will 'dearest' seem presumptuous? I scratch it out and replace it with 'dear' instead.

I describe how she's been missing her entire life, how we searched for her even before she was born. I tell her about her parents: who they were and what they did, how proud of her they'd have been. I beg her, if she has any doubts about who she is, to listen and act upon them, no matter how confused she might feel.

Daniela reads it over for me. We tussle over words like 'lies' and 'truth' and 'pride' and 'love' and 'missing': which ones to include, which ones would be better left out.

When it is done, she suggests I send it to the television and radio stations that took up the matter three years ago, as well as to the Argentine press.

Daniela and Paulina go out to meet the others, and I sit on alone in my study, watching the slats of sunlight travel over the rug on the floor.

I want, I need to find my grandchild. I need to see her; I need just once to hold her in my arms. To me, her absence perpetuates an imbalance in the world, a misalignment in the seasons or the stars.

I do my best to imagine her, just as the children have done. She is half her father's daughter, I tell myself, not just Graciela's child. Yet though she barely knew her mother, she may be all of Graciela that has survived.

I take my glasses off and rub my eyes. Leaf shadows agitate the strips of fading sunlight; soon it is going to be dark. After England, night falls quickly – it still disconcerts me. Here in the impatient tropics, there is no time for dusk.

I'm faxing the letter to Teodoro when I hear my family return.

Mateo, face aglow, has his hands full of *alebrijes*. Luminous with kaleidoscopic markings, wood-carved dragons with lobster tails breathe fire across the kitchen table. Lizards like psychedelic unicorns scratch at horned and spine-covered monsters – surreal escapees from a dream.

'Out of my kitchen, the lot of you!' Daniela says, brandishing some weapons of her own.

Mateo transports his painted army to the living room, trailing detachable quills and dragon flames.

'Someone had to imagine them before they could exist,' he tells me, explaining the story of the hallucinations from which the first *alebrijes* were born.

Then, he hands me a parcel. A colourful claw carved from a tree-branch pokes through the racing news.

'That one's for Liliana,' he tells me. 'I chose it specially. I think it is one she would like.'

2

The Cave of the Hands, Patagonia
April 1996

Though her mother still hasn't adjusted to life without her roses, and though she was sad to say goodbye to Adriana and Paco, Ana is pleased they have moved from the suburbs to this light-filled apartment downtown. Her father, years ago and without telling them, had entered their name on a waiting list for officers; merit, or perhaps his car accident, which left him in hospital for months on end, had accelerated their rise to the top of it, and suddenly they had the option of moving in.

Ana finished her *bachillerato* a year ago and, with it, the long commute to school. In the summertime lull between school and university, she found herself spending more and more time at the club. Lots of people in their new building were members – they were all military families and knew each other anyway – and that included Lucas, who lived three floors above them, and whom Ana occasionally encountered at family events.

The Tennis Club has a fifty-metre swimming pool and that's where she started to notice him properly, while he was training for competition and she was trying to better her own speed. The glimpses she caught of him played havoc with her concentration. There he was, collecting his towel from the poolside; there again, fair hair every which way, calves and pectorals shifting under tawny, summertime skin.

There was something in his profile that fascinated her, some purity in the cut of his cheekbones that was repeated in the line of his jaw.

She didn't know how to approach him; she didn't think she could dare. At home she waited in terrified hope for the elevator doors to open, relieved yet disappointed if he wasn't inside. She gravitated to the pool at times when he might be training, according to when she'd seen him there before. And at some point he must have recognised her, because one day he was short of change for the Coke machine and asked if he could borrow some coins.

Droplets nestled silver on the ledge of his collarbone. He looked at her through wet eyelashes, the irises washed to the palest sea-glass blue.

He was the first person she had ever kissed with any feeling, ten days later on their beach towels at the back of the Tennis Club lawn. They'd ended up with grass clippings in their hair and embossed on their shoulders, noticing only afterwards that the grounds had been freshly mown.

They've been together a year now – Ana, who has started law at university, counts from the day of the coins by the swimming pool; for Lucas it began the first time they went to bed. And Ana, at nineteen still diffident about her private life, has just told her parents that the two of them are planning their first holiday alone.

259

'Do you love him, darling?' her mother says, testing the moisture in the soil around the orchids in their pots.

'Of course, Mamá,' Ana says, knowing exactly what she means.

Her father has been friends with Lucas's father since they trained at the military academy, so he has no qualms when Ana tells him that she and Lucas are going to Patagonia, to a place she's been dying to visit because of a poster, to see some ancient rock art in a cave.

~~~~~

In a turboprop operated by the army, they fly south from Buenos Aires to Comodoro Rivadavia on tickets that Lucas's father managed to secure. From the midnight airport they catch a taxi to the bus station, where they have four more hours to wait.

They slump against each other on a row of plastic chairs that dip and rock with every fidgety move.

Too tired to sleep, Ana observes the somnolent station from an angle; it takes her a moment to decipher the bus company signs. '*El Condor*', she reads over one of the shuttered windows. Beside it, '*Lineas Puntuales: A Blue Star on the Road*'. A wall-map of Patagonia is dotted with *ñandú* birds, and right whales off the coastline, and llama-like *guanacos* picked out in plaster relief.

High above the entrance hovers the silver-rayed Virgin of Luján, blessing the travellers who pass beneath her in her stiff, isosceles skirts.

At twenty-past four, the first bus pulls into the station. As Ana sits up, the names of the coach companies skid like Scrabble letters back into their horizontal lines.

'Do I have to open my eyes?' Lucas asks.

'In a moment,' she says. 'I'll tell you.'

In the corners of the bus station there is movement. Shadows she hadn't noticed before change shape and then turn vertical; as if from the dead, bodies rise from the tiled floor. Oil workers, farmers, Indians, they rub their eyes and gravitate towards the counters, waiting to purchase their fares.

A light goes on at the Blue Star office window. Ana gives Lucas a nudge.

Ten minutes later, the coach's hydraulic doors sigh open and the two of them are scrambling up the steps. Video screens stare blankly as they burrow into their anoraks and pray for the heating to work.

Torn between exhaustion and curiosity, Ana struggles against sleep and is defeated. As the bus rolls south, her mind is filled with mysteries that later she isn't sure she has witnessed: the pitch of the night-time Atlantic; old men peddling newspapers under deserted street lamps; oil pumps probing the land like water birds, bloodshot eyes unblinking in the dark.

She awakens to dawn in what feels like another country: to skies drenched lemon-yellow and purple over landscapes like the bottom of the sea.

Mesas loom like reefs against the horizon, washed over by the night's retreating tide. Horses wade through the stringy light like creatures escaped from a myth. And in the distance, the shock of the *cordillera*, its razorback ridges juddering down South America's seahorse tail.

They pass a shrine to Gauchito Gil, the folk saint's chapel shimmering against the tundra under its drapery of crimson rags. Scarlet ribbons flap like wartime bandages against its blood-red breezeblocks in the wind.

Suddenly, in the middle of the highway, the bus decelerates, then groans to a halt. The day is overcast and there is no town, not even a building in sight.

Two men in khaki uniform mount the steps and work their way down the aisle. The metal of their weapons jars in the fuggy warmth.

They take Lucas's ID card and hand it back again; Ana's they stare at for some time. The guards make her feel nervous though there have been uniforms around her all her life.

'Don't be ridiculous,' Lucas says after the gendarmes have left, when she asks him if he ever feels the same. He slings his arm around her shoulder and grasps her breast through her clothes. 'We're going to need a bit of a siesta when we get there, don't you think?'

She pulls away and doesn't reply.

Dust scuds across the highway. She watches the guards march away an Indian they have escorted from the bus.

Later, she thinks, perhaps it is just tiredness, the overnight flight and the hours on the road, that made her irritable with Lucas. There is so much they have in common: their military families, the Tennis Club, even the place where they live. When his mood is good she likes his sense of humour. Then there is this thing about the look of him, the cool, sharp edges of his masculinity, that catches her somewhere between the ribs.

He straddles her at midday on the green chenille bedspread of the hotel in Perito Moreno, even before they've had time to take a shower. His urgency overcomes her doubts; she loves him after all, she reminds herself; her body slips into line.

Bed sheets kick and slap on the washing lines, while the poplars jab their boar's-hair branches at the sky. Ana remembers how they looked at sunset, stripped of leaves and luminous, like giant paintbrushes dipped in copper light.

At the end of town, Lucas, who picked up their hire car that morning, turns the vehicle around by the edge of a swampy lake. A few metres into the water, a sign that says 'Ice Skating Forbidden' has been hammered to the top of a stake.

They have more than 100 kilometres to go before they reach their destination. The pallid sun has given up for the day and, though it is still too early in the season, the radio is warning of snow.

Outside Perito Moreno they turn onto the RN40, an undulating ribbon of asphalt secured with white stitching to the earth. Ana thinks of it stretching behind them, all the way northwards to the border with Bolivia, and southwards down the leeward side of the Andes to the tip of Patagonia and the sea.

Out on the empty roads Ana had wanted to practise her driving, but she can see that prospect fading now that Lucas is behind the wheel. She can sense his exhilaration as the car flies over the tarmac, speeding through the gap between land and cloud.

After the urban corridors of Buenos Aires, with its vertical planes that obliterate the skyline, she feels her mind expand as the horizon grows. Oxygen fills her lungs and her pulse is racing as she opens the window, the sound of the engine lost in the rush of wind.

'Imagine living out here,' Lucas says. 'You'd go crazy in a place like this.'

She glances at him, and suddenly the feeling is back again, that sense of being out of sync. But then she smiles. That is so like Lucas, she thinks. Only he could feel hemmed in by all this space.

'You'd have to find something outdoorsy to do,' she says. 'Breed horses. Take tourists on expeditions.'

'You're not serious, are you?'

'Why not?' she says, teasing.

Before he can reply the car makes a sudden swerve. Ana thrusts her hand onto the dashboard to steady herself as the seatbelts yank and Lucas swears and jerks at the wheel and tries to avoid the gravel. Something russet flies in front of the fender and dives into the scrub.

'That was a pampas fox!' she says. 'Aren't they practically extinct around here?'

'Doesn't surprise me,' he says.

She watches the triangular head bobbing until it vanishes among the shrubs and the stones.

'You okay?' she says, her hand on his arm.

'Of course,' he says. 'Should have got him though.'

She shoots him a sideways look.

'Just joking, Ana,' he says with a cryptic laugh.

Twice they see armadillos scurrying like ambulances along the tarmac, and a falcon picking at the carcass of a third on the edge of the road.

They leave the highway on the unsurfaced road that leads to Bajo Caracoles, following it down into a canyon whose floor is scribbled with salt. Then suddenly they are up and out of it again, travelling along the lip of the crevasse. Far below, pockets of water glint like Indian costumes; the riverbanks blaze with gold as the trees that cluster there, the only ones they have seen since Perito Moreno, turn autumnal in the shelter from the wind.

They park where the road runs out. No one else has driven or walked in from the *estancia*, on Ana's map the only habitation for miles.

The weather is closing in. The wind that whips along the canyon carries the hint of ice.

She stands in front of the cave wall, eyes streaming with cold. Lucas lasted only a few minutes before retreating, shoulders hunched like a boxer's as he barrelled back up the pathway into the wind. But Ana, having come all this way after wanting so long to be here, is riveted by what she sees.

From every rock face, from a time that seems as ancient as the stone itself, they reach towards her: hands outlined in every colour, hands stretched open and striving upwards, hands like a cloud-lift of birds. She stares at the wall before her, trying to ignore the ringing in her ears. There are small hands like those of children, and hands with one finger missing, and hands superimposed upon other hands as if clapping or being held.

On the flight down from Buenos Aires she had imagined black and white and ochre, but not purple and vermillion, not these yellows and oranges and greens. She had not expected these multiple reverberations, colour overlaying other colours, new signatures laid upon the old.

She holds her own hand up to them. It could fit into the ghost of their hands.

Ana closes her eyes for a moment. She is overcome by a kind of vertigo, as if time were collapsing inward. These distant people, she thinks, had trodden the ground she is standing on; they had sheltered under this overhang of rock. They had expressed their sense of being in the most immediate way imaginable, stencilling their bodies onto stone.

She turns towards the mouth of the cave and looks down into the canyon, to the riverbed that will fill with the springtime thaw. Millennia ago they'd have descended a path like this one, and at the bottom of it, raw in the icy water, they'd have washed away the positive, leaving the negative like an insignia on the wall.

She shivers; the temperature is dropping; Lucas will be waiting back at the car. She is about to hurry after him when something catches her eye.

On the rock wall she sees one, and then another one –
solitary stick-figure hunters, and then a group of them, circling
in on their prey. Further along the rock face she discovers more
scenes: ambushes, *guanaco* herds in flight, a full moon hanging
whitely over the now-still beasts. Tracks have been drawn like
footprints across the ancient geology, like a map on the canyon
wall. She sees arrow-headed spears, and stone-carved *bolas*
strung with sinew flying towards the animals. It is all there, it
is all spelled out, drawn in mineral oxides on the rock.

And what it tells, she thinks, must be the world's oldest
story: the story of how they survived.

She feels shaken as she mounts the trail towards the car
park. It's as if some powerful force were pulling her off her
trajectory, confronting her with some mystery she has to
solve.

Behind her, the grey sky darkens over the canyon, tarnishing the silver ponds and the golden trees. The radio station
was right, she thinks. Any time now it will snow.

'Thanks for waiting,' she says, as she slides into the front seat
beside Lucas. The door slams shut in the wind.

He is twisting the radio dial for music, careening into walls
of static. He has become moody again, she can sense it; she
cannot work out what is wrong.

He gives up on the radio and starts the engine. The car
swings up the gravel track.

'Frankly, I don't know what you see in all this deadness,' he
says after a moment. In the side mirror she is watching the
crevasse get swallowed up by the land. 'Petrified forests.
Fossils. Rock paintings by Stone Age Indians. Everything is
over, here; it's vanished, finished, extinct.'

So he hasn't felt it, she thinks. He didn't see it, when to her
the place was thrumming with life. In a way it doesn't matter,

she tells herself; she doesn't share all his passions either, his obsession with Boca Juniors most of all. She knows how lucky she is to have him; she's not blind to how other girls react. What really counts is what she feels about him, she knows that, not whether they always agree.

They swoop out of the canyon and up into the folds of the plain. As they round the last curve, the horizon opens vastly before them, the great steppe offering itself to the cloud. And there ahead of them, in the lee of the hill on the roadside, cream-bellied and ochre-flanked against the tundra, a hundred *guanaco* stand grazing, watchful and timeless and graceful, under the purple sky.

One of them stands alone and higher than the others, close to the crest of the hill. Ears back, clear eyes scanning the distance, her nose twitches at the scent of the wind.

All the while, as Lucas sleeps and the Blue Star rumbles northwards through the nightfall, Ana thinks about the cave, she thinks about the paintings, she thinks about the hands she saw of people who so long ago disappeared.

In the emptiness between Caleta Olivia and the oil pumps outside Comodoro, she realises she will have to go back.

Not now, but sometime soon. To study the site. To work if she can with the archaeologists, and dig for what evidence is there. She wants to look for paint-pipes and the fragments of pigments; to uncover the remnants of cooking fires and spearheads and *bolas* – the evidence of survival, the instruments of life.

She didn't expect the cave to affect her so forcefully. It frightens her a little when she considers it, this feeling that seems to pull her to the past.

She thinks about ignoring it. Then she thinks about embracing it, about making this her path.

Lucas would hate it, she thinks. Her parents would be disappointed. To drop her law studies for this? They would see it as a terrible mistake.

But her friend Camila would love it. She would applaud Ana for striking out and being different. And Sister Rosario would encourage her, of that she has no doubt. The only nun Ana's kept in touch with since her school days, Sister Rosario would support her but also challenge her. She would say to her, as she always did: 'What else, Ana? What more is there? What does it mean?'

⁓

At dusk, the cave is empty. The only sound is the moaning of the wind in the entrance as it funnels down off the plain. The lizards are already hibernating; even the ants are huddling in their tunnels underground.

A lone *guanaco* negotiates the rocks of the canyon, old enough now to be expelled by the female herd. His toes leave tear-shaped prints in the sand as he picks his way down to the waterhole that winks glassily from the canyon floor.

Pegged to a crag above the cliff face, a falcon watches the *guanaco* descend. Night comes early this close to winter but there is light enough; he waits to see whether this passing beast will frighten any small creatures out of the brush.

A fox that nearly collided with a car at midday trots across the tundra. The scent trails led her further afield than she'd intended, but she is back on home territory now and knows where the hunting is good.

On the crest of a hillock she pauses. In the fading light the plains roll into the distance. Like the *guanacos* she's been following, she stops and sniffs the air.

The wind, though she doesn't know it, was named *Kóshkil* by a long-lost people whose language vanished when they did, with the exception of this last word. It whistles and howls in memory across the remorseless steppes.

This night, far to the south, it ruffles a forest of beech trees that fringes a river of ice. Restless, under unfathomable pressure, the ancient glacier stirs on its comfortless bed.

At first it is just one crystal that gives, but that is all it takes, one frozen crystal whose microscopic geometry slips, then all of them start to go. The façade creaks as the invisible fissure rips upwards, cracking through forty, fifty, sixty metres of ice. Below the surface, the secret hairline fills with water that prises it further open; the glacier tenses and rasps.

For a moment everything pauses, as if nature is holding its breath. There is a trembling as if in hesitation, then something rumbles, and the rumbling becomes a roar that echoes across the valley as the entire ice wall buckles and gives way. It shears off like the collapse of a row of skyscrapers, plunging and then rearing in an explosion of powder and glass. Shards of crystal plunge into the waters, then shoot back up before subsiding into the milky waves. Dust billows and falls; keels of ice collide amid the confusion. Mass and matter and gravity conspire in the shock of sundering, with only the beeches and the Jurassic earth arrayed in silent witness.

Halfway down the canyon the *guanaco* pauses, all senses suddenly alert. Through the pads of his feet he feels a tremor that has come to him over enormous distances, the vibrations travelling down to him through contiguous seams of rock. He leaps and bolts like a hare.

Forepaw curved to the air, the vixen doesn't dare move. She is aware of something shifting, some realignment underway. Periscope heads poke out of rodent burrows; ants stream from their underground nests in spite of the cold. Puzzled, wary, she waits another heartbeat. Peering between the tussocks, her golden eyes feel warm against the chill of the wind.

Then, under the thickness of her pelt, she shivers. The wind that was transparent becomes suddenly visible; in the movement all around her she sees it, whiteness streaking past her like spears. Across the glacier across the steppe across the canyon that the people visited, across the territory where she dug her burrow and last season weaned her cubs, across the highway where a bus is speeding northwards from the lake where nobody ice-skates, the clouds release their burden. It begins to snow.

~

3

Mexico City
April 1996

A flock of pigeons takes flight from the parish churchyard, looping once over its nougat walls. The jacaranda beside the bell-tower has burst into flames of purple; the colour leaps from house to house as if setting the city on fire.

Our jacaranda, too, has exploded into flower; against the window Daniela is framed like an Impressionist painting, and when we go outside we are bathed in amethyst light.

All across this suburb the scene is repeated, as if some signal had sounded and every jacaranda had obeyed. The sight of them lifts my spirits and fills me with a sense of possibility, as if the colour missing from the bleached-out sky had been restored in these clusters of bells.

There's a medical laboratory within walking distance of our apartment. The fatigue I've been feeling for the past few months doesn't appear to be lifting, and my doctor has finally agreed to order some tests.

I'm on my way home when some sort of commotion interrupts my thoughts. I scan the square around me, not sure I can trust my hearing, but nobody seems perturbed. Waiters in long aprons stand smoking outside the Guadalupana; beyond the whitewashed eucalypts, shoeshine boys joke and tout for business, their chairs like the perches that umpires use on the court of a tennis Grand Slam.

There is nothing, no conflict and no disturbance, no one calling for help.

When I hear it again, I am level with the carts of the *chicharrón* sellers, pork scratchings stacked like loofahs beside their tubs of quartered limes. This time, I am sure I hear my name. I turn, and see someone hurrying towards me, waving and limping slightly and holding his ribs with his hand.

I stare at him, and look again. The figure is familiar, but I cannot place him. I peer into his face as he nears.

'Hugo?'

I almost do not recognise him. Aged, eyes shielded by black-framed glasses, it is Hugo, my old schoolfriend Hugo, Hugo hobbling towards me like some latter-day Lazarus, the Hugo I haven't seen for twenty years.

'Osvaldo!' he says, puffing and nursing his stitch. 'You set a cracking pace, old man.'

'Hugo?' I can't stop saying it, as if repeating his name will tether him to the earth and make this apparition real.

Then suddenly we are laughing and embracing and I am holding him by the shoulders to steady myself and banish my disbelief. Those are indeed Hugo's eyes behind the thick-rimmed glasses; and it's Hugo's face, but crinkled as a paper bag.

'When did you start wearing lenses like that?' I say. Then both of us laugh out loud.

'Long gone, those little wire spectacles, Doctor. Though I must admit I'm still getting used to these.'

I can feel his back muscles working through the fabric of his jacket as he shakes his head and hugs me again and again.

He'd been talking to someone at the Gandhi bookshop when he saw me pass the window; it had taken a few moments to extricate himself, before he could rush down the street. When I didn't stop the first time he bellowed, he thought he'd been mistaken; the second time, all the pigeons took off and the street kids turned to stare.

Sight's not enough; I have to grip his forearm; I need the sensation of sinew and muscle to convince myself he is real.

'Do you live – ? What are you doing – ? How long have you been – ?' We speak through each other and over each other like politicians on the morning radio, unable to hear or be heard.

The outdoor terraces are set for lunch so we go inside a restaurant and order tequilas at the bar. The garden is an array of volcanic rocks and a row of cactus plants.

'I can't believe it, Hugo. The last time we spoke . . . I thought they'd come for you, too.'

'Oh, they came for me all right. But it's a long story,' he says.

He has lived in Mexico since getting out of Argentina, and when he arrived, just to be safe, he decided to change his name.

'So what do they call you here?'

'Enrique.' He laughs at my raised eyebrow. 'After Disépolo. Because they banned his music. But in this era of democracy, I answer to Hugo, too.'

I take the measure of how much he has changed. His eyes still sparkle, and in his wrinkled face I recognise his boyish smile. But his formerly light brown hair is silver, what's left of it, so that his eyebrows now seem bushier than before. They curl like feelers over the rims of his new glasses, as if they might somehow help him to see. But the incipient paunch he once fretted about has vanished, and the breeze billows under his jacket as he moves.

The limp, he says, is from a car crash on the road to Cuernavaca, when his car was on the wrong side of a truck that lost its brakes on the descent.

'Broken in two places,' he says, patting his leg. 'But you know me: indestructible.'

He fills in his story gradually: how after the magazine was vandalised, he was abducted en route to his parents' place, and held at Campo de Mayo for roughly five months.

Campo de Mayo, I think. That vast military complex, big enough to have its own airstrip, a dark hole in the fabric of the city when the rest of it is illuminated at night.

Inside, he was given what he describes as the full treatment. Then, inexplicably, he was released. The only reason he can identify is the least probable, the most fortuitous: that as a teenager he'd played football with one of the guards.

'It was either that or a mistake,' he says. 'I wasn't going to wait around to find out which.'

Emaciated, injured, he went straight to the docks and talked his way onto a cargo ship that turned out to be sailing for Hamburg. From Germany he flew to Mexico, where at least he spoke the language, and landed at Benito Juárez with nothing but the fillings in his teeth.

'Almost no one got out, from what I hear,' I tell him, 'not from Campo de Mayo or any of the others.'

'I know, Osvaldo, believe me.' He is quiet for a moment. 'You've heard about Scilingo, I suppose?'

I'd heard; how could I not have done? It was about this time last year. Daniela and I, along with all of Argentina, had listened in horror as the retired captain broadcast his confessions about the death flights. They screamed the following morning from the headlines of the Argentine press.

'At night, you know, even in solitary, I could hear the planes take off,' says Hugo. 'Never once did I imagine what they were for.'

We sit together in silence, back in the darkness of those years. Around us, the lunchtime restaurant fills; outside, a succession of buskers alternates the same three Beatles tunes.

I tell him my story, too. It is the first time in years I've spoken about my flight to Iguazú, about the two days I spent on the Argentine side of the waterfalls, trying to muster the courage to get across.

I've never recounted how surreal it felt, masquerading as a sightseer among the lianas and the slow-flying toucans, the rainbows arching like bridges across those thunderous cascades. The helicopters I could hear before I could see them filled me with terror, but everyone was drenched with mist from the falls and the steaming jungle; only the salt-hungry butterflies that lit on my hands knew I was sweating with fear.

Finally, I'd had to take the risk. There was a bus that ferried tourists over the bridge to the Brazilian side of the waterfalls. It was a Saturday; there was a match on the radio; the border guards were listening to the game. One of them, preoccupied by the fortunes of Independiente, glanced at me once, stamped my passport and sent me on my way. On Brazilian soil, it was all I could do to fight the urge to run.

But Brazil had its own military dictatorship and even there I wasn't safe. So I took the slow bus a thousand kilometres east to Rio de Janeiro, bought a ticket at a travel agent's and made my way to the airport that was bristling with police.

'And Yolanda joined you later on in Paris?'

He doesn't know; of course, he couldn't have heard.

'Hugo,' I say, 'Yolanda died. It was fourteen years ago.'

Behind his glasses his eyes grow wide, and for a while he doesn't speak. He traces circles around the rim of his glass as I tell him about Yolanda, about Graciela and her fiancé, then about their missing child.

Hugo was my best man at our wedding; later, he'd held both our newborn daughters in his arms.

'Osvaldo, I'm so sorry,' he says. He puts his hand on my shoulder. 'I had no idea.'

After a while I tell him about my search for Liliana, how I believe she is out there somewhere, an adult now, living her life as if in some parallel world.

'Which means Graciela isn't,' he says.

He states it matter-of-factly, a reporter, merely thinking out loud.

It takes me a moment to absorb what he has said, and then the blood drains from my face. It's as if it is needed elsewhere, to protect the inner workings of my heart.

'Why does that follow?' I say.

Hugo sees immediately what he has said. Mortified, he apologises, and backtracks, and tries to soften his words.

But I won't let go. I need to know what he knows.

Nothing, he has no information. What he's heard are only generalities, nothing specific, no facts. Nonetheless, I press him until he relents.

'She's not the only pregnant woman they took, Osvaldo. You know that, don't you? And once they'd parcelled out the infants, what reason would they have had to keep the mothers alive?'

As he speaks the logic becomes apparent. His words sink through me like a stone.

'I hate to say this, Osvaldo. But if they'd freed them, if they'd released the mothers, they knew they'd be storing up trouble. They knew the mothers would search for their children one day.'

Yet – they'd believed they'd be in power forever. Everything they'd done, they'd done as if there'd never be any reckoning. Surely it had no bearing, what the future, hypothetically, might hold.

Then, Scilingo's name returns. He'd worked at ESMA, at the torture centre where Inés and Graciela had been held.

'Hugo,' I say, and can't continue. In my deepest self I understand what he is saying. If Liliana is alive – as the Vatican said, as Inés confirmed – then Graciela must surely be dead.

I stare out at the jagged garden, the cactus plants, the rocks.

Deep down, had I believed till now that Graciela was still living? As long as there was doubt I could hold on to her; I could breathe life into the flame of her and keep that flickering alive. Implicitly I made my choice, and I chose disappearance. I chose the pain of it and the comfort of it, because the possibility of its reversal was right there in the word itself. Because the alternative was impossible to bear.

Then, some reflex in me rebels. No, I think. If she is dead, then take me to where she is lying; bring me her name on a list. Grant me a place where I can bury her and grieve for her, the way Eduardo mourns for his son.

What Hugo is saying is a theory: it's not proof and it's not an answer. I will not let conjecture extinguish my last remnants of hope.

Suddenly, Hugo himself looks stricken.

'Christ, Osvaldo,' he says, and his voice wavers. 'Was it my fault? Was it because of *Focus*, because we published those cartoons?'

I look at him, through the owlish glasses, at the panic in his faded eyes.

'Julieta blamed me for a long time,' I tell him. 'For a long time, I blamed myself. But there were other things . . .'

I tell him how Graciela and José were teaching in the *villas*, how the literacy programme was backed by the student union, how the union itself may have been backed by a Perónist group.

'I don't know how far it goes,' I tell him. 'God knows, it's hardly illegal to teach, though teaching the poor in the shantytowns, it appears, was considered subversion . . . It might have been my drawings – it might well have been. Or their names might have been pulled from someone's address book, or spilled under unspeakable duress. Or perhaps it was none of these things. Perhaps someone infiltrated their student circle, looking for people to denounce.'

'If that were the case, wouldn't you want to know who it was?'

'What for, Hugo? As a salve to my own conscience? To have somebody else to blame? I shoulder my responsibility either for endangering her, or for failing to protect her. If finding out could bring her back, perhaps it would be different . . . But I'm sixty-nine years old, Hugo, and what haunts me now is time. All I know, the few facts I have, relate to her daughter. They're all I have to go on. It's Liliana I have to find.'

Hugo nods.

'I don't know how to explain it, Hugo. I just keep thinking that finding her will bring me to Graciela, too.'

'To finding her, then, your Liliana,' Hugo says, and pauses, turning his glass between his fingers. 'To finding her, wherever she may be.'

Light-headed from the tequilas, we pay at the bar and emerge into the lunchtime square.

The day is heating up; through the haze I can feel the sun's bite on my face. Tourists are posing in pairs by the coyote fountain; the Aztec dancers with their rattling anklets are gathering under the arches; a crowd is forming for ice-cream in front of Las Nieves de Coyoacán.

'Hugo,' I say. 'There is still so much to catch up on. And I want you to meet Daniela – she's from Chile. She came with me from London.'

'And you both have to meet Cristina, and Nicolás – don't look at me like that! I know you never thought it'd happen, but I did finally get married and become a father. Young Nico is already fifteen.'

'Any more surprises, Enrique?' I say with a smile. There is such pleasure in finding him, in this random act of restoration, after so many missing years. 'Come home with me now and have lunch with us. I need a witness. I won't believe I've found you otherwise.'

We turn into my street, into a world that is snowing jacarandas. The trumpets sigh and flop onto the cobblestones, and gather in lavender drifts among the roots of the trees. Above us, the purple branches mesh into willow-pattern arbours, covering over the cracks in the porcelain sky.

~~~~

4

Colonia del Sacramento, Uruguay
May 1997

'I'll call you at six and get the coffee going,' Ana's mother had promised the night before. But Ana, who has always been slow in the mornings, still set her bedside alarm clock, knowing better than to run the risk.

She makes the coffee herself and heats the *medialunas* in the kitchen, moving carefully around the orchids her mother is coaxing into bloom. In the three years since they've moved downtown, orchids have replaced the roses her mother used to take such pride in; but sometimes Ana wonders whether she herself is the only one who waters the pots.

The aroma of coffee lures her mother to the kitchen where she leans against the doorjamb in her robe of shimmery mauve.

'Mamá, you slept in,' Ana says, kissing her on the cheek.

'I know, darling, I'm sorry,' she says. 'I think it's these new tablets they've got me on.'

Ana feels some tenderness towards her mother this morning. She is trying to cope, Ana understands that now; she knows her intentions are good.

'Have a lovely weekend, *corazón*,' her mother says, trailing Ana to the front door.

Ana turns to embrace her. In the doorframe that surrounds her mother, Ana glimpses something of the elegance that must once have drawn her father, the slender fall of her shoulder and neck.

'Good luck with the orchid people,' Ana says, hugging her goodbye. She reckons there's a fifty per cent chance her mother will make it to the Botanical Gardens this morning, to the glasshouse where her orchid class is held.

Ana leaves her waving from the doorway as she steps into the elevator. Her father had gone out before either of them had woken; he'd been expecting an early delivery at the warehouse that was taking up more of his time.

She presses PB and waits for the lift to descend. She guesses that Lucas, unlike Ana an early riser, will already be waiting in the hall.

They find an Italian restaurant just beyond the cannons that ornament one side of the square. There is a special with pumpkin gnocchi and tiramisù and Lucas, who loves both of them, is suddenly in a good mood.

'Are we on a romantic tryst too?' he says, scanning the couples around them who are holding hands and murmuring in the candlelight.

'Why not?' Ana says, and laughs. She has put behind her the despondency she felt in the museum that afternoon – a disagreement, not a dispute, about some Indian artefacts. They are on holiday, after all, this weekend.

He fills their glasses with the last of the red and gestures to the waiter for more.

It was a public holiday in Argentina, and they had taken the high-speed catamaran across the Rio de la Plata that morning. Here in Uruguay, in Colonia del Sacramento, they'd found cobbled streets full of flowers and lovers from Buenos Aires who'd escaped for romantic weekends.

It's not just the thought of romance, however, that prompted Ana to extricate Lucas from his regime of weekend sports. She's been putting it off for days now, but she has something she wants to discuss with him if only she can find the right time.

She waits till he is halfway through his main course before broaching what has been on her mind.

'Greece?' he says, and impales a piece of gnocchi on his fork.

'Yes,' she says. 'It's amazing, isn't it? They've actually invited me to come.' She is struggling not to betray her own excitement, at least until she can take the measure of his.

'It's on the other side of the world.'

'I know it is,' says Ana, smiling. 'There aren't any Greek ruins over here.' But her levity fades when she sees the expression on his face.

'Why does it have to be Greece?' he says.

'Actually,' she says, 'it doesn't have to be Greece, but they're the only ones who'd have me. I wrote to dig teams working in a dozen countries – Belize, Mexico, Jordan, Syria, Italy . . . It was only the Greeks who replied.'

Lucas doesn't comment or congratulate her. He says only: 'How long will you be gone?'

Her heart sinks. He isn't glad for her. Suddenly he is avoiding her gaze.

'It's only six weeks,' she says. 'I'll be back before you notice I've even left.'

'You wrote to twelve countries? You could have told me you were applying to go away.'

She feels a pang of conscience, and wonders if perhaps he is right.

'I wanted to,' she says. 'But what if none of them had worked out? It was all so hypothetical, until this one archae-ologist wrote back.'

'So what does that make me? Your consolation prize?'

'Of course not,' she says. 'There was no point in telling you if there was a ninety per cent chance I wasn't going anywhere at all.'

But he ignores her. 'If you loved me, you wouldn't be doing this,' he says.

'You know that's not fair, Lucas,' she says. This is not the way she'd imagined the conversation. After the initial surprise, she had thought he would be encouraging, that he would want what was good for her.

'And what's fair about your leaving me like this?' he says. 'What am I supposed to say: tell my friends you've found something better to do? That I'm dating the Invisible Woman?'

Sulking now, he is testing her. She can guess what is coming: he will push her to make a choice.

'It's only for a month and a half. Nacho and Geraldo will be overjoyed – you can watch football together all the time.'

'That's not the point,' Lucas says.

His mood has swung. She can feel his resentment brewing like the night.

'Why can't you be excited for me?' she says. He knows that she is switching to archaeology, that she's been through all this with her parents, that her heart is set on this change. 'It's a once-in-a-lifetime chance.'

'And obviously I'm not.'

'Lucas . . .'

'So you're going – you've decided,' he says. It's more of a statement than a question but she can hear the question in it.

And she can tell there is another behind that. She puts her hand on his but he pulls it away.

'This doesn't mean anything has to change between us,' she says,

'You don't think so? Maybe not for you.'

'Can't you just wait six weeks?'

'What, while you're off with somebody else?'

So there it is, that is the thing that is worrying him.

'What are you taking about?' she says. 'I'm going there to work, Lucas. It's you I'm going out with. It's you I want to be with.'

'Funny way to show it,' he says.

'Funny how little you trust me,' she says.

'Let's just see when you get back.'

Lucas spears the rest of his gnocchi in silence, and with exaggerated gestures knocks back the remainder of the wine.

Ana suppresses her disappointment and tries not to show she is hurt. She is too tense to eat anything else and they pay without having dessert.

The occasional street lamp only makes the black night blacker as they find their way back to their hotel. The leaves of the plane trees crunch underfoot as, an arm's length apart rather than arm in arm, they walk through the empty streets.

When they have undressed and gone to bed Ana tries to hug him, but Lucas turns to the wall. She can hardly believe this is still the same day that he kissed her amid a cascade of jasmine spilling over a gate.

'So when are you leaving?' he says after a moment. It's the only thing he's said to her since the restaurant, and he casts it over his shoulder without lifting his head.

'Not for a few weeks yet,' she tells him. The light from the street draws his profile in silver as it inches around the blind. 'Probably the beginning of July.'

He makes no reply.

'Let's not be like this, Lucas,' she says to the hunch of his back.

When still he doesn't respond she hugs him anyway. He pretends to be asleep.

5

Mexico City
June 1997

There is a scarlet box on the bottom shelf in the corner of my study; it came as a gift from Daniela with three new shirts inside. I reach for it now, then inhale sharply as the movement sends a bolt of pain through my joints. I sit back on my chair and rub my knee, and wait for the burning to subside.

Outside, the heavens are about to open; the sky is black and thunder is grumbling over the volcanoes. Churubusco is going to flood again; Daniela is miles away in Chalco, recording something about industrial pollution – she'll take hours to get home in the rain.

I lever the box onto the desktop and slide it towards me, my fingerprints transparent in its dust. This is where I store the items I am keeping for Liliana – not my search files, but the things she'll need to know about who she is.

When I fled Argentina I couldn't take anything with me, and when Yolanda died I couldn't depart with anything that might give me away. So it was Julieta who retrieved the family albums, Julieta who made me copies of the photographs, Julieta who helped me gather these things to keep for her sister's child.

Now I set about choosing pictures and organising them in a leather album, which I think of as a memory book. It will hold photographs for Liliana of her parents and her family, and the birthday cards her cousins made and sent to me to keep for her, and any other items we can find.

The last time Julieta came to visit, she brought an envelope of childhood pictures: Christmases with her cousins in La Plata, a holiday I'd long forgotten about in a house we must have rented by the sea.

There is a scallop-edged one in black and white of Graciela when she was a baby, sitting in a crocheted jacket inside her cot. She is staring into the camera with eyes so full of innocence I find it unbearable to meet her gaze.

There are others of her starting school, and one taken on her fifteenth birthday – a lanky teenager at home in the garden, with friends and Julieta and a guitar.

Under the arc of the reading lamp I sift through the other pictures: wedding photographs, various childhood scenes. Then I come to the one I love most of Graciela, the one Yolanda kept framed on her dressing table. It shows her under a willow tree, in probably the last photo ever taken of her, in the months before she disappeared.

José must have taken it when he stayed with us in Tigre, in that summer before the coup. There are times I cannot look at it, her flyaway hair turned curly in the humidity, her gaze drawn to something out of frame that's about to make her laugh.

I contemplate it for a moment now, and feel again the low dull ache of her absence, the places too tender to touch.

Of José himself there are only a handful of pictures. There is one that Eduardo and Maria sent me of all three of them. There is one of José finishing high school, and one of him and Graciela at a barbecue with friends.

So little, I think, to leave her, out of which to weave a life.

Just then comes a crack of thunder so powerful that the city pauses in astonishment, then whitens with the rain. Above my desk the light bulb flickers, considers its own extinction, and succumbs. When the electricity comes back in a few hours' time, I'll have to remember to reset all the household clocks.

In an envelope there are copies of the 'Missing' notices that I've updated for the newspapers every year. I place them in the memory book, along with the letter we published on Liliana's fifteenth birthday, and the other when she turned eighteen. I add in my yellowing copies of the articles the newspapers wrote about her, the mystery girl growing up with the wrong name.

In the darkened room I turn to the other objects. I have the *alebrije* Mateo chose for her, its appendages bundled together for her to construct. I have a shell necklace that Graciela once made for her sister, that Julieta found in a drawer.

And I have the clothes that Yolanda knitted for her grandchild, two a year for every year before she died. Julieta has wrapped them carefully with lavender and fresh tissue paper and I keep them in a basket of their own.

I try to imagine what else Liliana might need. Would she want report cards with remarks by Graciela's teachers? Her name on a swimming certificate? Her handwriting on a postcard she once sent home?

I don't have these objects and I don't know if Julieta found them, or if they've been lost in the upheaval of our lives. But what is certain is that Liliana will want more than these mementoes. She will want anecdotes of mischief and misadventure. The cadence of her mother's laughter. Memories that cannot be pressed into any book.

And as I sit there in the dimness, I reach for them, and reach again, and feel as if I am clutching at air. I cannot hear her intonation. I cannot remember the sound of her voice.

So this is how it happens, how people disappear. It is a transformation in those who are left to wait and wonder, a clouding of the mind so gradual you do not notice until its surface has turned opaque. There is no shock, no sudden realisation. Instead, it happens like this, on a Tuesday afternoon in an empty apartment, with a pile of fading photographs and the rain.

Graciela is alive in my memory, but my memory is starting to fail.

It's like diving for coins in the ocean. The things I try to remember slip between my fingers, they flash silver in the sunlight as they tumble through the blueness, discs of brightness blinking till they are swallowed by the dark.

What remains is all sensation. The softness of her skin as an infant. Awareness of her walking beside or behind us, and turning to find she isn't there.

I replace the lid and make room for the box and the memory book higher up the bookcase, pulling out volumes and piling them up on the desk. And as I lift and slide, it comes to me that forgetting is like a second disappearance, a slower one, that feels like a kind of betrayal.

Lightning flares again and illuminates the apartment. Thunder rolls so loudly that I duck my head. Beyond the study window, the world turns opalescent in the rain. Eyes peer from huddled doorways. Housemaids scurry up the steps of a battered *pesero* that ploughs through the lakes now fanning from the rubbish-choked drains.

Tethered to its perch, the panicked parrot squawks and screams for rescue. Moments later a door bangs open; the oldest boy dashes out to undo his lead. Bowed against the elements, he rushes back inside again, the bird perched like a falcon on his arm.

Against his back, against his skin in the downpour, the shirt that clings to his shoulders is transparent as a chrysalis wing.

6

Athens
July 1997

An overhead fan splices the darkness that pours through the open curtains. She is lying on the cool white sheets after her shower, exhausted by the flight, by the deluge of sensations, waiting for her hair to dry and her limbs to dry in the slow, revolving air.

Athens. Ana repeats the word to herself with a kind of wonder, dizzy with its heat and energy and light.

She has not yet completed her journey, but nearly. She has changed hemispheres, swapped winter for summer, left the safe circle of her world behind and exchanged it for something unknown. She is daunted and exhilarated, disoriented and jet-lagged, and wonders how she will ever be able to sleep.

The plane from Buenos Aires had landed early, and from her hotel room that morning she had set out to explore.

After the gloom of the Argentine winter, Athens was blinding. She couldn't tell if it was the dazzle of light off stone or the sun off the sea that affected her; the heat, or the rush of coolness as she stepped past a courtyard or an open door. She'd shucked off her sandals in a corner of the museum to feel its marble coolness under her feet. She'd drunk iced coffee in perspiring glasses in a city with a talent for shade.

There was, she thought, some current in the air that had infected her from the moment she'd arrived. It was in the bare-armed youths roaring past on motorbikes, in the streaming hair of their girlfriends as they gripped their thighs with their thighs. It was in the tang of the sea that wafted through the tobacco smoke and the pollution, in the way the skeletal Parthenon seemed to follow her down every street.

After nightfall, on the beachfront opposite the hotel, she had walked barefoot through the shallows trailing streams of phosphorescence, marvelling at the starbursts of white and purple light. Later, back in her room, she'd found that the seawater had embroidered her shins with small white circles of salt.

Her flight to Thessaloniki is due to leave mid-morning; the desk has promised her a wake-up call in case she oversleeps.

She phones her parents briefly, just to let them know she has arrived; hanging up, she feels suddenly alone. She is missing Lucas. They are still together, and since the trip to Colonia she has done everything to reassure him that she cares. Even so, he was distant with her right up till her departure, and declined to come to the airport to say goodbye.

Her mother, too, had taken some convincing about this journey, still hoping Ana would renounce this archaeology whim and go back to studying law.

'But you're only nineteen, *corazón*!' she'd said, when Ana had first informed them about her plans.

'I'll be twenty by then, Mamá,' she had responded, steeling herself against this holding, the emotional trap of their love.

She would lose a semester at the Faculty, she knew that, but later she'd be able to make up the units she'd missed. She'd been tutoring the neighbour's children for the past two years and had pooled the money with her savings to cover the fare.

'Oh, come on, it's only six weeks, Bettina,' her father had said. Ana had thrown him a look of gratitude for rallying to her cause.

She'd been close to him for as long as she could remember; she'd always been her father's little girl. Time and again he'd rescued her from her mother's failings: when her costume for the *chacarera* dance on National Day somehow got forgotten; when enrolment forms and excursion permissions got binned with the fashion magazines.

Occasionally, however, she wondered whether his encouragement was for her alone, or was just another salvo in the low-intensity conflict her parents had been waging for much of her life.

Still, when the time came for Ana's journey, all three of them had driven to the airport – the first time they'd gone anywhere together in years. They'd said farewell in the departures hall, her mother softly dabbing at her eyes.

'Mamá,' Ana had said, embracing her. 'Don't be sad – try to be happy for me.'

'I know, sweetheart, of course I am,' had come the reply. She'd made an effort to smile then and managed to blink back her tears.

Ana was wearing the two fine silver bangles her mother had surprised her with as a good-luck gift the night before her journey. She slid them back up her arm.

Her father had hugged her and told her to take good care of herself, and to telephone when she arrived.

His limp had all but vanished these days, though she pretended not to notice if occasionally she saw him wince.

Her love for him had deepened over the years since he'd had his accident, when she'd appreciated how fragile he really was.

She would have to hurry through this, she'd said to herself, or her resolution would come undone.

She'd left them there on the concourse. The automatic doors had opened and shut behind her; when they'd opened again she'd turned for one last glimpse of them and seen them walking towards the exit, two repelling magnets unable to touch.

Ana felt a pang of protectiveness towards her mother then, and shame at her own powerlessness to help. Whatever it was that seemed to hover over her, Ana sensed it was coming back.

As the engines revved, she had flattened her feet to the floor and aligned her body with the aircraft, with its colossal effort to lift them into the sky. She could feel it gathering speed along the runway. Then the wheels let go and the world she knew rushed sideways, as if the scenery of her childhood had been painted onto a tarpaulin that some mighty force of suction was hauling into the sea.

Under the hotel fan Ana sits up, fastens her sarong around her, and switches on the bedside lamp. Her documents are all together in a folder, beside the silver bangles on the table, and she takes them out for a dozenth time to check.

After flying north in the morning, she has an eighty-kilometre bus ride to a tiny place called Veria in the hills. In her notebook she has only a name, Anastasia Konstantinopoulos, that sounds more like a city, and a destination that sounds more like somebody's name.

It is a Saturday afternoon when Dr Anastasia Konstantinopoulos, intrigued as she later explains by the ex-convent girl
who'd written on pastel airmail paper from South America,
comes to find her at the airport in Thessaloniki. She inter-
cepts Ana in the middle of the arrivals hall, a young woman
pale with jet lag and the Argentine winter against the sun-
tanned, summertime crowd.

'Ana Bielka?'

'How did you know it was me?' says Ana, who hadn't been
expecting to be met.

Anastasia, sunglasses perched in a mane of black hair,
smiles and taps her temple. 'Intuition,' she says.

The airport is on the far side of the city and they crawl for
ages through the pre-siesta traffic, a flash of blue at the bottom
of every side street, before reaching the road that will carry
them to the mountains, west.

They take the back roads at high speed with the windows
down because Anastasia hasn't had time to get the air condi-
tioning fixed. Hair flying, Ana rides in the passenger seat with
her mouth half-open to ensure enough oxygen gets in.

Over the noise of the wind, Anastasia, in a turquoise shirt
that matches the sea that keeps eluding them, tells Ana about
the dig house they'll be living in and the city that they are
excavating, and all the dramas enacted within its walls.

She tells her about the palace, built to dominate the valley
and resonate in kingdoms far beyond. She tells her about the
theatre, where actors performed Euripides and a bodyguard
assassinated a king. She tells her about the necropolis, where
the marble vaults of the Ancient Macedons lie among jar
graves from the Iron Age, dug there eleven centuries before.

'There are at least three hundred burial mounds at Aigai,'
says Anastasia, 'the most famous, of course, being the cluster
of royal tombs.'

Ana's eyes widen as Anastasia recounts what they'd discovered inside: golden grave goods tumbled to the floor where the wooden tables had crumbled; an oak-leaf crown of beaten gold in a golden chest that was inside a marble sarcophagus. And under the crown, among the disintegrating fibres of purple cloth, the bones of Philip, the murdered monarch – the father of Alexander the Great.

Ana tries to imagine the moment: the sealed tomb broken open, air rushing into airlessness, a step where no one had trodden for two thousand years.

'One day,' she says, 'would it be possible to take a look?'

Anastasia nods. 'The four royal tombs have all been emptied for restoration, but there is one I could probably take you into. Sadly, it was looted in antiquity, but the decoration is magnificent. We call it Persephone's tomb.'

'So you know who occupied it?'

'No, the name comes from the mural inside it. You'll see.'

The coastline curves away behind them and the plain they are traversing loses itself in endless fields of corn. Gradually, as they near the mountains, the corn gives way to orchards that grow denser the further west they go. They cross three rivers before they wind up through the foothills of Mount Pieria. Thessaloniki has long since slipped below the horizon, and not even the climb towards Veria can give them a glimpse of the sea.

They pass the Veria turnoff and traverse the low slope of the hills. Roadside chapels and banks of oleander flash past them as they drive down into Vergina and out the other side of it before turning onto a dusty road. It crosses a stream and some fallow fields before sweeping in an arc up the hill.

'This, we believe, is the old Aigai road,' Anastasia says. 'Those roofs you see in the distance – that's Palatitsia. For centuries, long after Aigai was obliterated, the name of that hamlet was the only indication that there had ever been a palace here.'

Soon they come to a cattle grid, and a gate that is obscured on either side by a pair of anarchic figs. Fruits like hard green doorknobs thrum against the sides of the car.

They pull in at the front steps of a villa that rises behind a giant terracotta urn. An enormous bougainvillaea surges out of it, splashing its crimson blooms across the wall.

Ana climbs out of the car and stretches, and breathes in the summer air. The afternoon is pulsing with cicadas; the breeze is husky with dried grass. Beside the house, the scrolled up flowers of a spreading bush – angel's trumpets, somebody later tells her – point like exclamations at the sky.

'Welcome to Greece,' says Anastasia, smiling broadly. 'The house is a bit rough and ready, but isn't too uncomfortable. First we'll get you settled, and I'll introduce you to the others at dinnertime, and tomorrow we can discuss what you'd like to do.'

Ana thanks her and is about to ask about her backpack when a student saunters over, rubber flip-flops slapping on the steps. Over dusty shorts, he is wearing a Guns N' Roses T-shirt whose insignia is so faded that it looks like he's got it on inside out. His limbs are brown from working in the sunshine, and around his neck is a red bandana that is clearly a relic from better days.

He and Anastasia chat in Greek for a moment, then she hands him the keys so he can retrieve Ana's luggage from the car.

'I have to make a couple of phone calls, so Dimitri will show you around,' says Anastasia, plucking a leaf from a basil plant as she mounts the veranda steps. 'Not only is he a first-rate archaeologist, he's the only one who knows where everything is.'

The dig house has two floors, with wide balconies overlooking the valley on one side, and the slopes of Mount Pieria on the other. Like the rest of the buildings in the village, the walls are mustard-yellow and the roof tiles terracotta, as if all of them had been built from a single kit.

'It's an old farmhouse they had renovated a while back,' Dimitri says when Anastasia has gone inside. 'It's quite cool inside in the summertime, but in winter it gets freezing up here.'

He looks a little older than she is, and speaks English with an accent she cannot identify, and shakes his hair from his eyes with a sideways movement like someone who has water in his ears.

'Is that how long you are staying?' she says, in the summer heat unable to imagine how this country could ever be cold.

'I might have to,' he says. 'It depends how my fieldwork goes.'

She wants to ask what he is researching, but he has hoisted her backpack onto his shoulder before she can formulate the phrase.

'Come on,' he says. 'You must be shattered. I'll show you which one's your room.'

'Eshattered?' she says.

He looks at her with a semi-amused expression on his face. 'You know. Knackered. Bushed. Done in.'

She nods, not sure whether he is mocking her, and follows him up a staircase and along a corridor that is dark after the brilliance outside. As her eyes adjust, she notices the loose swing of his hips, the muscles working in the backs of his calves.

He sets her pack down against the wall of her room. A sliver of light pierces the shuttered windows, shoots like an arrow across the floor.

'There you go,' he says. Twin holes peep at her like a snakebite from under the arm of his T-shirt, revealing the sudden intimacy of brown skin. 'There are showers at the end of the hallway, and there's an outside one behind the bamboo fence that's just beyond the terrace, if you want to relax a bit.'

'I might just sleep for an hour,' she says.

'Sure, this is a good room for sleeping.' His eyes sweep over the wooden wardrobe, the mirror by the window, the bed pushed up against the wall. 'This was my room last year.'

Ana finds herself blushing for no reason as she steps back to let him pass. Then he pivots on the threshold, remembering he has forgotten to ask her name.

'Ana. From Argentina,' she says, grateful for the gloom of the hall.

'Dimitri-from-England,' he says, and thrusts out a hand whose calluses scratch her a little, like bark. 'Welcome to Antiquity,' he adds, doing a half-bow with his palm on his belly. 'If there's anything you need, don't hesitate . . . We wish you a pleasant stay in the royal city of Aigai.'

He shoots her a smile that illuminates the hallway like a flashlight and leaves her seeing doubles of him before she realises he is no longer there.

She is turning into her room when she hears his voice again, calling up from the bottom of the stairs. 'I forgot to say, Stella has dinner ready by eight, and we have beers beforehand, whenever people wander in.'

She calls down her thanks, and closes the door. She leans her forehead against it for some moments, exhausted by the journey and all the things she has seen and smelled and heard and is still absorbing, still blinking his silhouette from her eyes.

7

Aigai, Greece
July 1997

The sun pounds the back of her head through the hat that Stella had found for her, on a peg behind the villa's back door. Ana finds the light here overwhelming, sometimes even in the early morning; as the sun cranks higher, the air itself seems to split into shards of white.

After the one day Anastasia insisted she spend acclimatising, Ana now rises with the workmen in the still cool light of dawn. Though she has never been good at getting up early, here she finds she can do so without an alarm clock if she sleeps with the shutters open, letting the lightening sky and the distant roosters ease her with less violence into the day.

Once she is awake, she pads down to the kitchen and boils the water for coffee that she has learned how to make the Greek way, poured over a jug of grounds. She drinks it out on the veranda, watching the valley awaken with her arms folded into her windcheater as the colour creeps into the hills.

Although their numbers fluctuate, roughly a dozen archaeologists are staying at the dig house, and one by one they shuffle downstairs, yawning and rubbing their eyes.

Ana catches a lift with the first of them and by seven she is out at the site. Old Ioannis and the other workmen, who cross the village on scooters untroubled by mufflers, are always there before them, leaning on their spades and smoking while they wait for instructions to start.

Anastasia has assigned Ana to the new trench they have opened in the *agora*. The red tips of the survey pegs that mark out its perimeter make it look like a circus has decamped, or is about to arrive.

'Trust them,' Anastasia tells her, nodding towards the labourers who have set to work in the herringbone tracks that the earthmover has left in the dirt. 'No archaeologist will ever know this soil as well as they do. They are farming people. They have worked it all their lives.'

She asks Ana to shadow Dimitri since he is an English-speaker, and as a graduate student he is experienced enough to teach her the techniques she will need.

Her day is spent sifting through layers of dirt where the topsoil has been wheelbarrowed away. Dimitri explains to her about stratification, about cuts and backfill and edges, and the best technique for brandishing a pointing trowel.

He is patient with her questions, and does sketches to clarify issues of context and record, tearing pages from the notebook that he keeps in the pocket on his thigh. Her bedside drawer in the dig house, where she keeps her silver bangles, soon fills with his biro-scribbled thoughts.

She stops to stretch her back, and looks out over the burial ground where unknowing farmers for centuries have been ploughing and reaping the fields. The sun dyes the blond grasses pink in the long light of morning, then peroxides them white as it climbs.

After the first week she feels as if the trench has etched itself into her body; in bed at night, she can identify its angles like a ghost in the ache of her limbs. Her socks leave a lasso of dust about her ankles and her cuticles are inked with blackness that no amount of scrubbing will remove. Only after she peers down the table at lunchtime, and sees the same circular tattoos around everyone's fingernails, does she change her mind and wear them like a badge of belonging.

She veers between exhaustion and exhilaration. Every fragment they find, every chunk of masonry no matter how scattered and broken, has a context, is a part of a sentence they are striving to construct. After the abstractions of her law books, she loves the jigsaw-feel of piecing together a mystery, of starting the day not knowing what she'll know by the end.

She has begun sketching their finds and discovers she has some talent for it. Perhaps, she thinks, this path could lead to a place worth going to, as if the road she was on beforehand were somehow out of kilter with who she was.

And always at 2.30 p.m., when the screech of cicadas is deafening and the heat-warp makes it impossible to continue, they call it a day and head back to the villa for lunch.

People converge from all over the dig site, from the palace and the *agora* and the tombs. They rinse off the soil at the sink under the wall of jasmine; they flick water at each other like school kids; they jostle for chairs at the table under the ripening grapes. In her apron with its one torn pocket, Stella darts among them, passing around trays of meat or fish or vegetables she has baked or fried or grilled. To Ana, sitting at one end of the table, they could be a crew on the set of a film.

It is only when she glances up and catches Dimitri watching her that Ana realises he's been observing her from afar. She has been sawing through the suckers of octopi, decapitating sardines that the fish van brought that morning to the village, piling Olympic rings of onion on the side of her plate. He catches her eye with an amused smile and she blushes, to her own annoyance, when she is handed a rosy-cheeked peach.

After lunch she pointedly ignores him, skipping coffee and vanishing upstairs. Through the shutters, Ana can hear the clickety-click of backgammon being played down on the veranda, cicadas applauding dementedly in the heat.

In the shade of her room she peers at her face in the mirror. Even despite the dimness she seems altered, though she cannot describe in what way. Would Lucas be able to identify it? she wonders. Would he see more clearly than she can whatever it is that has changed?

When she thinks about him, now they're apart, what comes to her is mostly an impression, like a photograph taken in close-up because she couldn't stand back far enough to see. She misses him, and the missing tugs like a knot between her belly and her heart. But when she tries to picture him at a distance – across a room, say, or walking towards her over the lawns at the Tennis Club – she cannot seem to get him into focus. It's as if the rapport she has with him is intimate, or exists not at all.

She is tired, she tells herself; the sun out on the dig today was scorching; it is rest she wants, not thought. But when she kicks off her boots and stretches out on the bed that was once Dimitri's, it is Dimitri's smile that troubles her siesta sleep.

Anastasia comes over to them during the morning, when they are clearing a new foundation in the top trench, and asks Dimitri if he can spare his new assistant for an hour.

She turns to Ana, who squints up at her in the sunshine and pushes the hair out of her eyes. 'They've finished cleaning the mural in the tomb I told you about. I wondered if you wanted to come and see.'

Ana is already out of the trench and laying down her trowel on the table where they annotate their finds.

Anastasia shoots a quick smile at Dimitri. 'Well, I gather that's a yes,' she says.

They drive the short distance to Vergina and park beside the restoration workshops where Anastasia has her office, close to the royal tombs. Once the archaeologists had finished their excavations, they'd rebuilt the hill over a concrete dome where the museum was now taking shape.

Anastasia rummages in her desk for a flashlight, then they are waiting outside in the sunshine for the guard to unlock a door into the side of the hill. A tremor runs through Ana when he opens it; she sees a passage sloping downwards into the darkness, like a journey into the underworld itself.

'Ready?' Anastasia says. 'You shouldn't find it too claustrophobic, but they are still fixing the wiring, so it's going to be pretty dark.'

Ana finds herself speaking in a whisper, and finally not speaking at all. The darkness inside is absolute; they have taken a bifurcation that has obscured the light of the entrance, and no sound penetrates this deep from the world outside.

They follow Anastasia's cone of light that loses intensity as it jumps along the walls. It is cool inside, and smells of silicon and earthiness where the new construction meets the old stone and the soil.

Anastasia leads them down the turnings that they take from the museum's entrance as if she could do it without a flashlight at all.

Jumbled slabs of limestone rear into view and vanish, then the base of a shrine, ruined when it was plundered, that had yielded the marble paw of a lion. Then they are climbing a staircase up the side of a wall and peering over the top of it, between a parting in two mighty beams of stone.

Ana isn't sure what she'd been expecting, but it was nothing as drama-filled as this. From one surface, the wheels of a chariot seem to be flying towards them. Grappling with the reins in one hand, a wild-haired man is gripping a near-naked woman who is trying to break free from his grasp. Thunderbolts descend beside a second man who is racing ahead of the horses, while in the background a maiden crouches, one hand held above her like a shield.

'Do you recognise it?' says Anastasia. 'It's the abduction of Persephone.'

Ana takes in the vibrant colours: the reds and yellows and purples against the chalk-white surface, a frieze of flowers in a faded blue suspended over a blood-red wall.

'And the man with the horses?' she says, peering through the discolouration on the mural's left-hand side.

'Hermes, the messenger who accompanied the dead to the afterlife, leading Hades' chariot to the west.'

The torchlight plays around the chamber. Depicted in ashen tones on the adjoining wall, a woman huddles on a lonely rock, facing the abduction scene.

'That's Demeter on the left,' says Anastasia. 'The artist portrayed her not as a goddess but as a solitary mourner, bereft at the loss of her child.'

There are what look like three other figures on the opposite wall – the Fates perhaps – but the plasterwork is too damaged to be sure.

The frescoes flicker in the torchlight. Here in the subterranean darkness, this talk of the Underworld, of beliefs already ancient when they were adopted in archaic times . . . Ana shivers. She has that sense again of knowledge shimmering somewhere in the distance, tantalising but always out of reach.

'Come on,' Anastasia says after a moment. 'There's something I want to show you before we go.'

They descend the steps and enter the chamber and gaze at the paintings close up.

'See where the artist did his sketches?' Anastasia says. She points to the confident arcs, the fluent lines that Ana sees are not lines at all, but incisions made directly into the plaster. 'He mapped it all out while the surface was wet, then adapted his brushstrokes as he went.'

Ana sees, and understands what she is seeing. Right here, just as in the cave in Patagonia, the trace of a hand on a surface, a long-vanished artist at work.

'Are there any hypotheses about who it was built for?' she says. 'It has a feminine feel to it, wouldn't you say? All these women on the walls.'

Anastasia nods. 'It was looted in antiquity – when we opened it up, we found the bones had been scattered over the floor. The forensic lab tests showed that they belonged to a young woman and her new-born infant. She was in her mid-twenties and must have died with the baby, shortly after giving birth.'

Her mid-twenties, Ana thinks, and pauses. Hardly any older than herself.

'Nikesipolis – that's who we think it is. She was Philip's fifth wife.'

They stand in silence for a moment, watching the torchlight play over the eastern wall. Demeter, the grieving mother, looks down at them from the lilies and the hyacinths and the griffins adorning the frieze at her feet.

Ana considers her for some moments: a love so fierce it stopped the earth from flowering, anguish and tenacity entwined.

In the quietness, she glances over towards Anastasia and is startled. In the gleam of the flashlight, just for a second, her eyes look like they're glistening with tears.

But suddenly the beam is dancing around Ana's ankles, illuminating the chamber entrance, the path to the outside world.

'Ready to go?' Anastasia says.

They turn the final corner. An oblong of daylight beckons from the end of the passageway: a mosaic of luminous emerald, a lapis-lazuli sky.

Seconds later they are bursting through it, out into the midday heat. After the coolness underground, after the darkness of the tombs, they are hungry for it, for children shouting and insects buzzing and seedpods cracking open in the sunshine, for the scent of herbs and ripening plums and the summer air caressing their skin like fur.

⸺

Two days later, Dimitri, who is taking the measurements of what may have been a kind of storehouse, turns to ask for Ana's help. Shovel propped against her hip, she has her back to him and her arms in the air as she struggles to twist her hair into a knot.

'What's that, Ana?' he says.

She half-turns towards him, elbows raised, trying not to let the shovel slide.

'What's what?' she says.

He is squinting at her in the brightness, looking at the right side of her head.

Her hand follows his gaze and goes to the spot behind her ear reflexively, as if she were only now discovering it herself.

'Oh, that's nothing, I've had them forever,' she says. Her fingers flit over the markings, the ridges hard as Braille.

Her unruly hair, grown to her great frustration even curlier in the heat, falls back from where she is winding it as she darts to catch the spade.

'Three in a row like that. Those little crosses. You'd almost say they were scars.'

'They're not scars, they just look like scars,' she says, her voice a little sharper than she'd meant.

He raises an eyebrow as she digs in the shovel that stands like a punctuation mark in the dirt.

'What can I say?' she adds, softening her tone. 'I've always had them. They've been there since I was born.'

'So what are they?'

'Oh, just some sort of birthmark apparently,' she says, hearing even as she says it a certain lack of logic in her words.

'Hmm,' says Dimitri. He is about to add something, then changes his mind and presses the end of the tape measure into her hand.

'Can you hold it down for me?' he says, indicating the length of a line of stone. 'Take it as far as it will go to the end.'

She pins it to the earth where he has asked her and waits for him to note the distance down. A grasshopper catapults onto the toe of her boot, then catapults off into the weeds.

'Maybe you had stitches,' he says after a moment.

Her mind has drifted and it takes her a second to realise he's still talking about her marks. It's not as if she ever really thinks about them, though over the years she has tried to catch a glimpse of them with an awkward alignment of mirrors over the bathroom sink.

'Estitches?' she says. 'As in an operation?'

He smiles. 'Why not?' he says. 'Maybe they planted a chip.'

'I suppose that would explain the exceptional brain power. I'd always wondered,' she says.

'Or . . . perhaps you played noughts and crosses in the womb.' He extends the stripe of yellow centimetres and backs further down the trench. 'It can get boring, I understand, hanging around waiting to be born.'

'Are you accusing me of cheating? Of stashing a few spare crosses behind my ear?' She holds her end of the measure in place and feels it pull taut again.

'Lucky for you it wasn't Scrabble,' he says.

'I don't know. Aren't X's worth a lot of Escrabble points?'

'Say "Scrabble" again,' he says.

She blushes and screws up her nose at him. He is always teasing her for the way she pronounces words that begin with an 'S'.

With his left hand Dimitri slides his notebook out of his pocket, then pats a series of others in quest of a still-working pen. 'Hey, perhaps they're not letters at all,' he says. 'Maybe they're Roman numerals.'

She rolls her eyes. 'What, so thirty's my lucky number?'

Pen between his teeth, he can't respond for a moment as he slips the book back into his pocket. Then he has another idea.

'Hey, what if it's a serial number? You know, like an etching. Like a print.'

She laughs out loud. 'Oh, sure, number thirty off the production line. You'll be saying they've cloned me next!'

'Well, now you mention it . . .'

She shakes her head. 'And there I was, thinking I was unique.'

He stops and looks at her, turns on her the flash of his smile.

'You are unique,' he says. 'In fact, I think they've got to be three asterisks – you know: "Take note of this girl".'

'Only because she's dangerous,' says Ana, flushing and trying to frown as she releases the end of the tape-measure that makes him jump as it whips through the dust to his feet.

8

Acapulco, Mexico
August 1997

'It's four hundred kilometres, Osvaldo,' Daniela is saying. She is standing before the cupboard in the hallway, bath towels folded in a tower under her chin. 'It'll be four hours on the road at least, and that's if the traffic is good.'

'I know, I know,' I say. 'But when did we last go to the coast?'

In the thin air trapped beneath the volcanoes, the city is weary with humidity that makes the pollution harder to bear. It is not as bad as the windless days we had at the end of winter, when the pollution levels were peaking and the rains had not yet come. But Daniela, struggling daily through the city's traffic-clogged arteries, is still emptying bottles of eye-drops against the slew of irritants in the air.

She throws me a sceptical glance, then levers the bath towels in.

'We both need a break,' I tell her, 'and we haven't been to the sea since – when was the last time? It must be more than a year.'

'We went to Xochimilco two weeks ago.'

'Xochimilco isn't the sea!' I laugh, recalling the pink-and-yellow party boats chugging along the waterways between the market gardens, on the remnants of the Aztec lake.

Suddenly she smiles. 'You know what this conversation reminds me of?' she says. 'That time we went to Skye.'

'It's not nearly as far,' I protest, then realise she is teasing me when she extracts a pair of beach towels from the pile. 'Anyway, as I remember it, beach towels are purely optional for the places that get a mention on the Shipping News.'

Beneath her lightness, I know she is concerned about my health. The doctors have run more tests on me but have found nothing to explain my lethargy, and I don't know whether to be anxious or relieved. I know she fears the distance will exhaust me; she knows I fear she's exhausting herself with all the demands of her work.

Still, despite my constant tiredness, my spirits lift at the thought of seeing the coast. After the altitude of Mexico City, after its rainy-season chaos, a few days down at sea level will do us both good.

It's an odd-number licence plate day, so Hugo drives Cristina's Golf and we set off together in a two-car convoy to the sea. A relative has been urging them to use his holiday house on the cliffs near Acapulco, so Hugo has invited us to join them for a few days. Nicolás is accompanying them because of his new-found passion for surf.

The Autopista del Sol rolls in a long black stripe off the volcanic plateau and down to the open plains. Hugo is a speedy driver but we manage to catch him up at the toll booths, and tail him to the roadside markets he has plotted for us to stop at on the way. At the first of them, on the outskirts of Tres Marías, we drink cocoa-flavoured *atole* from ceramic cups under the benevolent eye of the Virgin of

Guadalupe; at the second we order fried blue-corn tortillas and demolish them elbow-to-elbow with the truckers.

'You know,' I say, as Cuernavaca fades into the distance, 'we should get Arturo and Carla to come over one of these days. And bring Santiago with them.'

'Do you think they'd come? All these crime stories tend to put people off a bit.'

'If they were with us they'd be fine. Maybe we could get Julieta to bring the family over too. Santiago and Mateo are nearly the same age. I'd love it if the two of them could meet.'

'We'd need a whole *hacienda* for everyone,' says Daniela over the top of her sunglasses. 'Are you sure you could cope with the whole extended clan?'

'Why not?' I say. 'Mexico is full of enormous families. And *haciendas*. We could get them over for Christmas perhaps, or Easter. We could find a place in Valle de Bravo, or maybe Tepotzotlán . . .'

The Pacific rears up to meet us as we wind through the Sierre Madre, down into Acapulco, then out along the coastal road. Palm trees shimmy like dancers above the shacks on the city's outskirts as we climb the headland, parallel to yet out of sight of the sea.

I open my window wide. The air pours in with smells of mulch and ozone, and overripe mangoes caramelising in the tropical sun.

We overshoot the turnoff, and almost reach the lagoon on the far side of the promontory before we can double back. Then we lurch down a track that's been ribbed and cratered by rain and other vehicles, sea-sawing between glimpses of blue.

Ahead of us, Hugo taps his horn to signal our arrival. Eyes opaque with cataracts, in a cowboy hat that could swallow him, a caretaker shuffles towards us and drags open the one-legged gate. We park the cars at the back of the house and leave them purring in the shade.

From this side, the house looks simple: whitewashed walls and a bamboo fence scribbled with passion-fruit vines. Hibiscus flowers blaze from the bushes that screen the house from the wind.

The generator chugs to life and the caretaker turns on the hot water; he nods without expression as he takes his leave. Dust billows at his feet as he shuffles back up the driveway, hemming his trousers with ivory chalk.

I place Daniela's bag with mine on the edge of the decking while she goes to fetch her sunglasses from the car. Hugo and Cristina are inside, doing the ritual furnishing-check for scorpions; Nicolás, in the kitchen, is rummaging around for something to eat.

The front of the house is nothing like the back of it – it is a sleight of hand performed with glass and light. Sliding doors open it partly or entirely to the ocean. From the bridge of a ship at nightfall, the windows must glow molten in the setting sun.

In a glass bowl on the wooden table, a fallen moth is embalmed in a sunken candle. Worn wicker chairs slump like old ladies at a Christmas party, spirals of cane pooling around their ankles like stockings.

I turn to face the water and then step backwards, arrested by the view.

From the end of the decking the edge of the world drops away. I take in the gulf of air, the silver lip of the horizon, the shifting corrugations of the sea. The loss of perspective is vertiginous; I feel higher even than the clouds. Far away, a cargo ship labours along the curvature of the earth; beyond it, the azure world disintegrates into mist.

An ocean gull hangs beneath me, coasting weightless on the thermals, then leans into the wind and climbs. For a moment, before the current lifts and carries him past me, we are eye to eye in the breeze. I can almost see my reflection in the convex jet of his pupil; his shadow as it passes over me is cool as an eclipse.

Daniela sees him too as she comes to stand beside me; I can feel the smooth bands of her rings when I take her hand. Neither of us speaks as we listen to the crash of the sea and the riffs of the wind that snatch away the crying of the gulls.

'How are you feeling?' I ask her after a moment; she had insisted on driving all the way.

'I feel fine,' she says, exhaling and stretching her back. 'As long as all this oxygen doesn't knock me out.'

Far below, black rocks glisten in the tide-heave, combing the kelp like hair.

'What a place for a house,' she says, staring into the distance.

I nod, and circle her with my arms.

In the evening the five of us have dinner out on the terrace, our bodies thirsting for the breeze. It is hotter here than in Mexico City; the wind has dropped since sundown but the temperature has barely fallen; inside the house we are in for an airless night.

Heaped in a translucent midden on the serving dish, empty prawn shells glister like broken light bulbs. Candlelight plays on the bellies of the weeping beer-bottles; the rings they leave on the wooden table evaporate as we watch.

The conversation rises and falls, our laughter carrying in the dark. Nicolás surprises us all by turning in early; he's got a friend to see in the morning to sort out a board. Cristina, meanwhile, tells us about the house, how it was left to her uncle long ago by the architect he built it for, a man with a passion for dolphins; how she spent half her childhood watching for them from the deck.

With Hugo, who seems more cynical these days, there is still so much to catch up on, as if talking could patch over the ways in which we have changed. Yet there is an understanding to the friendship we're rebuilding, perhaps because we knew each other as children, before life took over and bent us different ways.

Still, there is one thing I've been wanting to put to him, and the fact we haven't already broached it makes it that much harder to start. But finally, when Daniela is stretching her legs and Cristina is hunting for cigarettes, I find a moment to ask.

'Hugo,' I say. 'Have you had any word from Heriberto, or Marguerita and Diego, or any of the others we used to know?'

Hugo's dancing eyes turn sober.

'I lost touch with Heriberto about the same time you did, Osvaldo, and for a long time I thought he had disappeared. But then a year or two ago I heard a rumour – someone said he got out more or less when we did and went to Barcelona, where he is still critiquing movies under a pseudonym.'

'Do you think it's true?' I say.

Hugo shrugs. The way he raises the tufts of his eyebrows puts even more creases in his brow.

Heriberto, I think. His battered Borsalino and poison pen that laid waste to modern film.

'I hope he made it,' I say. I hope he got to Barcelona and is raging pestilential against all Hollywood post-1949. 'What about that girlfriend of his . . . Sofia, wasn't it? Did she go with him to Spain?'

'Sonia, I think,' says Hugo, smiling and shaking his head. 'Sofia was one of her predecessors. It drove her crazy when you mixed up the names.'

I colour slightly. I remember vaguely, now that he says it – and Hugo, or maybe Heriberto, kicking me under the table for getting it wrong.

'I haven't been able to trace her,' he says. 'But I don't have a lot of leads for her – I didn't know her very well at the time.'

I hold my breath. 'And Diego? And Marguerita?'

Daniela comes back and sits beside me, leaning her shoulder against mine. Cristina's cigarette glows redly, tracing neon subtitles in the dark.

Hugo clears his throat. 'All I know is that they went underground pretty soon after they shut down the magazine: new names, new jobs I presume, a new town . . .' He stops for a second. 'Can you picture it: Diego, disguised as a redhead with the help of a self-dye kit?'

He smiles, then frowns as we think of him: Diego, our brainy, impractical friend.

Then, his voice drops. 'After all these years they haven't resurfaced,' says Hugo. 'I've asked around whenever I've been back. I've even tried to visit Diego's parents, but when I eventually found the house, the neighbours said another family had moved in long ago.'

His words trail off.

Diego, dear Diego, our short-legged schoolfriend with his long-sighted theories for setting the world to rights. And Marguerita, with her incisive mind and what Diego called her Spanish temperament, who rendered him too tongue-tied to propose.

'The last time I saw them was with you, Osvaldo,' Hugo says. 'That night at the Paradiso.'

The candle sinks into its rind. A lace-wing moth darts over the flame that flutters to some rhythm of its own.

How long ago it was, I think, how unknowing we all were. None of us had had any clue how close we were to the abyss.

'What about Gustavo?' I say after a moment. 'Do you think he's still predicting the end of café life as we know it, while measuring out those cognacs at the bar?'

It's an eternity since I've thought about Gustavo, forever at the helm in his impeccable apron, complaining as he swapped out the cassettes.

'I've never returned to the Paradiso,' Hugo says. 'And now, when I look back, I wonder . . .'

'You wonder?' I say.

'You know,' says Hugo. 'If he was trustworthy. I always felt he was at the time, but now – I don't know. I honestly don't.'

'Trustworthy?'

'With so many of them working for the police . . .'

'Gustavo?' I can't think it, I can't bear to, not Gustavo. Informing? On Diego and Marguerita and Heriberto? On Hugo, too? On me?

The sea crashes on the rocks at the foot of the cliffs. I only become aware of it now, of the sound of the waves, though they have been breaking beneath us all along.

We sit for a time thinking our separate thoughts, and after a while Hugo and Cristina announce they are turning in.

'Leave the glasses – we'll do them in the morning,' Cristina says as we bid each other goodnight.

Hugo, silhouetted in the half-light, slides the curtains across the windows; Cristina switches on a lamp inside the door.

Daniela and I lean against the rails at the end of the decking, staring out at the now-black sea. The lights of a single fishing boat shine bravely, dwarfed by the mighty dark.

'Do you think you'll be able to sleep after all that talk?' she says when the house is quiet.

'Perhaps not right away,' I say. 'I might stay out here for a little while.'

'Do you mind if I stay out with you?'

I turn to her. 'Come over here,' I say.

I thread my arm around her waist as we stand there, her hair soft against my face, watching the fishing boat turn and head out to sea.

'It's a kind of guilt, isn't it?' Daniela says after a moment. 'Being here, with all that we have. Being alive.'

'I know,' I say, and hug her to me. 'And at times it seems to me so random, who gets and doesn't get to survive.'

She turns to look at me, her dark eyes catching some light I haven't noticed, bright against the duskiness of her skin.

'It's never going to go away, is it?' she says.

I can only shake my head.

The imperfect moon has climbed higher now and hangs over the ruffling sea. It looks like the doorway to another universe, a manhole with its cover off, the stars like dazzling rust-holes in the sky.

I think about my missing daughter, knowing in some part of me that she must be gone, yet unable to let her go. I think about my missing granddaughter, out there somewhere, twenty now, and starting to shape her life.

I think about where I'm standing, on a cliff on the edge of the vast Pacific, and still not high enough to see.

'I wonder if we'll ever find her,' I say. 'Liliana, I mean. This whole process, this stop-start searching . . .'

Moths flop against the window, maddened by the beacon Cristina has placed inside the door.

'Do you ever contemplate the possibility that it might not happen?' says Daniela, speaking gently. 'You know, that you might never get to meet?'

'All the time, Daniela. Every day of my life I struggle with it, the hopelessness of it, my inability to accomplish this one thing.'

Acapulco glows behind the headland, throwing its other-worldly halo into the sky. The moon scatters its luminescence like a trail of aluminium onto the sea.

'At the same time, though,' I continue, and pull her closer, 'I can't give up. Even if I wanted to. Even if I decided to.' I look at her, trying to explain. 'It's not just atonement. It's as if this search, this need to find her, is about something bigger than my own life.'

I think about my parents, who died so long ago, about my father's battles to earn a decent living on our behalf. I think about the despairing soil his own father left in Italy; how my mother's family fled during the First World War. And it angers me, and it steels my resolve, because the disappearance of Graciela, and absence of Liliana, feel like the negation of all that they had struggled for, of all they'd renounced and endured and striven for: so that their descendants could survive.

'I understand, Osvaldo, truly. If I didn't know what had happened to Sergio, if there'd been the slightest doubt . . . I know that I could never have let it rest.'

And it occurs to me that the conversation tonight must have been hard for her to listen to, that our wondering about our vanished friends must have stirred up memories she doesn't talk about that people her own hall of the missing.

I hold her against me and rest my head against hers. I think how the battles she fought before I knew her must have wounded her before they made her strong.

'Daniela,' I say, but cannot finish the sentence.

She lifts her face a little from my shoulder.

'What is it?' she says.

I shake my head, then kiss her, and murmur '*te amo*' into her hair.

9

Aigai, Greece
August 1997

They hear him before they see him chugging up the hill with a throbbing sound that causes even the tractor-drivers to turn. He slogs up the final rise and rattles over the cattle grid, shaving a handful of figs off the trees by the gate. He skids to a stop in a two-door car that is even more battered than Anastasia's; the handbrake when he yanks on it cries out like a creature in pain.

With one hand on the windshield that is missing a windscreen wiper, he levers himself over the gearstick and into the passenger seat. Weaving an arm through the passenger window, he cranks open the door from outside.

Graffiti etched into the car's dust-furred exterior reveals an ancient layer of bodywork that might once have been maroon. Inside, a shovel and an interesting piece of driftwood lie among yellowing newspapers, while dozens of tins of various sizes are arrayed along the back seat.

'They're those glazes,' Vasilis says as Anastasia hugs him, one of her eyebrows raised.

Vasilis already knows Dimitri so Anastasia introduces him to Ana, who can tell she is going to like him right away. His curly hair is receding like scrub in the path of a sand dune, his eyes are permanently crinkled as if he's just finished laughing, and the creases in his clothing are white with ceramic dust.

Arm in arm with Anastasia, he tells them about his journey from the island where he has a workshop, and he and Anastasia have a house. It had taken him a day longer than planned to get here because the ferry had broken down in one of the ports.

'It is very beautiful on the island right now. You must come,' he tells them. Ana has to listen closely; he speaks English more slowly than Anastasia does, but with an accent twice as heavy. 'The beach is right there in front of the house and the water is really very perfect for swimming.'

'Hey, don't tempt away my workers, Vasilis,' Anastasia says. 'But seriously,' she turns to them, 'Dimitri, you know this already, but Ana, you too: both of you are welcome any time.'

In the late afternoon they sit at the table out on the terrace. The dig house changes character on the weekends, with most of the archaeologists heading down to Thessaloniki for a break.

'So is she still forcing you to poke around in the dirt for broken pots when you could have any of the new ones I am making?' says Vasilis, as Dimitri passes him a beer.

'Actually, at the rate he destroys his work, his pots are not too different from the ones we're digging up,' Anastasia says.

'Quality control,' he says with a laugh. 'I should make a donation of all my fragments to the cause.'

Vasilis explains how, long ago, he'd studied with a Japanese ceramicist who, at the end of the year, announced a special exercise: that they were to destroy all the objects they had made.

'The thought of it was devastating,' Vasilis says. 'Smashing up things for which we felt a little proud. But in a strange way, once we'd done it, we felt – how do you say? – liberation. His idea was to be teaching us humility. He wanted us to be seeking perfection, but not to be caring so much about material things.'

'Even though you were trying to perfect material things,' Ana says.

'How can I explain?' Vasilis says. 'He wanted us to take the lessons he taught us deeply inside of us, and not to stop with the objects we had made. And perhaps he was also wanting to teach us, in such a way like this, that nothing lasts. No matter how beautiful it is.'

'At least nothing but the debris and the ruins,' says Anastasia. 'Fortunately for archaeology.'

'I don't know if I could do that,' says Ana. 'It seems like such a brutal way to learn.'

'Perhaps that's the point,' says Dimitri. 'That story reminds me of something one of the diggers told me last year . . . You remember Niko, Anastasia? He'd just finished his military service.'

Dimitri is sitting sideways, his bare feet propped on the rung of Ana's chair. Ana thinks in an absent way how tanned and square they are, how much she likes their shape.

'Yes, of course,' says Anastasia. 'I invited him back, but he'd lined up some job in the islands this year.'

'Well, he had this grisly story about a military academy, some place in America,' Dimitri says. 'They made the cadets who were training there adopt an animal for a pet. It could be any animal they wanted – a kitten or a puppy, a hamster, anything. They had to look after it for a year, and at the end of it, all of a sudden, they were ordered to kill it. In any way they chose.'

Ana recoils. 'That's horrible,' she says.

'The idea was to toughen them up for the deeds of war.'

'My father's in the military and I've never heard of that sort of thing,' Ana says. 'Can you imagine what that would do to you?'

'I guess that's why,' he says.

'Yes, but you'd stop being human.'

'I'm not saying your dad is like that. But what do we civilians know? Maybe soldiers have to know they can do that sort of thing if they want that sort of career.'

'Or maybe such a career is attracting people who already know they can do it,' says Vasilis. 'Certain types of personality . . . But in any case, I think that story's apocryphal.'

'What makes you say that?' says Dimitri.

'In Japan I heard something nearly the same. We were talking one time about the military tradition of *seppuku*, and then somebody mentioned the same story as you told, only it was in the country of Saudi Arabia. I think it's one of those myths that endures a lot because they are possibly so believable. But to say frankly, I can't imagine military academies having much room for pets. Animals, they are too anarchic. As well, they try to escape.'

As he speaks, a memory suddenly wells up in Ana's mind: fur like graphite mink, oversize violet eyes. The kamikaze kitten that her father once brought home for her, in spite of her mother's allergy to cats. The kitten she had adored with the full force of her eight-year-old's heart, the kitten that had suddenly disappeared.

'Ana, stop your wailing. These things happen in order to toughen us,' her father had growled, his anger halting her in her stride. He had never spoken to her like that before, never threatened her before with his hand. Weakness, she was learning now, was what he hated most in life; she must never cry, never show distress.

Anastasia puts down her glass. 'What a grim discussion for so glorious an evening,' she says. 'I'm going to make some mint tea, if anyone wants some. We've got a whole lot of it growing outside.'

'I'll go,' says Ana, jumping up.

She feels disturbed by the turn of the conversation, all this talk about the destruction of living things. She wants to stand in quietness for a moment, by the laurel tree in the stillness of the herb garden, breathing in the pungent scent of leaves.

After dinner they stay up late, finishing a bottle of wine that Vasilis remembered he had left in the boot of his car. There is a picture of a Santorini fresco on the label: renditions of lilies on a Minoan wall preserved for three millennia under ash.

They update Vasilis on the dig-house gossip, and how the museum is shaping up. Anastasia and Dimitri argue back and forth over who must have occupied one of the tombs. Though they are speaking English for her sake, Ana drifts in and out of their arguments until they agree to a truce.

The grapevine casts odd shadows over their faces in the light from an upstairs window; it is still hot enough to sit out in short sleeves. Above the trellis, over the brow of the hill, a shooting star darts and expires.

Dimitri sees it too, his eyes afire from all the sparring.

'This is the best time of year for spotting them,' he says. 'In fact, there's a great place for watching them back up the hill, if anyone's in the mood for a walk.'

Vasilis and Anastasia decide to turn in, but Dimitri is already reaching for a flashlight and struggling with the blankets that are tumbling out of the cupboard in the hall.

Though he never specifically asked her, and she never really responded, Ana, who is wide-awake and restless, has been drawn into his orbit and is following as a matter of course.

'You'll need proper shoes for the shortcut,' he tells her in the hallway. 'We'll go along the road for some of the way, but for the rest, it's just a rough track.'

She goes upstairs to find a sweater, and jimmies her feet into her boots. Puffs of dust erupt like tiny smoke signals as she yanks the laces tight.

The night is still outside the dig house and the jasmine wall exhales its force field of scent. In the yard, the Persian silk tree strokes the air with its tassels while the angel's trumpets, unscrolling whitely in the darkness, calibrate their radar to the sky.

Serenaded by insomniac dogs, they crunch down the drive and along the road that is white in the airless night. Ana switches on the flashlight when they reach the path, which veers off at an angle into the scrub.

Blackberries snatch at the blankets Dimitri is carrying over his shoulder. Roses shake their rosehips at them like the knuckles of cranky old men.

Ahead of them on the hillside, a pair of symmetrical pine trees stands like a folded cut-out against the sky. The moon when it finally rises is a fingernail sliver above them, which Dimitri says is perfect since it won't outshine the stars.

'That was a blue moon we had at the end of July, old Ioannis tells me,' he says. 'Hard to believe there's been three full moons since June.'

'Why do they call it "blue"?' Ana says. 'In Spanish we say the same thing.'

He shrugs. 'It's probably one of those expressions that have been around so long that nobody remembers any more.'

'Like living in a village called Palatitsia without realising there was once a palace up on the hill.'

He smiles. 'That's pretty much it,' he says.

'It's strange, though, isn't it,' she says, 'how we're always losing our connections to the origins of things.'

'Which I suppose is why we're up here digging. To try to get some of them back.'

They walk single-file along the path that follows the contour of the hill, then rises steeply towards its crest. Near the top she stumbles and he throws out a hand to steady her; she sees the muscles in his forearm flex as he grasps her arm for a second before letting it go.

Where the path widens they walk side by side, making it easier to talk. He asks her about Argentina, and how it happened that a girl from the *pampas* had landed in northern Greece. She protests that she's not a *gaucha* but a city girl, even if she's not too bad at riding. She tells him about her life in Buenos Aires, about a trip she once made to a cave in Patagonia, about the awe that she sometimes feels around ancient things.

'I've felt that too,' he says, and Ana shoots him a glance, not sure if he is mocking her again.

He stops walking. The moon slips higher, thin as a paper crease. Yet his eyes seem to pick up the light from somewhere; she catches their shine in the dark.

'The first time we opened a grave it was overwhelming,' he tells her, and she realises he isn't teasing after all. 'It was an Iron-Age one . . . you know, those enormous jar graves, where they placed the whole body inside. You could see the drinking cups, the earthenware pots laid out in a row by the family, the necklaces that had disintegrated into lines of beads.'

The air is motionless; a moth crashes into his side and flutters away.

'I wasn't prepared for it, for that sense,' he searches for the word, 'of intimacy. It was very humbling, like glimpsing the truth of something that's small and private, tender even, but at the same time immense and profound.'

He looks at her, earnest and then self-conscious at his earnestness, then shakes the hair out of his eyes. 'That must sound a bit crazy,' he says.

'No,' she says. 'I'd love to see something like that.' She has never even seen a tomb being opened but she can imagine it; she thinks she understands.

'It just gives you perspective on things,' he says. 'Maybe it's obvious, I don't know. It was as if I'd suddenly understood some fundamental fact about being human. That this is what we do, what each generation does for the one that goes before it – this need we have to lay the dead to rest.'

She nods. She remembers the funeral they'd had for her Polish grandmother; how her mother had wept, though it wasn't *her* mother who had passed away; how her father had managed to get through the day dry-eyed.

Dimitri follows her where the path turns level, chatting as they walk. He tells her he is half English and was born in London, but that all the summers of his childhood were spent in Greece. He tells her he has two brothers and a sister, that he is the eldest child. He tells her that his mother's family had had to move to England during the time of the Colonels, and that's where his parents met.

'What colonels?' Ana says.

'You know, the dictatorship. Back in the sixties.'

Ana is silent. She wonders if their dictatorship was anything like Argentina's, if there'd been terrorists and subversives here, too.

'What about your family? Do you have brothers and sisters?' he says.

She shakes her head. 'There's only me,' she says.

'So how did your parents get together?'

It takes her a moment to recall their story: the military connections in her mother's family, her father introduced to her mother by a mutual friend.

'It must have been weird growing up in a military family . . .' he says.

'Do you think so? I don't have much to compare it with.'

'Well, they must have been pretty strict with you as a kid.'

'I don't know – they didn't send me on forced marches or anything,' she says with a laugh. 'But I suppose they were strict in some ways. Convent school. Plenty of nuns, not a lot of discos. If I went to a party they had to talk to the parents first, and my father always picked me up at ten.'

'At ten! Didn't that drive you mad as a teenager?'

She shrugs. 'Perhaps it should have. But as an only child I was always pretty close to them. At one point I nearly lost my father in an accident – his car ended up wrapped around a tree after some guy sped into him at an intersection – and for whole chunks of my childhood my mother was pretty unwell. I never wanted to do anything to upset them, and, especially when I was smaller, I was always wanting my father to be proud.'

Dimitri takes that in. 'And I suppose they are pretty conservative – church, politics and all that,' he says.

'Church – that was mainly when I was younger, though we still had plenty of it at school. As for politics, my father doesn't believe in all that human rights stuff, if that's what you mean – not after what the terrorists tried to do.'

'Which terrorists?'

'You know, the ones who tried to turn Argentina over to the communists. Like Che Guevara in Cuba – he was an

Argentine, you know. In the seventies and eighties there were subversives like him all over Argentina, hidden within the general population. My father was on the side of rooting them out.'

'So he's a bit of a hero, your dad.' He says it neutrally, sending her a sideways glance.

'I've always looked up to him, I suppose.'

'And what about you, what do you think?' he says.

'About what?'

'About politics.'

'Well, I'm not all that political. But of course I'm against things like Communism and Socialism. And though I don't like everything about Menem, I admire him for pardoning the generals after the dictatorship, instead of punishing them for doing their job.'

There is a crumbling wall and they scramble over it, careful on the wobbling stones. Dimitri gives her his hand and changes the subject when they land on the other side.

'It's odd, it's as if for half of my childhood I didn't really have a mother,' says Ana when Dimitri asks her what she is like. 'When I was small we used to do things together – silly things, like painting our toenails and looking at magazines, and sometimes she'd plait my hair. Then – it's as if there were a gap for quite a few years.'

'A gap?'

'Until my father's accident. I mean, my mother was around all that time, of course, but she spent weeks on end in bed. Then, one day soon after his car crash, she seemed to just snap out of it. He took ages recovering in hospital, so it was just her and me, and we grew a lot closer then.'

'How old were you at the time?'

'Oh, about fourteen. It began when my mother was given some tickets to the opera, so we went to see *Madama Butterfly*.

Then on Sundays we started going to movie matinees – we went quite a lot . . . I began to understand her a little bit more.'

'Understand her?'

'You know, why she was always so unwell . . . I started thinking. Once, when I was about ten, we were working in the garden, and she came out with this extraordinary thing.' Ana pauses. 'She said that I'd had an elder brother. That he'd arrived prematurely and had died shortly after he was born.'

'They'd never told you before?'

Ana shakes her head. 'I don't suppose they had any reason to. But it rocked me, somehow, as if they'd been keeping some big secret from me. I suppose after bugging them for so long about wanting a little sister, I'd grown used to thinking of myself as the only one.'

They'd stopped walking so he could hear her finish her story.

'Are there secrets in your family?' she says, looking up at him.

'If there are, then I don't know them – which doesn't mean there aren't any – just that they're very well kept.'

'Which I suppose is the whole point of secrets,' she says.

'Except that eventually they tend to slip out.'

She trips on a rock but catches herself, and where the path narrows they continue in Indian file.

'So why are you called Dimitri?' she says. 'Are you named after anybody in particular?'

'My grandfather, as it happens, though I never knew him. He died in the war.'

'I'm sorry,' Ana says.

He nods. 'What about you?' he adds after a moment. 'Is Ana a big family name?'

'Actually it's Ana Lucia,' she says, 'but nobody calls me that. In fact, when I was small I wanted to be called Liliana – and don't ask me where that idea came from – it's not as if we knew anyone by that name. Apparently I kept insisting, but people kept forgetting, so that finally when I was given a baby doll, I gave her the name instead.'

He holds back a spiny bush to help her get past.

'And how did you learn to speak such good English?' he says.

'It's not *that* good – I'm making mistakes all the time,' she says. 'But in my school we started English early and I really loved it. Then later I had a great teacher, one of the nuns in fact, who lent me books – you know, poetry and things.'

Feet luminous with dust, they scramble through the last of the bushes and emerge on the Aigai road; up ahead is the turn-off to the palace. The way is barred by a padlocked gate to which Dimitri produces a key.

Ana stares as he inserts it into the lock.

'Where did you get that?' she says.

'Connections,' he says. 'Follow me.'

He hitches open the gate for them to slip through, then pulls it shut behind them, leaving the padlock swinging on its chain.

Arm aloft like a scorpion, an earthmover is parked on one edge of the site. A giant elm overlooks the sleeping valley; at its foot, hessian bags for topsoil lie folded in stacks. Beyond the tree, looming out of the darkness, she sees the hull of the workshop where the archaeologists clean and record their finds.

'Over here,' says Dimitri. She turns and sees him leaning over a sheet of corrugated iron. 'Can you grab the other end?'

They drop it to one side with a violent clattering, then shift a second and a third. Beneath them, protected from the weather, Ana sees something mysterious, a square surrounding a circle that is marked by an elaborate border, and within it, a swirling design. She squats down to touch the surface. As fine as any painting, it's a mosaic created from tens of thousands of minute river stones.

Dimitri shines his flashlight towards the perimeter. In a wedge of colour, lotus blooms protrude from leaves and tendrils; an eight-petalled flower radiates from the centre with stamens picked out in slender lines.

The lamplight plays into the corners. In each, there is an ethereal figure that Ana cannot initially make out. She looks closer, sees a flower that opens like a lily and then transforms itself into a woman, her robes tapering off in a flourish of elaborate scrolls.

'It's beautiful,' she says, looking at the pearl-grey folds of clothing, the coral of her mouth and skirt.

'I thought you'd like it,' Dimitri says, treading on an acanthus flower.

'You can't walk on it!' she says.

'Why not?' he says. 'It's a floor!'

She stares at him.

'Don't worry, we won't damage it. They've removed the plastic sheeting because the restoration is finished – every last pebble is locked in place.'

Already he is covering the central motif with the blankets. Tendrils escape from under them like waves from beneath a raft.

She steps gingerly onto a vine.

'You see,' he says. 'It's safe.'

Cross-legged on the blanket, she feels the curve of the stones under the palm of her hand and is surprised to discover they're still warm.

Dimitri stretches out beside her and stares up at the blue-black sky.

'Can you believe this was the largest building ever constructed in Classical Greece?' he says. 'It once had two storeys of colonnades; it was bigger than the Parthenon itself.'

She gives him a sceptical look.

'It's true!' he says. 'You'd have been able to see it for miles. Maybe even from the sea – it's receded now, but the Aegean was a whole lot closer in those days.'

'People will try to overdo the neighbours,' Ana says.

'Outdo,' he says with a smile. 'You're not wrong about that. Old Philip got the palace completed for his daughter's wedding so he could impress all the foreign dignitaries he'd invited. Only then he got bumped off, at dawn down there in the theatre, in front of all his guests.'

'And – don't tell me: the wedding ceremony turned into a funeral ceremony, and then into a coronation ceremony, and the rest is inside the Great Tumulus.'

'Okay, okay,' he says, laughing. 'I know I go on too much. Sometimes I can't help it – I just love this place so much.'

Ana stretches out beside him on the blankets on the palace floor. She lies among the flowers that Philip's household must have gazed upon; stares up at what must be the same stars.

'What do you think they used this room for?' she says.

'Banquets. It was one of the king's dining halls, apparently. I bet he brought everyone in to show it off.'

'He sounds a bit flashy, this Philip,' Ana says.

'I know – but what do you expect from a king?'

The palace is on a plateau halfway up the hillside and the night unfolds above them, and falls away before them, across the plain to the out-of-sight sea. They lie with their dusty feet towards the mountain, facing away from the lights of the valley, and wait for the shooting stars.

'Do we get to make a wish?' she says.

Warm in the windless night, Dimitri has rolled up his sweater and offers it to her now for a pillow. She takes it, conscious of how close he is in the shadow, his skin like some velvety substance against the pallor of his T-shirt in dark.

'Not until you've seen three of them,' he says.

'I'm up to two already – I saw two of them back at the house.'

Another light streaks across the startled sky.

'Hey – no cheating,' he says. 'Sputniks and satellites don't count.'

'It wasn't an Esputnik,' she protests.

'Say "Sputnik" again,' he says, but she screws up her nose instead.

They amuse themselves trying to identify the constellations, Dimitri making her laugh with his made-up names.

Low on the horizon, a light flares and soars and is extinguished. Like a needle, another threads the stars along its arc. Then another, and another, some brighter, some mere pinpricks that scratch the sky's glass dome for less than a heartbeat before vanishing into the infinite dark.

'What makes a shooting star shoot anyway?' she says.

'Like all stars, the prospect of an audience, wouldn't you say?'

'All these attention-seekers,' she says. 'I think I might go for a walk.'

She raises her legs so that her clumpy boots are silhouetted against the sky.

'Hey, wait for me,' he says, sticking his legs up parallel to hers.

'Hurry up, then,' she says, then after a second: 'Actually, I feel a bit dizzy up here.'

'Just don't look down. Keep your eye on the horizon. Like on a boat.'

'Why, are we going somewhere?' she says.

'We're there already: the Celestial Disco. Care for a twirl?'

They try it for a bit but the music is lousy – too many wind chimes and bells.

'Let's get out of this dive,' Dimitri says. 'There's got to be a tango club nearby.'

'You dance tango?' she says.

'Of course not,' he says. 'I'm English. I thought you were the Argentine.'

'I've never taken a tango lesson in my life.'

'You mean you don't have a licence? I don't think my insurance will cover me . . .'

'Then I'm afraid you'll just have to wing it,' she says, giving an airborne side-kick with her heel.

'Steady on, I'm only a beginner,' he says.

'Then watch you don't step on my toes.'

She can feel the warmth of his skin where the hairs on their arms are touching; she is still laughing when he takes her by the hand.

His fingers are wider than hers and the skin on them is roughened from the dig. She remembers his calluses from the day they met, when he introduced himself in the dimness of the upstairs hall.

She leaves her hand in his, allowing it, wanting it, but knowing she cannot divide herself, nor hold at bay a growing sense of contradiction she has been trying to pretend isn't there.

She will have to tell him; she should have already told him; she is delaying the moment she has to tell him that someone is waiting for her back home.

The Persian silk tree casts odd shadows down the driveway from the single lamp illuminating the veranda, and the scent of jasmine carries faintly on the summer air. Things have changed subtly between them by the time they stumble past the damaged fig trees, and crunch up the drive and around the back of the house to the door with its ear-splitting creak.

Dimitri is whispering to her in the hallway. The cavernous house is silent, the entire world asleep.

She has told him about Lucas on the long walk back but it's as if he hasn't heard or doesn't care.

'We only have one life, Ana.' He is leaning over her outside her doorway, one elbow propped against the wall. 'We have this time, this moment. We do not always get another chance.'

Everything in her is aware of him: the warmth of his body; the scent of him, of dust and sweat and cotton that has softened after drying in the sun.

She isn't good at this. She feels loyal to Lucas and wretched about it; she feels too torn to act upon her feelings; cannot decide what she will regret more later on.

Yet Dimitri has unsettled her. She is not the sort of person who breaks her promises, she reminds herself; she had given her word to Lucas and meant to honour it; she'd been brought up never to waver when she should be loyal.

Dimitri waits as she struggles with her confusion, her wanting and her sense of duty, her unreadiness to act.

'Ana,' he says, then pulls her towards him in a hug. She rests her weight against him, her head against the hardness of his chest.

And after a moment she realises something that before she hadn't sensed about him: that he would wait for her, that he would wait all the time that she needed, that he would wait for her for as long as it would take.

She lets him kiss her, just once, on the threshold of the room that still feels to her, like the bed in which she is sleeping, like the view over the valley from her window, as if it is all in some way really his.

At breakfast, when she comes downstairs for coffee in the watercolour morning, there are shadows around her eyes. She smiles at him, and hopes he cannot tell she hasn't slept.

10

Mexico City
November 1998

Blink blink blink.

The night is dark and the street outside is silent.

It is a nondescript hour on the wrong side of midnight in Mexico City, when the last *mariachis* are trudging home and the first shift-workers are struggling into the day.

If there are to be burglaries tonight and crimes of passion, they've been committed. If the dance floors of the *salóns* have promised romance, it's all been found. It's a lost hour when the clocks have slowed and time is fluid; when shapes are shifting and no one can be quite certain that they've seen what they've seen.

It's the hour of truth and the hour of reckoning. It's the hour when luck is decided or luck runs out.

Blink blink blink.

Behind the door of a study in a second-floor apartment, its view obscured by the branches of a spreading jacaranda, the small red light on a fax machine is winking. It's not an hour for sending or receiving faxes – unless they come by error, or from another time zone, or bring in information that cannot wait.

Daniela finds the coversheet in the fax tray the next morning, with the law firm's crest at the top of it and Teodoro's corkscrew initials halfway down. Page one of three, it says, and she lifts it out and turns it over, but only a single page of it has arrived.

It seems strange to her, because this machine has always printed backwards – its 'special feature,' the salesman said, was to finish with the coversheet on top. She opens the paper feeder to see if anything is concertinaed in its entrails, then flips it shut and gives it a thump in case something is stuck in its craw.

When nothing happens she glances around the office; no sheets of paper have strayed onto the table or floor. She shrugs, and tosses the coversheet onto the pile for recycling, telling herself that it must have been sent by mistake.

She is logging into her computer when from the corner of her eye she sees it: one, no, two sheets of paper that have glided half under the couch. She bends down to retrieve them, then steps into the light to read them. She needs only to skim the first line.

'Osvaldo!' she cries, dropping everything, bursting into the living room, spinning around, remembering, then leaning as far as possible through the window overlooking the street.

'Osvaldo!' she shouts at the top of her lungs, not caring who else in the neighbourhood might hear. 'Osvaldo! Osvaldo! Come back!'

Buenos Aires, 21 Nov. 1998

Est. Teodoro Bonifaccio,

I am writing this letter to you, in confidence, in response to a notice I stumbled across some months ago inviting anyone with certain information to get in touch.

What I am about to tell you has been weighing on me since January, when quite by chance I saw your ad in El Clarín. It brought to mind an incident that took place many years ago, perhaps fourteen if my memory serves me, and which troubled me not a little at the time. I had forgotten all about it in the interim – until I came across your advertisement, so I cut it out to think about what to do. Unfortunately, events in my own family diverted my attention, but it is those same events that are prompting me now to write.

What I read in the paper was an appeal for help in finding a missing person. It concerned a girl born in 1977, and it mentioned the presence of some distinguishing marks located behind one of her ears.

Back in the 1980s, my husband and I lived next door to a couple whose little girl used to climb the fence to come over and play with our boys. One day – I remember it quite vividly because of the scare it gave us – the kids were messing around in the swimming pool, smacking the waves with paddles while stirring up a whirlpool, when the girl was injured by a blow to her head.

The wound was bleeding quite profusely when my husband – who God be thanked was passing and saw the accident happen – fished her out and brought her inside. We propped her up at the kitchen table, and I fetched a bottle of Mercurochrome and a bag of cotton-wool balls. When the bleeding stopped, I was relieved to see that the cut was not a deep one, but as I twisted back her hair to dress it, I remember getting a bit of a shock.

Behind her right ear was a set of marks exactly like the ones you describe. They looked to me like scars in the form of crosses, dark pink and raised a little – and as the mother of boys, I am familiar with how scar tissue looks. When I remarked on it, however, the girl – who was still a little groggy – said it was simply a birthmark, which struck me initially as strange. Then I wondered whether she might have been a forceps delivery, and for some reason needed stitches, and might indeed have been marked like that at birth.

Still, something left me uneasy, and I was tempted to raise the question with her mother. Her father, however, was some big shot in the military, and when I mentioned it to my husband he cautioned me against it, saying it would be more prudent not to get involved. This would have been early 1985 and the girl – her name was Ana – would have been about seven or eight years old at the time – an age not incompatible with that of the person you seek. After that we saw her a lot less frequently. Her parents were very protective, and I suspect that after this incident they ordered her to stay away. She was a sweet girl, however, and when she got a little older, she'd sometimes drop by after school to say hello.

FAX: Page 3 / 3

Her mother, Bettina, who was often unwell, had a thing about cultivating roses. I seem to remember she was into grafting – from time to time, if she was home alone, she would point out her successes over the fence.

They were an odd couple in many ways. Victor was a singularly intense person, and though Ana completely doted on him, I never saw them together much as a family, and personally, I never felt *comfortable when he was around. He ran some odd kind of antiques business besides his military position – Bettina said it was a project for when he retired. All I can say is that he was well prepared, because he started it way back under the Junta. Ana often accompanied him there on Saturdays, and somehow he kept it going even after his car crash, which incapacitated him for the best part of a year.*

Around the time Ana turned sixteen, the family moved to a military apartment downtown. Ana came around to say goodbye to me and Paco – he's my eldest – and Bettina left a forwarding address in case we got stuck with their mail. She also gave me their phone number – because of her husband's position, she said, their details were never listed in the directory. I still have the slip of paper, which I actually found this morning, curled up in the paper-clip jar.

I must stress that I cannot be sure that this is the girl you are looking for, but I am including the contact details Bettina gave me should you wish to follow up.

Late though it may seem, I'm writing to you now because, earlier this year, Paco was involved in a motorbike accident. Sitting beside him in the hospital with his body encased in plaster and cross-stitches above his eyebrow, I suddenly remembered Ana's markings, and how uncomfortable they'd made me feel. And because we'd come so close to it, and I'd had plenty of time to consider it during my vigil at his bedside, I began to get some inkling of what it might mean to lose a child.

I know nothing more of Ana's family circumstances, though Bettina once confided that she couldn't have children when I asked if she was planning any more. It never occurred to me to ask whether Ana had been adopted. Perhaps after all she was not.

But if she were, and if your client is looking for a child who grew up with markings as odd as these ones, then perhaps this information will help.

As I mentioned, I would be grateful if you would keep this letter confidential. I am, however, including a card with my telephone number should you wish to discuss it further. You will find Ana, Bettina and Victor Bielka's details on the back.

Yours sincerely,

Adriana Martín
Encl.

11

Buenos Aires
December 1998

A gossamer rain is falling over the night-time garden, invisible until it is caught in the kitchen light. Constanza doesn't notice until she feels it on her face; when she goes indoors to find a coat, thousands of tiny beads of it sequin her silver hair.

There is a twinge in her back that she's rubbing as she returns to the bottom of the garden. She has untangled the floppy tape measure from the reels in her sewing basket, and she aligns the metal end of it against one of her overgrown walls. With the rubber tip of her walking stick she nudges a rock to hold it, then unrolls it into the middle of the lawn. It lies there like a strip of barrier tape delineating the scene of a crime.

Pinpointing the spot with a clothes peg that she'd found on the kitchen table, she pulls the tape measure in again, then lays it out in roughly a perpendicular line. She makes allowances for the agapanthus that luxuriates in her flowerbeds, and measures the distance carefully between the peg and the perimeter fence.

She adjusts the peg's position, then double-checks the coordinates against the ones in the back of her atlas, adjusting till she feels the distances are right.

Then, in a part of the lawn not far from the pomegranate tree, she tosses down her gardening cushion and lowers herself gently onto it, steadying herself with the back of her outdoor chair.

Beside her, she lays out her instruments: a pocket lamp, a knitting needle and a trowel.

The needle she uses to probe the soil around the peg the way she'd test a cake to see if it's done. She is breathing a little too heavily, and her arthritic knees are hurting, and she begins to worry when she fails to strike anything hard. She stops and reconsiders, then starts again, but this time more methodically, stabbing the number eight needle in north–south, east–west lines.

Suddenly she meets resistance; the needle buckles and nearly breaks. Withdrawing it, she then uses it to feel her way around the obstruction. Then she picks up the trowel in her good hand and begins to saw a circle into the soil.

The grass roots are denser than she remembers so the going is tough and her grip slips off the handle several times. She jars her wrist and curses, and bites her lip as she waits for the throbbing to subside. She should have worn her gardening gloves, she thinks to herself, but she is not about to go hunting for them now.

Finally, the patch of turf comes free and she shifts it sideways. She shines the torch inside the hole, startling a millipede that uncoils itself and dives into a forest of roots.

Again she prods with the needle, then takes the trowel and digs deeper, quickening to the sound of metal scraping on tin. Carefully now, she works about the circumference, surprised how deeply they'd dug the first time around. Then, wedging the trowel beneath it, she levers the container to the surface till it pops out of the soil and rolls onto the grass by her knees.

In the drizzle that is starting to fall more heavily, Constanza stares as if astonished to have found anything there. Fingernails muddied by the digging, she wipes the dirt off the outside of the jar and shines the flashlight into it, then holds it up to the light of the house.

The glass is opalescent with the curiosity of subterranean creatures that have nuzzled it in the dark and gone around. The metal lid has rusted but not rotted and, as far as she can tell without her glasses, the jar is free from condensation on the inside.

She brushes the earth back into its hole and pats the puck of turf back into place. Slowly, mindful of her knees, she leans on the chair and winces as she eases herself to her feet. She slips the jar into her apron pocket where it clinks against the tape measure and the peg.

Her back twinges again so she rubs a little warmth into it, and stretches a little, then reaches for her stick. She replaces the trowel on the outside table and, chuckling now, takes the flashlight and the old glass jar indoors.

She has only to prise it open, but that proves harder than she'd thought. She bites her lip and says *ffffffffff* as she concentrates, and inserts her bluntest knife blade under the lid. She takes a towel and covers it and tries to twist it open, but the rusted metal sends bolts of pain ratcheting up through her wrist.

When the ache subsides, she boils the kettle and tries to steam it open, but even then the container will not give. She considers wrapping it in a cloth and looking for her hammer but is nervous about splinters of glass.

Constanza sits for a moment to catch her breath, and rubs her wrist, waiting for the strength to return. And while she sits, beside the coffee cups hanging from their double row of pegs above the table, she calculates – eighteen years it must be, eighteen years under the garden lawn, eighteen years to rust.

Finally she decides to re-boil the kettle and pour some more hot water over the lid. She lays a damp cloth over it, inhales sharply, and twists with every fibre of her strength. Pain sears her tendons and tears through the inflammation in her joints, but the jar falls suddenly open in her hands.

She exhales slowly, chasing away the burn of it, then smiles in triumph when at last she opens her eyes. She squeezes her wrist and elbow, massages the pressure points in her shoulder, and shakes out the tension in her hands.

The scrolls of paper are still wrapped in their plastic bags, and she extracts them. Suddenly it comes back to her: the day – sometime after that episode at the kindergarten – that she and Yolanda had sat at this same table wrapping each item in baking paper before sealing them in a gherkin jar.

Now she discards the external layers encasing the individual scrolls. With trembling hands she braces for disappointment: for pages glued together, or gnawed to lace, or decomposed into dust.

But when she peels them open, the pages curling back on themselves like wood shavings, she finds each one intact.

Folded, faded, but still legible, the documents they got from the kindergarten are all in there – copies of the enrolment form, two sets of medical data, and the birth certificate, signed beneath a military stamp.

Constanza peers at the signature now, bringing it close to her glasses under the light. This time, it looks familiar. She has seen it on other certificates belonging to other children that the Grandmothers had had questions about.

And there are other things. A paper pouch with a single strip of negatives. Photographs, three of them, in black and white, one blurred but two quite sharp. They are the photographs Yolanda had taken outside that kindergarten, of a little girl who had raised her arms to show her the paint on her hands.

Constanza stops sifting through the documents. She removes her glasses and rubs her eyes and thinks about her friend. She remembers how anxious she'd seemed as she approached them, after the march in the Plaza de Mayo, the very first time they'd met. She remembers the look on Yolanda's face when she'd shown her the marbles in her bag. She remembers the clack of Yolanda's needles as they criss-crossed Buenos Aires in *collectivos*, how she always seemed to be knitting something new.

And she remembers the terrible day she came across her, motionless and crumpled on the stairs.

Constanza sits there awhile in the stillness, missing her and remembering her, knowing that she was doing this for all of them, that any child found was found for all of them, but that especially she was doing it for her friend.

Then she shakes herself. She shakes off her longing for her own still-missing daughter and her grandson, and takes herself back to her task.

She flattens out the birth certificate and the enrolment form and the medical information, pinning them down with the sugar bowl and the pepper grinder and the coffee cups she takes down from their pegs.

And beside them she lays out the fax that Osvaldo has sent her, a letter written by a woman called Adriana Martín.

Constanza's faded cornflower eyes go back and forth behind her glasses. She examines the documents again and again to make sure.

Ana Lucia. Bettina. Victor Losada Bielka.

The names match up. All the names are the same.

So Yolanda had found her. She had photographed her missing daughter's girl.

Constanza stops and cautions herself: they have known disappointment before. We cannot know beyond a doubt, she reminds herself. We cannot be certain of anything until she has done a DNA test.

Still, it all adds up, she thinks. The tiny crosses that the midwife described to Osvaldo. The names on the kindergarten papers. And at last, the thing that links them: the letter from Adriana Martín.

She is ready to soar from the rooftops. She has to call Osvaldo in Mexico City. She wants to illuminate the metropolis and turn on all its fountains and dance all night in the rain.

But she sits at the kitchen table a moment longer, under the old-fashioned clock with its easy-to-read face and the empty spaces where she has removed her cups from the wall.

Yolanda had found her granddaughter. All those years ago she had found her and was never to know.

Constanza rubs her knees where they are aching from all that kneeling in the garden, then reaches for the phone.

PART V

THE HERACLES CROWN

June–September, 1999

Athens

Late June 1999

Lights. Passenger announcements. Words that look like algebra on newspapers, on electronic screens. You want taxi? We buy dollars! You speak English? German? Swedish? Overpasses. Underpasses. Revolving turrets of sunglasses. The sun. The blinding light. The barren land.

She squints into the heat haze and hoists her scarlet raincoat over her shoulder. Behind her, jets descend or clamber into the sky.

There are trains, somewhere. She is working from memory. She remembers, she thinks she remembers the way.

At the end of the train line, a port, and a tide-surge of people. A shipping office in an air-conditioned building that shocks after the diesel-choked heat. Morning ferries, night boats, flying dolphins. A ticket for dawn and a grimy hotel in the crook of an oily street.

She is coming apart. What felt whole is now fragmenting. She can find no foothold, nothing solid to grasp.

The Aegean
Late June 1999

Vasilis looks up at the sound of the gate, his wet hands gloved in clay.

A woman, the figure of a woman, is moving towards him. He notices first that her clothes are all wrong for the weather; absurdly, she is carrying a raincoat, and limping on a broken heel. If it weren't so far, he'd swear she had crossed the entire island in a pair of unwalkable shoes.

The late-afternoon light has turned the bushes golden; her shadow is as lean as the tallest ones as she stumbles down the path.

He rises from the wheel that continues to spin without him and moves towards her. Puzzled, he looks again, thinks he recognises her face.

'Ana?' he says.

He catches her by the shoulders with the inside of his wrists, his palms turned outwards like wings.

~~~~

The summer house has no hot water so Anastasia heats some in a cauldron on the stove. She mixes it into the bath, then tests it with her elbow the way she would do for a child.

There are towels on a stool and soap in a dish that is glazed the colour of Japanese jade.

She makes sure Ana has what she needs, then leaves her, and returns with a small pile of clothes.

'I hope these fit,' she says, shaking out a nightdress, a swimsuit left behind by a long-ago visitor, a plain and a patterned shift dress, a scarf.

Anastasia hides her surprise at how much Ana has changed. Two years ago she was full of vitality, and on the cusp of life.

Ana looks at her but cannot bring herself to speak.

She has never been to the island but she remembers the name from Vasilis's stories, and from the postcard Anastasia sent from their summer break. She still had it in the bottom of her handbag when she threw herself into the taxi in her street.

In the port she asked directions at a taverna. Click-clicking worry beads, an old man with a wind-hollowed face showed her on a map on the wall.

Anastasia gives her a sachet of something that fizzes furiously in a glass of water. She tells Ana it will help her get to sleep.

She wakes in the night and turns, confused by her dreams, unsure whether she isn't still asleep. She lifts her head, searching for something familiar: the glimmer of a lamp, a rod of light under a door. All that comes to her is a paler square of darkness, a window hovering at some indeterminate distance like a painting suspended in mid-air.

A car approaches and recedes on a distant roadway; far away a donkey brays, and, nearer, another responds.

The throbbing in her head has subsided but her limbs are aching, still. Her blistered feet are tender and the bed sheets scratch the sunburn on her skin.

She places her hand on the coolness of the wall beside her. From beyond it, expectant as a breath being held, comes only the silence of the motionless sea.

When she stirs again she hears the murmur of voices. She lies there staring at the ceiling. In its whiteness she loses all sense of depth.

She turns again to the wall.

The door moves softly on its hinges and Ana opens her eyes. From the intensity of the light coming in through the window, it might be late afternoon.

Anastasia looks at her, not quite masking her concern.

'What time is it?' Ana says. It's the first time since she got here that she's spoken; her voice is fainter than the breeze.

'It's nearly five. You've slept for three whole days.'

'Is it Thursday?'

'It's Friday today, what's left of it.'

Ana drops back onto the pillow. Everything in the room is white: the walls, the bedding, the cloth over the jug on the table, the curtains with their handmade lacework band.

'It's peaceful here,' she says.

Anastasia considers her for a moment. She wants to ask but sees it is still too soon. Instead, she enquires if Ana is hungry.

Ana's responses come slowly, as if barely accessible to herself.

'No, but thank you,' she says. 'I only want to sleep.'

Anastasia sits on the side of the bed. She is not sure if it's the sleep of exhaustion that Ana is seeking, or sleep of some other kind.

'I thought you might like this,' she says.

Ana elbows herself up against the pillows.

Anastasia watches her as she sips from the cup, then places it on the nightstand by the bed.

'Thank you,' she says. 'For letting me stay.'

'You're welcome here, you know that,' Anastasia says, observing the shadows in Ana's face. She looks bleached against the pillows, even her freckles seem faded, her hair turned hospital-limp. She seems drained of everything, strength, concentration, energy, as if merely standing would be asking too much.

Anastasia places a hand on Ana's forehead and peers into her eyes. They are duller now, not the blue-green they turned that summer on the dig site when the sunshine put colour on her skin.

'Ana, are you all right?' she says.

Ana looks at her as if returning from some great distance.

'I'm just so tired,' she says.

Again she sleeps, tormented by dreams.

Through them, she hears the wind pick up, hears it caressing and then pushing at the pines.

A rooster crows on the edge of her slumber; the rising sea disturbs her, answering the wind.

~~~

'How is she then?'

Anastasia and Vasilis are in the kitchen, their conversation disguised by the running tap.

'Much the same, I think,' says Anastasia.

'But has she said anything?'

'By way of explanation, you mean? No, I'm afraid. Not yet.'

She turns off the tap and sets down a colander of tomatoes, skins the colours of sunset, patched with woody scars.

'It's just the way she got here,' Vasilis says, 'blown in by the wind like that. No luggage. No proper shoes. It's as if . . .'

'. . . I know. I've been thinking it too.'

'Well, what is she running away from? To have shown up halfway across the world without any warning . . .'

Propped against the table, he has his shoulders to the window so that he is framed by the green of the terrace, and beyond that, the blue of the sea.

'It could be anything, Vasilis. I don't think there's any point trying to guess.'

She passes him a cucumber for peeling. The skin flays off in long thin strips that lattice the cutting board in green.

'I just worry that we ought to contact someone,' he continues. 'Does anyone even know she is here?'

Anastasia pauses over the cutting board, and leans on the handle of the knife.

'I was wondering the same thing,' she says. 'Though my instinct is to wait, at least until we learn what's happened . . . She is an adult, after all. It's not as if she's a runaway child.'

Vasilis makes a small green haystack of his peelings, observes the ostrich-leather puckers in their skin.

Alerted by the sound of chopping, a beach kitten pokes its head between the strings of seashells to see what might be available to cadge. Anastasia claps her wet hands sharply and the triangular face withdraws.

She dries her hands and goes over to Vasilis who is now standing with his back to her, slender against the outdoors' turquoise light. A sailboat in the distance clips the crests of the waves.

'She may have come to us for a reason,' Anastasia says softly, weaving her arms beneath his arms and folding her hands across his ribs as he gathers the stray cucumber wheels. 'She'll tell us when she's ready, don't you think?'

She rests her chin on his shoulder.

'Okay,' he says, still worried. 'Let's give her a little more time.'

3

The Aegean
Early July 1999

It is not until the next morning that Ana finally makes her way downstairs.

Vasilis sees her descending the steps from where he is sorting through plums in the kitchen. He sees her brittle ankles, the plasters over her blisters, as she emerges into the light.

She is thin as a heron in her borrowed nightdress, barefoot on the cold grey flagstone floor.

The plums are perched in a colander, or piled up in a tureen; still more are awaiting triage among the pages of last week's news. Vasilis is peering over the half-moons of his glasses, one hinge replaced by a safety pin, selecting which ones should be stewed.

Their skins are such deep purple they've turned blue under their halo of whiteness. The surface resembles frost, he thinks, like the glaze he is trying to perfect.

'Sit down – have some coffee,' he says as if she has always lived there, as if her presence now were an unremarkable thing.

He slides the coffee pot across the stove and pours its contents into a mug.

'Milk?' he says, a tin with triangular perforations poised over the tongues of steam.

She nods and sits on the old wooden chair beside the window. It squeaks on its rickety joints.

Everything about her seems precarious. He tries not to stare but she is translucent almost, porcelain-faced, salt-scoured. He is still adjusting to the new reality of her, trying to reconcile this apparition with the girl he met at Aigai, the one Dimitri fell for, the one who dug up the handle of a vase and thought it was a question mark in the earth.

A narrow cat weaves between her ankles. With its damp nose it kisses her twice on the calf muscle; on stone-cool paws it pads over the tops of her feet. When she lifts it to her knees it retains the form of a parabola long after she releases it, put out at being moved.

'Are you feeling better?' Vasilis says. He wants to ask more, but now that he has the opportunity he feels a sudden reticence, as if he shouldn't intrude.

She nods again, stroking the fur. 'I slept a lot,' she says.

'We noticed,' Vasilis says. 'Anastasia tried to rouse you a couple of times to see if you wanted to eat.'

She looks surprised. 'I didn't hear anything,' she says, wincing as the cat pincushions her thigh. It turns three times in a circle then settles against the crook of her arm.

'He likes you,' Vasilis says. 'Normally they are taking days to decide.'

'He hardly weighs a thing,' she says, fingertips sunk in tabby stripes. A young cat, he is still half-kitten really, all pipe cleaners and sinew and coiled determination to survive.

'You'll have to meet the whole extended family,' Vasilis says. 'Luckily, they are mostly free from parasites, but Anastasia still won't have them being in the house.'

'Should I take him out?'

'Keep him for now. Just don't say I said so,' he says.

Outside, kittens are stalking each other in the bamboo clump or sunning themselves on the pebbles between the pines. Paws tucked into a W, a tortoiseshell cat ignores them from her lookout on top of the hull of an upturned boat.

'So many pets,' Ana says.

'They're not pets, believe me,' Vasilis says. 'They're all blow-ins and vagabonds and strays. Word's gone out that they can treat this place like some sort of animal sanctuary, and so they are coming in. That one with the limp – see that black and white one – one week ago she turned up here and is never letting me out of her sight.'

'Maybe she is just showing her affection,' Ana says.

'I think she thinks I'm her bodyguard. If I walk up the path, she is following me; if I glance at the car, she is leaping into it ahead of me, even though she is terrified of roads. She is riding in the back window while I am driving, and is sitting there while I am doing whatever I am doing in the town, waiting till I am ready to drive her home.'

'So she's your guardian angel,' Ana says. 'Or maybe you are hers.'

'Well, she's picked the wrong person – I'm a very second-rate angel,' Vasilis says. 'It's curious though. She won't let anyone touch her, yet for some reason with me she is not showing fear.'

'What is her name?'

'They don't have names,' he says, with some animation. 'I don't want them to be having the wrong impression.'

'It doesn't seem to have deterred them.'

He laughs. 'You're not wrong about that.'

An old Labrador-cross lies prostrate in the shade of Vasilis's worktable, oblivious to the felines and the occasional wasp.

'What about him?' says Ana, gesturing with a nod. 'Is he a vagabond too?'

'That old fellow? No, he's on holiday. He is living up in the village, but Nikos and Eleni are having to go to Athens for a couple of weeks.' He shrugs. 'What can I do? They bribed me with a mountain of plums.'

One of them rolls off the table like a depth charge and somersaults across the floor. Ana mouths a silent 'Ow' as the tabby awakes and fixes his claws to her thigh. She prises herself free, then tickles him till his jackhammer purr resumes.

A lifetime's supply of cat crunchies slumps in a bag against the terrace wall. Four ducks sashay towards it while they are talking, taking it in turn to peck at the rent in its side.

Vasilis shrugs. 'They all eat it. The pelican will be here next. They are all just helping themselves.'

While he is speaking he fills a jug and sloshes the contents into various water bowls, squinting as the aluminium refracts the light. The Labrador opens one eye and lifts his head, then lowers it as Vasilis passes, his sandals slapping against the flagstones like fish.

'Tough being a dog, isn't it?' Vasilis says, resisting the urge to scratch him between the ears. A pair of kittens tumble in a headlock across the yard.

'Anastasia will be down for a break in a moment,' he says, returning the jug to the kitchen and upending it on the rack. 'Usually she is working in the mornings while the house is staying cool.'

The triage of plums is over. A second colander is brimming, and a full cauldron is waiting on the stove.

Vasilis looks at Ana. 'Do you feel like eating anything?' he says. 'There's plenty of bread if you like.'

She shakes her head. 'I'm okay,' she says.

Still, she has made progress, he thinks. She has come downstairs in daylight; she has had something like a normal conversation. Surely this must be a good sign.

Vasilis leaves her pinioned by the sleeping tabby as he goes outside to tackle a problem with the kiln.

⌇

Heat is creeping into the day. Barefoot on the terrace, a bead of perspiration races down Ana's ribs beneath her nightdress. The wind has dropped; the pines are stiff as telegraph poles and the blue-grey leaves of the olive trees angle their edges to the sun.

Already the cicadas are tuning up against an orchestral undertone of bees.

And yet, still numb, these things she barely notices. Most of the time the outside world is peripheral to her, impinging at most by accident: the night-time sea, for instance, that slips into her dreams and interferes with the rhythms of her sleep. She wonders why she stops hearing it in the daytime, why once dawn breaks she is scarcely aware of its sound.

Like the sea, the roar of traffic was always present in Buenos Aires; even in the new apartment, from streets away, the rumble of cars and the lament of sirens provided a kind of soundtrack to her life. But the urban racket never invaded her dreams the way the sea does, and she could sleep right through the cacophony oblivious to its clamour and cries.

Immediately she douses these thoughts. She will not think about Argentina. This is why she has come here. She will not let it sidle in.

She stays up only half the day. By lunchtime Ana is exhansted again, and barely eats, and doesn't re-emerge from siesta.

'She had a bad night,' Anastasia says. 'I could hear her turn and turn.'

Vasilis has found what is wrong with the wiring and is fixing the kiln so he can fire in the next few days.

Friends come by in the evening and they have dinner outside on the terrace. They drink rosé and finish off the lamb and eat dark plums in syrup out of small glass bowls. Still Ana doesn't come down.

The light of a single fishing boat rises and falls across water that unfolds in the dark.

When Anastasia looks out over the terrace the next morning, Ana is swimming.

She has borrowed a pair of flip-flops to crunch across the shingle, and left them beside the half-buried log that separates the pebbles from the sand.

The saltwater stings Ana's eyes but buoys her; she had forgotten how weightless she feels in the sea. In the shallows, rings of sunshine flit across the sandy floor.

There is marble in the hills and the sea is aglitter with mica. In the glare of the sunlight, the seabed is scattered with stars.

Afterwards she stands dripping in a bath-towel on the terrace, shreds of sea-grass clinging to her skin. Anastasia lifts aside the curtain of rattly seashells and Ana smiles at her – the first smile she has managed since she arrived.

~

Ana emerges onto the terrace with a water jug and glasses from the kitchen. At the outside table, Anastasia is topping and tailing green beans, their strings peeling back like rip cords under the blade of her paring knife.

Burned hollow after last night's dinner, a candle slumps in the middle of the table; a collection of periwinkles, arranged in a circle, surrounds it like a castle under siege.

'Shall I finish them for you?' says Ana, her glass atilt on the tabletop's blisters of wax.

'Could you?' says Anastasia. 'I'm running a bit behind plan.'

Ana sits and slides the chopping board towards herself. Anastasia passes her the bowl, then goes indoors to check what she's left on the stove.

From the window Anastasia glances out at her, in the green light sitting sideways at the table, head bent to her hillock of beans.

Will this be enough? she wonders: Sunshine? Swimming? Sleeping? Hands busy at some practical task?

4

The Aegean
July 1999

Anastasia looks up from her computer.

Ana is standing one foot on top of the other in the door-
way, her hair still damp from her shower after the sea.
Self-conscious in her shift dress, she is unsure whether
Anastasia will mind if she interrupts.

'I knew that blue would suit you,' says Anastasia, smiling
as she gestures to a chair. Beached like a shipwrecked galleon,
it is Anastasia's favourite reading chair and the only truly
comfortable one in the house.

Behind it, the window sunk into the whitewashed wall
looks like a cube of sky.

Ana lifts an open book and some papers off the armrest
and places them where Anastasia indicates, in a pile on the
rug at her feet.

'Anastasia,' she begins, then falters, trying to order her
thoughts. 'Something happened. Before I left. In Argentina.'

Anastasia straightens, her smile shading into a look of concern while Ana seeks a way to explain.

'I got a summons to go before a judge,' Ana says at last. 'In his chambers at the Palace of Justice.' In her pocket she has found a soft yellow ball that the kittens like to play with, and she squeezes it now in her hand. 'When I got there, he told me that someone had made a *denuncia* . . . how do you say it? . . . . a denunciation.' She grips the ball hard. 'About me.'

'A denunciation?'

'A formal accusation. Someone, it seems, has declared that I am not who I think I am.' She trembles slightly, hearing herself say it for the first time out loud. 'He said that my birth date was not my birth date. That my parents were not my parents. They are saying that my life is a lie.'

It takes Anastasia a moment to understand what she has said.

Suddenly Ana is fighting back aftershocks of feeling: anger alternating with distress. 'He said that what I am doing is illegal. That it's breaking the law, going around with a false ID.'

Anastasia hears her unhappiness mounting as she speaks. 'Slow down, Ana,' she tells her. 'One thing at a time. Did he say who your real parents were?'

Ana drops the ball that bounces twice and rolls against the bookcase. She can't bring herself to meet Anastasia's gaze.

'He didn't give me their names,' she says, almost in a whisper. 'He just said they may be *desaparecidos*. Disappeared people. Which means subversives. Fanatics who plant bombs and kill people and die in shoot-outs with the police.'

Deprived of the ball, Ana is twisting her fingers as she speaks. The skin along her forearm is puckered like a zipper where one of the kittens has scratched.

'It was horrible, Anastasia,' she continues. 'He knew things. He knew I had these marks' – Ana turns her head and twists her hair back – 'and he said they had some photographs from my childhood. They must have been spying on me for years.'

'Show me again,' Anastasia says.

Ana leans forward, lifts back the sweep of her hair.

'I don't understand how he even knew I had them. But he said they were scars, and that they knew how I came to have them there.'

Anastasia sees the marks, sits back.

'He said they were from my mother, my real one. That it was she who put these cross things on my skin.'

'Your mother? Why would a mother do that?'

'God knows,' says Ana. 'Nothing he said made any sense.'

'And the pictures?'

'I walked out before he could show me.'

'Ana,' she says. She draws her chair close and takes Ana's hands in her own. 'Look at me now. What's your feeling about all of this? Could any of it be true?'

'I have to go to hospital to find out,' she says, misery sliding into her voice. 'They want me to do a blood test. A DNA thing. So they can prove whose daughter I am.'

Anastasia waits.

'It's a lie,' Ana says. 'It's all made up. It's got to be all lies.'

Anastasia considers the possibility. 'It's a strange way to operate, though, don't you think, if somebody's lying? To lie through a judge, I mean.'

But Ana isn't listening, or doesn't want to hear.

'I don't know what to do,' she says, anguish permeating her words. 'They are my parents. They are good people. I don't want them to go to jail.'

Anastasia is startled. Ana's logic is lurching in directions she cannot pursue.

'What makes you think your parents would go to jail?'

'Because that's what it's like in Argentina,' says Ana. 'It's happened before. There was a big case a few years ago – it was all over the TV news. They accused this couple – the father was a police chief – of adopting a child illegally. They'd found some problem with the birth certificate. The judge insisted they'd stolen the child as a baby and threw the parents in prison.'

Then Ana speaks about her mother's fragile health, how her father is two years from retirement, how devastating such an accusation would be.

'They do it to military families, to police families,' she continues. 'It's a revenge thing. Human rights people are behind it – my father once explained it to me. And now it is happening to us.'

Anastasia lets the silence pool between them. There is too much in what Ana is saying for her to advise her, too much she doesn't understand.

'Did the judge say that this was your situation?' Anastasia says eventually. 'That you were subject to an illegal adoption, too?'

Ana tries to recall what exactly was said. She rewinds the fleeting film of their encounter: the silver-haired judge with his cold-edged voice; the prim psychologist with her bow-necked blouse; the desk with its high-backed chairs. What comes back to her is the speed of the conversation, and the intensity of the ringing in her ears.

'What I remember is what he said about my identity,' Ana says finally. 'I can't remember what he said about my parents, whether he accused them of any crime.'

Her words hang in the air a moment, tilting and revolving like kites.

'Do you not think you should look into this?' Anastasia says at last. 'Even if it's just to confirm who you are?'

'I already know who I am,' Ana says, surprising herself with the sharpness of her tone.

'So – you're not going to do the test?'

'How can I do anything that might make trouble for my parents? And just imagine if it *were* true – why would I want to find out that I come from a family of terrorists who were more interested in planting bombs than they were in me?'

Anastasia hears her anger and begins to apprehend what she's been going through, grasps its implications almost better than Ana herself. She sees the shock, and the wrench on her deepest feelings, the doubt that threatens to shatter her sense of self.

'Anyway, if they were terrorists, then they're probably dead,' says Ana. She swallows hard. 'I don't want some bit of paper that replaces my living parents with dead ones.'

Anastasia goes over to the window and opens it. The cawing of a seagull floods the room.

'Are you sure the test isn't obligatory?' Anastasia says, pausing to look at her before going back to her chair.

Ana pulls an envelope from her pocket. There are smudges on the outside and creases that show that it's been folded and refolded many times.

She hands its contents to Anastasia who examines the formal lines of Spanish, the stamp of the judiciary, the court's Buenos Aires address. Though she doesn't read the language, she can identify a telephone number and the address of an immunology department at a hospital, and a date that looks like a deadline by the end of the year.

'Do you think they can they force me to do it?' says Ana, her voice suddenly afraid.

'I don't know how these things work in Argentina. But this is a court order, isn't it? Generally speaking, that's not something you should ignore.' Anastasia folds the letter and passes the document back. 'Did you tell your parents you were going to see the judge?'

'I showed them the summons. My father kept offering to accompany me, though he'd have had to take time off work. But I told him there was no need for it, that they probably just wanted to talk to me about something going on at the university, or maybe the Tennis Club.'

'And afterwards?'

'I didn't see them. When I got home my father was at work and my mother was out.' She looks up at Anastasia. 'I tried to ring Lucas but he wasn't answering, so I grabbed my passport and ran. I thought they were going to come after me. I thought if I could reach the airport, I might get a stand-by to Paraguay, or Brazil if a flight left sooner. Then, when I reached departures, there was a plane that was leaving for Athens, and I'd just got your postcard . . .' Ana gives her a helpless look. 'I know it was crazy, but I couldn't think clearly. I couldn't think who else to trust.'

'Of course you are welcome, more than welcome, to stay with us,' Anastasia says. 'I just hope your parents haven't reported you missing to the police.'

Ana shakes her head. 'I left them a note,' she says.

'Saying?'

'That I was going away. That they shouldn't worry. That I love them.'

Anastasia nods.

'And now?' she says after a pause. 'Have you thought what might be the best thing to do?'

'I don't know,' Ana says. There is wretchedness in her voice. 'I just want it all to go away.'

Anastasia picks up the yellow ball and squeezes it, tossing it backwards and forwards as she thinks.

'Ana,' she says after a moment, 'I don't know much about your country. I have no idea about your family and I don't know what happened when you were a child. But it seems to me that if the judge says there has been a denunciation, then someone must be looking for you. Or for someone they think is you.'

Ana groans. 'Perhaps,' she says. 'But I don't want to be found.'

Anastasia searches her face. There is fear in it, and resistance like a wall. Suddenly she sees the extent of Ana's disorientation, as if love, empathy, instinct, every point on her emotional compass, had lost alignment, that she no longer had her bearings, nor any place to land.

Anastasia reaches over to her and folds her in an embrace.

'There will be a solution, Ana,' she says to her, not knowing how but repeating it and trusting it because she cannot think what else to believe.

~

It is morning, and Anastasia and Vasilis are drinking coffee out on the terrace; Ana is floating in the sea. Eyes shut to the sun that is already blinding, she is a creature neither of land nor water, suspended under an aquamarine sky.

Vasilis has found her an old pair of swimming goggles. They are cloudy with scratches but now, when she swims underwater, she can see.

Beneath her, catching the sunlight, sand-glitter sparkles like Christmas. Sea urchins bristle like ordnance left over from the Second World War.

Anastasia has told Vasilis what Ana has told her, about the crosses and the denunciation, about the things she has to decide. Now he is pondering the circumstances, trying to order the facts in his mind.

'This is only the half of it – that's my feeling,' Vasilis tells her, toying with the base of a ceramic bowl that had broken in the kiln.

'Half of it?' she says.

'Look, I'm not familiar with how justice works in Argentina, but it doesn't seem to me as if it's just some lawyer making a threat. It's a judge, an investigating judge by the sound of it, and a judge wouldn't call her in without good cause.'

Anastasia weighs his words. There is more to it, she senses it too, though she doesn't know what. She waits for him to go on.

'What is she now . . . twenty-two, twenty-three?' he says. 'Which means she was born in . . . what? . . . seventy-seven or seventy-six. Wasn't that the time of their Junta, not long after ours? It just makes me wonder, that's all.'

'Makes you wonder what?'

'When there's been a power grab it sets the tone, doesn't it? It filters down that things are there for the taking, especially when you're on the winning side. Does she really know who these people are, these parents she's so concerned about? I'm just saying, it's something to bear in mind.'

'I don't think she is questioning who they are – I don't think she even accepts that she might be adopted. Why should she? The first she'd ever heard about it was from this judge, and clearly she's suspicious of his motives. I think she just panicked and leaped on a plane.'

But Vasilis's mind is turning and he hardly hears.

'Just supposing she is adopted, and they never got around to telling her. Well, why didn't they? Isn't that how it's done these days? There's no reason to keep it secret, especially once she'd become an adult.'

'Oh, Vasilis, there could be any number of reasons. Perhaps they were intending to. Perhaps the longer they left it, the harder it got.'

He shoots Anastasia a look over the top of his broken glasses. 'Or – perhaps they had something to hide. Maybe it wasn't actually an adoption,' he continues. 'Maybe it was something else.'

'Such as?'

'Kidnapping? I don't know. Did they buy her? Was there some kind of theft? Those crosses, for example – if you thought your child was going to be stolen, wouldn't you try to mark it in some way?'

Anastasia looks at him. 'That's a bit of a leap, isn't it?'

'I'm not saying that's what happened. Just that it might have. I wonder what this father of hers did during the regime.'

'He's in the military,' Anastasia says. 'She told us at Aigai that time.'

Vasilis stares at her. 'I'd forgotten that,' he says. Then, anticipating her reaction, he adds: 'Of course it might not mean anything. Or, on the contrary, it might mean quite a lot.'

Anastasia tells him what Ana told her: that her father was still active, and wasn't intending to retire for another two years.

'Which must put him roughly in his early sixties,' Vasilis says. He does a swift calculation. 'So, back in the nineteen seventies – mid-career.'

Anastasia fires him a warning glance. 'Beware of conspiracy theories, Vasilis,' she says. 'Ana's got enough on her mind.'

She goes to finish her coffee but finds it's cold, and shivers despite the heat building into the day. She looks out beyond the terrace to where Ana has started swimming, clean strokes shattering the glassy sea.

Let her swim, she thinks. Let her stay in the sun. Let her get strong.

Ana has just refilled the enamel basin with the hose beside the bamboo when Anastasia wanders up from the beach. After siesta, she is planning to go to a village beyond the headland and wonders if Ana would like to come for the walk.

'It'll be dry in half an hour in this heat,' Anastasia observes, as Ana pegs her spare dress to the line. The teenage tabby scutters sideways as the drips patter onto the ground.

Ana is washing her clothes in the garden. The water, dazzling in the brightness, is scalding for the first few moments where the hose has lain in the sun.

This mention of another village makes Ana nervous. There are stretches of time when the world still feels opaque to her, when her mind turns inward to what feels like empty space. Then, this place is enough for her: the terrace, her small white room, the narrowness of her days.

Now, she feels confronted. She isn't sure she is ready for the outside world.

'It will take us about forty-five minutes,' Anastasia is saying, 'that's if we go along the beach. I need to pick up a few provisions, and you might like to take a look in the shop.'

'I don't know, Anastasia . . .'

'You don't have to decide right now. Just think about it,' she says. 'It'd be nice to have your company. But see how you feel later on.'

Ana's tiredness is back and she just wants to sleep all afternoon. Yet she should go; she needs things . . . She thinks of the clothes she's been borrowing, of half-a-dozen items she hasn't brought.

Anastasia goes crunching over the pebbles to the terrace, plucking a leaf from a basil plant by the back door.

'If you come, we'll take that dog,' she calls back through the strings of seashells. 'We might have to drag him along the beach, but it's about time he went for a walk.'

~~~

At the end of the second bay they come to a sailors' chapel built on a low spit of rock. Ana attaches the Labrador to his lead, and his lead to a rusty water tap, where Anastasia orders him to stay sitting in emphatic Greek.

A bouquet of herbs has been fastened over the doorframe. The door complains as they push it open and enter, waiting for their eyesight to adjust. The darkness is aromatic with pine needles and incense, and the metallic odour of silver tarnishing in the damp sea air.

Anastasia inhales deeply and turns to Ana. 'Do you smell it?' she says. 'It's only like this by the sea.'

Ana, taking in the arches and the darkened murals, the elongated eyes of the saints on the iconostasis, breathes in the scent and nods.

A thicket of candles emerges from the sand in a filigree holder, some of them burned down to the quick. Aslant, the icons watch as Anastasia drops some coins into a moneybox and selects a couple of tapers from a tray. Asking Ana to hold them, she fills the air with phosphorous as she finally succeeds in lighting them with matches the humidity has turned soft.

'That one's for you,' Anastasia says, taking the other candle from her hand. Ana, surprised, looks up in thanks, and cups the flame that flickers in a current of air. Then after a moment, she places the taper next to Anastasia's in the sand.

Later, where the rocks become impassable, they join the road for a little way, passing a dusty taverna half-hidden in a depression among the pines. The Labrador barks at the pelican that sometimes visits their beachfront; it stares and yawns obscenely from where it is standing guard.

The shop lies beyond the taverna, above a sandy beach beside a cluster of holiday homes. Among the inflatable rings and light bulbs, Ana rummages for her size in flip-flops, then goes through the underwear box. She adds toiletries and a sundress that she tries on behind a curtain, heaping them in a pile by the till.

She has just enough money for everything, including the chickpeas and the detergent for Anastasia, despite Anastasia's determination to pay.

'Let me, please,' says Ana, her hand on Anastasia's forearm. 'I'm imposing enough as it is.'

Anastasia frowns her disagreement, but Ana has already handed across the notes.

The Labrador's claws click like backgammon counters on the concrete as he goes to anoint the signposts and the trees. Down on the beach, Ana frees him to investigate clumps of seaweed and lumber up to his haunches into the sea.

Two old men are drinking ouzo at the taverna when they pass it again. The pelican has shifted his vigil to the kitchen door.

On the last stretch of beach, Anastasia shakes back her hair, lets the sun warm the lids of her eyes. She had wanted to give Ana the chance to talk some more if she'd felt like it, but instead she has been quiet again, still troubled, on their walk.

Anastasia looks over to where she is trailing through the shallows, her patterned dress hitched up with a purple scarf. The bag of supplies she purchased in the village swings beside her, in low arcs over the water, almost grazing the tops of the waves.

5

Mexico City
July 1999

I move mechanically through the arc of my days. I pare my life back to routine and adhere to it, its automatisms sustaining me rather than the other way around. What weighs on me is this waiting, which I worry is not waiting at all but something inconclusive that each day further abrades my shored-up hopes.

Where is she? The question churns through my sleep, it harries my waking hours.

In response comes only silence. To still my thoughts, I divide my life into practical tasks and dissect them into their smallest constituent parts.

I wake early and lie there listening to Daniela's breathing, trying not to disturb her before her working day begins. Restless, I rise half an hour before she does, and after my shower dress quietly in the bathroom, then go out into the still-fresh morning to bring home the bread that she likes. I arrange the cups and bowls on the breakfast table, and have the coffee waiting by the time she has dried her hair.

Later, when she has gone out to tape an interview, I sort through the bills and paperwork, then try to focus on reading or a lecture I have to prepare.

Sometimes I meet Hugo for lunch and he tells me about his family, about Nicolás, still living at home, still trying to find a job. Sometimes we talk about Mexican politics; there is an election coming and Hugo, ever the journalist, is excited. He hasn't ruled out, after seven decades, the chance of a change of regime.

'We are living in historical times, my friend,' he tells me, eyes sparkling behind thick new spectacles, fingers drumming on Formica or wood.

I shake my head. 'When have we not?' I say.

I listen, I go through the motions of enthusiasm as he pours another shot of tequila into the blue lip of my glass.

Daniela is worried about me, I know that. She has sent me back to the doctor, who has sent me again for testing. Each time they find nothing to report.

Lethargy seeps into my limbs. My spirits drag behind me like a stone.

I cannot get beyond it: how close we came; how deep the silence since.

If only, after those long months preparing our case with Teodoro, we'd asked an intermediary – Patricia, perhaps, or one of the other Grandmothers – to break it to Liliana gently. We should never have confronted her directly with the law.

She must be so angry. The thought of it is more than I can bear.

That is what consumes me as I cross the square, barely noticing the shoeshine stands or the fruit vendors with their cups of thick-sliced mango, chilli powder speckling the flesh like rust.

I am not ready. I am not yet able to accept that we have lost her, though everything tells me I should.

I turn in circles, knowing but disbelieving, unwilling to begin the letting go.

6

The Aegean
July 1999

'Ana, come and look at this,' Anastasia says.

Ana is leafing through a book on the Santorini frescoes. In Anastasia's study, the cube window is deepening to violet; the nightfall wind is flustering over the water, restless as it always is around dusk.

Anastasia flicks through the files on her computer. She has something she's been wanting to show Ana for a while now but has hesitated, not certain if it was yet the right time. Now, her screen fills with a single photograph, a vessel filled with dirt and the threads of roots and flashes of something luminous, the distinctive colour of gold.

'What is it?' Ana says.

'We discovered it at Aigai last year.' Anastasia pulls up the next frame. 'Now,' she says, 'do you see?'

Ana gives a small gasp.

'It's exquisite, isn't it?' Anastasia says. 'It's like the one that Philip was buried with, only smaller – the same oak leaves, reserved for royal males.'

'You found this at Aigai?' Ana says. 'I thought you'd finished excavating the royal tombs.'

'It wasn't in a royal tomb. It was Ioannis who found it – in the new trench we sank, a few feet across from where you and Dimitri used to work.'

Ana colours slightly at the mention of Dimitri's name.

'I don't understand,' she says. 'Were there tombs in the middle of the *agora*?'

She can picture the scene so clearly: the smell of freshly turned earth, the wheelbarrow tracks across soil newly stippled with footprints, and old Ioannis in the midst of it, hands knotted over his shovel like rope.

'No, that's just it. That's why this discovery is so strange.'

She calls up another photograph. Against the murk and decay and debris, Anastasia traces the edge of a golden leaf on the screen with the end of her pen.

'It was buried in a ditch beside the sanctuary. This picture was taken the moment we opened it – the whole container was waterlogged, but you can see where the acorns are attached by their thin gold wires.'

She shows Ana how the copper vessel was rusted through on the outside, while the golden one inside it remained fully intact. She explains how, when they unsealed it, the oak-leaf crown was sitting on a layer of ashes; how the finesse of its craftsmanship was typical of the Macedonian workshops, down to the veins in its crenellated leaves.

Beneath the golden crown, they'd discovered fibres of purple fabric, and the golden discs that once had been sewn into it, found only in royal graves.

Anastasia pauses for a moment, clicking through the photos on her screen.

'And beneath all that there was something else,' she says, pulling up another shot. 'They were all still there, all carefully placed. We found his cremated bones.'

Ana blinks.

'Do you know who it was?' she says.

'We sent the bones to the lab for testing, and the results are just starting to come in. From the size and formation of the pelvis in particular, they have concluded the body was that of an adolescent male, somewhere between fourteen and seventeen.'

Ana breathes in sharply. It seems astounding to her that after two millennia, an age could be attributed with such precision.

'Surely that narrows it down, then,' Ana says. 'There can't have been too many Macedonian princes who died in adolescence at that time.'

'It narrows it down, certainly. But there is only so much the lab can tell us. The pit debris gives us a rough idea of timescale. But neither can give us a name.'

'Do you know how he died?'

Anastasia shakes her head. 'No, though there is a slim chance the lab will come up with something – which is why we haven't yet publicised the find. There are still a few more tests they want to run.'

The purple window has darkened now, turned the colour of Indian ink.

'If he was a prince,' Ana says, thinking aloud, 'why wasn't he buried with the rest of the royal family? Why did they go to all that trouble – the crown, the royal fabric, the whole cremation – if they were only going to bury him in a ditch?'

'That is why it's so puzzling,' Anastasia says. She hesitates a moment. 'To me, as an archaeologist, there is something almost disturbing about this find.'

'Disturbing – in what way?' Ana says.

'A rogue burial of a royal male – of all places in Aigai, the ceremonial capital with its huge necropolis . . . It makes no sense, when you think how organised their cemeteries were and how sophisticated their funeral rites. Yet there wasn't even a stele to mark the place.'

'So – do you think the vessel was stolen?'

'A robbery? No; the crown would have been the first thing to go. And there was no evidence of any displacement in the strata, suggesting there was no later attempt to dig it up. I can't help wondering whether there was some reason he had to be buried discreetly. Or indeed, whether it was a burial at all.'

'What else could it be?' says Ana.

'Concealment. Removal, perhaps, from an original site for its own protection . . .'

In a flash Ana sees where this might be leading.

'Like the ransacked grave at the front of the royal cluster?' Ana remembers passing it by torchlight, its façade looming like a temple out of the darkness, when Anastasia took her to see Persephone's tomb.

'For instance.'

Ana is already imagining it: barbarians, despoiling the grave, attacked by loyal Macedons who had rescued the vessel and hidden it, perhaps before fleeing themselves.

'It's only one hypothesis, and perhaps not even that, just speculation,' says Anastasia. 'At the very least the dates would have to square up. And tomorrow might produce some other find that makes us jettison that entire line of thought.'

'But surely . . .'

Anastasia interrupts. 'You'll be interested to know that there is another hypothesis about this crown, even if some consider it far-fetched.'

Ana looks up, intrigued.

The most obvious candidate, Anastasia tells her, is Alexander IV – the son of Alexander the Great, who was murdered along with his mother at around the age of fourteen. But his remains, most archaeologists concur, have already been discovered, in the unlooted tomb beside Philip's.

Ana knows about this second grave: oak-leaf too, the golden crown around the silver urn that held the prince's bones.

'Well there was, by some accounts, another son.'

On his military campaign eastward, Anastasia tells her, Alexander was believed to have fathered a child by a Persian, a noblewoman called Barsine who, when she'd lived in exile, had been one of his childhood friends. The boy, who grew up with his mother, was said to have been named Heracles; he would have been Alexander's eldest child.

'During the power struggles that took place after Alexander's death,' Anastasia continues, 'Heracles was said to have been mentioned as a potential successor – alarming a man called Cassander, who had designs of his own on the throne. By one report – and there is only one, recounted by a much-later historian – Cassander sent orders for Barsine and Heracles to be killed and privately buried. He wanted no state funeral. The idea was to have them quietly disappear.'

Anastasia pauses. 'Heracles would have been seventeen at the time. And that has led some to speculate that these may be his bones.'

Ana looks at her. 'And that this is Heracles's crown.'

Anastasia nods.

'I hasten to add that there are a great many problems with this hypothesis,' she says, 'first and foremost being our uncertainty as to whether Heracles was fictional or real.'

She runs through the counterarguments. Ana listens, and weighs them: against the age of the bones, the anonymous grave, the oak-leaf crown with the purple shroud denoting a royal male.

How young he was, she thinks. To put a name to the crown, to the bones it wreathed . . . She hadn't expected this field to become so *personal*, to acquire so intimate a feel.

'As an hypothesis, it seems to fit,' Ana says.

'Which is half the attraction, of course. But you know we need more than that. Some corroborative text, some confirmation. It's not enough, a single account written several centuries after the fact.'

'But you have the material evidence,' says Ana, surprised by her own vehemence. 'You have all the material evidence you could possibly wish for. How can that not be enough?'

'Yet it isn't, not now, not today,' says Anastasia. 'We need some other element that takes us, if not beyond all doubt, then closer to reasonable supposition.'

She sighs, and picks up a shard of pottery from her desk.

'All we have, Ana, are these random fragments that the earth yields up to us from time to time – each one meaningless on its own. As archaeologists, our job is to establish their context, to find the links between them and improve our techniques for reading them – not seize upon the first explanation that appeals. On the contrary, we have to be most sceptical of the hypotheses we hold most dear.'

'But how can we ever hope to state one fact with any conviction? There isn't going to be convenient corroborative evidence all of the time.'

'No, not even most of the time. So all we can do is dismantle, reassess and build on what others have deduced before us, and the most we can hope for at the end of it is to lay one tiny pebble on top of the cairn.'

'That someone may come along and demolish.'

'And that's the way it should be, Ana,' says Anastasia. 'When new facts rise to the surface. When new tools refine our understanding. When new relationships are found.'

Later, sitting alone on the beach as the waves caress the darkness, Ana thinks about the crown.

Something about it moved her. Its beauty, certainly. How delicate it was. Its mystery.

A murdered youth in an unmarked grave, in a place where nobody could mourn.

～～

She jolts awake in the night.

Outside her upstairs window, the sea is milky with moonlight.

Something has haunted her sleep. Not a dream as such. A bass chord still sounding after the melody has faded. A feeling that has lingered from the day.

Something Anastasia had said. A word that the judge had used.

Disappear. Disappearance. Disappeared.

～～

7

The Aegean
July 1999

They were all murdered, she reads later on.

Two days later Ana is lying in a hammock rigged up between the terrace and the pines. She has cleared away the dishes and helped wash the plates from lunchtime, the forks with one prong lifted, the knives with mismatched curlicues on their ends.

Vasilis is in the kiln room tossing out the pots whose glazes have buckled, salvaging those that have come out intact. Still limping, the cat that has adopted him ties knots around his ankles in flashes of black and white.

Ana has found a book about Alexander in English and is reading it in borrowed sunglasses in the garden, its spine propped up on her chest.

At Aigai she'd learned what had happened to Alexander's father; she'd stood in the very theatre where Philip's assassins had struck. It's what happened to the rest of his family for which she is unprepared.

Also murdered in the two decades after Alexander's death were his mother, three of his siblings, both his wives, his son, and if the account that survives is reliable, his mistress and his firstborn, Heracles.

A fourth sibling – his half-sister, Thessalonike – died later, she discovers, murdered by one of her own sons.

Ana has had no idea. Regicide, matricide, infanticide, homicide, forced suicide: it's all there, she thinks, all the permutations. A dynasty that violence stalked.

She lies the book down, gazes out over the tranquil sea. Beside her, a bee turns in panicked spirals, then lands on the stalk of a wild flower that should but doesn't bend beneath its weight.

She cannot take the measure of it. The ruthlessness of such deeds.

She picks up the book again.

Shortly before Alexander lay dying in Babylon, a messenger set off from Macedonia. Cassander, she reads, had known Alexander from boyhood; the two had studied with Aristotle in Pella. Cassander's father, furthermore, was a general so loyal to Philip that Alexander in turn had made him regent when he set off on his battles in the east.

It is no longer known what news Cassander was bringing to Alexander, what message his father had sent. Ravaged by grief or battle wounds, by typhus or perhaps malaria, Alexander had only a few days to live. There in Babylon, on a July day in 323 BC, he finally succumbed to his fevers, poisoned perhaps by the hellebore plant that may have been prescribed as a cure.

Cassander saw his opportunity. Yet it would take him eighteen more years to usurp the throne; twenty-two before he felt himself secure. The murder of three of Alexander's closest relatives lay before him; Barsine and Heracles would make it five.

Only Thessalonike was spared. Cassander took her for his wife, fathered her sons and eventually made her Queen of Macedonia. She outlived Alexander by twenty-eight years.

Ana pauses. Thessalonike. In Aigai, Ana had stood in what they believed was the tomb of her mother. She had marvelled at the painting of Persephone that had decorated its long-buried walls.

Cassander, as it happened, had only eight years to enjoy the power he had so relentlessly craved. Within three years of his death, Macedonia would slip between the fingers of his children and Thessalonike would be murdered in their feud.

A speedboat emerges from behind the headland. Its pale wash lingers behind it like a jet stream on the surface of the sea.

Ana is remembering the palace at Aigai, the mosaic floor with its tendrils and lotus-flower women. She remembers the theatre terraces, hunched under their blanket of grass. She remembers the sanctuary where she and Dimitri were digging, and Demeter's lonely vigil, and all the tombs asleep under the feathery blond fields.

It was a coveted kingdom, she sees that. And covetousness had soaked its soil in blood.

The oak-leaf crown shimmers in her mind like an apparition. What chance would Heracles have stood? she says to herself.

A wreath like that.

You could crush it under one foot.

8

The Aegean
July 1999

At the far end of the beach is a half-sunken jetty where the old men occasionally go to fish. It is late morning when Ana finds herself walking towards it and, drawn to some disturbance in the water, goes to the spot where earlier in the day a fisherman had been casting his line.

Something is bobbing about in the brightness. She stares at it, leans out over the railing, tries to make out what it is.

Trailing a streamer of pinkness, its glass eye fixed on a passing aeroplane, a decapitated fish head grimaces and laps at the waves. What looked like a single creature she now sees is a mass of minnows; the surrounding water is boiling with gobbling mouths.

Ana stands for a while and watches it, fascinated and at the same time repulsed. Then abruptly she turns her back and walks across the shingle, sits in the shade of an upturned boat.

Her back to the hull, she goes over the things in her mind that are certain.

She has parents she loves.
Without a test there is no proof she is adopted.
There is no need for anything to change.

These, she tells herself, are the facts.
What she hadn't been counting on are the doubts.
Despite herself, despite the depth of her reluctance, she is sifting her memory for lies.

'Mamá, where do babies come from?'

'You know where babies come from, darling. They come from their mamá's tummy.'

'And how do they get inside?'

'That's God's decision, darling. He's the one who decides.'

'What was it like when I was in there?'

'Well, you kicked a lot to show you wanted to come out.'

'Did it hurt when I kicked?'

'Babies only kick gently, darling. Luckily they aren't born with any boots.'

'Mamá?'

'Yes, *mi corazón*.'

'When can I have a baby sister?'

'Oh, darling, why do you want a baby sister?'

'Magali has one. So does Rodrigo.'

'Well, you don't have to do everything the same as them.'

'But I want one, Mamá. Magali says that hers sleeps in the cot she used to sleep in, and now they both sleep together in Magali's room.'

'That's nice, darling. Now pass me Teddy – do you want him or Liliana tonight?'

Was that how it went? She is delving into the past, hauling it to the surface like an anchor chain encrusted with all its barnacles, all its strings of weed.

What else was there? Lies, half-lies, or just omissions that festered in the cracks between fact and supposition? Had she assumed things that no one had corrected? Was she the only one who hadn't known?

Her febrile mind is at work. She is scouring every fissure in search of proof.

There were the words they had used, for instance, spontaneously and frequently; words they'd used to designate and define.

'I want you to grow up like your father,' he'd tell her, if ever she came home in tears from some schoolyard slight. 'Cut the snivelling. Never let them think you are weak.'

'Just tell them that your mother is unwell,' she'd say to Ana, the gardening club waiting on the phone.

Even amid the tensions: 'You can't snap out of it, can you? Not even for your own daughter's sake.'

Mother, father, daughter. The names that were also relationships had meshed them into a family, and never once had it occurred to her that their use might have been usurped.

She knew she didn't resemble them, not really. She didn't have her father's height or her mother's figure; she didn't have their hair or eyes. But her skin was not so different from Bettina's, she'd said to herself on the rare occasions she'd considered it, and Victor's cheekbones were not unlike her own.

Silvery and bloody in the water, the rotting fish head glistens and revolves in the sun.

And if her parents really weren't her parents? They must have had good reasons for their silence. Otherwise, how could this make sense?

Stigma. It must have been to shield her from the stigma. In the playground. From her schoolfriends' parents. From the ranks of the nuns with their punitive eye for anyone who failed to conform.

That must have been it. They loved her; they love her still; they hadn't told her only because they cared.

And yet, the doubts keep tugging at her, gently at first and then insistently, sucking at her skin with fishy mouths.

Why wouldn't they have told her later, at fifteen, or eighteen, or twenty-one?

Did they really believe the truth would drive her away?

She feels a surge of love for them. She must reassure them: she would never forsake them simply because of her birth.

Perhaps, after all, they'd had no information. Or – perhaps they had had information they'd wanted to protect her from.

Ghoulish, the fish head propels itself around the pier. Frenzied and flashing in the sunlight, the multitude keeps feeding, the surface bubbling with gaping lips and seething with the thrust of their tails.

And if she *were* one of them, a child of the disappeared?

It is beyond imagining. It runs counter to all her values and everything she's been brought up to believe.

She'd have that taint, of course. A secret defect. A deformity in her genes.

A picture suddenly comes to her, of a stain creeping across her neck like algae in bloom across a pond.

She shudders. No, she thinks. She doesn't want any other story. If there is some other truth about her birth, well, so be it. She doesn't need to know.

⁓

Anastasia is sitting on the terrace reading when Ana pads around the corner, a spidery bouquet in her hands.

'They're for you and Vasilis. For being so generous. For letting me stay,' she says. Then, diffidently: 'I stole them from the garden, and some from the edge of the road.'

Wild flowers veer in every direction, mixed with daisies and herb-sprigs and jasmine, and plumes of grasses at jaunty angles, in amongst the aniseed and the weeds.

'They're beautiful,' says Anastasia, smiling at what she can see of Ana through the petals and the spikiness and the twigs. 'Hold on to them for a moment, would you? I've got exactly the right vase.'

She takes one of Vasilis's amphorae from the living room and fills it at the outdoor tap. Then she places it beside the turquoise bowl that is sitting on the outside table, and together they tame the unruliness into an almost-symmetrical shape.

For panache they add a red hibiscus. Then Ana vanishes around the side of the house and returns with stalks of rosemary and a handful of flowers she has no name for, heavy with purple petals.

'It still looks a bit dishevelled,' she says, poking in the last stems where she can.

Anastasia laughs. 'They *are* wild flowers,' she says.

Sugar-drunk, freighted with bright saddlebags, a bee procrastinates over the vase. It circles, and they stand still for a moment to see where it will land. They breathe in sun-dried aniseed and jasmine that is cut with the tang of seaweed, the scent so light they barely notice it because it is every day all around them, in layers on the flinty air.

It's a good day, thinks Anastasia, glimpsing something of the Ana she used to know. She has talked with Vasilis and they've agreed to let her stay till the end of summer if she needs to, to allow her to make a decision about what to do.

Now she wonders whether inside Ana something is shifting, whether she is resolving something or accepting something – or whether this lightness is only momentary and she is about to slide back.

＊

9

The Aegean
July 1999

'Ana,' he says. 'To inspire you to take up pottery. Come and see.'

Ana looks up from where she is scraping carrots in the kitchen. She places the knife beside the chopping board and dries her hands on a cloth.

They go crunching over the pebbles, Vasilis leading, Ana a few paces behind. She follows him past the olive tree with the split in it, past the deckchairs and the coffee table set up between the pine trees, past the bar he has fashioned from driftwood and coils of thick sea-rope. Where garden meets shore, they pass the table set up for a seafarers' banquet, the plates and bowls and goblets all ghostly with salt.

There is a gate in the fence and they go through it, and come to a hillock of sand. Vasilis prods it with his sandal until part of the surface subsides.

'These ones, by the way, aren't mine,' he says, exposing a midden of pottery shards. Sea-eroded, some bearing faint traces of brushwork, terracotta fragments lie tangled among the grass roots, baking in the cobwebby sand.

'I didn't think you'd been around that long,' she says, kneeling. Lozenges of Hellenistic pottery slip between her hands.

He smiles. 'It's all just rubble now,' he says. 'And in winter, the sea is coming up. You can see how damaged everything is.'

'How long do you think it's been here?'

'Well, I did consult an expert,' he says. 'Anastasia is saying the reddish ones probably go back to the first century. But given how broken everything is and how the sea has got to it, it's not a significant find. Which is a bit of a relief, to say the truth, as I'd rather not see this crockery ditch turn into one of your digs.'

Ana smiles in turn and picks out a few more pieces. They are brittle, and light as cuttlebone, and clink like pieces of glass. She arranges them like a crossword but none of them, either by shape or line or thickness, bears any resemblance to its neighbour; they are fragments that belong together but do not fit.

'Actually, nearby there is what I am thinking was an ancient kiln,' Vasilis says. 'They'd have had a small workshop close to it. And, of course, the forest for getting fuel.'

Ana starts; the ceramic pieces slide from her knee and land like miniature mileposts in the sand.

'They turned their pots right here?' she says.

'A little further over, not far. In fact, because of all the rubble, I am thinking this is the place they were throwing away the ones that came out broken – you know, like landfill, for holding the sand in place.'

'When did you find it?'

'I don't remember finding it – we've always known about it. The house has been here many years. My mother, my mother's mother, even her grandparents, they knew.'

'That long?' she says.

'That's not so long, when you are talking about Greece.' He laughs. '*Keramikos* – of course it is a Greek word. But it is coming from the most ancient version of the language, from the language of the Mycenaeans, maybe eighteen centuries before now.'

Ana feels light-headed. It's as if, after the cave in Argentina, she is poised on another fault line, as if the past is sliding forward to meet her, here, on this sliver of coastline, on this shelf between the mountains and the sea.

The ancient jigsaw pieces don't connect, not directly, not to each other. But they connect with something larger, some continuity that has Vasilis making ceramics in the same place as these forgotten craftsmen, its long lines reaching backwards down innumerable generations, to some horizon that keeps beckoning her to turn.

'Deep down you know, don't you?'

A voice from her unconscious, rising up through her sleep.

'You know it's true. Otherwise you would never have fled.'

She jackknifes awake. Whose thoughts are these, whose words?

She is bathed in sweat. The sheets cling to her limbs and her tongue is like cloth in her mouth.

The window scrapes softly as she opens it and leans into the cool night air. The sea's slow breathing soothes her till her heart aligns with its rhythm and smoothes the ragged edges of her thoughts. A breeze that's scarcely a breeze creeps into the room, lifting the dampness from her skin; it turns her shaking into shivering till she stills it with a blanket from the chair.

Inside the house there is the sound of creaking as someone turns in their sleep. Outside, a rattling of pebbles, the furtive tread of a cat.

Slowly her hand travels to the side of her face, slides back the weight of her hair. Then gingerly, half afraid she'll find them tender, she allows her fingers to search for the cross-shaped ridges, trying to read what they say.

What comes back to her is the gravity of the judge's voice.

'Ana, those three crosses behind your ear . . .'

Rigid as a mast, she'd sat there listening.

'. . . it was your mother who put them there.'

She'd understood the truth of it immediately; it had hit her in an explosion of light. Not the mother she had grown up with. The mother she had never known.

The revelation had disabled her senses: blinded her, rendered her deaf, amnesiac, mute. Against its incandescence, she had turned her back and fled.

Gently she allows her fingers to caress the scarring, the triangle spaces between the ridges, this place on her that her mother's hand had touched.

Outside, she can see the darker shadow of the mountain where it drops into the water, and above it, stars like perforations in the sky's great dome, letting in the light.

Deep down, she thinks, she knows, she has always known, and doesn't know how she does. But through the wrought emotions and torn allegiances she feels it, knows she is somebody else's daughter and understands it profoundly, like something inscribed in her bones.

10

Mexico City
August 1999

Daniela has her diary open among the coffee cups on the living-room table and is flipping through the pages weeks ahead. Outside, the trees are dripping; the rain has stopped as suddenly as it started and the city has a rinsed-out feel.

Last week, we had another earthquake, a small one, though in Puebla it brought down some buildings and the dome of a church. Now I can hear the scrape of the doorman's ladder as he drags it across the hallway, covering up the cracks in the walls with what he calls his anti-seismological paint.

'Carla says they can come over in mid-December. She's got some time off then in any case, and Arturo will be on sabbatical – it's just Santiago they're not sure about.'

'Does he know Mateo's coming after all?'

'Yes, she's told him. But reading between the lines, I suspect there might be a girlfriend on the scene.'

'Well, maybe he could bring her,' I say.

'I'll suggest it. But they're only students, remember. They're not going to have much cash.'

'They know, don't they, that if they can cover the flights from Paris, they wouldn't have any expenses once they were here?'

Daniela nods. Hugo and Cristina have arranged for us to borrow the house near Acapulco over Christmas, and Daniela is starting early, hoping to get everyone to come.

I know she is doing all of this for my sake: as distraction from discouragement, to stave off my despair. And I go along with it for her sake, though my heart isn't much in anything these days.

What I want is a single thing: some sign – the merest indication – that Liliana is all right.

'It's Pauli I feel a bit sorry for,' Daniela is saying. 'For a four-teen-year-old, it won't be much fun on her own.'

'Hmm,' I say, already drifting.

'Osvaldo?'

'Pauli . . . oh, yes,' I say. 'Well, if Hugo and Cristina come to visit us, maybe Cristina will bring one of her nieces along.'

I think of all Paulina's drawings in the memory book, the annual birthday cards. She had wanted so much to find her missing cousin. She has long since considered Liliana to be the sister she'd never had.

It torments me now to think of Liliana: the shock, perhaps the harm we might have done to her, the starkness of the way she was told.

I still don't understand why the judge couldn't have sent the police round to take a genetic sample from her home. Surely a toothbrush, or a hairbrush, would have yielded the material that could end the uncertainty . . . But Teodoro had insisted it couldn't be done that way. Liliana wasn't a suspect; no sample could be removed without her consent.

Soon I will have to explain it to Eduardo, to Yolanda's family: that although we nearly found her, it went wrong at the crucial moment; how improbable it is now that we will ever welcome her home.

Once a week, hope flickering, I telephone Teodoro. Once a week he tells me the same thing.

No, she has not made contact with the judge.

No, there is no indication of how she is.

No, there is no sign she has done the test.

〜

The Aegean
August 1999

Anastasia has to run some errands, and send some emails from the main town on the island where the Internet connections work. There are cash machines, and pharmacies, and a cybercafé if Ana needs them. Or she could just come along for the ride.

Ana feels a shiver of apprehension. She should go; she should check her messages; email Lucas; perhaps get in touch with her parents. Part of her would like to see the island. But she is still ambivalent. She isn't sure she is ready to reconnect.

In the end she decides not to make a decision: to go, but to see how she feels once she's there.

Vasilis is trying to extricate himself from the ever-tightening circles that the cat-with-a-limp is tracing around his feet.

'Sorry, my friend. Today you have to stay and guard the fort,' he says, shaking off the loops like coils of rope and then, because the lock on the door is broken, swinging his legs through the jammed-down window of the car.

Sliding across the gearstick, he winds down the side window in order to release the passenger door that cannot be opened from inside. Ana ducks and swivels onto the back seat's peeling vinyl; Anastasia clears a space in the front among the work boots and the wood blocks and the stones.

'Ballast,' Vasilis says by way of explanation, in response to the look he gets.

He apologises for the missing handle that prevents him from closing his window; Anastasia lends Ana a scarf to stop her hair from whipping her eyes in the wind.

The engine turns over three or four times before kicking to life in a rolling start down the hill.

In the coruscating heat, the island billows around them like a sail. The road hugs the coast at first but then veers inland, passing the rump of a squat, white chapel that looks as if it's been moulded out of clay.

Ana closes her eyes as the car labours up the foothills. Light strobes the inside of her eyelids as they pass through a forest, its shade aromatic with resin. The new pine leaves are citrus-green against the scars of last year's fires.

She is not thinking; she is tired of thinking. Let the world flow around her like a current around a river stone.

On the far side of the forest they burst onto a plain where the crumbling walls of a ghost town were returning to the rocky land.

'There are ancient sites in this valley, too,' says Anastasia, turning in her seat. 'A while back they uncovered a sanctuary to Demeter, on a rise in the potato fields.'

'You know what the give-away sign was?' Vasilis says, peering at Ana through the crack in the rear-view mirror. 'Whenever you see a Byzantine church that is incorporating chunks of marble, you know where they got it from.'

Anastasia laughs. 'It's true,' she says. 'They carted off all sorts of ready-made pieces: column capitals, lintels . . . Of course you still have to locate your sanctuary, but once you get your eye in, and start looking at the land the way the Ancient Greeks did, it's not hard to lay down an exploratory trench as soon as the harvest is in.'

The island, Vasilis explains, is shaped like an apostrophe; now they are above the curve of it, looking down from a saddle in the hills. A pause in the Mediterranean, thinks Ana, punctuating the wind-squalls on the waves.

'Which way is Athens?' she says.

Over the broken windscreen wipers, Vasilis orients her through a latticework of insects. 'It's over that way, about five hours by boat.'

'You can't see it yet, but the port is down to the right,' Anastasia says. 'There is also a coastal road, a surfaced one, that takes you there via the town up ahead, but this route is more direct.'

The afternoon ferry is pulling the island towards it like a dragnet, hauling the inland traffic down to the port. Ana can see how the ferryboats impose their rhythm on the days and seasons, animating the waterfront tavernas, signalling the hour with their foghorns, alerting those with rooms to rent that it is time to hurry down to the pier.

The road sweeps down, then up towards the town that clings to the side of a mountain. At its highest point, a ruined fort tilts perilously over the Aegean; sun-bleached houses huddle in its shadow below. Even from afar, Ana is struck by the way they cleave to impossible gradients; another earthquake would shake them into the sea.

The car hiccups to a halt under a eucalyptus tree that is tattooed with elongating hearts. A pair of mongrels squabble in the dust as Vasilis does a half-twist out of the driver's window, then walks around the front of the vehicle to let his passengers out.

They have arrived at the end of siesta. Grandmothers shuffle into courtyards to pluck herbs for the afternoon's cooking. Children lunge at alley cats, or lurch on plastic tractors over cobblestones outlined like hopscotch games.

Vasilis is going to see his mother. Anastasia has brought her laptop so she can email from a café in the *platia*, but first she accompanies Ana on a tour of the streets.

Under grapevines, in the lanes in front of their houses, women chat on folding chairs while geraniums burst like supernovas from plump ceramic pots. Backgammon counters race across boards under the cafés' fluorescent lights.

'Come and meet us back in the square when you're done,' says Anastasia, leaving Ana by the cybercafé door. 'You'll see us outside at the restaurant I showed you. We'll probably stay for dinner, if you'd like to, so don't feel you have to be in any rush.'

Ana hovers on the doorstep, watching Anastasia retreat down the uneven cobblestones, and is suddenly overwhelmed by reluctance to step inside.

Bent double, patting the white stonework the way an actor might seek an opening in a backstage curtain, a shrunken old woman shuffles her way downhill. Ana watches, and waits until she passes, then steps back into the street. She will walk for a while, she tells herself, before pulling back any curtains of her own.

She can feel her calf muscles stretching as the town's main artery carries her uphill. The Blue Note Bar and the Aeschylus Café give way to hardware stores stocking everything from nail varnish to paint. Soon the flagstones twist around silent houses; hibiscus bushes and trellises peer over head-high walls.

Patchwork kittens loll beneath a citrus tree in the patio of a derelict house. One of them, in white and ginger camouflage, is losing a battle with a lemon that he is trying to bat away. He presses his belly to the concrete when Ana tickles him on the forehead, flattening his wingnut ears. His dandelion fur is soft as pollen, light enough to blow off in the wind.

The afternoon hangs torpid between the houses and Ana is sweating with the climb. A donkey stands immobile beside a cement mixer, its panniers overloaded with bricks. Bandy-legged widows rummage for pegs in courtyards hyphenated with washing.

Soon, the street becomes so narrow that Ana has to turn sideways to fit between the buildings; it leads to a square the size of a handkerchief beside a church with its back to the sea. From above, the houses she has walked through fit together like an Escher drawing: their roofs are also footpaths; their arches also bridges; their façades also steps.

Above her looms the scaffolding of the ruined fortress, and a seabird holding its own in the scudding breeze. Between the houses, she glimpses the bay fanning out from the foot of the cliffs and, far below on the beachfront, stick-figure barmen sweeping a disco floor. Jaunty as cocktail umbrellas, a row of parasols studs the curve of the shore.

The afternoon ferry retreats towards the horizon, trailing its smudge of smoke like a tattered flag.

Beyond the church there is one final corner, where the last house huddles against the rock. Ana rounds it, and is almost felled by the onshore wind that strikes her with such force she can hardly breathe. Gasping, she sways on the ledge over-hanging the clifftop, while the harridan wind wheels about her, clawing at her hair and clothes. Her stomach drops, and the world falls away beneath her; in the yawning gulf of blueness, all distinction is lost between sea and sky.

And on the crest of that wind, in the crush of its speed, the things that she has been holding at bay rush back at her; the chasm on which she is standing, between cliff and heave of water, brings the same vertigo as the judge's words. There is the same velocity, the same sense of things collapsing, the same sense of impossibility at what she is being asked to do.

She stands there, hesitating, on the edge of the azure world. And suddenly she sees herself plummeting, past laden donkeys and playing children and black-clad women pegging out the laundry: a female Icarus plunging into the sea. She could do it; it would be that simple. Just lean into the wind.

But instead, she inches away. She moves step by tiny step along the rampart. Her mouth is dry and her hands are frozen in spite of the pulsing heat. She reaches a tree at the end of the ledge and clutches it, and lowers herself onto the sun-warmed stone.

And as she rests there, head and heart both pounding amid the dazzling light and the wind-rush, she comes to a decision.

She will not do it.

She will not do the test that the judge has ordered.

She won't untangle the double helix.

She will not use her body as evidence to condemn the people she loves.

⌐⌐⌐

There is one booth free at the cybercafé when she gets there, in the corner at the back beside the door. She'll just check for any messages, she tells herself; she does not even have to reply.

411

It's been weeks since she has looked at her email; the screen takes a moment to open, then judders as the messages rain down.

She scythes through the weeds of spam, deleting, deleting, trawling for the messages she should keep.

There are a dozen from Lucas.

'*Where are you?????????????????????*' he writes in the subject space, a chorus line of question marks expanding with each resend.

Several from Mónica at the Faculty, about a seminar she'd been planning to attend.

A warning from her bank in Argentina, after the airfare all but emptied her account.

One that surprises her, from Dimitri. She hasn't heard from him since Christmas. She is aware of a rush of pleasure, and decides to keep the message from him till last.

There is a short one from her friend Camila, inviting her to a movie on a Saturday that has long since passed. And another, given her silence, asking whether anything is wrong.

She asks the bank not to close her account.

She asks Mónica not to count on her for the seminar.

She apologises to Camila and says she will be in touch.

Lucas's latest one she opens, and closes, and thinks about. '*Please ring*' is all it says. Though it sounds like a plea, she can tell how angry he is.

She doesn't want to call. She isn't ready to speak to anyone in Argentina, or tell anyone where she is.

But Lucas knew she'd had an appointment at the Palace of Justice. Lucas she cannot ignore.

She taps out a response. '*I had to travel urgently. The judge said I may be the child of* desaparecidos. *I'm thinking what to do.*' She reads it back and knows it sounds surreal, and probably inadequate, but she wants it out of the way. '*Don't worry,*' she adds, and hits send.

She hadn't expected his response to come so quickly. Succinct, in Times New Roman black on white, in twelve-point characters on screen.

'*Surely you don't believe all that crap about the disappeared?*'

She stares at it a long time. That, though expressed more crudely, is what she too had always thought.

It's what was said in the circles they both moved in, in the apartment building they lived in, at the Tennis Club where their families spent weekends.

'It was a war, for Christ's sake!' her father would roar, the house keys jumping on the sideboard as he thumped the arm of his chair. 'There's always collateral damage – just look at Iraq,' he'd say to anyone who was listening, as the TV filled with pictures of Desert Storm.

She'd never really given it much attention. The subject didn't concern her and in the end it bored her. The 1970s, with its bombs and its bad haircuts – it was all so long ago.

Of course, there were those students at university . . . everyone knew their parents had disappeared. Ana recognised a couple of them by sight but kept her distance; she felt awkward in their presence and vaguely embarrassed on their behalf.

And now? It is possible, she knows.

She gazes at the screen. She feels upset by Lucas's message, and decides she isn't going to respond. However this resolves itself, she senses he isn't going to understand.

Then, a long way down, in a thicket of junk mail ads for surgery and pharmaceuticals, she sees a message she's missed.

It's an email from her father, a single one, dated two days after her flight. She takes a breath and clicks.

'*Ana, darling,*' she reads.

They got her note; they hope she is safe; they are worried about how she is.

'*So,*' he continues, '*we found out what that judge was after: while he had you in there, he sent his "investigators" round to visit us. They showed up at the apartment and made your mother dig around for documents, then took her off for questioning. In my case, they had the audacity to turn up at work.*'

So they know, she thinks. They've been told.

'*They are lying, Anita darling, you must know that. It's all political, and these "human rights" judges have an agenda. Well, it wouldn't be the first time, as you know. Don't worry, we will fight it, believe me. Your uncle Ramón has put me in touch with an excellent lawyer; it will be most enlightening to see how they present their case.*'

Ramón, her godfather, her policeman uncle who wasn't really her uncle. She remembers those birthday games of Blind Man's Bluff.

Her father is furious – she can hear his scorn in every line. And his fury fills her with relief. He will use his connections in the military. He will make all this go away.

'*You are our precious daughter, Ana: you always have been, you know you always will be. Do you remember the night we drove all the way back to the picnic ground to find that doll you'd put to bed in the forest? The fun we had on those weekends riding horses? That crazy kitten I brought home for you that used to fly out of the trees? I can't tell you how much I love you, darling. You've always been your papá's special girl.*'

Shame shimmers behind Ana's eyelids. Her instincts had misled her: she can't have been adopted. How could she have thought otherwise?

'*Your mamá isn't taking it very well, as is only to be expected, I suppose. If her health deteriorates any further, we'll be laying that at that judge's door, too.*

'*She doesn't speak to me much at the best of times, as you're well aware, but it would do her good to see you. Perhaps you could go on one of your matinee outings again.*'

Anxiety about her mother twists Ana's heart with guilt. She had doubted them, she had abandoned them, just when they needed her most.

'*They will try to get to you, Ana, but you must be strong, the way I've always taught you. I know you will be; you've always been a good girl. We won't let them tear this family apart.*'

And he signs it: '*Love always, your papá.*'

Her eyes trail over her father's message, then halt at his last words.

What's that got to do with it, she wonders. Her being 'a good girl'?

She looks at her watch – she has lost track of the time. She should get back to the square.

She is about to log out of her messages when she remembers the one from Dimitri. It is getting late, she needs to get going . . . It is sitting near the top of her inbox, dated only a couple of days before.

Hey Ana,

Haven't heard from you in a while. How are things in BA? Hope you're in fine fettle and the research into the Cave of the Hands is taking shape.

My news, such as it is, is that I've finally submitted the opus, which means defending in Dec. or Jan. I can't wait till it's out of the way. Now I'm looking for some sort of fellowship – assuming they pass me, of course. No idea where I'll end up, but hopefully it'll be some place with sunshine and ruins.

Anyway, your country's in the headlines again over here. The mention of Argentina always makes me think of you – not that I need an excuse ;)

Send me a sign of life. Any plans to come to London? It's not so good for star walks but it'd be great to see you again, and now I'm (nearly) free of the thesis I can take you on a tour of the sights.

Yours ever,
Dimitri

She smiles. So Anastasia hasn't told him. He doesn't know she is back in Greece.

Under a P.S. he has pasted a link to an article. '*By the way there's a Bielka in this,*' he's added. '*Presume it's no relative of yours.*'

She clicks on the link, and it opens to a page in a British newspaper.

Spain Seeks to Extradite 48 Argentines Accused of Torture, 'Dirty War' Crimes.

She doesn't need to read beyond the headline to the list of names, the allegations, the acts.

Her mind lurches.

In the photograph, above the military uniform, she recognises his face.

~~~

From where they are sitting at an outside table, Anastasia sees her stumbling towards them, between the kids on bikes and the eucalyptus trees in the square.

'Ana?' she says, standing up.

Ana barely makes it to the washroom at the back of the restaurant before her stomach heaves.

In the mirror her face is ashen. Her skin is clammy and her eyes look black and out of all proportion to her face.

Night falls as they drive home hardly speaking, returning the way they came over the unsurfaced road.

As they climb the last rise before the house, the car's one working headlight picks up a bundle on the side of the road.

Black fur, white paws, a dark slick on the side of the head.

Vasilis groans as if it were he who had been hit.

Anastasia puts her arm around Ana's shoulder and helps her inside. Hungry, the Labrador lumbers over to greet them. The cats blink awake and stare with eyes that gleam from various lookouts around the terrace.

Through her misery and the chaos of her feelings, Ana understands why Vasilis doesn't give them names.

The next morning she watches from her window. He wraps the bundle in a hessian sack and buries it behind the bamboo.

'It's my fault,' he says, when he returns indoors. 'I should have let her come.'

12

The Aegean
August 1999

Thousands of kilometres across the Mediterranean, beyond the plateaux and the wadis, beyond the caves of the swimmers and the herders and the dwellings of the djinns in the sands of the Libyan Desert, a vicious wind awakes.

On the island, the day starts hot and turns still hotter and the breeze cannot temper the heat. It is 30C before breakfast and the mercury keeps climbing. The fields of straw bleach whiter and the bamboo hisses ignitable in the wind.

By noon the sky is citric. Ominous as tanks, clouds the colour of sulphur roll in from fires on other islands. Birds fly like bullets to their roosting places and the last cicada falls silent as the wind picks up and smears the air with rust.

The kittens stare wild-eyed from where they're hiding under the dinghy, while the sea-bobbing ducks make landfall and crouch among the rocks on the shore.

'*Sirokos*,' Vasilis says. The Sirocco wind, the fire-carrier, laden with Saharan sand.

The Labrador wedges himself between the barrels beneath the workbench. Vasilis rescues the goblets from the seafarers' table and Anastasia goes from room to room bolting the shutters of the house.

In the villages and around the island, women are gathering up beach towels and dragging in children's toys. The priest leaves the incense burners smoking beside the altar as he flaps through the emptying streets.

On the hillsides, the conifers creak and lean. Bees dock in their hives and ants stream down frantic highways to their nests. Underwater, sea anemones shrink into rock fissures. Further out, the bigger sea fish dive.

Light has acquired a new prism. Under a burnt-orange sky, indigo and green vanish altogether from the spectrum.

The Sahara settles on everything: rooftops, the windscreens of cars. Out on the clotheslines, forgotten bed sheets twist into orange cocoons.

At about 5 p.m. the wind shifts, and the sepia world turns dark. The sea churns. Fat drops pockmark the beach like vaccinations.

At the top of the town, rain patters onto the flagstones, then beats harder, sweeping up the dust in rivulets that lift the moths and the geranium petals and carry them off like spoils.

Everything now makes sense about the angle of the streets and the aspect of the houses; the rivulets become a cascade that nothing will obstruct. At the foot of the town, the cascade becomes a torrent as it joins the creek that's swollen with the runoff from the mountains, dislodging whatever it encounters as it hurtles through the half-pipes to the sea.

The deluge has turned the world to darkness. Lightning cracks the sky like crockery. Thunder roars its fury in reply.

Hobbled, without shelter, the only creatures left outside are donkeys that stand where they've been tethered, blinking the streams of water from their eyes.

On a distant hill, a solitary cedar brandishes its limbs at the sky.

In her bedroom, under a shutterless window turned purple by the dark sky's bruising, Ana's nausea gives way to numbness and a premonition of grief.

Is this true? she thinks. Is this what her father did?

It is beyond her comprehension. It cannot be the same man.

Her heart recoils and she is full of fury. It fills the cavity in her chest where she loves him still.

Where did the newspaper get this name: the Wolf?

What does he know about her parents?

What is she to him – vengeance? An extension of the battle zone?

She is sliding. Beneath her feet is nothing. The earth is giving way.

~

The salt stings her eyes and her lungs are on fire and every stroke is a whiplash of anger. She wants to exhaust her body, to exhaust her mind so there is no room for any more thinking.

She listens to her breathing from the inside as she hacks into waves that have not yet subsided after the storm. The sea writhes brownly after the tempest and is still not done with its effects. Curtains of sand billow and evolve into pillars that glitter with mica. The columns part with a sigh as she cuts through them, the water sifting grittily in her ears. Under a pewter sky there is no measure of depth nor any sense of distance, the light itself unsure.

Between the heave of her breaths an image floats towards her, as if parting the shreds of seaweed that hang in the clouded sea. It's an image from her childhood, from a story that has always puzzled her: a woman who, in turning, was turned into a pillar of salt.

So what, one last curious glance? But now she hears in it a warning against attachment, an urging to sever ties.

The saline water buoys her but the waves are higher now and striking without rhythm; she tries to shift direction in the deepening troughs. The headland, she senses, is somewhere to the right of her, but it's been out of sight since she left the lee of the cove.

Suddenly another memory breaks the surface, released in her lashing of the waves. It's a single word, and now it's returned she remembers where she heard it, that it's been hovering over her fitful nights like a warning pitched too high for human ears.

Represor.

It didn't stay with her because she could make no sense of it. In that office in the Palace of Justice building, she couldn't attach it to anything she knew.

But now, after the article Dimitri sent her . . . Torturer? The father she had always loved?

She crosses pockets of warmth and pockets of cold and works hard to fight off the chill. Every third stroke she tries to breathe but her hair has come loose and is now in her eyes, now over her mouth; she needs all her concentration not to flail.

The swell bears her up, then tosses her in its angry roll. She has lost her rhythm and is losing traction in the current that keeps on shifting; its drag on her means she cannot turn back to land.

Suddenly, above the roar in her ears and the wrench in her lungs, she hears something on and off again, something there and gone again, a motor and a sound like shouting, intermittent in the slapping waves. Then the hull of a boat looms over her and somebody's hand is gripping her, hauling her in.

'Ana, For Christ's Sake!' His eyes are wild, his face distorted; he is terrified he might have been too late.

In the bottom of the boat, on its metal struts, she lies coughing, she lies fighting for air.

She was half a mile out when Vasilis finally reached her and turned the boat to shore.

13

The Aegean
August 1999

She is sitting in the living room with Anastasia and Vasilis. Night falls earlier now; the lights are on indoors and the reflections in the windows blank out the terrace and the sea.

'You can't know what he was or wasn't involved in, Ana,' Anastasia is saying. She is trying to calm her, trying to help her absorb the possibilities gradually, unsure what she might have to face. 'You probably won't know for sure unless it goes to trial.'

'Or you ask him yourself,' Vasilis says. Anastasia shoots him a look.

'How can I ask him these things?' Ana says.

'How can you not?' says Vasilis.

Anastasia draws her chair closer to where Ana is sitting.

'You can ask him about your original parents,' she says. 'There must be something he knows.'

'Though it is possible, if he has a lawyer, that he's been told not to talk to anyone,' says Vasilis.

'Not even to me?' says Ana.

'Especially not you.'

Ana is wavering. Above all, she is worried about her mother – she still thinks of Bettina as her mother – and particularly about how she will cope.

'Ana, listen to me,' Vasilis says. 'This mother of yours – Bettina – might well have been complicit. I find it hard to believe she didn't know.'

Ana flinches and Anastasia frowns at his words.

'She needs my support right now,' Ana says, and then, with a surge of anguish, remembers that she cannot help.

'Ana, may I ask you something?' It is Anastasia, softness in her voice.

Ana turns.

'You must take this with the love and respect you know I have for you. Would you listen to me if I asked you to stop thinking about Victor and Bettina just for a moment, and consider what this means for you?'

'It's not about me right now,' Ana says. 'I'm not the one who might have to go to court.'

'I have to disagree with you, Ana. I would say that this is absolutely about you. It's about the most basic truth of your existence, as it is for any of us – knowledge of where we come from, of who our parents are.'

'I don't think I need this information, Anastasia. I've got along fine without it until now.'

Anastasia pauses, then speaks slowly. 'But now you know there is a question. There is a doubt, and that doubt changes everything. It will haunt you for the rest of your life.'

'Maybe so, but I don't think that allaying it should come at so high a price.'

'All knowledge comes at a price, Ana. That's why it's worth striving for.'

'Even when it affects other people? Even when it affects the lives of the people I love and who love me, who've given me everything I have?'

'I'm not telling you what to do, Ana, and I don't underestimate for one second how difficult this must be. But haven't you already made your choice? You came to Greece in the first place because you had chosen a field dedicated like no other to the quest for knowledge about the past. We both know how hard it is to establish any ground we can safely say is solid, even with all the material evidence in our hands. Yet this truth about your life is within your grasp, and your response is to turn your back. What wouldn't I give to run a DNA test on the bones that might have been Heracles's, if that could prove it was him. But we can't, and it's too late, and it may never be possible to draw a line in the Aigai dust that says: "This is Heracles. A dynasty ended here." Your identity, on the contrary, can be proved, and that depends on no one but yourself.'

'It's not cowardice, Anastasia, if that is what you are saying.'

'Then what do you call it, Ana?'

'Love. Loyalty. Gratitude. I owe everything to Victor and Bettina. I don't think I could live with the guilt.'

'You have no idea how the truth will make you feel, either on the first day you hear it or over time.'

'That's just it,' Ana says. 'I don't want anything to change.'

'But it already has, Ana.' Vasilis sits forward in his chair. 'Have you stopped to ask yourself why Victor and Bettina are never telling you the truth? Have they ever offered to help you find your family? Have they made any attempt, even now, to explain?'

'They are probably trying to deal with their own crisis.'

'That's what I mean,' Vasilis says. 'So stop running away from yours.'

~

She finds Anastasia on the beachfront, drying off after her morning swim. Ana comes and sits beside her on pebbles that are still chill from the cool of the night.

'How are you feeling?' Anastasia says, making space for her on her towel.

'I'm fine.' Ana looks up and manages a smile. 'How was the water?'

'Glorious – you should go in,' she says. She can tell by looking at her that Ana hasn't had much sleep. Then, after a pause: 'I'm sorry if we lectured you last night.'

'You didn't lecture,' says Ana. She is picking out small round stones and tossing them into the water that has finally recovered its calmness after the storm. 'What I feel, what to do – it moves around so much. Sometimes I wish I could just go to sleep until the whole thing has gone away.'

'I thought you'd already tried that,' Anastasia says.

'Well, maybe I should give it another go.'

Anastasia shakes her head. 'And miss out on this, another week of life?'

Ana gazes out over the water at the headland, at its mother-of-pearl reflection, at the distant island floating in the morning mist. It's as if, until this moment, she hasn't been able to see it, that her eyes have been shut to its beauty, to the depth of its peace.

'You'll have to forgive Vasilis for being a bit sharp yester-day,' Anastasia says. 'He cares about you as much as I do. I know he didn't mean to sound harsh.'

Ana gives her a rueful look. 'It's okay,' she says. She casts another pebble into the water, listens for the hollow sound it makes. 'He is probably right, I know.'

'I think you scared him a bit when you swam out so far the other day – both of us, in fact.'

Ana swallows. 'I'm sorry,' she says. 'There was so much . . .'

'I know, Ana. But you're our guest, and if anything had happened . . .'

Ana feels ashamed. She hadn't considered anyone else. She hadn't even considered the risks.

'This is your life, Ana,' Anastasia continues. 'You mustn't be so reckless with it again.'

They let the silence linger, broken only by the plop-plopping of Ana's stones. One of the beach kittens stalks through the grass and over the shingle, weaving through the A's Ana has made with her knees.

'You know I have a daughter just a few years older than you,' Anastasia says after moment.

Ana starts. 'A daughter?' Anastasia has never mentioned her before.

'Michaela. There is a picture of her when she was smaller, in the study. She's not Vasilis's; she's from my first marriage, a long time ago. She's twenty-six now. Her father took her to America when she was eight years old and decided not to bring her back.'

Ana stares. 'That must have been terrible,' she says.

'I tried for years to bring her home, but it was hopeless. The courts here couldn't do anything . . . These days she's got some boyfriend and they're both mixed up in drugs. She doesn't return my calls. I went over once to visit her, but she refused to see me.' Anastasia pauses, staring out to sea. 'Even now, not a day goes by when I don't miss her. I don't think I'll ever stop missing her; I don't think any mother ever does.'

For a long moment Ana is silent. She doesn't know if her real mother ever missed her.

And in that silence, everything that's happened slowly settles, and with it, every thing that's been said. And though it runs counter to all she has ever been taught, to all she has strived to do, to everything instilled in her for as long as she can remember, Ana lets the tears come, lets them fall.

The waves trip on the beach and rake the kelp along the headland. Far above them, high enough to see as far as Africa, a seagull hovers with wings outstretched, its face turned into the wind. The barren slope of the mountain towers as it has for millennia over the blue-grey sea.

She cries and the tears keep coming and Anastasia sits with her arm about her without speaking or trying to stop her, letting her weep.

Later, when Anastasia is chopping mint leaves in the kitchen, Ana asks her a question that has been on her mind all morning. Anastasia hugs her and gives her assent.

At the end of siesta Ana hitchhikes into town. She catches a ride on a rattling truck that is carrying crates of cucumbers down to the port.

From the Internet café halfway up the rain-rinsed hill, Ana sends a message.

'*Dimitri,*' she writes. '*Please come.*'

14

Mexico City
August 1999

Whose hands are these?

It's when I'm washing the glasses in the kitchen, the slanting light opaque through the steamed-up window, that I notice them, as if for the first time seeing them, these unfam-
-iliar, old man's hands.

Hard-nailed, they are, and marbled with purple filaments, and dappled with faded watermarks on skin that shades to jaundice where the knucklebones pull it taut.

I lift these hands from the soapsuds, turn them into the light.

The mark is still there, the polished indentation. The ghost of Yolanda's ring.

On the back of my hand, the fine bones work like hammers inside a piano, the sinews tugging like strings.

Once, they were the hands of a surgeon, I think to myself, their capabilities precise. They were the hands of a husband also, once; of a father, an adolescent, a boy.

And they have done what was in their power. They have made mistakes and tried to rectify them. And in the course of a lifetime they have tried to do some good.

But there are things that have been beyond them. They have tried to salvage sight where it was failing; they have tried to help the almost-blind to see. But where sight was most badly needed, they failed to make anything visible, and there are broken things they will never be able to mend.

There is no help for it, I tell myself. It is not enough to want something, to strive for it over all my remaining years. What we have lost can never be recovered. What I want, what my granddaughter wants – these things will never be reconciled.

And so it comes to me, a slow acceptance like the sun's reluctant slide into the ocean, that the two of them are gone from me forever. That in losing Liliana, we have lost Graciela, too.

How did she die, my daughter? The things I've heard about and read about, the things that Inés spoke about: these things must have happened to her.

She was tortured: with wires, with electricity. She'd have been chained, brutalised – God help me – probably raped. But allowed to live, until she had given birth. Then, within days, the Pentothal injection. Shoved into an aircraft. Pushed.

I stand there a moment, leaning on the draining board, swaying with the certainty of her death. The ending must surely have come years ago, yet over all this time I've held on to her; it was I who was unwilling to see.

The water vanishes. The wine glasses steam and drip on the rack as the sunlight shifts, clouds over.

And I find that I am weeping, my tears mixed with the steam and the fog on the window. Irretrievably, inconsolable as a child. Over the glasses, over my failure as her father. Over all that was beautiful in her. Over her abbreviated life.

⁓

15

The Aegean
Early September 1999

Ana spots him the minute the crowd from the afternoon ferry sweeps onto the pier. Through the clouds of exhaust from the impatient trucks she sees him before he sees her, his face still pale from the English summer. And suddenly, his luminous smile.

Through his T-shirt when she hugs him she can feel the warmth of his body; she remembers his height as he stands beside her, the Dimitri smell of his skin.

'You've cut your hair,' she says, suddenly nervous, saying the first thing that comes into her head.

'Special occasion,' he tells her. 'Hey, I've even given it a wash.'

'Don't tell me – you finally got rid of the Aigai dust.'

'At last! And I binned that bandana, too. The new look is more London sophisticate – what do you think?'

She takes in his sandals, his T-shirt and jeans.

'It's not all that different,' she says, a little dubious.

He laughs. 'I knew you'd be impressed.'

He is here, she thinks, beside her on the jetty in the ordinary sunshine; she picks up his rucksack to anchor her heart to the earth. But quickly he takes it back from her and swings it over his shoulder, leaving her to grapple with her heart on her own.

They stand awkwardly before the taverna where Ana first asked for directions, waiting for the bus to reverse. In term time it also does the school rounds, crossing the island with adolescent hieroglyphs etched into its carapace of dust.

'The summer hasn't been too bad to you,' Dimitri says as they sink into a seat by the door. He is looking at the tan on her skin that has turned her green eyes bluish, at her flyaway hair lightened by the sun and the salt.

She isn't sure he is right, but now isn't the time.

'Welcome to my hideout,' she says.

Anastasia has left a note of welcome. Vasilis, she says, is planning to cook this evening, but they won't be back till after dark.

Dimitri goes for a swim in the opaline water, then stretches out on the sand. Beach grit sticks like sesame seeds to his ribcage that rises and falls as he breathes.

Ana sits beside him in the rays of afternoon sunshine, watching the bay transform itself into colours she cannot name.

'Thank you,' she says, 'for coming all this way.'

He turns his head to look at her.

'It's great to see you,' he says. 'I got your message and left as soon as I could get a flight – though I'm intrigued what the mystery might be.'

She hasn't yet explained why she wrote, all the reasons she needed him to come.

'There's one thing, though,' he continues before she can answer. 'On the flight over I realised I should have asked you.' He props his head on his elbow. 'How's Lucky Luke these days?'

'Lucas?' she says. She thinks about him with a pang, and flushes. She hasn't spoken to him yet, but needs to – they haven't communicated since their one brief email exchange. Over these past few weeks of turmoil she has come to realise that the person he believes he is in love with bears little relation to her self.

'I don't know about Lucas,' she says. 'I think that he's in love with some other girl.'

They talk for a long time. Against the starkness of the island, in the calm of the early evening, she tells Dimitri everything that has happened: the reasons she had for coming here; the decisions she has to make.

He listens gravely and without interruption to all the things that she says.

When she has finished he gives her a look she cannot interpret, and then he extends his hand.

'Swim with me,' he says.

They wade out into waist-deep water, then swim to the edge of the bay, then float in star formations staring up at the sky. The sea is still as a lake and the sun, as it slides behind what might be clouds or islands, gilds their faces with copper light.

When they are close to shore again they both stop swimming. She feels his arm as it slides about her waist.

'Hello, sea goddess,' he says.

She feels the smoothness of her skin against his skin, like silk, warm against silk.

He scoops up a strand of seaweed with drooping pendants and drapes it about her forehead. Its clamminess sends a frisson down her spine.

'There, you see. Emeralds. I bring you offerings from my dwelling in the deep.'

She rolls her eyes, then tries to glimpse the knobbles he has used to adorn her, but all she can see is a blur of rusty green.

'And there I was, thinking you dwelled in London,' she says.

Her heart thumps loudly against her ribcage; she dares not look down at the ripples it must be dispatching across the Aegean.

Seawater beads the hollows of his neck, his shoulders. Her fingernails are pale as moons against the brown skin of her hands.

'I remember you,' he whispers, to her, to the mountains, to the listening breeze, as he kisses her, and pulls her back to him where she is drifting, both of them trembling now as he holds her, close in the shivery sea.

Their footprints have long since dried on the terrace when the car pulls in across the gravel, its one good headlight greeting them with its permanent wink.

Anastasia hugs Dimitri like a son and Vasilis embraces him like a long-lost friend.

'It's been too long,' Vasilis says, pleased to have another man around.

He discovers a tray of ice in the freezer and they pour measures of the vodka that Dimitri has brought them into the tallest glasses at hand. Vasilis retrieves the chair that he has borrowed again for his workshop, and flicks off the dust with an expert switch of a towel.

Dimitri is sitting so close to her that Ana can feel the warmth of him, the fine static hairs on his arm.

Anastasia is telling them how they'd driven Vasilis's mother over to Agios Georgios for a baptism, in the mountains on the inland road. The chapel was so small that only the priests could fit inside it; the congregation had to stand with the baby on the pine needles outside.

Then she and Dimitri talk a little about London, and Ana, dislodging the kitten that adopted her on her first morning, goes inside to give Vasilis a hand.

She has instructions to fetch some rosemary from the bush she once trimmed flowers from next to the gate. At the top of the path she turns and stands a moment, inhaling the night aromas, watching the lights of a tanker glide by on the now-black sea.

She can just make out the ancient pottery midden, the table for phantom seafarers, the place where the silvery log lies sunken among the pebbles on the beach. She can hear the breeze in the bamboo stand where Vasilis buried the black-and-white cat that once sought sanctuary there. She sees Dimitri and Anastasia, their faces lit up brightly on the terrace, and Vasilis emerging from the kitchen with an over-sized bowl in his hands. The windows of the house glow golden in the darkness, like the bridge of a sturdy ship.

Things are shifting inside her, falling at last into place.

The night is still warm so they eat outside with the hurri-cane lamp hooked up to a nail in the wall. Ana feels calmer than she has in weeks, thanks to Dimitri and the vodka and the sea.

Anastasia wants to turn in early. She makes up a bed for Dimitri in the living room in case he needs it, and leaves an extra blanket on the chair.

The sheets on Ana's bed are cool against their limbs as they lie there, salt-skinned, messy-haired, half-awake. They've left the window open and the mosquito coils are smouldering and the bed is all tangled with legs.

'It's really you,' she whispers, not daring to believe he is there.

They speak in subdued voices, no louder than the breeze in the pines.

They doze and turn, restless, unaccustomed this night to the presence of the other in their sleep. He wakes with her breath on his neck, her arm across his ribs, and lies there silently, thinking.

'Ana,' Dimitri says, searching for her again in the last languid hours before dawn. He can see the line of her hip, the curve of her shoulder, the three raised crosses at the back of her ear where she's swept up the weight of her hair.

She turns to face him. It's as if she has been waiting for him a long time, already awake. She turns, and moves under his hands.

He'd go anywhere she asked him, he realises, this green-eyed girl he found in the Aigai dust.

He will help her; they've discussed it; isn't this what researchers do? They will call Madrid and Buenos Aires, find out more from the newspaper in London. There must be people in Argentina who can help.

He dreams and wakes, and listens to the unfolding of the sea. It is not yet daybreak, just something preparing to alter in the quality of the light, when he whispers to her again.

'All these things you've told me about your family, about your known and unknown parents.' He hesitates. 'It's okay, Ana. It's just your story. It's just what happened to you.'

She looks at him, a thousand things in her eyes.

He puts his finger to her lips. 'You will still be you in the end.'

He is stroking her hair now, soothing her, ironing away her questions with the slow even movements of his hand. He is aware of her need for someone outside all this to lean against, for some intimacy of her own to draw courage from, with the ground in constant motion beneath her feet.

'You will still be you,' he tells her. 'Whoever you are. Whoever you turn out to be.'

EPILOGUE

ALL THAT YOU ARE

1999

Buenos Aires
October 1999

A young woman walks into the Palace of Justice building. Her hair is shorter now; she has cut it because everything is changing anyway and nothing after this moment will be as it was before; even so, she is dismayed to find that her curls are no easier to tame. Her skin still has colour in it, and the memory of salt, and the feeling of morning sunlight on the surface of the sea.

In the back of her mind, something bright is shimmering: the golden leaves and acorns that might have been Heracles's crown. In her pocket she has a shard of pottery, sanded, sea-eroded, and a small round pebble with mica in its veins. There is a scratch on her arm, fading now, where a beach-kitten clawed his way into her affections. Her eyes look bluish-green because she has spent so long in the sunshine, but they are weary with all she has been deciding.

She makes her way into an office. Her back is straight because she has settled on a course of action, and now she is determined to see it through. She has given blood; the judge has the results; but even before she went for the test, she knew.

She sits in a high-backed chair that is upholstered in leather and dimpled with fat leather studs. She hasn't spoken to Victor or

Bettina but she will speak to them; she knows if she goes to them now, to these parents she has always loved, then she will falter, that in the tumult of her feelings, on the high narrow bridge she is crossing, she will lose the courage to do what she has to do.

Beside her, a few paces away, sits an elderly man with his hair brushed back, and glasses in tortoiseshell frames. Does she look like him? she wonders. Is there something in the arc of his forehead? The shape of his face? His hands?

She sits side-on to him, observing him and wondering. If he had truly wanted to find her, she says to herself, then why had he waited so long?

He looks at her, over the fifty years and the generation that lies between them. He is seventy-two and she is twenty-two and she has disarmed him. He is terrified that she will vanish again, that he will lose her again. He is like a child again, dumbfounded by an apparition.

Nevertheless, he holds himself with dignity. He is trying to contain the emotion he feels and the immensity of all that he's been carrying, on his own behalf and of those who didn't make it to this place.

They have found her. She is here. She is here.

It's in the slightest things. The height of her. The way she holds herself. He wants to stare but stops himself though every part of him is yearning.

There was a child that lived.

She has turned to him and is looking at him with eyes that are new but are also familiar. Graciela, he thinks for a second. His heart ricochets. She has Graciela's eyes.

She can tell he has dressed carefully this morning. He has knotted a tie around a collar that is too loose for him. He has shaved and put on a jacket that she suspects has been bought for the occasion, but she can see how thin he is. A stick figure of a man. Nothing to him but sinew and bone.

442

She doesn't know what he expects of her, this grandfather, but for love it is far too soon. She feels defensive towards him, this stranger who has upended her life.

Then she remembers what Dimitri said last night when he called to encourage her: that her life was upended long ago, perhaps even before she was born. She has been falling so long she scarcely remembers it starting; perhaps since the day she stood in awe in the cave in Patagonia, when the past had first called out to her. Or perhaps a long time before.

And she is scared of what she will have to slough off, some part of it, or all of it, she doesn't know yet; a lifetime, and all she has known of love.

But when she looks again she meets his eye and senses the kindness in him. Perhaps it will be all right, she thinks. Perhaps he will understand.

There is damage all around them, they both know that. It will take time. It will all take time.

He puts his hand to his jacket pocket, checking for the hundredth time the flatness against his shirt. He has the photograph of her father that Eduardo has entrusted to him. He has the picture that José took of her mother under the willow tree in Tigre, so long ago he wonders if it was really theirs or somebody else's life. And he has the photographs Yolanda took of her that time when she saw her painting, one autumn under a jacaranda tree when she was a tiny girl.

Will she shun him? Will she scorn him? Will this first time be the last time he sees her face?

He holds himself back; he will not be the first to speak. He has waited this long, as Teodoro said: what matter a few seconds more? He doesn't want to hurry her, he doesn't want to frighten her. He will do nothing that causes her to flee.

And yet he cannot help it: loving her, though they haven't met and he doesn't know the slightest thing about her; loving her, because anything else is now beyond him; loving her, because he doesn't have a choice. Her preciousness to him is inexpressible: the mere fact of her being alive.

She is not Graciela, he knows that. And yet within her, something of Graciela still lives.

When she speaks to him she will ask him the simplest things. Who her parents were, she wants to know. Who she was at the start of her life.

He hasn't known how to prepare. He has spent two decades searching for her, believing in her when it was scarcely possible to imagine her, and now he feels at a loss. He can focus on only one thing.

He has said it a thousand times, he has said it over and over, he has rehearsed it because this of all possible outcomes is the only thing he is certain she will want to ask him, and he wants her to be proud of it the first time it reaches her ears. Two surnames, one each for her mother and her father, and the first name, which was the last thing and the only thing her mother was able to bestow.

And if anyone happens to be passing by the courtroom on this bluest of Argentine mornings, or be waiting alongside those who have long been waiting for her, with Eduardo and Constanza, with Julieta and Daniela, just outside the door, they might hear it too because he will say it with only the slightest tremor, with everything that has been in his heart over all these years of searching, with all he knows of constancy, with all he knows of love.

She turns to him, this woman who is his granddaughter who has unmoored him.

Her voice is calmer than she feels inside but it breaks, because she cannot hold it.

'Tell me who I am,' she asks him. 'Tell me my name.'

ENDNOTE

Between March 1976 and December 1983, the Grandmothers of the Plaza de Mayo estimate that approximately 500 children were born in clandestine detention centres or taken from their families and appropriated by members of the security forces and friends of the Junta. Most were subject to false adoptions and brought up with falsified identities. At the time of writing, the Grandmothers had recovered 121 of them, some in other countries in Latin America. Roughly 400 remain missing to this day.

The incidence of child theft has a long and dark history, and over the past century it has recurred for political, ideological, racial, religious and criminal reasons around the world. The theft by Nazi SS officers of an estimated 300,000 'racially valuable' children from orphanages or from their parents in Poland, Bohemia, Moravia, Belorussia, Ukraine, Slovenia and the Soviet Union during the Second World War is perhaps the most notorious example, but it is not the only one. Australia, Canada, Ireland, Spain, Switzerland and the United States are all among countries that have experienced eras of child theft. In some instances, cases are estimated in the hundreds of thousands.

In 1989, thanks largely to the efforts of the Grandmothers of the Plaza de Mayo, what have become known as the Argentine clauses were incorporated into the United Nations Convention on the Rights of the Child. Those clauses, articles 7, 8 and 11, enshrine in international law the rights of children to the protection and preservation of their identity.

The convention remains the fastest and most widely ratified human rights treaty in history.

HISTORICAL NOTE

In the course of this novel, I have taken liberties with some elements of the historical record, shifting chronology in the following cases:

in France, the idea of organising a boycott of the 1978 World Cup in Argentina arose in October 1977 rather than January as I have it in this account;

I have imagined the sighting of an Argentine military spy, at an exile group meeting in Paris in March 1978, after the case of Alfredo Astiz, the naval officer who had already infiltrated and betrayed the Mothers of the Plaza de Mayo in Buenos Aires. In fact Astiz was recognised in Paris a month later, in April 1978, and was later found also to have been present at the counter congress on cancer, held in Paris in October that same year;

Antoine de Saint-Exupéry's *The Little Prince* was officially banned from Argentine schools in September 1980, but I have advanced its proscription at Yolanda's school to July 1976, since titles by Saint-Exupéry were included in the big book burning in Córdoba in April 1976, the first of at least three such incidents. The Junta also drew up lists of songs and performing artists whose work was censored, an eventuality reflected in Gustavo's curtailing of the music he played at the Paradiso;

The request by the Spanish investigating magistrate Baltasar Garzón for the extradition of 48 Argentines suspected of crimes against humanity during the 1976–83 dictatorship took place in 1997, rather than in 1999 when Ana learns of it in the novel;

In this book Osvaldo gives a blood sample to the Argentine genetic database in 1986, when the database was in fact set up a year later, in 1987. However the grandparent index, whereby a genetic sample from an individual's grandparents could be used to establish identity in the absence of such material from the parents, came into use several years earlier, in 1984, and was therefore in existence when both Osvaldo and Eduardo gave blood at the Hospital Durand in Buenos Aires;

I have accelerated the pace at which the results of DNA tests were typically returned. Although today it is much more rapid, in the 1990s and 2000s, some cases took as long as a year.

The golden oak-leaf crown, which according to one hypothesis may have belonged to a possible son of Alexander known as Heracles, was discovered in the *agora* at Aigai, in northern Greece, in 2008. I have shifted its discovery back a full decade, to 1998.

In May 2012 I attended a session in the trial of the ex-generals Jorge Videla and Reynaldo Bignone and the former ESMA obstetrician Jorge Magnacco in the courtrooms at Comodoro Py in Buenos Aires; testimony in and around the case, which established the theft of children as a systematic process under the 1976–83 dictatorship, and my visits to some of the former clandestine detention centres in Buenos Aires – particularly ESMA – inform the section in Graciela's voice, and the part in which Inés Moncavillo recounts her experiences.

ACKNOWLEDGEMENTS

The late Argentine poet Juan Gelman was the first of various sources of inspiration for this novel, and I owe him heartfelt thanks for the long afternoon we spent talking in Mexico City back in April 2004. Osvaldo's visit to the Vatican I borrowed from his experience; the quotation on page vii comes from the introduction to his anthology, *En el hoy y mañana y ayer*, published by the Universidad Nacional Autónoma de México.

In Argentina, I had the honour of holding several discussions with Estela de Carlotto, President of the Grandmothers of the Plaza de Mayo; with Rosa Rosinblit, the group's Vice President; and with Taty Almeida, one of the founding Mothers of the Plaza de Mayo. To each of these extraordinary women, my most heartfelt thanks. Warmest thanks must also go to Victoria Montenegro, Juan Cabandié and Macarena Gelman, each of whom contributed to my understanding of the diverse paths by which some of Argentina's stolen children have found their way home.

Leopoldo Kulesz, Hugo Paredero and Luba Lewin have been the most generous of friends, both during my time in Argentina and beyond. Romina Ruffato and Caroline Uribe were always ready with expert responses to my questions, and Diego Lluma very kindly arranged for me to spend a memorable day in the shantytown, Villa 21. Yamila O'Neil graciously provided me with a sense of what life is like for a young generation living with disappearance. In Patagonia, Hugo Campañoli was an expert guide to the Cave of the Hands.

Innumerable kindnesses were also extended to me in Greece. Angeliki Kottaridi and Ioannis Graekos, of the 17th Ephorate of Prehistoric and Classical Antiquities, showed me over the dig site and the museum at Aigai, and allowed me to witness the opening of a jar grave. Kathy and Vassilis Koutelieris, Petros Demeris, Yanna and Michael Hignett and Theo Nomikos extended variously friendship, insights into archaeology, explanations of the declensions of Greek names and knowledge of island life. My imagining of Vasilis's island workshop was partly inspired by that of the late ceramicist Yanni Komboyannis, a gifted artist and generous human being.

In Mexico, I owe sincerest thanks to the poet Pedro Serrano, not least for the seasons of jacarandas, and to Carlos Beltran, for explaining the workings of mitochondrial DNA and for references concerning the Argentine diaspora.

In France, Alicia Bonnet-Kruger was a font of knowledge about the Argentine exile, most generously sharing her own life story and her moving letter to the Argentine Congress. Cacho Kruger and Frieda Rochocz were also unstinting with their knowledge and accounts of their own experiences.

For background to Osvaldo's profession, I received expert guidance from consultant ophthalmologist Dr Richard Packard in London, and from Dr Robert Kaufer and Dr Gunther Kaufer in Buenos Aires. Any misapprehensions that have worked themselves into the text, however, are my responsibility alone.

Frédéric Niel has been a generous and erudite sounding board from the novel's beginning. Antoine Colonna, Chris Nicholson and Fiona Ortiz opened the first, crucial doors that opened so many others in Argentina. Ann Brothers, Caroline McLeod, Sylvain Piron, Gyongyi Biro, Paul Myers, Ann Collier, Chris Knight, Brian Childs, Patricia Ochs, Andrew Johnston, Henry Jackson, Chris Welsch and Marti Stewart all sustained me variously with their insight, humour and goodwill. To each, my most heartfelt thanks.

To Barbara Trapido, Gillian Stern, Linda Healey and David Miller I owe special thanks for their thoughtful readings of the novel's earlier drafts. Helen Cross, Joan Michelson and Neva Micheva provided insightful comments on parts of the manuscript. I am deeply grateful to Ellen de Bruin, Paul Steenhuis and Clay Adam, whose friendship provided a vital counterbalance to the dark places I sometimes had to enter during my research.

I would like to express my gratitude to Ledig House in upstate New York for the residency which allowed me to complete an important part of this novel, and to the *International New York Times*, which kindly gave me leave to attend. Sangam House in India generously provided time and space to complete the final revisions.

Everyone at Bloomsbury has been a delight to work with, but I must particularly thank Angelique Tran Van Sang, Rachel Mannheimer and Lynn Curtis for their meticulous editing, and Alexandra Pringle for her insightful observations at every stage from this novel's earliest days.

ALSO AVAILABLE BY CAROLINE BROTHERS

HINTERLAND

'An illuminating and timely story that highlights the plight of refugees ...
A book that haunts and shames in equal measure'
GUARDIAN

Two young boys cross a river in the middle of the night. The river is also a
border, and their lives depend on this journey. With nothing but the clothes on
their backs, Aryan and his little brother Kabir travel by truck, boat, train, bus
and on foot across a Europe they desperately hope will offer them a future they
can no longer wait for in Afghanistan. Kabul-Tehran-Istanbul-Athens-Rome-
Paris-London – this is the route they cling to, the mantra they repeat in their
prayers, and the only option they can see before them.

Hinterland is the story of two ordinary brothers whose courageous gamble
brings home the devastating human consequences of war.

'Caroline Brothers' stark, unsentimental novel is one everyone should read'
DAILY MAIL

'Harrowingly exposes the hidden world of migrants ... The emotional as well
as geographical borderlands are sensitively delineated in this visceral and
moving debut'
INDEPENDENT

'Brothers' elegant prose holds sentimentality at bay, complementing some
impressive reportage'
FINANCIAL TIMES

ORDER YOUR COPY:

BY PHONE: +44 (0) 1256 302 699; **BY EMAIL:** DIRECT@MACMILLAN.CO.UK

DELIVERY IS USUALLY 3–5 WORKING DAYS. FREE POSTAGE AND PACKAGING FOR ORDERS OVER £20.

ONLINE: WWW.BLOOMSBURY.COM/BOOKSHOP

PRICES AND AVAILABILITY SUBJECT TO CHANGE WITHOUT NOTICE.

BLOOMSBURY.COM/AUTHOR/CAROLINE-BROTHERS

BLOOMSBURY